Here We Go
Again, Boys

Here We Go Again, Boys

J. Allen Clary

ABSOLUTELY AMAZING eBOOKS

ABSOLUTELY AMAZING eBOOKS

Published by Whiz Bang LLC, 926 Truman Avenue, Key West, Florida 33040, USA.

For information contact:
Publisher@AbsolutelyAmazingEbooks.com

ISBN-13: 978-1945772245 (Absolutely Amazing Ebooks)

ISBN-10: 1945772247

Here We Go Again, Boys

Chapter 1

While the Baker Boys were toasting and choking on their drinks and celebrating the success of their latest mission, Colonel Travis pulled Gunny Baker aside and said; "I have another mission for you and your men."

Gunnery Sergeant Alistair Baker stood five-nine and weighed roughly 160lbs. He had lost close to thirty-pounds on his last mission, so his uniform hung limply from his shoulders. He had also lost three of his men. The Marine standing before the colonel was expressionless, a vision of lean, raw power in a uniform, angry at the loss of his men, and eager for another crack at his enemy. "We're ready when you are, Colonel. Just say the word."

The conversation didn't last long, but it was noticed. As soon as the squad cleared the colonel's tent, the men quickly congregated around their boss, all the while, pushing Corporal Kirby to the forefront, to ask that all important question. "Go on, Corporal. You're the man with the extra stripe." The appointment was unanimous, so the corporal sheepishly responded to the challenge. "What's up, Gunny? We're going to Sydney, right?"

Hopes were still high despite the immediate silence.

Sergeant Stamper didn't say anything for a few seconds. His gaze was fixed on Gunny's expression until the light of comprehension flickered on. His quickly thought-out appraisal concerning his friend's expression also had him shaking his head. *Damn. Here we go again.* "You look like you volunteered us for something. Where are we going, Gunny?"

Stone-faced as usual, Gunny replied. "To the halls of hell and back, Roger. Codename: Boogeyman Island."

Now, a month and a half later, the men of Baker's squad were drooling at the prospect of once again attempting to spend two weeks in Sydney. Almost an entire year has passed since they had eyeballed a woman not wearing a uniform. Yes, they had earned that trip to Australia many times over, yet not all of the Baker Boys would be making the trip. Two were left on the island they had died on, buried beneath the waves of Boogeyman Cove. It was a hard mission. A tough mission, and now it's over. It was time to lick their wounds and heal.

About every thirty minutes, Captain Rogers brought the *Longfin* up to periscope depth and then raised the antenna mast to check for incoming messages, his normal routine during the quiet times. On this particular inquiry, the *Longfin* received a startling message: "Proceed to these coordinates and rendezvous with Cactus Three. Orders in route. Red King out." Less than a minute after receiving the transmission, the submerged boat was moving west towards a small clump of beach some three-hundred-miles west of Boogeyman Island.

After a two and a half day journey, the sub arrived at the rendezvous coordinates and sent a coded message to a Catalina PBY, flying boat, circling off in the distance, at about 20,000 feet. Bobbing up and down on the surface, the sub was exposed to all, and extremely vulnerable to a surface attack. The crew of the sub manning the surface weapons were forced to wait an anxious thirty-minutes before the airplane finally flew into view and splash-landed about thirty-yards to starboard of the *Longfin*. While the plane was on its landing approach, Captain Rogers was in his quarters discussing the second message with Gunny. The apologetic smile on the sub skipper's face was the first hint that bad news was about to arrive. "Sorry, Gunny. It looks like you boys will miss the trip to Sydney again."

Gunnery Sergeant Baker shrugged his shoulders as if

not sending the Baker Boys to Sydney was nothing more important than throwing a cigar butt on the ground and stepping on it. However, inside, behind his stony expression, he was not happy. The men had lost a lot of weight on their last mission. Only three of the squad had reached 140lbs before they were shipped off again. The men needed meat put back onto their bones and a chance to blow off the tension of war. Generals, however, are generals, and they love it when their subordinates follow orders without question. The Baker Boys were fast becoming General Swift's favorite unit.

"Don't let it bother you, Skipper; it's just part of the game. Just fill us with lots of coffee and a side order of steak and eggs, and we'll be good to go. Any indication on what the orders read?"

"No, Gunny. Your orders are on that PBY. That's about all I know. Too bad you can't go to Sydney. I was looking forward to tossing a few with you. I guess that'll have to wait until next time."

Before their conversation could continue, there was a knock and then an interruption. "Skipper, we're all set. Ready when you are." Immediately after the announcement, the executive officer handed his captain a sealed manila envelope.

"Thank you, Commander. I'll be there in a minute.

~ ~ ~

The rafts had been unloaded quickly and were in the process of being deflated and buried. This part of the landing was second nature to the Baker Boys. Hit the beach, unload the supplies, and bury the rafts, bam, bam, bam. The strange sounds emanating from a new breed of mammal to the island was also second nature to the Baker Boys as well.

While the men unloaded the rafts, they were privy to the sounds of countless bird calls and other creatures of the jungle, especially the two legged creature known as Uncus

Samus Marineus. This mammal creature was well known for its ability to walk great distances in knee deep mud, under heavy loads without any complaints, and upon waking, it sang such beautiful songs as: "Dames, broads, chicks, damn what rotten luck. Man, they were just waiting for us to... Oh shit, Gunny's glaring!" And it died a quick death, just as efficiently and just as silently as burying the rafts.

When that chore was finished, the Marines gathered around the man in charge, and the introductions were made. Two new appointed volunteers were added to the ranks of the Baker Boys, and Thomas Banan was finally on his way to Australia.

Banan was in a lot of pain and running a fever, and to put icing on the cake, he was also seasick and dead broke. Besides losing his plantation to the Japanese, empty-handed was not how he envisioned leaving the island. His version of his exodus had him departing the island a wealthy man.

Sergeant Michael Thomas was a good Marine. He had cut his teeth on Guadalcanal and a few other skirmishes, but what made him stand out, was his love for blowing up whatever needed blasting. That particular talent was why he was chosen for this mission. He was very, very good at making things disappear amid erupting explosions.

PFC Daniel Choctaw, on the other hand, was chosen for his ferociousness in battle. He didn't care how he killed his enemies or what weapons he used just as long as he killed them. He was a vicious, brutal Marine in battle.

Now it was time to head for the cave.

"Red Robin, this is Dirty Bird, come in, over."

"This is Red Robin. Go ahead, Dirty Bird."

"Red Robin, this is Dirty Bird. We are hit and covered. I repeat, we are hit and covered. All is good."

"Roger, Dirty Bird. Understood. Good hunting. Red

Robin out."

"All right, Marines, let's get these supplies to the cave. Chief, you and Geronimo get out front. The rest of you grab something and get moving. I want his stuff in the cave before daylight."

"How come those two guys ain't carrying something?" Gunny heard the comment PFC Choctaw uttered. It was made to no one in particular, just a thought expressed out loud. Sergeant Stamper always took care of the petty annoyances for Gunny. This chore was also second nature. "When you become a real Marine, you'll understand. Now quit complaining, PFC, and get to work."

The rest of the Baker Boys just smiled. They were all thinking along similar lines of thought: *Boy, is that big lug in for a surprise*

~ ~ ~

The squad didn't get the supplies into the cave before sunrise. They were an hour late. Still, it took a lot less time coming up the west side of the plateau than it would have had they gone up the east side. A lot less time. And since Kirby's radio conversation shortly after reaching the plateau, Gunny was no longer concerned with how to dispose of the wooden crates some of their supplies came in. The crates would make great kindling.

The Japanese had placed one of their infantry squads on the plateau, but they hadn't heard from the plateau squad in almost a week. That mishap occurred because Corporal Kirby was in a submarine at the time, one-hundred-feet below the surface of the Pacific, so he couldn't call in a spot report. When the squad arrived on the plateau, he immediately rushed over to the radio and sent a false report to the Japanese commander in charge, and by accident, was just in time to stop a patrol from checking up on that squad. Now, the Marines could breathe easy for awhile.

5

Thanks to the Baker Boys, the last Jap on Plateau Flat Head was killed just a few hours before their previous mission ended. However, the Japanese command had no idea their men on Flat Head had been killed. Thanks to Corporal Kirby's studied knowledge of the enemy's language, and by using the radio the squad captured, he was able to convince the Japanese commanders that they still had a squad positioned high on the mountain plateau, nick-named, Flat Head. Then their mission ended.

When the squad left the island, the men had no idea they would be going back just a few short days later. The squad thought they had left Boogeyman Island, never to return. Then they received new orders: "We're going back to the cave gentlemen. Corporal Kirby, when we reach the top, get on that Jap radio and see what's cooking. Let them know that they still have a squad on that chunk of rock."

"Aye, aye, Gunny."

~ ~ ~

Right from the start, PFC Fox didn't get along with PFC Choctaw, but what was closer to the truth, PFC Choctaw didn't like the scout. His size and his status with the squad had a lot to do with Choctaw's attitude. The shorter man from Swain County, North Carolina, could hardly be called average size. He was small for a Marine. He might reach 5' 7" if he stood on his tiptoes, and maybe 120lbs if he had rocks in his pockets. It was because of his determination and his scouting skills that he was reluctantly accepted into the Marine Corp, not to mention the influence his family had over some of the state officials.

This mental picture Choctaw concocted of Fox was what he was seeing in his mind, what he perceived as a scrawny little lightweight, protected by the squad. PFC Choctaw, on the other hand, was 6' 1" and weighed about 190lbs. Much bigger than Fox.

Everyone in the squad knew what the little scout was

capable of doing, so they just left the situation alone, smiled, and watched. Gunny was also aware of the impending trouble between the two PFC's and was about to set things straight with PFC Choctaw. Nobody messed around with the chief as long as Gunny was alive, but before he could do anything, Sergeant Stamper stopped him.

"Al, you know I'm behind you all the way, no matter what. But I think you should let the kid handle this one by himself."

"You really think so, Roger?"

"Yes I do, Gunny. You watch and see, Al. I'll bet this is one lesson that ugly pug will never forget."

"I sure hope you're right, Roger. I just don't want to see the boy get hurt. He's barely eighteen."

Sergeant Stamper stared at his friend for a moment before he replied. "That eighteen-year-old kid you're so concerned about has more Jap kills under his belt than all of us combined. I'm not worried about him," and the conversation ended. Gunny, however, was still troubled.

Towards the evening of the third day after the Marines arrived back on Boogeyman Island, trouble began to brew between the two PFC's, and Choctaw was the flame. Only three Marines were outside the cave by the radio tent: Corporal Kirby, PFC Fox, and PFC Choctaw. Sneering, the big Marine made some comments about Fox. "So, you're the gunny's pet are you? Do you run to Gunny at night when you're scared?"

Corporal Kirby didn't like the direction the conversation was heading, so he stepped forward in defense of his friend. "Leave him alone, PFC."

Smiling, the chief looked at the corporal and shook his head. "Stay out of it, Lance. I don't need a wet nurse."

A deriding snicker interrupted the two friends, so they turned to face the culprit. When the offender spoke, his intent was obvious. "Maybe you should go get Gunny,

Corporal. We wouldn't want the PFC to get scared, now would we?"

Corporal Kirby stared at the big Marine for a few seconds, then his eyes narrowed, and he stood up straighter. "Maybe you should pick on someone more your size, PFC?"

"Maybe you should shut up, Corporal. This is between me and him."

"Stand down, Lance," said Fox. "Just stay out of the way. I'll handle this."

In ones and twos, the little clearing by the radio tent was quickly filled with excitement in no time. How the Marines knew what was about to happen was anybody's guess, but they were there nonetheless. Rumor has it, however, a good Marine can smell a fight from a great distance, without the use of radar.

PFC Fox was standing about six-feet away from PFC Choctaw, completely oblivious to the taunting words. He was looking past the big man's right shoulder, staring a hole through nothing and smiling carelessly. To PFC Choctaw, the scout looked as if he didn't think anything was going to happen. *Boy, is he in for a surprise*, he thought, smirking confidently to himself.

PFC Fox was staring past the big man, trying to remain aloof and unconcerned, yet he was cringing inside because of his opponent's size. *Oh wow, he's a monster. Damn; this one's going to hurt.*

The other scout had his own ideas. The hair on the back of his neck was standing straight out. He was only an inch taller than Fox, but he outweighed the little scout by over twenty pounds. Sizing up the larger man, Geronimo felt he could beat him severely. He was having a difficult time just standing there, unable to stop the confrontation and keep the sour-ass from beating on *the wolf* (Bonito's nickname for PFC Fox, but no one knew about that nickname except Bonito).

For a couple of seconds, the Apache scout stood staring at the chief's foe, measuring him up, planning his first strike. His planning, however, was interrupted by an overwhelming desire, and he found himself stepping towards the taunting Marine, stating his intentions. "Even the stoutest tree will fall with enough well placed blows. You are no different." Before he could finish baiting his trap to draw the PFC into a confrontation, Gunny interrupted. "PFC Bonito. You and Corporal Kirby go back down into the cave and bring me back a carton of smokes. You know where my rucksack is, so don't come back without them."

"But, Gunny, you don't..."

"Now, you two!"

The two Marines answered as one, "Aye, aye, Gunny," all the while shaking their heads on their way down to the cave. Disgusted was an understatement. "Damn, Geronimo. You need to slow down your attack. I bet twenty bucks on the chief, and..."

"Quiet," whispered Bonito, "I have an idea. Gunny said don't come back without them, right? He doesn't carry cigarettes on a mission, so it's a set-up. All we have to do is to adapt, improvise, and scamper up to the ledge with my carton of smokes. If we get caught watching the fight, we can always say we were on our way up with a carton of cigarettes."

A moment of silence went by before there was a reaction to Geronimo's words. Immediately after the moment of silence, a wild scramble ensued, and within seconds, the two Marines lay perched on a lower ledge, peering over the crest, waiting for the fight to begin.

Sergeant Thomas was standing off to the side, watching Gunny and somewhat concerned after he noticed the difference in size between the two men. "Are you sure you want this fight to happen, Gunny? I've seen what this man can do with his hands."

"Sergeant Thomas," said Gunny, "don't you have your firecrackers to look after?"

Now that everyone was aware of what was going to happen, PFC Choctaw began his taunting of Fox again without even trying to hide his comments anymore. It looked to Choctaw as if the squad had high hopes for their undersized scout, and this assumption added fuel to his already burning desire to beat the little Marine to a pulp. Still, the man from the Carolinas paid no attention to him. Smiling, he just stood there, staring past PFC Choctaw as if the man wasn't even there.

"Are you sure about this, Roger?"

"Yeah, Al. I'm sure. You remember what happened when the chief fought Bonito, don't you? That one turned out to be a draw. Geronimo is a hell of a lot smarter than this bum is."

Now the situation was starting to heat up. One second the scout was smiling, looking unconcerned, and in the blink of an eye later, he was circling PFC Choctaw, staying away from the man's right hand. Circling on the balls of his feet and waiting, he was only a little over an arm's length away from PFC Choctaw.

Without warning, both men charged at the same time, and the fight was on. PFC Choctaw was deceptively quick for his size and sent the scout spinning crazily to the ground with a left hook. The little man from Swain County looked like a thrown rag doll when he landed flat on his back. He hit the ground hard, shook his head, and, smiling carelessly, stood up. "I hope that wasn't your best shot," he said, but the chief wasn't feeling as stout as his words. In fact, he was seeing a multitude of stars. *Damn, that hurt.*

PFC Fox had a lump already forming on the right side of his face, but PFC Choctaw was also wounded. He was bleeding from his nose and his mouth because the smaller man had beaten him to the punch. Wiping the blood away, he moved towards the scout, but with a little less swagger in his taunts. *Those two punches hurt! And what did that little man say? I hope that wasn't your best shot!*

Fox was back on the balls of his feet, still moving away from his opponent's right hand. The smile on his face was no longer careless: it was tight-lipped and determined, and it had PFC Choctaw somewhat distracted. *What is this little man up to?* Without warning, PFC Fox attacked and caught Choctaw by surprise with a sudden blur of quickness, and Daniel Choctaw's head snapped back twice. Confused and dazed, the big man slowly picked himself up off the ground. Not knowing what just happened, he looked around at the onlookers, wondering which one blindsided him. The squad just smiled at him.

Still somewhat disconnected from coherent thought, he slowly turned his gaze back to Fox. *This little man knocked me to the ground?* With that sudden realization, his temper began to rise, and it overrode all common sense thinking. He had lost the initiative and his focus, and he had no idea on what to do next. He had been sidetracked by his temper, and the distraction threw off his timing; greatly agitating him even more.

The fight was slowly shifting in favor of the scout, thanks to Choctaw's disconcerted state. For every punch Choctaw threw at Fox, the little man landed two, three, and sometimes four punches. Only one out of every three punches the big man threw at Fox landed, yet that one punch still hurt and bruised.

Choctaw's face was beginning to show the results of the little man's speed and power. But the bigger man's punches were also taking their toll on Fox. His whole face was swollen. It looked nasty, and the scout was slowing down. All of a sudden, he went twirling and gyrating to the ground from a good, solid, right to the cheekbone.

So far, throughout the entire ten minutes of the fight, the rest of the squad had stayed quiet. No cheering, no shouting, no urging on, but when Choctaw landed that solid right to the side of the little scout's head, everyone let out a loud, ooohh, man! Gunny, however, didn't stop at ooohh man. "Damn, Roger. I bet that jarred his brain!" And it did.

Sergeant Stamper was looking at the chief when he shook his head and said, "I believe you're right, Al. I think I heard something rattle when he got hit."

The chief hit the ground on his butt. Dazed, he sat where he had landed for a few seconds before he tried to get up. He made it to his feet on his third attempt, but he was a bit wobbly when he tried to walk. His legs didn't look strong enough to carry him back into the fight. Gunny was about to put an end to the fight, but Sergeant Stamper grabbed his arm.

"Wait, Gunny. Look at his eyes. He's not done yet."

Gunny was still arguing with Sergeant Stamper, so he missed what happened next.

Wow. This guy hits hard. I gotta come up with some way to end this fight now, or he'll beat me to death. Fox shook his head, trying to get rid of the cob webs that the big man implanted in his brain. Then he had an idea. *Well, here goes nothing.*

He could have stood up on his first try, but Fox was stalling. When he got up on his third attempt, he knew what he was going to do. Slowly, the scout wobbled towards the big man. He looked as if one strong breath from Choctaw would put him on the ground.

Daniel Choctaw saw the little man awkwardly stutter-stepping towards him and thought, *I've got this fight. All I have to do is hit him one more time and he's done.* With that thought in mind, he threw caution to the four-winds and rushed straight at Fox, his mind only on throwing the ending punch. *That little man hits hard. I gotta end this now.* The chief's misshaped face and that last solid fist to the head fueled the bigger man's, rising confidence. All of a sudden, the little man's legs weren't so wobbly anymore. In fact, PFC Fox was attacking with everything he had left in him.

He saw his opportunity while Choctaw was charging at him. As soon as the big man's left foot planted, and before the power behind his punch could develop, David Little Fox, attacked. The ferociousness of his attack took the taller Marine by surprise. One punch right after the other landed over and over again on the larger man's face, like two pistons firing, rapidly smashing his opponent's confidence. PFC Choctaw was so overwhelmed he was unable to defend himself against the speed of the attack and very quickly began pawing at the air, trying to block the little man's punches. Then bam, the chief changed his target and caught the big man in the mid-section with a hard right. Immediately, Choctaw lost his wind and almost doubled over.

The man who barely weighed more than a rucksack, hit his challenger in the gut two more times before he threw three wicked punches to the big man's face...bam, bam, bam. Two went to the jaw, and one solid uppercut landed right under the point of the Louisiana boy's chin. Helped along by the clash of teeth, the collision of fist-to-chin sounded like a baseball bat hitting a home run ball. Then came a round-house right to the temple. *Splat!* The big man's head was jarred back violently to the right and he staggered back about four or five steps before he hit the ground on his butt. The bruiser from the bayous stayed upright for a few seconds, before he fell backwards, his head bouncing off the ground. And there he remained, unmoving.

PFC Fox stood where he was until he was sure Choctaw was out cold. Then, he, too, crashed to the ground on his hands and knees. His arms buckled, and he fell face-first to the ground, exhausted, his arms no longer able to function.

The plateau erupted with such cheering that you would have thought Charlie Keller had just blasted another homerun. The shouting and cheering lasted almost three minutes before the two sergeants were finally able to quiet the Marines down enough to be heard. Fifteen minutes later, all were back inside the cave, discussing the fight, except for Corporal Kirby and PFC Bonito. They were caught watching the fight without Gunny's carton of smokes in-hand, so the two men were forced to stand outside, monitoring the radio while the rest of the squad was inside the cave, enjoying the festive mood and basking in the aftermath of the fight.

"Damn you, Roger. You made me miss the end of the fight."

"Too bad, Al. That's what you get for not listening to me. I told you he'd whip him, but you wouldn't believe me."

The two friends argued back and forth for almost ten-minutes, before they were interrupted by the radio. Colonel Travis was on the horn, and he had their marching orders. The Baker Boys were to rendezvous with a sub in three days. Submerged, the sub would head up the west coast of the island and dump the Marines off about three miles from the Poloba naval facilities. There was an airfield nearby the colonel wanted harassed.

Chapter 2

The submerged sub was heading north at about four knots. Their drop off point was still over twenty-hours away, a very long time for PFC Fox. He hated subs, he hated large bodies of water, and he hated the confined spaces of the sub.

PFC Choctaw's face still showed signs of the fight. Even after three days, he looked a mess. He had cuts everywhere and his left eye was still swollen almost shut. His face resembled a puffer fish because it was so swollen and multi-colored. The men of Baker squad didn't much care for the big Marine, mainly because of what he did to the chief. But if the two of them were put side by side, he looked far worse than the scout did.

The airbase the Marines were targeting was situated on the northwest corner of the island. The Japanese had spent a lot of time and effort in building and camouflaging this base. Their defenses around the base were strong and also well camouflaged, so the hidden positions had to be mapped.

The fuel and ordinance was being stored somewhere in the jungle on the east side of the base, and so far, the allies have been unable to destroy those stocks. Gunny's mission was to remedy that situation. "Find where they hide their fuel, Gunny, and blow the whole thing to hell. Good luck, gentlemen, and good hunting."

The sub was under orders to return to the drop off point every three days for two weeks. At the end of those two weeks, the sub would depart for good, with or without the Marines. So, Gunny was cracking two whips. "We have two weeks to get this mission done, people, so we're going to burn the candle at both ends until we know our jobs inside and out. I'm not going to miss that sub because we haven't finished our assignment due to piss-poor preparation. Now listen up and pay attention. Don't make me throw a boot at you because you won't like what's attached to it."

Sergeant Stamper interrupted the gunnery sergeant before he could continue. "You know, Al. The way things are looking, HQ is probably going to wait until after we've mapped out all the positions before they decide to send someone back in to destroy the damn things. And guess who will be the lucky screws that get that mission?"

"Yes, Roger, I believe you're right. Maybe we should just go ahead and plant the charges, blow up the positions, and forget the mapping. But you know colonels, they want to be the man giving the orders."

During their cruise to the target, Gunny drilled the squad over and over again, using the aerial photos taken by the flyboys. The photos showed all the known defensive positions and everything else that was visible from the air. The rest, the Marines would find out on their own. Sometime around 0330 hours, Gunny received a message to report to the maneuvering room.

"Yes, Skipper, you wanted to see me?"

"Yes, Gunny. The mission has been scrubbed. My orders are to take you back and drop you off at the pick-up co-ordinates. When you get back to your cave, you are to contact command for further orders."

"Aye, aye, Captain." Gunny didn't know whether or not to jump for joy, so he glanced around the maneuvering room, instead.

Captain Weaver paused for a second, then he asked a question that wouldn't leave him alone. "What happened to your two PFC's?"

Gunny usually talked to higher ranks with his normal

stone-faced expression. On this occasion, however, his face cracked and a smile emerged before he could hide behind his, gunny, glare. "They got a little over excited during a hand to hand training exercise a few days ago. They're all right, just a little bruised up."

Laughing, Captain Rogers shook his head and said. "A little? I'd hate to see what happens when they go at it for real."

The sub arrived back at the rendezvous point around 1030 hours and was forced to wait for the sun to go down, but it wasn't until 2200 hours when the sub actually surfaced. After a twenty-minute delay, the Uncus Samus Marineus were paddling their way back to the beach.

"At least we got the chance to eat food we didn't have to scrape out of a can, or kill and cook before we ate it."

"Yeah, that was the only good thing that happened on the tour. Maybe we should write the cruise line and complain about the rest of the service."

"Hey, Gunny? How come they scrubbed the mission?"

"I don't know, Corporal. They just did."

The squad was getting close to the beach now, and they could see the whiteness of the sand.

"Gunny, there's someone on the beach."

"Are you sure, chief?"

"Yeah, Gunny. I'm sure."

Gunny didn't hesitate. "Sergeant Stamper."

"Yeah, Gunny?"

"Someone's on the beach. We stop here."

Within seconds, the whispered word had been spread and the Marines quit paddling. Now they had to wait and see.

"Let's get these rafts tied off. Sergeant Stamper, move towards that little island over to your two-o-clock. We'll stop there and figure out what to do next."

"Aye, aye, Gunny."

That little island he was talking about was actually just a little spit of land with a few coconut trees on it. There was no real cover anywhere on the tiny piece of real-estate, but about three-hundred yards to the northeast was a silhouette of an island that looked like it might have some decent cover on it. The Marines took over an hour and a half to arrive at the larger island, and it had the cover they were hoping for. In fact, it resembled the chunk of rock they had just spent the last thirty-four days on, but on a much smaller scale.

~ ~ ~

Fox climbed down from a tree and handed the binoculars back to Gunny. "I can't tell if they are tracks, Gunny. There's just too much distance between us and the island. But my guess is that somebody was definitely on the beach last night. I noticed a dark line leading from the jungle to the edge of the water. Then it goes over the beach like somebody was walking around."

Deep in thought, Gunny stared off in the direction of Boogeyman Island. *If there was somebody on the beach last night, then who the hell was it?* Shaking his head over the puzzling mystery, he paused for a moment before he turned to face the squad. "All right, gentlemen, spread out. Let's check for Japs. PFC Bonito, see if you can scrounge up some water, or something to eat. The rest of you get moving, and stay sharp. Sergeant Stamper, take charge of the men, I've got some planning to do."

"Aye, aye, Gunny. All right Marines, you heard the man. Snap to it."

Gunny, still deep in thought, turned to face the ocean.

"I'll go, Gunny."

"Huh? What?" He turned back towards the voice. It was PFC Fox. "You'll go where?"

"I'll go back to the beach," replied the little scout.

"All by yourself?"

The chief was so floored by Gunny's response that all

18

he could think of to say was, "Yes dad."

Now it was Gunnery Sergeant Baker's turn to be surprised.

"Excuse me, Gunny. I'll go with him." PFC Choctaw wasn't smiling because his face hurt too much. His cheek muscles were refusing to work without a great deal of painful protest, so he was wincing while he spoke. "The little man's arms aren't strong enough to paddle all the way to the beach and back. He'll need someone big like me to help him."

Staring intently at the big Marine standing before him, Gunny responded. "Now why would you want to help PFC Fox?"

"It's personal, Gunny."

"That's not a good enough answer, PFC."

"Gunny, I've never lost a fight until I ran into the likes of him, so I owe him."

Gunny's eyes narrowed, but before he could say anything else, PFC Choctaw beat him to the words. "Don't worry, Gunny. My face is still too sore to tangle with him again. Hell, I can't even talk without pain. That little man hits hard. I'm not about to go through that again. Not without a damn good reason. He hits hard, Gunny."

Then the chief interrupted. "Gunny, he's right. I probably do need an ox along to help out. He can carry me back to the beach." What the little scout was doing was painful as well, but that didn't stop him from showing off his pearly-whites.

"I'll go with him, Gunny."

All three Marines turned, and there was PFC Bonito, leaning up against a coconut tree, with his thumbs hooked in his web belt. "I'll go, Gunny. I don't trust this Choctaw character."

Gunny looked at PFC Bonito for a long few seconds before he responded. "I thought I told you to find us some food, PFC?"

The Apache scout just shook his head. "Gunny, I won't be able to find anything until those clowns quit stomping around. With all their thumping around, they're scaring everything to the other end of the island. Besides, that damn Cherokee can't do anything without me. He'd just get himself lost if I wasn't around to help him."

"Thanks for the vote of confidence, Geronimo. If anything happens, I'll be sure to duck behind the Ox. He's big enough to stop a bullet and survive. Besides, you'll probably get seasick. The ocean is much bigger than a bathtub, don't you think?"

Shaking his head, Gunny looked at his two scouts. *Damn. They act just like my brothers.*

~ ~ ~

The raft carrying the two Marines slowly headed towards the big island, sometime around 2030 hours. The sea was a bit choppy with the wind blowing from the east. A storm was brewing up, and it looked like it was going to be a dandy one. By the time they reached the beach, they had been blown off course, three-quarters of a mile west of where they wanted to land. The two men had to carry the raft, fully inflated, to where they originally wanted to land because no one thought to bring along CO_2 canisters so they could re-fill the raft. The rain hit twenty minutes after they landed.

The going was tough with the wind blowing, so it took Choctaw and Fox over an hour to reach their destination. By 2300 hours, they were at last on their way inland following a faint trail. Because of the rain, the tracks on the beach were not much more than indentations in the sand, but they were definitely made by a human.

For over an hour and a half, the two men sloshed their way through the pouring rain and the dense jungle finally to stand at the edge of a kunai grass clearing about sixty-yards from the base of the plateau. They had just removed their packs to take a short break, but that short break never took place. The two Marines were suddenly jumped by three shadows that materialized out of nowhere. PFC Fox was immediately taken to the ground by one of the attackers before he had a chance to react. The other two attackers went after the big Marine.

The struggle was short and sweet. At least for the two American's, it was. The big man was attacked from his left and right without the slightest warning. His reaction, however, was almost instant. The silent attacker, coming in from the right, jumped on the taller man's back, trying to strangle and distract him from behind, while his partner skewered the big meal-on-feet from the left. That strategy, however, didn't work out so well for the colleague. The man coming from the left ran into a very hard thrown, straight-shot to the nose and immediately crumpled to the ground. Every bit of power the big man possessed went into that punch. The man wearing feathers was dead before he hit the ground.

As soon as he had one opponent down and out, Choctaw grabbed a handful of his second foe's hair and feathers, and then jerked him over his shoulder until a cannibal was dangling directly in front of him. Immediately, the Louisiana brute grabbed his attacker just above the left knee with a vise like grip, and still holding on to his assailant's hair, the big bruiser hoisted his terrified enemy high above his head and threw him into the nearest tree. The cannibal's screams were abruptly cut short when he hit the tree. Despite the loudness of the rain storm and the collateral sounds of the struggle, the big man from the bayous heard his opponent's bones cracking when the poor soul slammed into the tree. By the time the unfortunate man-eater hit the ground, he too was dead.

PFC Fox was still struggling with his antagonist when

PFC Choctaw finished up with his two assailants. The big man quickly reached over and grabbed the chief's adversary by his hair, and yanked him off his feet, slamming the unlucky man-eater hard to the ground on his back. Without any hesitation, the beast of the bayou immediately, swung his balled-up right fist downward like a sledgehammer and crushed the stunned man's chest. A couple of minutes went by before the last assailant finally died. His death, however, went unnoticed.

PFC Choctaw was grinning from ear to ear until he saw PFC Fox down on his hands and knees, puking. The scout's left shirtsleeve was darker stained than the rest of his rain drenched shirt and immediately caught his attention. Two finger snaps later, the big man from Louisiana saw a reflection and then a knife sticking out of the wounded Marine's arm. Immediately, he ran over, grabbed Fox by his shirt collar, pulled him to his feet, threw a left to the chief's chin, and put the little man's lights out. Gently, he lowered the injured man to the ground, pulled the knife out, and doing the best he could, bound up the wound. Once the wound was wrapped well enough to stop the bleeding, he hoisted "little man" onto his shoulder, grabbed his carbine and headed back to the beach and the raft.

~ ~ ~

PFC Fox woke up to a rising sun. For some reason his chin hurt like hell. When he tried to move, his left arm exploded in pain. Immediately, a bout of nausea swept over him like some massive wave and he started puking again. Then he heard something that sounded like held-back laughter.

"See, Gunny," said PFC Bonito, "what did I tell you. I let him go on his own for a change and he goes and gets himself hurt. What's a fellow to do?"

After his nausea had subsided somewhat, PFC Fox looked around and saw nine Marines staring down at him.

Then PFC Choctaw spoke up.

"I'm disappointed in you, little man. As hard as you fought against me, you let that little scratch put you down. You should be ashamed of yourself."

Almost immediately, the little scout remembered what happened. "YOU HIT ME," he roared. "That's why my chin hurts so much. You hit me when I couldn't fight back. As soon as this arm heals I'm gonna take one of those trees and beat you over the head with it."

Then it dawned on him. They were on the little island. "How did I get back here?" He laughed, realizing the only way he could have gotten back...PFC Choctaw. *Owe! Don't laugh, stupid! It hurts!*

The Marines had managed to capture almost two gallons of rain water in their ponchos, but that wasn't going to last long under the baking sun. By late afternoon, the chief was walking around again, and the men were now starting to call him *little man*. That is, until the big man put a stop to that misunderstanding.

"Nobody calls him little man except me. If you got a problem with that, then take your best shot. One at a time or all of you at once, it makes no difference to me." The look on the big Marine's face told everyone that he meant business.

Sergeant Thomas was a little uneasy with the way the bantering was going. To him, it appeared that hostilities were about to break out on all fronts. Gunny, however, didn't think so. In fact, he was laughing so hard his words were delayed a few seconds. "Why waste the time? Just shoot the Ox and be done with it. It'll be a lot less painful for us to just shoot him."

"Nobody shoots the Ox except me!" shouted Fox. "I owe him for bouncing his fist off my chin. Anybody has a problem with that and you can take it up with him." The chief was pointing at the big bruiser from Baton Rouge, Louisiana: PFC Daniel, the Ox,

Choctaw.

The Marines stayed on the little island all of that night and all through the next day. Corporal Kirby kept an eye on the chief's wound just to make sure it didn't go septic, and he was under orders to make sure the wounded scout had an ample dose of his, hand-me-down, heals-all, elixir.

Listening to the little man tell what happened after he had three large swallows of the stuff had the squad laughing so hard they had to run off and hide just to calm down enough to hear what Gunny had to say. The man in charge only lasted a few seconds longer before he, too, was forced to leave the scene of laughter. The thought of war or any of its associates was left in the dark recesses of their minds, and for a quick few minutes, they were human again.

The setting sun was the signal, so the Baker Boys made preparations to head back to their cave. When the sun finally went down, they hauled the rafts onto the beach, loaded them up with what supplies they had left, and around 2200 hours, they pushed the rafts into the surf and headed north.

"Damn he snores loud." Everybody in the squad snickered at the sudden comment. And then Sergeant Stamper whispered some additional words of wisdom. "He sounds like an old Evinrude. Maybe we should put him to good use and stick his head in the water." The soft laughter only carried a few feet, and despite having to paddle to the big island, morale was good. Gunny could feel it. He could also hear it in the squad's bantering.

"That was funny, Roger. I'm impressed."

PFC Fox was lying in Gunny's raft, passed out, and snoring loud enough to wake the ocean waves.

Chapter 3

The tiring paddlers were halfway to the island when the first shadow came into view. It turned out to be a Japanese destroyer, and it scared the hell out of the Marines. It came so close to the flimsy boats that the bow wave almost swamped the lead raft. The first enemy destroyer was followed by three others, one right after the other, and it turned the men's peaceful sea venture into a panic driven nightmare.

Frantically, the Baker Boys paddled as hard as they could to get out of the path of the fast moving Japanese ships, all the while praying to their maker, as was Gunny. His prayer, however, was shouted, and it was heard by everyone. "Roger, why the hell didn't you see those ships coming?" Almost immediately, his prayer was answered.

"I didn't see those ships coming because your big ass was in the way."

They barely managed to survive. The wave from the last destroyer pushed one of the rafts into the other two, almost capsizing all three of them and knocking PFC Bonito into the sea. In less than a minute, though, he was hauled into one of the rafts spitting, sputtering, and swearing up a storm. What the Marines didn't know was the enemy had decided to evacuate most of their regiment because they were no longer able to support the size force they had there. Just like on Guadalcanal, they were using destroyers to evacuate their troops. However; unlike Guadalcanal, the enemy was leaving behind a small garrison force to maintain a presence there.

"What the hell's wrong with those Japs? They almost ran us over!"

Gunny's face cracked and a smile began to form at the same time he replied. "Be glad they didn't see us, Geronimo, or they would have run us over for sure. Besides, we're not back in the states. There are no traffic lights out here, and we're the enemy."

Throughout the entire trip back to Boogeyman Island, the squad ribbed Geronimo relentlessly. Even Gunny got in on the fun. It wasn't until they hit the beach that PFC Fox finally woke up. He had missed all the fun.

Trying to get the chief up the mountain with his bum arm proved to be quite a chore. Finally, PFC Choctaw just threw the little man over his shoulder and started climbing. He also took a ribbing from the rest of the squad. "Come on ya big ox, you can do it."

"Hell, who needs a mule when we've got him?"

"Ox hell, we've got Paul Bunyan's beast. Look at him, a big ugly ox without horns. Somebody put a rope on him quick before he gets away."

The big man from the bayous had fought his way into the squad, the most amazing thing was the fact that he lost the fight. That big Louisiana brute had lost the fight, but he won the respect of every Marine in that squad because of what he did for PFC Fox after he lost the fight.

Now it was, nobody messed with the chief as long as the Ox was around. Gunny just shook his head. *Damn. What a goldmine of Marines these men are.* Just for a moment, he stared at his Baker Boys until a bug flew into his eye, forcing him to wipe away the imagined, bug-induced, tears. "Damn Bugs." And again he shook his head.

The Marines could hear Colonel Travis laughing over the radio. On the colonel's end, it sounded hilarious, but on the squad's end it wasn't quite so funny. The destroyer episode wasn't far enough into the past for them to laugh about it yet.

"How hungry are you for this recon, sir?"

"Very hungry, Gunny. If the Japs have evacuated their troops from their base, then we might just land some men there and bring you and your boys back at the same time."

"That sounds good, Colonel, but like I said, my lead scout is hurt, so it will be at least a couple of days before he'll be ready."

"ASAP Gunny. The quicker you get this mission over and done with, the quicker you get off that island."

"Understood, Colonel. Dirty Bird out."

Gunny looked at Sergeant Stamper, somewhat disgusted. "I sure hope it wasn't the Colonel that thought up that call sign. I'd be really disappointed if he did."

"I don't think it was the Colonel, Gunny. I think it was some kid fresh out of college trying to impress some general who thought up that one."

Gunny shook his head and patted his friend on the shoulder. "Thank you, oh man from Pitt. Your words of wisdom are heartwarming." Then he turned his attention to the squad. "All right, Marines, listen up. It looks like we have one more mission to accomplish before we leave this hellhole, so..." Immediately, pandemonium broke out and cheers erupted. Gunny stopped spreading his good news because the cave roof threatened to collapse from all of the uproar.

~ ~ ~

"The place looks deserted, chief. What happened to all of the Japs? This place used to be crawling with them."

The chief was just as puzzled when he replied. "They must have been on those destroyers that almost ran us down, Corporal."

The two Marines heard a soft snicker to their left and turned their heads, waiting for what came next. The bruiser from the bayous didn't hesitate. "And you were snoring like a banshee, little man."

Bonito's expression almost matched the bigger man's

facial exertions, just a little less humor crinkles around the eyes. "Yep, you slept through the whole thing. Missed all the fun too."

The Ox immediately turned towards Bonito and said. "What are you laughing at, Geronimo? You were the one who decided to take a swim in the ocean about that time."

"Don't call me that, you big ox, or I might just show you how it feels to really get whipped."

"Any time Ger..." The interruption was sharp and to the point.

"Shut up, Ox. Both of you. You'll give us away. This isn't a hide and seek game you know. These boys fight to the death, and there's a hell of a lot more of them then there are of us."

Corporal Kirby's whispered response was just as heated as the chief's. "If I wanted to see the Three Stooges, I'd go to the movie house to watch them. Now, all of you shut up."

"Ox, you stay with Corporal Kirby. Geronimo, you head around to the right and see what you can find out. I'll go around the left side and do the same."

"Hey, chief. You forget who's in charge here."

"Yeah, you're right, Corporal. I forgot my manners, sorry. What do you want us to do?"

Corporal Kirby tried to answer as stone-faced as Gunny, but he failed miserably. Instead, his face lit up. "I'll stay here with the Ox. Chief, you go to the left, see what you can find out. Geronimo, you go to the right and do the same. Don't be gone too long, I get nervous sitting beside this big ugly beast."

The chief was nodding his head while whispering his appreciation. "My kind of Marine. Always accommodating." However, the light-hearted humor didn't last long.

"Who are you calling a big ugly beast, you witch doctor?"

"Ox!"

"Yeah, little man?"

"Can it. Corporal Kirby's your boss. Don't give him any trouble."

Smiling, the big man from Louisiana, replied. "Aw, he's no trouble at all little man." Immediately following the smile, a sinister expression crossed his face at the same time he snapped his fingers. "Just like that, little man."

"Whose side are you on, PFC?"

"I'm a Marine, Corporal Kirby. A U.S. Marine. That's whose side I'm on."

"Good," whispered the corporal. "For a minute there, I thought I was going to have to whip you hard."

The big man smiled again, then patted the corporal on the head. "No problem at all, little man."

~ ~ ~

The Japanese were unaware that they were being watched. The slightly under-strength company, roughly 160 men, had enough supplies to last them about a month. Once they were out of provisions, they would have to rely on the northern bases to truck-in their stores. Like it or not, they were now on their own.

The Japanese set up most of their defenses facing east, towards the beaches. Their mortars were in the middle of their defensive positions, but not all of their defensive positions faced towards the beaches. Some faced the jungle. The mortars were positioned so that they could support the beach defenses, as well as, the jungle defenses.

~ ~ ~

The two scouts were about to move out, but stopped when they heard excited shouting. Looking at each other, they all had the same question in mind. *What the hell is going on*? Less than a minute later, they found out. One of the enemy squads sent out on patrol was returning, and with them were three captives. Their prisoner's hands were tied behind their backs, and each captive was coupled to one another by a rope tied around their neck. The length of rope, linking the three men together was short, forcing them to walk awkwardly.

"What are they shouting about, Corporal?"

"I can't understand what they're saying right now, chief. They're too far away."

A minute or so later, the corporal's face went pale and he turned to face the scout. "They've captured some Marines, chief. They found them wandering around by the bridge."

"What else are they saying?"

"I don't know. You need to get us closer so I can understand what they *are* saying."

"Geronimo, you cover the right. The chief and I are moving in closer so I can hear what's going on. "Ox, you go back and get Gunny. Tell him the Japs have captured three Marines, and we're going to try to set them free. That ought to get him moving faster."

Within seconds, PFC Choctaw had disappeared from view.

PFC Bonito moved off to the right, and at the same time, Kirby and Fox started moving straight towards the squad leading the captives. Forty minutes of sneaking about went by before the two men were within ear-shot of the two enemy soldiers talking to each other.

The squad leader was talking to one of his superiors, explaining what happened when he noticed his prisoners had collapsed to the ground. "Excuse me, Sergeant Kato, while I put these Yankee dogs in their place." The junior NCO violently flung his empty fist up in the air as if he was jerking something off the ground, and at the same time, he began yelling at the three captives. "You yellow dogs, how dare you sit before your betters?" Brutally, the men were yanked back to their feet, choking from the violent jerk on the rope tied around their necks, their dispirited eyes staring back at their captors.

The prisoners themselves looked in really bad shape, and the Japanese were treating them with brutal disdain. They didn't appear as if there was much fight left in them. They looked as if they had given up on life. Corporal Kirby turned to look at PFC Fox.

"No heroics, chief. Nobody does anything, understand? We wait for Gunny."

"Aye, aye, Corporal. Damn. Did you see that? Did you see what the Japs just did?"

"Yeah, chief, we saw it." The scout didn't like it, but an order was an order, and Corporal Kirby was in charge. "Go find PFC Bonito and have him report to me, then you go back and guide Gunny here. Understood?"

"Aye, aye, Corporal."

~ ~ ~

Gunny and company were hunkered down at the edge of the jungle, waiting for the sun to go down. They were discussing the best way to go about freeing the three captives. Then PFC Bonito hit Gunny with a haymaker.

"You have something to say, PFC?"

"Yes, Gunny," replied Bonito. "It's about the Lieutenant, Hawks, and Garcia."

"What about them?"

"They are still alive, Gunny."

Somewhat surprised, the gunnery sergeant from Oklahoma hesitated before he replied. "I thought you said they were dead?"

"That's what I thought, Gunny. I waited for over an hour for them to show up, but they never did. I even went down to the beach and waited for them, thinking maybe they got hurt or something, but there was no sign of them anywhere. The Japs were getting too close, so I left."

"How do you know they are alive?"

31

"Because I saw who the Japs captured. It's the guys, Gunny. The lieutenant was still wearing part of his underwater rig."

"Are you sure, Marine?"

"Yes, Gunny. I'm absolutely sure."

The man in charge stared at his scout for a long few seconds and then slapped him on the shoulder. "It's okay, Jose. You didn't know. You did as much as I would have done under the same circumstances. Shake it off, Geronimo, and forget about it. They're alive, and we're going to get them back. Now listen up, people. This is how we're going to do it."

The Marines began arming their escape route, sometime around 2130 hours. That part of the preparation was Sergeant Thomas' job. Gunny's plan of action was simple. Corporal Kirby, the two scouts, and Sergeant Thomas would go after the prisoners. Once they were free, the four men would carry the wounded northwest until they ran into Gunny and the rest of the relay team. The four Marines would then take over the relay race until they ran into the east-west trail, where they would stop and rest.

Bonito and Fox were staying behind as a rear guard, just long enough for Corporal Kirby and Sergeant Thomas to scamper to their next position, in order to cover the retreat of the two scouts.

"Sergeant Thomas, you have your demo set?"

"Yes, Gunny."

"Everyone ready?"

"Yes, Gunny. We're set to go."

Gunny gazed at his men for a brief moment and then issued his normal final briefing words. "Good! Let's get it done."

~ ~ ~

The three prisoners were being held in one of the bombed-out buildings. The roof was gone, but the walls were still somewhat intact, except for the wall facing the jungle; there was a large, gaping hole where the back door used to be. The American lieutenant was being slapped around by a sergeant known to the Marines: it was Sergeant Akira Kato. The interrogating officer was Lieutenant Yoshida, another enemy acquaintance of the Marines.

PFC Fox was beginning to regret his decision not to shoot Kato when he had the chance. Turning to PFC Bonito, he looked him square in the eye and said, "That Jap is mine. If you get in the way, I'll beat you till you're blacker than blue."

PFC Bonito stared back at the chief for a moment, and was absolutely stone-faced when he replied. "It's first come first serve, little man. If you get to him first, I'll leave it alone, but if I get to him first, don't get in my way."

The two scouts stared intensely at each other for a long few seconds and then relaxed. The chief spoke up first. "We'll talk about this again when we reach the trail. Right now, let's free our friends."

Sergeant Thomas was laying his little diversions with a smile on his face. To him, it was such a pleasure working with explosives; especially when it concerned blowing up his enemies. Forty-minutes elapsed before he was back with the other three Marines.

"Listen, you guys, the other plunger isn't working. For some reason it's not producing an electrical charge, so don't forget to take this one with you when you leave. It's the only one we have that works so don't forget it."

~ ~ ~

Because of the condition the three prisoners were in, the question and answer session didn't last long. The interrogation session was over ten minutes after it started, and all three prisoners were lying unconscious on the floor, still tied up. The four Marines were just inside the jungle and intently watching their enemy.

The interrogators left the building and headed for another bomb damaged building about forty-yards away, leaving only two sentries to guard the prisoners. One was standing guard inside the bombed out structure, and one was outside, by what was left of the front door.

PFC Fox was watching the building the two interrogators had entered. Something was not right. He couldn't explain why he felt the way he did; it was just a feeling he had. Abruptly, his eyes narrowed and his focus sharpened. *Was that a shadow that just slithered into the jungle?*

He was just getting ready to investigate the shadow, but was stopped when he saw the same two Japs leave the building. One of them he recognized as the officer asking the questions. The other one could have been the tracker, but he wasn't sure. The two enemy soldiers walked another thirty-yards before they entered another bombed-out structure, but this one had a tarp stretched over part of the building. *Could it be their headquarters?*

The Swain County scout was annoyed. He still had this nagging feeling that something wasn't right. Turning to face PFC Bonito, he started signing.

Something is wrong. I feel it. Why would they leave three prisoners so weakly guarded?

You may be right. Let's move back into the jungle and wait.

Good idea, Jose.

Corporal Kirby had no idea what the two scouts were signing, so he just waited, somewhat awed at their talents. And then the chief whispered softly. "Corporal, something's not right. We need to move back into the jungle, now."

Corporal Kirby looked first at PFC Fox and then at PFC Bonito. Both scouts looked worried. "Okay, let's go."

After few minutes of quiet slinking passed, the three men were hiding in the shadows of a large, vine-covered tree. They waited, but not a sound was heard. Forty-minutes went by before they headed back to where the three prisoners were being held, but not to the same place they had been watching from. Another thirty-minutes of silent scampering passed before they were crouching down, about twenty-yards from the structure the prisoners were in.

~ ~ ~

The Marines were waiting and watching what was going on, just inside the jungle. While they were watching, they saw the same two enemy soldiers leave the tarp-covered structure and walk directly to the building the prisoners were in. One of the two men squatted down and grabbed one of the prisoners by his hair. Pulling the prisoner's head up a few inches off the ground, the enemy interrogator looked into his captive's face, and then let go of the man's hair. The impact of his head hitting the floor could be heard by the four men hiding in the jungle twenty yards away. The unconscious man didn't move, didn't make a sound. After checking the other two Americans the same way, the two enemy warriors left, walking back to the tarp covered building.

"Are they dead?"

"No, I don't think so, Corporal. If they were dead, they wouldn't keep those guards posted there. Maybe the guys are hopped up on something? That could be it. It looks like we'll be carrying those guys out of there. They definitely don't look like they can make it on their own, that's for sure."

Corporal Kirby fixed his gaze on Fox for a moment, then issued out his order: "PFC Bonito, you, me, and Sergeant Thomas will do the carrying. Chief, you watch our backs. We go in ten minutes."

The wind was starting to pick up again, and it was coming from the east. "It looks like it might rain. Do you want to wait and see if it does?"

"Yeah, Jose," replied Kirby. "Let's give it about thirty more minutes. Here's how we do it. Chief, you take care of the outside guard. Geronimo, you take care of the inside guard, and put out the light. I'll help Sergeant Thomas with one of the wounded. PFC Bonito, you help me with someone, and you chief, help Geronimo with the last man. Then we all head out the back with the chief here covering our asses. Don't wait around for anybody. As soon as you get someone on your shoulder, head out the back door. Got it?"

Corporal Kirby saw the affirmative nods and gave one of his own. Now, the only thing left for the four of them to do was to wait for the rain to begin. But rain or no rain, thirty-minutes from now, the game would begin.

A few minutes after Corporal Kirby came up with their game plan, the wind picked up. In the open areas, it was gusting up to 30 mph, blowing everything wildly about. Shortly after the wind kicked-in, the rain hit, and it was coming down so hard, it put out the kerosene lantern.

"Chief, Geronimo, get going, now. Come on, Sergeant Thomas. Follow me."

In less than a minute and a half, the two enemy guards were dead, and Sergeant Thomas was on his way out through the large hole in the back of the building. Following ten steps behind the sergeant was Corporal Kirby, and two steps behind the corporal, was Geronimo. Fox waited until Bonito had cleared the back of the building before following after the three men. So far, everything was going according to plan. Of course, the wind and the rain were a big help.

The opening team of the relay reached the first plunger, and so far, there was no sign of pursuit. PFC Fox waited for a couple of minutes, just to make sure, and then he took off after the escapees, taking the plunger with him. After a ten-minute scurry, they met up with Gunny on a tributary path leading to the foot bridge.

Immediately, Gunny and team took the still unconscious men from the now very tired trio and headed towards the east-west trail. PFC Choctaw, in the mean time, handed the type-99 Japanese light machine gun to Corporal Kirby in trade for the unconscious PFC Garcia, and then he hurriedly caught up with the rest of the group. While the rescue relay sprint was taking place, Sergeant Thomas was quickly attaching the wires to the plunger the chief brought along with him. When he was finished, he sat back and waited for hell to arrive about thirty-yards to the right of Corporal Kirby's position. Fox and Bonito were already on their way to their next location.

Gunny had planned on having to help the three captured Marines, but he hadn't planned on carrying three unconscious men. The task was proving to be a quite a chore.

Abruptly, and without warning, the quiet, rain swept jungle was blasted awake by small arms fire. For some reason, the hiding Japanese hadn't seen or heard Gunny and his men when they passed by their positions, but they definitely heard the two scouts running up the trail, so they opened up on them.

The enemy had misjudged where the two scouts were because the rain distorted the sound of their running, so instead of hitting the two men and cutting them to pieces, the Japanese ended up firing behind the running Marines, which allowed the Americans time to slip into the jungle.

Corporal Kirby and Sergeant Thomas heard the shooting and realized that the Japanese had somehow gotten behind them. The master of blast immediately set off the first three distractions, after which, he frantically removed the wires from the plunger, and took off running after Corporal Kirby, but not along the trail, they were running through the jungle, using the jungle foliage to hide their movement.

Within a few minutes, the shooting had stopped. Instead of finding dead Marines scattered all along the trail, the enemy found nothing but dead mud. Because of the excitement of the situation and the dead mud, the Japanese belatedly found that they had also managed to kill one of their own men and wound three others. When he saw the dead and wounded, Sergeant Kato was furious. "How did this happen? Why were these men out of position?" Then his eyes narrowed. "Who gave the order to open fire?"

"I did," said a sergeant.

Sergeant Kato was still a bit agitated when he turned to face the squad leader. "Who gave you permission to give that order?"

The junior sergeant stood at attention, surprise written all over his face when he answered. "I heard the Americans running up the trail and thought they were going to get away, so I ordered the men to open fire."

The once disturbed jungle was disturbed once again, but this time by a single shot, fired by a very agitated platoon sergeant. "Nobody moves!" shouted Kato.

Not a single one of his men moved. After what they just witnessed, they were too afraid to even breathe let alone move anywhere. However, before the jungle could regain its composure, it was disturbed yet again, but this time by the blast of a Japanese light machine gun the Baker Boys confiscated from the enemy up on Plateau Flat Head and by the sharp, heavy bark of an M1 Garand. The dumbfounded Japanese warriors started dropping like flies. Just as abruptly as the shooting began, the gunfire stopped. And once again, the jungle went silent.

This is not going according to plan, thought Sergeant Kato. *I start out with twenty-six men, and now ten of them are dead and four are wounded.* He screamed at the dark, silent jungle, shaking his head in anger and frustration. Turning to his wounded, he shouted, "Get back to headquarters, you're no good to me now, and leave the dead where they lie. They can't help us either."

The chief heard the captured machine gun firing and ran toward the muzzle flashes. He almost got shot for his trouble, but he was still able to stop the two Marines from firing before they gave away their position. The Japanese commander had bungled his only chance to eliminate half of his enemy in one fell swoop.

The four Americans quietly headed southwest, trying to get as far away from the enemy as they could before they changed course, and attempted to catch up with Gunny. The rain helped and hindered them in their efforts, but mostly it helped. Keeping to the shadows, the rain camouflaged their movements, enhancing their efforts to remain hidden in the background.

~ ~ ~

Sergeant Kato was now down to just twelve men, all that remained of the two squads he had been assigned to carry out his mission. Twelve men to go after a handful of Marines who had so far, proven that they were a very formidable force, a very capable squad of warriors that had given their enemy a black eye many times over the past several weeks.

The enemy platoon sergeant had a feeling that the Marines were no longer close to them, but the tenseness of the situation still lingered. His gaze searched the jungle for nothing more than something to do. Deep in thought, he shook his head, exasperated, frustrated almost to temper tantrums. What he had thought was going to be the perfect ambush, had turned into a foolish, wasted effort. Now he was forced to track down the Yankee animals in order to kill them all.

Using a shielded candle to see by, he scoured the ground, trying to make sense of all the tracks. Following the trail to the west, he finally came to a place that had only four sets of tracks. The deepness of the boot prints had him smiling to himself, pleased at his discovery. Just as he was turning to head back to his men, he remembered the firing from the south. The men he placed in ambush positions only had one light machine gun, and he had seen its barrel protruding from the camouflaged position. The short burst of firing came from the south.

The twelve-man detachment was still standing in the middle of the trail, soaking wet, but they dared not move for fear of getting shot by their raving lunatic of a sergeant. The senior sergeant's ruthlessness was beginning to show.

Sergeant Kato studied the trail as much as the rain would allow him to before he headed back to his men. He knew that as hard as the rain was coming down on the trail, the tracks of his enemy would be washed out in no time. He showed his anger at the situation again by the way he ordered his men to move out. They were now more afraid of him than they were of the American Marines.

Chapter 4

A few minutes after arriving at the trail, the four Marines discovered that the Japanese had already been there and gone. The two scouts made a quick area-search for any surprise stragglers the enemy might have been left behind, then the four of them headed for their next objective. They still had over a mile to go before they reached the footbridge spanning the river the chief crossed and had his little encounter with the crocodiles. That little encounter occurred before the footbridge was built. Once across the narrow bridge, they still had another three miles before they reached the start of the mountain pass. They knew what the head honcho's plan was so they didn't need to follow his tracks, but what the four men did need to do was to make sure Gunny wasn't bothered by the enemy. That was their part in the plan.

When they finally made it to the footbridge, the rearguard paused. Directly in front of them was the perfect place for the Japanese to lie in wait, for their enemy to get half way across the bridge and then open up on them. It was definitely time to pause and scope the area out.

Corporal Kirby had been put in charge because he'd earned the chance over and over again. Now he had one of those decisions to make that could cost the life of one or more of his men. "Chief, I need you to make sure the Japs aren't waiting for us on the other side."

"You want *me* to go across that bridge? What, are you nuts? Those Japs don't like me, Corporal. They might just start shooting at me on purpose. Then I'd have to jump in the river to keep from getting shot. Once I hit the water, I then have to worry about those damn crocodiles."

Corporal Kirby stared at the chief for a few seconds, and for the first time, successfully managed a stone-faced expression. "Okay, skinny, I've got a solution for you. You take off down the bridge. When you reach the halfway point, turn sideways. You're so scrawny that when you turn sideways, they'll never see you."

"Oh you're hilarious, Corporal, really hilarious. They'll see the reflection off my teeth and start shooting anyway."

Sergeant Thomas could only shake his head in wonder. *Damn. Now the clowns are wearing the uniform.*

PFC Fox was almost across the bridge. He only had about twenty-feet left to go, but he had been stopped dead in his tracks. *To hell with the Japs. This monster looks hungry!* There wasn't much he could do without giving himself away, so he started backing up, his carbine at the ready.

The three men had been watching the chief, ready to open fire in support if they needed to, but unexpectedly, the scout just stopped and started moving backwards. The three men looked at each other, puzzled. Then Sergeant Thomas asked. "What the hell is he doing?"

The other two answered at almost the same time. "I don't know."

The foot-bridge was close to sixty feet long, and now, because of his slow retreat, the little man still had about forty feet to go before he reached the other end. Without warning, Corporal Kirby stood up.

"Holy cow! Look at the size of that thing," he whispered harshly; absolutely stunned at the size of the creature.

Bonito and Thomas could now see what Kirby was staring at. The corporal spoke first. "What are you doing, chief? Don't bring that thing over here."

"Well, what do you want me to do with it, Lance? I'm not about to let it eat me."

"I don't know. Throw something at it."

"Throw what? My carbine?"

"Damn, chief. Why are you asking me? Just shoot the damn thing," whispered Kirby.

"Yeah, sure, and bring every Jap on the island down on our necks. Why don't you guys think of something? He looks awful hungry to me."

"Damn you, chief. I'll shoot you if you bring that damn thing over here."

Out of nowhere, a black shafted arrow slammed into the wooden planking, humming softly after the impact, about four inches in front of the crocodile's long, narrow, snout, causing it to suddenly jerk away. That little flinch was all it took. The crocodile was barely able to stay on the bridge because of its body width. When it jerked in surprise, part of its body slid off the bridge and then the rest of it followed, and with a loud splash, it was back in the river again, five-feet below the bridge.

"What the hell's the matter with you guys?" whispered Fox. "You were going to let that big-ass head full of teeth eat me, weren't you? You'd rather that thing ate me than try to help me. What's wrong with you?"

"Calm down, chief." whispered Kirby. "Geronimo chased the crocodile away before it could eat you, so there's nothing to get so excited about, now is there?"

The words hit him like a brick to the face. Shocked, the chief stood motionless for several breaths, staring intently at Corporal Kirby, absolutely refusing to believe what he just heard. "Who? No he didn't, you're lying. He couldn't have. Damn it, Lance. Why didn't you stop him?"

That damn, Apache. Now I suppose I gotta thank him for what he just did.

Gunny was having a hard time carrying the lieutenant because his left hip was beginning to hurt him. It seemed that he'd been carrying around lieutenants his entire career, but having to actually carry one on his shoulder was a bit ridiculous. The thought brought a smile to his face. *At least this lieutenant's worth carrying.* The gunnery sergeant's thoughts, however, were interrupted by a sudden burst of gunfire to his rear. His first thought was to stop and help out, but like Sergeant Stamper pointed out. "Those guys are back there fighting so that we can get away. You'll piss them off if you interfere, Al. They'll think you don't trust them enough to do their job."

Sergeant Stamper was right. They were Marines, and what they were doing was their job, so, the gunny kept his men moving, but before they went another thirty-yards, the shooting stopped. Then he heard the yelling. Almost immediately, a cheeky smile appeared, and words of wisdom spewed forth. "You know, Roger. I do believe that Jap's really pissed about something."

Sergeant Stamper smiled, but was interrupted before he could reply. Abruptly, the two sergeants heard a single shot, followed a moment or so later by the sudden outburst of automatic weapons' fire. Two blinks later, that too, stopped after a few seconds or so, and the jungle was silent once more.

"Gunny, I'll take the lieutenant, now." It was PFC Jones.

An involuntary, "Ahh," escaped from Gunny when he felt the weight of the lieutenant's body lifted off of his shoulders. Now that PFC Jones was carrying the junior officer, it was up to the gunnery sergeant to cover the rear. Visibility was very low due to the heavy downpour, so he stopped for a minute or two to wait until his men were well out of sight and then started following them. Half an hour went by before he caught up to Sergeant Stamper.

Gunny led everyone into the jungle and then he pulled up for a much needed break. While the PFC's took their break, the two sergeants moved up the trail towards the footbridge. Earlier, on their way to rescue the three Marines, the squad had been forced to cross the wooden-planked causeway. The Japanese had placed guards at each end, but those two guards only held the Marines up for about a minute thanks to the two scouts. Now, Gunny and Sergeant Stamper were making sure the enemy had not replaced their guards.

"It looks clear, Gunny."

"Okay, Roger. You stay here and keep an eye on things while I go back and bring everyone forward."

Sergeant Stamper's expression was almost as stone-faced as Gunny's. "Don't get lost, Al."

His facial muscles straining mightily, the gunnery sergeant from Oklahoma bowed as he replied, his hand sweeping majestically towards the ground. "I will heed your words of wisdom, oh Roger of Pitt."

"Oh shut up you overgrown loudspeaker. Damn! Where are all the good comedians when you need one?" Get out of here, Al, before I shoot you just to put me out of my misery."

The two Marines had been together for a long time. Too long thought Gunny. But there wasn't anyone he'd rather have covering his back.

Instead of finding his men in the jungle where he left them, Gunny found them moving up the trail, all five of them. PFC Choctaw was in the lead when they met. "I'm sorry Gunny," he stammered. "The lieutenant here wouldn't listen to me. He said he'd be damned if he was going to let a Marine carry him anywhere. He said it was the Navy's job to carry the Marines, not the other way around."

Gunny smiled and nodded his head before replying. "That's fine, PFC. He's a good squid."

Turning towards the good squid, the gunny held out his hand and said; "Nice to see you puttering around. How do you feel, sir?"

Smiling drunkenly, and missing the gunny's out-stretched hand on his first attempt, the lieutenant's reply was a bit slurred. "Like I'm swimming in a barrel of oil, Gunny. I feel like my body's made of rubber. What happened? I think they drugged us, Gunny."

PFC Garcia was just standing there, with a blank expression on his face, but PFC Hawks was casting wild frightened glances at the jungle. It made Gunny sick to see his two Marines in the condition they were in.

Halfway through their last mission, during one of Gunny's supply rendezvous', the Marines were handed new orders and a Navy lieutenant. The idea was an experiment, so the lieutenant asked for volunteers and Garcia and Hawks stepped forward.

The Japanese found a small natural harbor on the southeast coast of the island, so they built it up, turning the small nature-made anchorage into a fully functioning supply port. The mission of the three men was to blow up three ships that were anchored in the bay. Applying underwater demo to the hull of multiple enemy ships was the experiment. One of those ships was an ammo transport, tied to the dock. Another was a small supply freighter anchored in the center of the inlet, and the third was a Destroyer anchored close to a narrow, shallow channel; the only entrance into the cove.

The experiment was somewhat of a success. The three ships were blown up as planned, but the timers malfunctioned, and the under-water demo went off prematurely, almost killing the three men setting the charges. Their dysfunctional state was a result of that premature detonation.

PFC Hawks' wild frightened glances, however, were the results from a different horror. Also during their last mission, Gunny and his boys, along with Sergeant Kato and two of his men, were captured by cannibals. Bonito was on the scout at the time, so he was better able to avoid capture. After capture, PFC Hawks was forced to watch while the cannibals began eating his best friend, Ted Lewis, as fast as they could cook the poor man. Geronimo, however, ruined their lengthy dinner plans and the Marines escaped, taking their Japanese enemy with them.

In thanks for saving their lives, Sergeant Kato agreed, upon word of honor, to return to his headquarters and not continue the chase until after he heard from Gunny. Three days into the agreement, the boys of Baker squad retaliated, leaving behind explosions, and a smoldering, cannibal village. When they left the ruined village behind, they walked away with two bows and almost two dozen black shafted arrows. And the signal was heard by Sergeant Kato, dissolving the word of honor agreement.

"Nice to see you up and around, sir, but it's time to go. Sergeant Stamper is waiting for us at the crossing, and the Japs are coming up behind us, so we need to move fast."

Only ten-minutes had elapsed before the Marines were crossing the foot-bridge. Although the three men were now able to walk, they were still in need of help. They were like children on bicycles for the first time. They needed Marine Corps training wheels to help keep them upright, but at least they were alive, and they were free of their Japanese tormentors.

The relay team took almost four hours to reach the mountain pass, but by then, the effects of the drug had worn off enough to allow the three men to walk without help. Gunny stopped for a short, five-minute breather before they headed up the mountain trail. He now had seven men, but only four of them were armed.

Gunny's first impulse was to head west, straight to the cave instead of using the mountain trail, but he finally decided to stick to the original plan. The climb up the east side of the mountain was brutal and treacherous, and with the condition his Marines were in and the conditions they would have to climb up the mountain under, they would probably still be struggling up the mountain when the sun came up. They could very well be exposed for all to see, plus the four men following behind wouldn't know that he had deviated from the plan.

The enemy squad was about twenty-minutes behind Gunny when the boys of Baker squad started up the mountain trail.

The trail itself stretched across the mountain from east to west for about three miles, but it was by no means easy. The rain was making it extremely difficult for the men to maintain their footing, so they were unable to move very fast. This slow pace would allow the Japanese to gain some ground on them, but then, they too would have to face the difficult task of climbing up the mountain trail, just like the Marines.

~ ~ ~

The two scouts started up the mountain trail with Fox in the lead, followed by Corporal Kirby, and then Sergeant Thomas. It was slow going for the four men. They were climbing in single file, huffing and puffing while they struggled from rain-drenched tree to rain-drenched tree, trying to maintain their balance. The rain had slowed down to a steady drizzle, but the footing was still treacherous and slippery as ice. They would take three steps and slide down two.

The climb from the base of the mountain to the top of the pass was almost 600 feet. Even with the trees to help them, it was still a hazardous ascent. At the pace they were forced to climb, the scramble was going to be long and hard before they reached the summit.

The four men had been struggling up the trail for almost an hour when they heard a muffled explosion. They stopped for a second to listen, but nothing else happened. They started climbing again after a couple of minutes, but they didn't advance very far before the chief whispered an alert. "Japs! Hit the ground!"

Through the breath-holding silence, they could faintly hear the ranting of a very agitated Jap. Corporal Kirby had crawled up beside PFC Fox, hoping, to see what was going on.

"What are they saying, Corporal?"

Kirby's face was all lit up when he replied. "It's not they, chief, it's him."

"Him?"

"Yeah," replied Kirby. "That sergeant is pissed at having lost more men, and it sounds like he's taking it out on the men he has left."

PFC Bonito was wearing a hopeful expression on his face when he spoke his thought out loud. "Maybe he'll shoot his own men and save us the trouble."

The four men laughed quietly, easing a bit, an extremely tense situation.

"What happened?"

Corporal Kirby looked at Sergeant Thomas. "I'll bet a whole month's pay that Sergeant Stamper left the Japs a little present. We're going to have to be more careful from now on, guys, because I think he'll be leaving a few more surprises for those bastards."

"Hey, chief, I need you to skinny on up there and find out how many Japs we're up against."

PFC Fox stared at Kirby for a moment or two before he replied. "Geeze Corporal, you've been around Gunny too long. You're starting to sound just like him."

Kirby's face lit up just long enough to express his appreciation for the compliment, then his face lost all expression. "Thanks, chief. Now get going you worthless Marine, and don't get caught."

49

Corporal Kirby was still carrying the captured machine gun so he moved off the trail to the left with Sergeant Thomas, while PFC Bonito moved off to the right of the trail. Bonito was laughing to himself. *I sure am glad it's him and not me. That Cherokee is probably going to end up with twenty or thirty pounds of mud in his pants low-crawling through this shit.*

PFC Fox inched his way toward the site of the explosion, scampering from shadow to shadow until he was forced to hit the ground and low-crawl to the spot of the blast. Silently, he moved into the shadows along the left side of the trail and stopped to listen. At first, all he could hear was the steady plop, plop, plop, of the raindrops falling from the leaves and hitting the ground. Then he heard ragged breathing. He stayed where he was for another ten-minutes before he was satisfied that no one else was there. After one last eye-search he crawled toward the sounds of the heavy breathing, but before he got there, the fight for breath had stopped.

PFC Fox stood up and looked around. He found three mangled bodies lying on the path, and another one off to the right side of the trail, the source of the labored breathing he had heard. But the man was now dead.

The light rain was not enough to wash out the tracks yet, so with the first light of a new day, PFC Fox was able to make out some of the tracks. Then he froze, and his eyes narrowed. He had seen those tracks before…many times. Deep in thought, David Little Fox looked up the trail through the dawning light. *So, he's the one chasing after Gunny. Good. Maybe I'll get another crack at him.* With that thought still on his mind, he headed back down the trail.

Chapter 5

The anchor of the relay, the seven escapees, had finally made it to the other side of the mountain pass and were moving southeast through the flat lands of the jungle. Only two or three more hours separated the hunted men from the cave, but they still had the problem of the Japanese who were following them. The Marines heard their first surprise go off, but they hadn't heard the second one go boom. That meant that either the enemy hadn't made it that far yet, or they had discovered the second surprise and bypassed it. Either way, Gunny knew he had gained some time on his pursuers; he just didn't know how much.

~ ~ ~

Sergeant Kato was beyond rage. He was now down to eight men, and they were so exhausted they were unable to go any further until they had a long break. Even he was feeling the need for a breather. That's what had him so frustrated, his own inability to go on. After an hour or so of rest, he pushed on after the Marines. The situation was no longer a matter of ridding the island of the Americans. To Sergeant Kato, his fight with the Marines had become personal. His sense of honor had been violated, and all that mattered now was that he be victorious. Death meant nothing to him. His men meant nothing to him. They were just a tool to be used to satisfy his sense of honor.

He saw the string too late to stop two of his men from kicking it, but he was able to warn the rest of his men seconds before the two explosions went off. Again, the Marine dogs were showing how treacherous they were. Then he smiled. *My enemy is very smart. Each time we run into a trap, they gain a little more time.* Again he smiled, but this time it was not a very pleasant smile. His enemy had failed to hide their trail like they had in the past.

~ ~ ~

The Marines were still trudging along through the jungle when they heard their second surprise go off. It was a beautiful sound to the men. It meant that their pursuers were now not so numerous anymore. More than anything else, however; it was a morale boost, giving them a renewed sense of urgency, a fresh surge of energy in their step. "Ha! I'll bet he's pissed! Too bad you ran out of presents, Sergeant Stamper. I like the sound they give off. Boom, and one less enemy to worry about. I like that sound. Boom!"

"Damn, Al. Have you been hitting Kirby's elixir again?"

Seven very tired Marines finally made it onto Plateau Flat Head, just in time to make a mad dash to the cave before the rain hit. The wind had picked up again, along with the rain. The Marines had just barely made it to the ledge leading to their digs when the rain hit, but it didn't matter anymore. A few minutes later, they were as snug as bugs in a cave.

The in-mountain hideaway was almost empty of supplies. What supplies they did have were taken out of the crates so that the wood from the crates could be used to build a fire to dry out their rain drenched clothes. Just that thought alone birthed all kinds of excitement. *Dry socks, dry boots, dry skivvies, and dry uniforms. Dry everything!* What a wondrous display of enthusiasm and emotion the men put forth. With the rain, also came the thought that maybe their trail up the mountain would be washed away. Maybe they would lose their pursuers long enough to finally wear dry clothes again.

The thought of warm, dry clothes, however, lasted just long enough to become a wistful dream. The time spent thinking about their present situation was also at an end.

No more dodging fights. The Baker Boys were tired of running, tired of being forced to avoid a fight because of orders. They felt it was time they went toe-to-toe with their enemy, to show them who they were up against.

Gunny, however, wasn't ready for a reckoning yet. He still had four Marines somewhere out in the jungle. And until those men made it back to the cave, he wasn't going to do anything. Besides, he knew that his two scouts would want to be in on the action, and he didn't want to disappoint them.

Twenty-minutes after the Marines made it into the cave, Sergeant Kato discovered the trail up the mountain. He found it by accident. He was tired and a bit clumsy. He didn't lift his foot high enough to clear the rock completely, so he tripped face forward to the ground, and there, under an inch of rain water was a boot print. It was pointing up the mountain. He found several more boot tracks, and they were all facing towards the top of the mountain. The enemy tracker smiled, and then his smile tightened. Standing up, he took several steps backwards, thinking to himself. *Had I not fallen, I probably would have thought that this was another of their false trails.*

The clouds were starting to cover the top of the mountain with a thin white blanket. Staring up at the rapidly deteriorating conditions, a vicious smile appeared on his face. He had fought under similar conditions in the past, and had always been victorious. Bringing up his past victories also fortified his growing confidence that he would emerge victorious from the next battle as well.

Gathering what was left of his men, they started climbing. After a difficult, two and a half hour struggle up the side, the seven Japanese warriors were crouching down, cautiously searching the top of the plateau for their elusive foe. The enemy troops were hunkered down about a hundred-yards from the radio tent, but it was no longer standing. The tent had been blown over by the previous night's storm, along with the makeshift table and the captured radio. The area looked deserted, but Kato knew that was wrong. He knew that his enemy was somewhere on the top of this mountain, and he was determined to find that enemy no matter how long it took him.

Was that smoke? Immediately, he stopped. He had just caught a brief whiff of smoke, but then it was gone. It had happened so fast that he was unable to determine which direction it came from. Taking a more determined look around, his gaze shifted towards Pot Belly Ridge. *Maybe it came from the north? The jungle looks a bit thicker in that direction, a good place to hide a fire.* So, with that thought in mind, Sergeant Kato headed north, away from the cave.

~ ~ ~

PFC Fox was about a hundred-yards out in front when he heard the second explosion, so he waited a few minutes for everyone to catch up with him before he went to see what had blown up. Forty-minutes of cautious walking brought them to the scene, where they discovered two dead enemy soldiers. PFC Fox turned to face Corporal Kirby and said, "Corporal, if we don't hurry up the pace, Sergeant Stamper's booby traps are going to end up killing all the Japs before we get a chance to fire a single shot."

Corporal Kirby was conquering the knack for stone-faced expressions, so when he replied, he threw the little scout into a panicked tailspin. "Then I suggest you quicken up the pace, don't you think, chief?"

PFC Fox stared back at Corporal Kirby for a few seconds, then he reached up and removed the corporal's helmet with his left hand and patted him on the head with his right hand. Then the chief smiled deviously. "You have hair on your head, so you can't be Gunny. Damn, Lance, lighten up. You're scaring me." And the pace quickened.

Thirty-minutes into their quickened pace, the scout noticed some movement up ahead. He was only able to see a little color here and there, but nothing definite. Two hours went by, and he was still unable to identify who was moving up ahead. Whoever it was, they were in a real hurry all of a sudden and had not taken a break in the last couple of hours or even slowed down. It wasn't until the four Americans were halfway up the mountain that Fox finally caught a glimpse of who was in front of them. He immediately signaled, and within seconds, all four men were hugging the side of the plateau. A few minutes ticked by before the four Marines were together again.

"It's that Jap tracker, and he's got six men with him."

"I don't think there's anything we can do about it right now," whispered Corporal Kirby. "They'd have us by the horns if we started something from here. Let's wait until we get on top before we try anything."

"Corporal, we don't have the moxie to take them on anymore. At least, not head to head. We lost that Jap machine gun up on the trail when you dropped it in the mud."

"Hell," whispered Corporal Kirby, "I don't know how to take the damn thing apart to clean it, so why should I lug that stupid thing around if we can't use it?"

The little scout was wearing a somewhat devious expression on his face when his next words spewed forth. "I have an idea, but you might not like it."

Looking at PFC Fox, the corporal decided that his scout was right; he wasn't going to like it. So, with a deep sigh he replied. "Okay, chief, let's hear it."

Immediately, the little man turned to PFC Bonito and whispered his question. "How many arrows do you have left?"

"Four," was the other scout's immediate answer.

"That gives us seven all together. Only one of us can

miss once."

Corporal Kirby shook his head. "I don't like it already."

"Oh, come on, Corporal, you haven't heard much more than a question yet. Give me some time, here."

Kirby looked at Fox and shook his head. "Maybe I don't want to hear it, chief." After a short pause, the corporal gave in. "Oh, what the hell. Okay, chief, let's hear your idea."

A few minutes after their discussion ended, Corporal Kirby was slinking his way to the cave, to explain the plan to Gunny, while the two scouts headed for the Japanese, who were wandering around somewhere near Pot Belly Ridge.

The clouds had dropped below the top of the mountain, giving the jungle covered mountain top an eerie ghostlike appearance. The wind had stopped altogether, but it was still drizzling, and despite the rain, it was still hot and clammy on the floor of the plateau.

Gunny was not a very happy Marine. When he heard from Corporal Kirby what the two scouts had planned, he hit the roof. "You let him talk you into that, Corporal?"

"Their plan is a good one, Gunny," replied Corporal Kirby, "and besides, it was my call. I had to make a decision and I made it."

Gunny looked at Corporal Kirby for a few seconds while he thought about his corporal's response. *Where did he come up with the guts to make that call?* Turning away from Kirby, he smiled, *Well, I guess he is ready.*

~ ~ ~

Kato was shaking his head at an ominous feeling that came out of nowhere. *Something is not right. I can feel it. It's too quiet, too still.* Abruptly, the ghost-like eeriness of the jungle was shattered by the howl of a wolf. It was a lonely, chilling sound that struck fear into the hearts of Kato's men and sent chills rippling through the sergeant's body. *Sooo*, he thought, *the fox is back.*

Everyone in the cave also heard the howl. They knew who it was, and still, it sent shivers through everyone inside. Gunny's smile was grim. *Good hunting, Marines.*

Corporal Kirby spent thirty-minutes arguing his point, but he finally convinced Gunny to let the two scouts handle the Japanese. "This is their kind of weather, their kind of fight, Gunny."

Of course, the rest of the squad stood solidly behind PFC Choctaw. "Come on Corporal, there's too many of them out there. Those Japs are going to kill that little man!"

Corporal Kirby's quick response was brimming with confidence. "No, Ox, you're wrong. The Japs didn't bring enough to do the job. Besides, Geronimo is out there watching the chief's back." Then came the fastball; strike three. "Think about it, guys. If you go out there now, you might get one, or both of them killed." And so ended that argument.

A few minutes after the squad's discussion ended, Sergeant Stamper walked over to Gunny, his pearly-whites were showing brightly when he asked; "What was it you said to Corporal Kirby? Oh yeah. You let him talk you into that?"

Gunny replied, but his attempt at humor was weak. "Oh, shut up, Roger, and get out your map."

~ ~ ~

PFC Fox stood about seventy-yards northeast of Kato's position. PFC Bonito was standing about the same distance, but he was southwest of the Japanese.

"Hey, Tojo. Why don't you tell your men to stay out of it and just you and me fight it out?"

A mocking laugh echoed for a few seconds, then Sergeant Kato answered with a question. "Are you challenging me like I read in one of your western books?"

The chief's reply was a bit less than complimentary, and it was intended, deliberately, to piss off his enemy.

"Hey, you catch on pretty quick for a sergeant."

You arrogant dog, thought Sergeant Kato. "Where is your friend, the other Yankee dog?"

Still smiling deviously, the Swain County scout replied. "Oh, he's probably standing right behind you by now."

It was an involuntary act, and Sergeant Kato's face turned deep red after he caught himself turning to look back over his shoulder. Now he was getting more than just a bit agitated. "You arrogant fool! My name is Akira Kato, and I will cut out your liver and feed it to the pigs!"

Bonito was shaking his head and smiling. *That Cherokee can sure piss a man off when he wants to.*

"Hey, Tojo, you going to call off your men, or do you want me to kill them first? Maybe one of them might get lucky, and you won't have to come out and play."

How dare this Yankee dog talk to me this way? He is deliberately taunting me. Sergeant Kato was furious. His whispered words were harsh when he spoke to his men.

"Find him and bring him to me. I will cut out his heart while he watches."

Reluctantly, the six men stood up and moved out into the Jungle.

Sergeant Kato followed his men with his eyes until they had moved out of sight. His expression was full of vicious hate and his thoughts were merciless. *They will make a good distraction for me*, he thought. *While the Yankees are fighting them, I will hunt the Americans down, and kill them one at a time.*

The chief waited only a minute for Kato's answer, and when the answer didn't come, he quietly moved south. It was time to talk with Geronimo.

After the birdcalls, and a few minutes of sneaking about, the two scouts finally met. "I don't think he liked your insults," whispered Bonito.

"I think you're right," answered Fox. "I heard a lot of movement before I left cover, so I think he sent his men out after us."

"Great, let's give them something they haven't heard before."

"Good idea. Give me thirty minutes to get back over there, and then you can start singing."

PFC Bonito had to struggle hard not to laugh. "If I start singing, it'll scare even you away." A minute or so later, the two Marines smiled, shook hands, and parted company.

The conditions were really spooky, sneaking through the misty rain and clouds, where every shadow could be the enemy. PFC Bonito had his neck of the woods to cover, PFC Fox had his, and the *Pot Belly* rocks were the dividing line – the birdcalls were the identifiers.

The Pot Belly rocks got their name because they resembled a fat man's beer belly. Pot Belly Ridge got its name because it looked like the rocks were hand carved to the shape they were, and formed into an age old idol. An age old idol that over time had crumpled to the ground in large chunks of scattered ruin.

A shadow was moving towards Fox, and then that shadow turned into a form. It was the enemy. Silently, the scout moved in behind the shadowy figure and was about to strike when his instincts kicked in, and he instantly dropped to the ground, a move that might have saved his life. Immediately following his sudden drop to the ground, someone tripped over him and plunged head long into some vine entangled foliage, and a dull thump was heard. The chief stayed on the ground, unmoving. A living shadow among the deeper shadows.

The form Fox had been stalking heard a noise to his rear and turned, firing as he turned. But there was nothing there. He failed to see the Marine scout lying on the ground only three feet away. Slowly, the enemy turned and continued on, shaken up because of what just happened.

Fox waited where he was for about three or four minutes before he rose to his feet, and again, began to stalk his foe. *That was close. I might not be so lucky the next time. Whoever tripped over me must have had quite a surprise when I dropped to the ground so fast. I'll bet it was Tojo himself.*

PFC Bonito heard the shooting and started moving northeast. His thoughts on the plan changed as soon as the shots were fired. *To hell with this idea, I'm gonna help. I'm not going to sit here and do nothing, while he has to fight seven Japs.* Gliding silently through the rain and low hanging clouds, he headed towards the sound of the shots.

Visibility was really poor on the jungle-infested plateau. The clouds covered the rocky, flat shaped mountaintop completely, dropping to two-hundred feet below the crest. It was eerie and unnatural in appearance. The trees would emerge between eye-blinks, and at first glimpse, they resembled the enemy each man was fighting, and each man was keenly aware that any mistake or hesitation would cost him his life.

The enemy had already lost three men. Two had been killed by PFC Fox and one was killed by a panic stricken soldier. It was a weird, strange situation and it was heart-pounding, almost terrifying.

A shadow appeared out of the dense cloud cover so fast that Bonito barely had time to react. The dull clash of the knife blades striking each other was somewhat muffled by the rain and cloudbank. Before the fight could continue, however, there was a whispered curse.

"What the hell are you doing? I almost killed you!"

The two Marines broke apart and then moved off about twenty-feet, both men shaking from the sudden spurt of adrenaline.

"You dream a lot, don't you," whispered Bonito. "I

couldn't sit there and do nothing while you had all the fun. Besides, this is my fight too, you know."

"Okay, Okay, but next time, warn a friend."

Unable to hide his smile, he still managed a whispered reply. "I'm coming, Little Fox. There, now you've been warned."

"Thanks for the warning, Geronimo."

The two Marines spent the next ten-minutes discussing their new plan of action. That plan was simple: kill all the Japs and get back to the cave.

Chapter 6

Sergeant Kato regained consciousness about ten-minutes after his collision. His neck and back hurt, but it was his head that was causing him the most pain. Not to mention his pride. He kept thinking to himself. *How could I be so stupid?* When he tripped over PFC Fox, he had run headlong into a tree on the other side of the vine entangled, jungle foliage, knocking himself out in the process. The shooting off in the distance told him where his enemy was, so off he went, heading towards the sound of the shots, his head pounding.

PFC Fox was still smarting over the fact that his left arm was barely able to hold Bonito's knife at bay. It was weak, and it hurt like hell. His weakness concerned him more than he cared to admit, but he wasn't about to back down from *this* fight. *I just have to be extra careful.*

PFC Bonito had also noticed the weakness in the little man's left arm, as well, so instead of following the plan they had come up with, he moved off about twenty-yards away, and then waited for the chief to move out. When the Cherokee scout headed north, he followed, shadowing his friend, all the while humming to himself, and thinking; *He'll probably beat me over the head with the closest tree handy, if he discovers what I'm doing. I'll tell him after our little war with the Japanese tracker is over.*

Silent as a hunting predator, the Apache scout moved from shadow to shadow, always keeping the *wolf* in sight. Quietly moving off to the northeast to give the chief some maneuvering space, he went on his own hunt. His goal was to keep the Cherokee's blindside, clear of the enemy.

A slight breeze started blowing in from the east around

2230 hours. As a result, the clouds covering the mountain began moving off to the west, but a much darker batch of clouds was moving in, with the possibility of bad thunder storms. Not a good night to be fighting a battle, no matter how small it was. But the little man from Swain County wasn't concerned about the weather. He was more concerned with the enemy he was about to attack.

The man Fox was stalking could feel that something was wrong, but he couldn't put a finger on it. Out of nowhere, an arm grabbed him around the throat, closing off his air. Then he saw a shadow of movement, a gleam of reflection, and death instantly followed. Fox quietly laid the man down onto the ground, out of his way, and then moved off a couple of yards to listen. Nothing unnatural could be heard. He was getting ready to move to the south, but stopped when he heard a scream. It was a terror filled scream that raised the hair on his arms; it came from somewhere close by, from the northeast. Moving about thirty-yards to the west, Fox hunkered down and then hooted like an owl. A few seconds later, he was rewarded by a return hoot. *Good*, he thought. *At least that last scream wasn't Geronimo.*

The soft call of a whippoorwill was followed shortly by the caw of a crow. The signal to meet was acknowledged, so the two Marines began converging on each other. It was a gathering to share information, such as, how many of the enemy were left. However, something caught the chief's attention, and he immediately crouched down beside a vine-covered tree, waiting and listening. *What was that?* Slowly, silently, he cautiously circled back around, hoping to get a look at his backtrail. *It must be Tojo. Bonito should still be to the northeast.*

He waited another couple of minutes before moving north. While he was searching his backtrail, he heard that same noise again. This time, though, the disturbance was to his right. The little man from the Carolinas turned to his right and waited in the shadows. He only had to wait a minute or so.

David Little Fox stood in the shadows and watched as his enemy appeared out of the murkiness directly in front of him. Then the chief took a step forward into view. "All this sneaking around because you're afraid to face me. No wonder you guys are losing the war."

Sergeant Kato stopped and stared at the little scout standing before him. *The arrogance of this puny little man.* His eyes narrowed and a sinister smile appeared on his face. "Here I am Yankee dog. Shall we begin?"

PFC Fox didn't say a word, but he had a menacing expression on his face when he closed to contact.

The two knives striking each other were the only sounds heard. Even the insects stopped their buzzing, but only long enough to place their bets. Over and over, the two knives spoke, scraping and clashing each time they came together. The two men were circling each other, and then attacking when they saw an opening, their knives singing dully when that opening quickly closed.

As if on cue, the two enemies paused to catch their breaths. It was a short pause, and then they charged at each other. The clash of the weapons striking each other, could be heard more than twenty-yards away as they parried each other's blows. Also twenty-yards away was PFC Bonito. He was standing, watching through parted vines while the *wolf* fought his foe. He wanted so desperately to intervene, but he knew he couldn't, not if wanted to keep the chief's respect. All he could do at the moment was urge his friend on, and try to control his sudden arm thrusts before he gave himself away. The urge to attack was hard for him to control.

Fox moved back a couple of steps, and the two warriors began to circle each other again.

"You are good, Yankee dog, but you will soon die."

The chief's left arm had started bleeding again from the exertion. It wasn't bleeding much now, but later on in the fight it could slow him down enough to give his opponent a serious edge. Smirking, little man replied. "You talk too much, Tojo."

The man from Swain County, North Carolina continued to sneer, but it turned serious, and then malicious. "You're holding your knife wrong, Tojo. You should have the blade edge-up so you can slice into your opponent. Bleed him useless. Then you can kill him easier."

Without warning, a thunderclap exploded, loud and close, and both men jumped. Then the rain hit. When the next blast of thunder erupted, it was accompanied by a quick series of lightning strikes, and they were popping all around the two combatants while they stood staring at each other. The weird strobe-light effect from the lightning strikes made it harder for the two men to attack each other. One second Fox was facing an enemy to his front, and the next lightning strike later, he was facing the same enemy, now to his right. The fight had turned into a strange and bizarre struggle.

Fox felt, rather than saw, that Kato had somehow managed to end up on his left. He didn't hesitate. He dropped low to the ground, and balancing on his left foot, he immediately spun around to his right. Backhanded, and with his right arm extended; his knife led the way until contact. The blow struck Kato coming in, just above his right hip. The knife went into Kato's side all the way to the hilt. It was a deep shocking wound that pretty much took the fight out of the enemy sergeant.

Now unarmed, the chief immediately scurried back a few steps and waited for the next lightning strike to light up the area, so he could see where his enemy had fallen.

Without warning, the plateau was lit up by a dazzling, three-second lightning show, and there was Akira Kato. He was lying on his left side, both hands empty, with a fourteen-inch knife sticking out of his exposed side. PFC Fox walked over to where Kato's knife lay on the ground, picked it up and threw it deeper into the jungle. Then he turned and waited for the enemy sergeant to die.

Kato took almost an hour to die, and during that time, neither man spoke to each other. The mortally wounded sergeant was in too much pain and shock to speak, and PFC Fox had nothing he wanted to say to his enemy. Just before Sergeant Kato died, PFC Bonito emerged from the mist and walked up to Fox.

"You all right, chief?"

"Yeah, Jose, I'm all right."

PFC Fox, with tears in his eyes, looked at PFC Bonito, and pointing down at his enemy, he said; "This is for Corporal Dent, PFC Spruel, and PFC Daily." Then he turned to face Kato. "You murdering skunk, you killed your last American."

Loose-limbed, the chief plopped to the ground cross legged, lowered his head, and began to cry. All this time he had carried the grief of losing his friends, deep inside of himself, never letting it out, never letting it rise to the surface. But in the last few minutes of the fight, he felt that his three friends were standing beside him, helping him to win his fight. Now, with the death of Kato, all his grief rose to the surface, and for more than twenty-minutes, he cried like a baby over his lost friends.

Dawn found the two Marines still sitting in the same place. PFC Fox was no longer crying, and PFC Bonito was waiting patiently, waiting for his friend to let him know that it was time to go. That's where Gunny and the squad found the two scouts, still sitting cross legged, two silent statues in the quiet stillness of the jungle morning.

Chapter 7

The Baker Boys finally did have their time in Sydney, and it was quite a bash. Two week's worth of Sydney crammed into four days was an amazing accomplishment. One tavern was completely closed down because the roof fell in ... on a bet.

"Hey, Ox. I bet a whole month's pay you can't move that support beam."

"Wait a minute. You're saying all I have to do is move that 10-by-10 and you'll give me your whole month's pay? How far you want it moved?"

"Six-inches ought to do it."

"All right, Jonesy. You're on."

Turning away from the bar, Choctaw smiled and said to the patrons; "You better leave in case the roof comes down." They didn't believe him until the roof came down on their heads.

The big Marine walked over to the squared, wooden support beam, located in the center of the tavern, and wrapped his arms around it in a bear hug and winked at the chief. "Watch this little man."

With his knees slightly bent, the bruiser from the bayous buried his chest against the beam, tightening his grip on it, as if trying to squeeze the beam into submission. Straining so hard his face was red, the big man struggled to straighten his legs and move the beam. Caught up in the moment, even the bartender was silently urging the big Marine on.

A sudden screech caught everyone's breath, and for a long few seconds, all was quiet, no clinking of glasses; nothing. Another squeal of protest from the nails lasted only a couple of seconds, and without further waste of time, the beam was ripped away from the floor. Several protesting cracks were heard overhead, and that was all the incentive everyone in the bar needed to begin evacuation. Only one man didn't make it out of the bar in time, but he did survive.

When the authorities arrived at the scene, they found the bartender trapped behind the bar, shaking his head, and still amazed at Choctaw's feat of strength. Everyone was astonished. When they were asked by the authorities what happened, they pointed to each other and said; "Ask him, I didn't see a thing." A bond of friendship had been formed with the Baker Boys, and a legend was born. The patrons of the Three Monkey's had no intention of sharing their legend or their memory with anyone but themselves.

Three weeks after leaving Boogeyman Island for the second time, the Baker Boys found themselves on another sub again. This time, however, they had no idea where they were going. It was a cloudy, moonless night. The boat was on the surface, gliding silently through the darkened waters at ten knots. Not all, however, was as quiet as the Pacific night. The chugging diesel engines of a ghost gray boat disturbed the soft Pacific night without recourse. The sailors manning their battle, surface, stations could see off in the distance, the darker shadows of an island slipping past them on the starboard side of the boat.

It was creepy. It was dangerous. Everyone onboard the sub was on edge. They were deep in enemy waters, riding on the surface. The whispered hail from the Chief of the Boat was filled with the tension caused by the situation. "Captain?"

"Yes, Chief."

"Radar is still down, sir."

"Well, keep at it Chief, were sailing blind here. Let me know as soon as you get the radar up and running."

"Aye, aye, Skipper."

Captain Weaver really had no choice at the moment. The subs' batteries were low and needed recharging. The only way to recharge the batteries was to run the diesels, and without a snorkel exhaust, the submarine had to travel on the surface. Although it was dark enough to hide the vessel from sight, their radar equipment had malfunctioned, which left them surface blind, unable to detect an enemy ship until it was in point-blank range of the boat, and far too late for the sub to submerge to safety.

Six-hours of agonizing tension still remained before sunup, providing the radar situation wasn't resolved. Six-hours would also give the sub skipper a little more time to charge up the batteries, and pray it was enough to travel submerged during the day.

The Baker Boys were on another mission, their sixth one. Onboard the submarine, only Gunny and the sub skipper knew where they were heading, and they were under orders not to disclose that information to anyone; including their own men. It was a top-secret mission that only six people knew about: Colonel Travis, the submarine skipper, and Gunnery Sergeant Baker were three of those six.

~ ~ ~

The squad was topside, spending the last few minutes of their fifteen-minute fresh air break, enjoying the cool, wind-swept spray of the Pacific on their faces. Then it was back into the belly of the sub. There were only six Marines under Gunny's command now. PFC Hawks and PFC Garcia had been deemed unfit for combat duty and were on their way back to the States. Jonesy was left behind in Sydney, recuperating from the broken leg he received when the roof of the pub crashed down on him before he could make his escape. Also, the experiment that Lieutenant Sterns had been sent out to do was somewhat successful, so he was on his way back to the command that sent him, leaving Gunny, lieutenant-less and happy again.

The Marines were on their way to the conning tower when disaster struck the sub. An enemy destroyer suddenly loomed out of the darkness, bearing right down on the helpless sub and colliding with it just behind the conning tower. The bow of the destroyer knifed its way into the hull, causing the bow and stern of the sub to fold back towards the sides of the destroyer. The force of the destroyer pushing the sub, against the pressure of the ocean waves, broke the sub in half. The sounds of the collision; and the screeching and rending of the metal hull were loud, until it was swallowed into silence by the vast emptiness of the dark Pacific spaces. The blaring horns on the Japanese destroyer was even louder as it knifed its way through the hull of the sub, celebrating a great death-blow. The destroyer didn't stop or even slow down to see if there were any survivors. It just kept on going and disappeared into the darkness.

Most of the men on the conning tower were crushed when that part of the hull slammed into the port side of the destroyer. While all these events were happening, the Baker Boys were knocked into the sea by the impact of the collision, just escaping the explosions and fires erupting from the stricken sub. The surface of the sea was instantly turned into a burning, boiling, cauldron of flames, motivated by the oil and diesel fuel that bubbled out of the stricken vessel. Seconds later, the stern of the sub slipped silently into the depths below, leaving only the bow of the boat still bobbing like a cork in the water, a floating chunk of gray steel, marking the spot where the ship and its crew had died. Then the bow also slid silently beneath the burning waves, and the fire silhouetted night grew silent.

The only survivors were the Marines, but they weren't telling anyone about the collision. They were unconscious, swaying up and down in the Pacific waves like a leaf on a slowly meandering river, their life vests securely fastened.

They should thank the captain for his insistence on wearing the damn things while topside, but they couldn't. Captain Weaver was dead, and so was their mission.

Nobody knew that the sub had gone down, so there would be no rescue efforts made. The survivors were now on their own. A few minutes after the stern went under, ship-board items began rising up to the surface. The floating wreckage of the dead submarine, a temporary grave marker showing the sub's final resting place.

~ ~ ~

Colonel Travis was sitting in front of his commanding general, toasting to the success of their most recent mission.

"Tom, your Marines did an outstanding job on their previous three missions. That is why they were chosen for this mission."

Colonel Travis tried to hide his pride-induced smile, but he wasn't very successful in that endeavor. "They didn't get much of a break sir. Only four days in Sydney? Gunny's boys slept the first day and half just to get that out of the way, and then what happens? The MP's find them before they can get past the first beer joint. That's not much time considering what they went through and how long they were on that island."

"Tom, why don't you give Sydney a break. Your boys closed down the first beer joint they came to. According to the owner it's going to take over a year to rebuild the place. We're lucky that's as far as they got. The MP's were only doing their job." Shaking his head, the general continued. "Hell, Tom, I agree with you, they didn't get much time, but we were handed a unique opportunity, and we had to act on it now. Your men were the closest and the handiest we had available. How long have they been gone?"

"They've been gone now for almost two weeks, sir. Estimates have them located here, about one-hundred-miles northwest of Bougainville, so we won't hear anything from the sub skipper for another week or so."

"Okay, Colonel, keep me posted."

"Aye, aye, sir."

Colonel Travis rose to his feet, saluted, and left the general's office.

He really felt bad about sending Gunny back out so soon, but orders were orders. Command needed to act now and the Baker Boys were the closest men within reach, so off they went. Their four-day leave was supposed to be two weeks, but that didn't work out. Their only choice wasn't so bad until they found out that they were going by submarine again.

Colonel Travis went to the closest pub and sat down at the bar. It was packed with Americans, British, Australians, and a host of other nations, all fighting for the same cause: to kick the Japanese all the way back to their home island and end this war.

The colonel's thoughts were interrupted by the barkeep.

"What'll it be, mate?"

Looking at the barkeep, he let out a big sigh and then answered. "Give me a double shot of Jim Beam, and no ice."

"You got it, mate!" answered the bar keep.

Colonel Travis took his double shot of bourbon and held it high in salute. *Here's to you Gunny. Keep your heads down and come back alive. All of you!*

~ ~ ~

The smell was awful. When Gunny opened his eyes, the first thing he noticed was the stench of a rotting sea turtle and it stunk to high heaven. When he raised his head up to look around, he saw three uniformed bodies lying on the beach, about thirty-yards away to his right. The three men didn't look as though they were alive. Slowly, because it seemed as if every muscle in his body hurt, he rose to his feet and started walking towards his men. Before he got there, one of them began to stir. It was Corporal Kirby.

By the time he got to Corporal Kirby, the other two bodies were also showing signs of life. They were Sergeant Thomas and PFC Bonito.

Gunny looked at Kirby. "Are you all right, Corporal?"

"Yeah, Gunny. I think so."

Smiling, the two Marines reached down and helped Sergeant Thomas and PFC Bonito to their feet. They were both in pain, but nothing serious. Gunny then looked around and spotted another body about fifty or sixty-yards away, to the left of the dead turtle.

"PFC, you and Sergeant Thomas head east and check the beach in that direction."

"Aye, aye, Gunny."

"Come on, Corporal. Let's see who that is."

When the two men were about thirty-yards from the prostrate form, Gunny recognized him; it was Sergeant Stamper. Rolling the man over onto his back, Gunny discovered that his friend had *tied* the life vest to his body because he was afraid he would slip out of it if he blacked out. Gunny smiled to himself, thinking; *always the cautious one.*

A minute or so later, the sergeant from Ketchum, Idaho opened his eyes and looked up at Gunny. Shaking his head, he cringed before he spoke. "I must have gone to hell if I'm looking at your ugly pus hole."

Gunny's face immediately cracked, revealing a hidden smile. Looking up at Kirby, he asked; "Corporal, do I look like hell?"

Corporal Kirby's reply was accompanied by a subtle laugh. "Yeah, Gunny. I'm afraid you do."

Not so stone-faced, Gunny looked back at Sergeant Stamper. "Well then, Roger, I guess you did go to hell. In the mean-time, we had better get off this beach before the Japs find us."

Then it dawned on the man in charge. He was two Marines short. *Where're PFC Fox and PFC Choctaw?*

Chapter 8

Gunny moved the squad into the jungle about sixty-yards and then took stock of the situation. Only the three sergeants had weapons other than their combat knives. They had their .45 automatics, but they only had seven magazines between the three of them. Not a lot of firepower for the five Marines.

After two hours of searching, the squad still hadn't found their two missing men, so they gathered up what items they could carry and headed deeper into the jungle. Their first order of business was to find some fresh water. That chore was given to PFC Bonito. Next, they needed to find out where the hell they were. Gunny knew they were somewhere on the southeast end of an island. At least, he thought it was an island, and judging by the position of the sun, it was almost noon.

The squad hadn't gotten very far when they heard the chugging of diesel engines. It was an enemy patrol boat, and it was heading towards the beach. The Japanese on sea-born shore patrol had spotted some of the wreckage scattered along the beach, so the patrol boat went in to investigate.

"All right Marines, grab what you can and leave the rest. Geronimo, keep an eye on the Japs, but don't get caught. Find out what they're up to and then get back to us, pronto."

While the four men were heading deeper into the jungle, PFC Bonito moved closer to the beach. Only three of the enemy had jumped out of the patrol boat to take a closer look at the wreckage. The half-hearted inspection took about five-minutes. Twenty-minutes and half a bottle of

Sake went by before the patrol boat finally moved on.

"Roger, why are you still wearing that thing? We're running around on dry land now. You don't need that vest anymore."

Some of the crates had items the men might be able to use, but for the most part, the rest was useless. "Hey, Gunny, if we tie enough of these life vests to the island, maybe it won't sink into the Pacific?"

"Hear that, Roger? Throw that thing away. We have more than enough life vests to keep this island floating for weeks."

Bonito did find some boxes with uniforms in them, but they were navy uniforms, so wearing those items was out of the question. However, they could be used for something else besides bandages.

Barely an hour after the patrol boat left the debris littered beach behind, the stranded Marines heard an airplane engine. The man in charge could only shake his head, amazed at the quickly developing situation. *Damn. That was quick. We must have beached ourselves onto a major Jap island and they don't like it. They responded too quickly to be just routine reactions. They'll probably send in the troops next.*

The enemy plane took off from an airfield located on the northwest corner of the Japanese held island of Bougainville, about 120 miles southeast of the island the Baker Boys were now stranded on. The plane flew over the southern tip of the island for almost an hour before it headed for Rabaul, the main Japanese bastion in the Southwest Pacific Theater of Operations.

The pilot noticed the wreckage scattered up and down the beach and took pictures of the whole southern tip of the island before he headed northwest to refuel. On his way to Rabaul, located on the northern tip of New Britain Island, the pilot took pictures of the oil slick left behind by the sunken sub, and some of it was still burning. When the pictures were developed, the Japanese commanders realized that the report about a surface action and sinking of an American submarine from one of their destroyers was accurate. The pictures also showed there was the possibility that some of the survivors were now on the island, only sixty-miles east of New Britain; right in the middle of the strongest concentration of Japanese forces in the area.

Thirty-minutes after the Japanese came to that conclusion, a Daihatsu transport landing craft was sent down the west coast of the island. It was filled with over twenty Japanese troops. Their mission was to hunt down any survivors from the sunken submarine and either capture or kill them. That last part was left up to the discretion of the officer in charge. But the gunnery sergeant dubbed, "Deadeye" by those who tried to out shoot him, wasn't aware of any of these developments. Once again, he was only concerned with surviving. The Marines had to find a way to survive long enough, to get off whatever island they had landed on. And Gunny was still missing two men: PFC Fox and PFC Choctaw.

~ ~ ~

"Gunny, do you hear that?"

"Yeah, PFC, I hear it. Geronimo, go find out what they're up to. Corporal, you go with him." Immediately, the two Marines took off towards the beach.

Gunny's face was cracking wide, showing off his pearly-whites, when he said; "Hey, you two. Remember. No shooting."

PFC Bonito was somewhat taken aback by Gunny's comment. "What are we supposed to shoot with, Gunny? We have no weapons."

The laugh was immediate, but the words took longer to spring forth. "Don't shoot off your big mouth and get caught."

Sergeant Stamper exhaled and shook his head. "Al, you're a Marine Corp gunnery sergeant, not Bob Hope. Stick to what you do best. These guys might panic and run if you crack too many bad jokes."

"I wasn't cracking a joke, Roger. I was spreading words of wisdom. There is a difference, you know. All right, you two, we'll head north a couple hundred-yards. If the Japs start heading into the jungle, catch up to us. Be careful out there."

"Aye, aye, Gunny."

While the two men headed back to the beach area, Gunny moved north through the jungle. It seemed to the Marine Corps gunnery sergeant that he spent more time in the jungle than anywhere else. *Maybe I should start calling the jungle my home.* Shaking his head at the thought, he continued heading deeper into the tangled mess he was tempted to call, his own.

The going was tough for the Marines. The terrain they were moving through was rocky and infested with vines, trees, and every other plant imaginable that would impede or stop their progress. The conditions were almost as bad as the island they had just recently spent forty days on. After moving about two-hundred-yards deeper into the jungle, the Marines began to see what they were really in for. They thought they were walking through flat jungle terrain until they noticed that the jungle had inconspicuously risen up around them. Some of the jungle covered ridge looked to be over two or three-hundred-feet high.

"Look at what we just did, Gunny. We could get trapped here like a bunch of rookies."

"Yeah, you're right, Roger. I didn't notice the jungle rising around us until you just mentioned it. We need to find an escape route out of here in case the Japs come after us. You cover the east. I'll take Sergeant Thomas with me, and head west. We'll meet back here in thirty-minutes."

"Aye, aye, Gunny."

~ ~ ~

"I count twenty-three rifles and one officer, Corporal."

"Yeah, and they're unloading supplies, so I guess they plan on staying for a while."

PFC Bonito whispered again. "Can you hear what they're saying?"

Corporal Kirby shook his head, somewhat disgusted. "That lieutenant is not very happy. He seems to think that this is all a waste of time. Let's go, Geronimo, the Japs are definitely looking for us. We need to get back to Gunny and let him know what's going on."

The two Marines cautiously left the beach area, heading deeper into the jungle, and all the while, Corporal Kirby was shaking his head. "Hell, we've been on this rock less than a day, and the Japs are already sore at us. We can't blame it on the chief this time." PFC Bonito, however, failed to hear the attempt at humor. His thoughts were elsewhere.

Two hours, and a lot of cursing later, the two Marines finally found Gunny. He had found a way out of the notch, but it turned out to be a tough, two-hundred-foot climb. They also discovered something that they hadn't run into on the last island they were on. Some of the plant life had teeth, thorn like needles that hurt like hell.

~ ~ ~

The enemy spotted the washed up debris and noticed some tracks leading from the beach into the jungle. Once they had their supplies offloaded, a squad was sent into the jungle. A second squad had been split up. Half was going north along the beach, while the other half was heading southeast. A little over an hour later, they all met back at their supplies. According to the sun there was still plenty of daylight left, so Lieutenant Watanabe formed up his two squads and headed into the jungle, following the boot tracks.

They found more of the wreckage about fifteen-minutes later. Crates had been opened up, and some of the contents were missing. The rest looked abandoned, as though they were left behind due to a hasty departure.

~ ~ ~

Gunny was hunkered down on the backside of the ridge with his men spread out to the left and right. The four Marines peered over the crest of the ridge, watching the two enemy squads while they searched the jungle for them. "If they start up the side," whispered Gunny, "we move south. I don't want to leave this area until I know for certain that the chief and Choctaw didn't make it."

Gunny turned at the tap on his shoulder. "What is it, Geronimo?"

"I have an idea. We can tie some of this Navy crap over our dockers to help cover our boot tracks."

"Do you think it'll work?"

Bonito was nodding his head when he replied. "Hell yeah, Gunny. It'll make our tracks almost as smooth as Grabal's tush."

"Okay Geronimo," he whispered softly. "Show them how to do it." Still low-voiced, he turned to Sergeant Stamper. "Keep an eye on the Japs. Let me know if they start up the ridge."

After a quick nod the sergeant whispered his response. "Aye, aye, Gunny."

~ ~ ~

The Japanese started up the ridge, so the squad moved south along the side of the rugged hillside, just below the crest. There was a marsh at the bottom, just below where the Marines were positioned, so they had to get past it before they could climb down to level terrain. The climb up from the notch took them over thirty-minutes, so the man in charge figured it would take his enemy about the same amount of time.

"Once we get past the marsh," whispered Gunny, "we can climb down off this rock and maybe circle back around the bog to the north. Once we get behind the Japs, we'll be home free for a while. What we need is a place to hole-up. We damn sure can't engage them, so we're going to have to stay at least one or two steps ahead of the bastards. Take point, Geronimo. Move out."

The going was tough for the Marines because they kept losing their footing and sliding down the rock-strewn hillside. The going was just as tough on the enemy, as well. They were being introduced to the thornier side of the island on their way up the treacherous hillside.

Once past the marsh, the five men headed down the rocky spine, stumbling their way from tree to tree. The way was hazardous and fast-moving, so they were forced to use the trees to keep their balance, and to keep from flying headlong down the side. They finally made it to the bottom of the ridge, only to discover that they had stumbled into a mucky bog that bordered the edge of the marsh. Not the perfect situation to be in.

"Geronimo, head south," whispered Gunny. "Get us out of this muck." So the Marines headed south again.

The two enemy squads finally made it to the top of the ridge and found indications that their mysterious island visitors were now moving along the side of the ridgeline, so they followed after them.

About twenty minutes after the five Americans turned south again, they heard a scream. Nobody stopped because that scream sounded pretty close. Somehow the Japanese had gained a little ground on them, but they lost that ground when one of their own lost his footing, and tumbled headlong down the side of the rocky incline.

When the tumbling soldier came to a stop, he found himself in the waist deep water of the marsh. When he tried to stand up, he couldn't because his leg was broken, so he tried to swim to the edge of the swamp. When his friends finally reached him, they found him limply thrashing around, gripped in the jaws of a twelve-foot crocodile. The two squads started shooting at the splashing menace and finally killed it, but their friend was dead when they got to him.

"Sergeant Takagi, form up a burial detail and get him buried."

"Hai."

After recovering the body of their fallen friend, they were forced to move south, away from the marsh. They took over thirty-minutes to move far enough away from the marsh to allow them to bury their friend. Once that chore was accomplished, they started moving again. Lieutenant Watanabe had not yet given up the chase. He could still see signs that their mysterious visitors were still out in front of them, so the enemy continued their pursuit.

~ ~ ~

After what seemed like hours, Gunny finally called a halt. Everyone was tired, and they were thirsty. Most of their gear was now residing at the bottom of the Solomon Sea, thanks to that enemy destroyer. However; they still had their web belts, and one canteen each. Not much at all considering they had landed on an enemy held island. Still, however dire the situation was, having nothing at all was much worse.

The Marines had been resting for only a couple of minutes when they heard something rustling around in the undergrowth. With their Ka-Bars ready, they spread out and waited. A couple of sweat-squirting minutes passed by before an Iguana type lizard came scooting out of the foliage, startling the bejesus out of the men before it quickly scurried away. It was almost three feet long.

"Did you see that thing? What the hell was it?"

Gunny shook his head. "*That*, Corporal Kirby, was a

damn big lizard."

PFC Bonito was rubbing his chin. "Maybe we should put a saddle on it and try to ride the damn thing."

Sergeant Stamper immediately shook his head and replied. "You might be able to ride that thing Geronimo, but the rest of us wouldn't be able to. We have longer legs than you do."

Feigning excitement, the Apache scout replied. "Just think, Sergeant Stamper. If we put a saddle on it, I'll be the only one riding it."

"Can it, you guys," whispered Gunny. "We've got Japs on out tail, remember? So let's move out, break time's over. Geronimo, get out front. Sergeant Stamper, you take the rear. All right, let's go Marines."

Because the enemy had stopped to bury their friend, they were now almost an hour behind the Marines. Lieutenant Watanabe was not very happy. They had been slugging their way through the jungle after the elusive strangers for almost ninety-minutes. Then, out of the blue, he had an idea.

"Sergeant Takagi, take your squad and head north over this ridge, then circle around and try to cut them off. I think our unidentified arrivals are heading back to the beach."

"Hai." replied Sergeant Takagi.

A couple of minutes later, Sergeant Takagi and his squad were struggling their way up the side of the ridge while Lieutenant Watanabe continued on, following the trail of the mysterious footprints.

Searching the jungle with his eyes, he could see, touch, and inhale what he had siding him on the hunt. The smell of death, the stench of rotting jungle, and the monotonous drone and buzzing of the blood-thirsty insects. *We are probably following survivors of that sunken sub I heard about, which means they are probably not armed.* The lieutenant was somewhat right on that thought, but his notion that they were sailors was completely wrong. The Japanese were hunting U.S. Marines, and they would not be taken without a hard, tough fight, armed or not.

Chapter 9

The two Marines were in bad shape. The Japanese had beaten them badly in hopes of getting the answers they were looking for, such as, how many more of you are there? But so far, the only response the enemy interrogator was able to get out of the two men was an occasional groan, and when the blows really hurt, a yell of pain, followed by a torrent of spitting and swearing. That last part was usually done by PFC Choctaw; PFC Fox didn't make a sound.

"Come on you little monkeys. Is that the best you can do?"

Of course, taunting the enemy didn't help either Marine's cause. In fact, it only pissed them off even more, particularly Captain Matsui. He understood and spoke English pretty well, but not good enough to pass for a Harvard graduate. His job was to gather information. How he did it was his business, and he was good at what he did.

Captain Matsui found out earlier that it did no good to talk to the smaller Marine. He refused to say anything no matter how hard he was beaten. But the captain only smiled. *Sooner or later, he will speak. They always do. It is only a matter of time before the pain becomes too unbearable. Then I will get all the information I need.*

The little Marine had passed out cold, at least, that's what Captain Matsui thought. The big one, however, was still somewhat conscious, though he was babbling like an idiot. He stared at the babbling idiot for moment longer before he decided it was time for a break.

"Come Kenji, it's time we ate. We will give these swine time to recover a little bit before we continue." The two men left the bamboo hut and headed for the officer's mess. It was time to sit back and enjoy the evening for a little while. It was still hot, but with a light wind blowing in from the east, it was actually an enjoyable evening. The humidity wasn't too bad, thanks to the breeze.

~ ~ ~

"Hey, little man? Are you all right? They're gone."

The chief slowly raised his head up to look at PFC Choctaw. What the big man saw turned his stomach. The scout's face was one big, sickly, yellow and purple bruise, stretched tautly from the swelling. Choctaw could barely see the guy's eyes. *Little man can definitely take some punishment, that's for sure.* But PFC Choctaw was also in bad shape.

"Hey, Fox. I'm tired of letting these little monkeys beat on me, so why don't you and me try to get out of here. Do you think you can make it?"

The chief didn't say a word. He just looked at Choctaw and nodded his head.

"Good!" replied Choctaw. "I'll have us out of here in a … ahh … couple of … ahhh…" Then with one last, hard-gut effort … "Minutes." Then snap! The bamboo chair he had been tied to split apart, spilling him to the floor. Wriggling quickly out of the ropes that bound him to the chair, he immediately rolled onto his side, curled up into a ball, and forced his tied up hands under his butt and over his curled up legs. His hands were now in front of his body. The bailing wire the Japanese had used to tie up the two Marines had cut deeply into his wrists and ankles, but even that didn't slow the big man down.

The guard outside the bamboo hut had heard the chair break, but he didn't know what it was at first, so he hesitated a minute or so before he went in to investigate. That minute or so of hesitation gave PFC Choctaw the time he needed to get his hands in front of his body. He was waiting beside the doorway when the guard entered.

The first sight that greeted the sentry was the broken chair, and then PFC Fox. Taking a couple of steps forward, deeper into the hut, he quickly realized that one of the captured Marines was gone. A nauseating knot of cold fear hit him in the pit of the stomach when he realized his mistake. *The escaped Marine is behind me*! By then, however, it was too late for him.

PFC Choctaw swung his still wired-up hands over the top of the guard's head to settle against the terrified soldier's throat. Instantly, he pulled the enemy to his chest, for more leverage, cutting off the flow of air, and immediately dropped to the floor, dragging the struggling guard with him, causing the sentry to drop his rifle to the floor. Quickly using his weight to his advantage, he rolled over, pinning the struggling guard to the floor on his stomach, and hurriedly pulled up hard against the flailing man's throat. A couple of minutes went by before the frantic struggle was over, and the enemy lay dead on the floor. In seconds, Choctaw had his ankles un-wired and was back on his feet, looking down at PFC Fox.

He knew that he was going to have to carry the little man. The chief looked as though he didn't have enough strength left in him to even stand up, let alone run. As quickly as he could, and with his hands still wired together, Choctaw grabbed the guard's bayonet and slid it through his belt, then he unwired Fox from the chair and slung him over his shoulder.

Using the bayonet, he cut through the bindings holding the back wall of the bamboo hut together, and with a quick glance to his left and right, silently disappeared into the jungle, heading northwest.

An hour after their hasty departure, PFC Choctaw ran headlong into a river. He ran right over the bank, into the river, and the fall-to-splash was a huge eye-opener. He was so concerned with running away from the Japanese, that he failed to see the embankment and tumbled headlong into the river. It took him a few seconds to find the chief, but when he did, he slung the little man over his shoulder again and tried to climb up the embankment, but it was too steep for him. In a panic, he began moving up river until he spotted the roots of a tree growing out of the embankment. Using the roots, he was finally able to reach the top of the embankment.

Where he came from, a river in this kind of terrain usually meant that alligators were around somewhere, but in this case, it was crocodiles.

Once he reached the top of the embankment, the big man didn't hesitate. He headed away from the river. It was now too dark to see much of anything, and he sure didn't want fight a crocodile under such unfavorable conditions, so he continued moving away from the river until he could go no further. Gently, he lowered the chief to the ground and collapsed beside the little man, exhausted.

~ ~ ~

Captain Matsui and Lieutenant Nakamura were on their way back to the bamboo hut, deep in conversation, but that conversation ended abruptly when the two officers noticed that the guard was not at his post, and the door of the hut was slightly ajar. Immediately, they drew their sidearms and quickly ran towards the hut. As they approached the open door, they cocked their weapons and then cautiously entered the hut. A loud curse erupted from Captain Matsui when he discovered that their two prisoners had escaped.

~ ~ ~

"Gunny?"

"What is it, PFC?"

"I found a place where we might be able to hole up for a while until the Japs move on. Once they get past us, we can head back and go around the marsh."

Gunny trusted his two scouts, so he didn't hesitate at the suggestion. "Lead us there, Geronimo."

A few minutes later, the Marines were hiding behind a wall of vines and thorn bushes, and Sergeant Thomas was shaking his head. "Wow, PFC. What a tropical paradise you've brought us to. It even comes supplied with toothpicks." But the Apache scout didn't hang around their new digs. Instead, he covered up their trail as much as he could and then continued on, leading their enemy on a merry chase. About fifteen-minutes into his little decoy trail he stopped, ripped off a piece of the Navy shirt he had tied over his boondockers, and stuck it on one of the thorn bushes. Looking back towards the oncoming enemy he thought. *That ought to keep them going for a while.* Then he began looking for a way to leave the trail without leaving any tracks.

Bonito was searching around, whispering to himself. A goading kind of whispering. "What I need is a low hanging branch." A few minutes later, he found what he was looking for. Grabbing hold of the branch, he lifted himself onto the branch, climbed over to the backside of the tree, and then dropped to the ground, about thirty-feet from where he left the trail. Smiling back on his handy work, he began to backtrack to where he left Gunny in their new thorny hideaway.

The Apache scout was about twenty-yards from the briar patch hideout when he heard his enemy talking. Immediately, he dropped to the ground and waited for them to pass. When they had passed completely out of sight, he rose up from the ground and moved into the hideout. He was greeted by three .45's and a corporal with a big stick in his hand.

Gunny's face cracked, and the beginnings of a smile formed. Nodding his head at Bonito, he said; "We'll stay here for the night and head out in the morning for the marsh."

~ ~ ~

Sergeant Takagi and his men were just cresting the ridge when the four Marines entered their hideout. A couple of minutes later, the enemy squad was on their way down the ridge and heading south. Although they were only about three-hundred-yards from the beach, the terrain they had to go through was tough going, and time consuming. Once they cleared the vegetable garden, then the rest of their walk was going to be much easier. Sergeant Takagi's squad took more than an hour to accomplish their goal.

"Lieutenant, look!"

Lieutenant Watanabe saw what the private was pointing at. A piece of clothing appeared to have been ripped off of one of the running survivors. The lieutenant's excitement was starting to grow. He could see they were getting closer to their prey. Now it was only a matter of time before they caught up with their elusive mystery visitors. *Hopefully Sergeant Takagi is on his way south to cut off the fleeing sailors, so we can put an end to this stupid mission.* He wanted to smile, but his surroundings stopped him. Looking up and around, he shook his head, resigned, knowing he had no choice.

"Let's go." he ordered, and the squad moved out with Lieutenant Watanabe leading the way. A couple of hours went by before he was standing on the last rise overlooking the beach. He saw nothing. The beach looked untouched. No tracks. No sailors. Just undisturbed, soft, white sand. Disappointed, he started down the rise, heading for the beach. By the time he reached the beach, his men were exhausted, so he took a break.

Twenty-minutes into their rest on the sand, Lieutenant Watanabe spotted some men moving towards his position. After a few more minutes had passed, he recognized who the men were. It was Sergeant Takagi, and he had no prisoners. He had only the men in his squad. Their prey had escaped. The two enemy squads made it back at their temporary supply base, tired and disgusted. And so ended a wasted day. All that the enemy troops got out of the deal was a tour of the jungle and lots of cuts and scratches. By the time the sun had fallen below the horizon, they had their fire going, and PFC Choctaw, with the chief over his shoulder, was making their break for freedom.

~ ~ ~

Captain Matsui formed his men up and was giving his instructions to Lieutenant Nakamura. The men standing in formation were seasoned veterans. They had fought through many battles, most of them in the jungles of Southeast Asia, and all of them against a tough opponent, so they knew what they were doing. But these Japanese soldiers had never faced U.S. Marines before. Going up against those guys was going to be a whole new experience for the Matsui troops. Especially against the likes of Gunnery Sergeant Alistair Baker and, as his unit was now known as, the Baker Boys.

~ ~ ~

PFC Choctaw slept like a baby throughout the night. Not even the snake crawling over his chest woke him up, but the sharp point of a spear poking at him, did—instantly. When he opened his eyes, he was looking at six island inhabitants, and they were all armed. Two had spears with wicked looking steel spearheads, and the other four were armed with bows. The big man smiled weakly, held up his hands in surrender, and then called softly to PFC Fox. But he didn't get an answer.

Fearing that the little man was hurt worse than he thought, he looked to where he had laid Fox on the ground the night before, but the little man was gone. He had disappeared into the jungle, and PFC Choctaw never heard him leave. The big man didn't know what to do. Then he heard a soft growl. *Oh shit.* And he cringed. So did the island inhabitants.

The islanders knew there was nothing on their home turf that would make that sound, so they started casting nervous glances into the jungle. Then they heard little chittering sounds, another sound not associated with the island. The newcomers, upon hearing the chittering, looked at each other, confused. *What's making those animal sounds?* All thoughts of PFC Choctaw were gone. Now curiosity was beginning to fester. Bowstrings relaxed, spears were lowered, and the big man let out a sigh of relief.

For a minute or so, the jungle was back to its normal sounds, but that normality was interrupted by another soft growl. This time it was behind the six strangers. Quickly, with bows and spears at the ready, they turned to face their rear and froze all movement. Surprise was an understatement. Swollen face and all, and standing right in front of them, was a little man, and he was smiling.

The islanders stood staring at PFC Fox, absolutely bewildered. Their expressions changed from surprise to anger and back to surprise. The little man had them stumped with his smile and his cut and swollen face. But the islanders didn't dwell on the chief's face. He was amazing the new arrivals with his animal calls. They didn't know whether to kill this little man or put a leash on him, so they just continued to stare at him.

After a short pause, PFC Fox screwed up his lips and began chittering like a chipmunk. The look on their faces went from indecision to complete surprise. They just stood there dumbfounded, staring at this little man making strange animal calls. Then their expressions went from surprise, to smiles. Great big, huge, cheek-stretching smiles.

The tallest of the five had a piece of red cloth tied around his head. When he spoke, Fox pointed to his ear and shook his head. "I don't understand your language." He did, however, figure out through the man's head nodding and finger pointing that more animal calls were wanted. Fox, grinning like a dad with a four-year-old child asking, "Do it again daddy," started chittering again. The five men began laughing like little children, and just like little children, they wanted more. PFC Fox gave them exactly that, and then some.

He was just getting ready to howl the wolf. Something he thought his unexpected visitors might get a kick out of, but he stopped when he heard someone crashing through the jungle, right towards them. It was another of the inhabitants, and he was whispering excitedly. No sooner had he appeared, when immediately, the unexpected visitors took off running. The only word Fox understood, was *Japans*.

~ ~ ~

The Japanese had waited for the sun to come up before they started out after their escaped prisoners. Lieutenant Nakamura was leading two squads. He could see where PFC Choctaw had stumbled around through the jungle, trying to get away from the area. The lieutenant was smiling over his discovery. *This fat pig will be easy to find. He stumbles through the jungle like a bumbling idiot.*

The trail the big Marine left through the jungle looked like a huge bull had trampled down the foliage. A little over an hour into their pursuit, the enemy discovered where the two men had gone over the embankment into the river. Staring down at the water, Nakamura was actually looking at nothing in particular, just contemplating the recent events. Then he noticed the crocodiles. A couple of them were down at the river's edge, where the two runners had fallen into the river.

Another smile crossed his face. *Maybe they were dinner for the crocodiles last night.*

The lieutenant spread out his men, and for the next hour, they searched the west bank of the river for over a hundred-yards in both directions. The Japanese, however, were unable to find where the Americans left the river. Another smile formed on the lieutenant's face. *Perhaps the Americans really were eaten by the crocodiles.* But thirty-minutes into their second search attempt, one of his men found where PFC Choctaw had come out of the river. He also found a Japanese bayonet lying on the ground.

Lieutenant Nakamura could see where PFC Choctaw headed deeper into the jungle after he left the river. The tracks were deep. Twenty-feet from where he was standing, he discovered the bailing wire used to tie the Marine's hands. There was blood still on the wire. *So,* he thought. *His hands are free now.* A smile crossed his face again. *No matter, you will be mine by tomorrow afternoon.*

So far, Choctaw's trail was easy to follow. He also found where PFC Choctaw had fallen to the ground a couple of times. *Judging by the crushed plants, the Americans must have stayed here to rest awhile before moving on.* Something out of the ordinary caught his eye, then his full attention. Staring at a crushed plant, he was puzzled as to what had crushed it, and why it was crushed facing a different direction. Dimple marks from combat boots should have told the story, but there were none. *Hmm.*

~ ~ ~

"Shh! Listen up!" Bonito's hand signal dropped the Marines to the ground.

"What is it, Geronimo?"

"Shh!"

The Marines listened for another minute or so, but they didn't hear anything. Gunny just stared at Bonito, stone-faced as usual, but his eyes were narrowed, betraying his irritation.

PFC Bonito looked over at Gunny. "Sorry, Gunny. I

didn't mean to be disrespectful. I thought I heard something that sounded a lot like PFC Fox."

"Are you sure?"

"That's just it, Gunny. I'm not sure."

Gunny sat contemplating for a moment and then whispered. "All right Marines, move out. Geronimo, keep a sharp ear out. Let me know if you hear it again."

"Aye, aye, Gunny."

Then all four Marines heard a faint owl hoot that stopped them in their tracks.

"Was that who I think it was?"

PFC Bonito shook his head like an irritated teacher. "That Cherokee never could call it right, Gunny."

"What direction did it come from?"

Pointing to the northwest he said; "Over in that direction."

"Are you sure that was PFC Fox?"

"Yes, Gunny." answered Bonito. "Like I said, he never could call it right."

The gunnery sergeant from Oklahoma was cracking a smile, and so was the rest of the squad. "Okay, Geronimo. Let's go get our missing Marines."

Chapter 10

"Let's go, Ox. The Japs are coming."

He didn't need to be told twice. The two Marines headed northeast until they came in contact the river again. From there, they followed the river north, hoping to find a place to ford, but the banks were too steep at this point. Twenty-minutes into their search, however, the two Americans found a place to ford the river, but it looked kind of dangerous.

The roots of the tree were about six feet below the riverbank where PFC Fox and PFC Choctaw stood. The tree stretched out across forty-feet of river, with the top of the tree resting on the opposite bank. During one of the flash floods caused by the sudden rainstorms, the roots of the tree had been washed out, causing the tree to topple over, and come to a rest on the opposite bank. The tree itself was covered with all kinds of green slippery stuff and moisture; the dangerous, part.

Slowly, the two Marines climbed down the embankment to the roots. After a couple of minutes, they were through the roots, and standing on the dead tree. The chief kept looking around, searching for any crocodiles that might decide to use the tree to cross the river ... like the crocodile that tried to cross the little foot-bridge on their last mission. When he didn't see any, he slowly stutter-stepped towards the opposite bank.

The footing was treacherous. It was almost as bad as walking on ice. The two men had to slide their feet forward along the tree trunk, one foot in front of the other, never lifting their feet off the surface of the tree. Otherwise, there was the very real chance of slipping off the tree, and plunging into the river.

PFC Fox was in the lead. With the two of them going across the tree bridge together, the tree had begun shifting around. Immediately, the chief stopped, then cautiously turned to face Choctaw. "Ox. Stay put. Don't do anything until I get across." Staring back at the big man from Louisiana, he could see the terrified expression on the Ox's face. He was such a large man, with such big feet. His shirt-front was already drenched with sweat.

The chief cautiously maneuvered his way across the tree bridge, taking almost twenty-minutes to reach the opposite bank. When he finally reached terra-firma, he started breathing again.

PFC Choctaw was a different story. Fifteen-feet up from the roots was where, what was left of the branches started. If not for the stubs of the branches, PFC Choctaw would have fallen into the river three or four times. His body was just not made for that kind of delicate walking. The Louisiana man took over thirty-minutes to reach the opposite bank. Just before he reached the other bank, the top of the tree, the part resting on the opposite bank, began cracking, causing sweat to squirt out freely from every pore on his body. The poor guy lost almost five pounds trying to cross the tree bridge. Sweat just drenched his uniform. With a big sigh of relief, the big Marine finally reached solid ground.

PFC Fox shook his head at the Ox, and smiled so big, his bruised and swollen face hurt.

The big man stared at Fox for a couple of seconds and then, he too, began to beam. Waving the chief off, he replied to the strange apparition appearing on the chief's swollen face. "Aw, shut up."

The two Marines rested on the opposite bank for about ten-minutes before they started heading east. Now that they were walking again, Fox thought about what they went through at the hands of the Japanese, and that thought angered him deeply. The two men had no weapons. PFC Choctaw lost the bayonet when he climbed up the embankment, and the Japanese had the chief's knife in their possession, something that was beginning to drive him mad.

Without warning, the little man stopped, then waited for the big man to stop and turn around. He didn't wait long. The Ox stopped and looked back at the chief, and was immediately floored after hearing the small scout's words. "We're going back to that Jap camp. I want my knife back."

"You're nuts little man. They'll just get their meat hooks into us again. I'm not going anywhere near that camp again. Not without a weapon."

"Suit yourself, Ox. I'm going back."

PFC Fox started walking again and passed by the big man, leaving him standing there, surprised at the sudden decision.

"Wait a minute, little man. I can't let you go back there by yourself. You'll just get caught again."

Fox stopped and turned around, and with a smile on his face said; "So you're going back with me?"

"Somebody's got to look out for you. You'll get caught without me."

The two Marines stared at each other for a couple of minutes until the chief began to laugh. "Are we going back, or are we just going to stand here gawking at each other?"

~ ~ ~

Lieutenant Nakamura was staring down at the trampled jungle plants. *The two Marines had definitely rested here. Hmm.* What had him confused were the extra tracks he found. There had been at least five or six other people standing around, but he couldn't figure out who they were until he noticed they were barefoot. *Are the inhabitants helping the Americans?* Then he shook his head in answer to his thought. *No, it's probably just coincidence. They must have stumbled upon the Americans by accident.* With that thought ruling his judgment, he searched the area with added thoroughness, hoping to find a more definite track and a clear-cut direction.

The barefoot tracks ended about ten-feet from where the lieutenant was standing, but another set of tracks were leading north. It didn't take him long to realize that the tracks heading north were from the big Marine. *He isn't stumbling around anymore.* So the enemy headed north, following the big man's trail. After thirty-minutes of struggling and searching, they found the tree the two Americans had used to cross the river.

When their short break was over, the enemy troops began crossing the tree bridge. The going wasn't as treacherous for the Japanese as long as they stepped where the two Marines had scrapped off most of the slippery, dangerous material. The trouble started when the two enemy squads were three-quarters of the way across the tree bridge. The top of the tree, the part resting on the opposite bank, started protesting to the added weight of the Japanese troops. The cracking was heard by everyone on the tree bridge. The soldiers in the rear started calling for their comrades to hurry up, before the tree gave way. "Hey, you guys. Step it up before we crash into the river!"

"Shut up back there. Your rantings are not helping matters at all. We can't go any faster because we'll end up in the river. Just walk softer!"

Lieutenant Nakamura and fifteen soldiers made it across the tree bridge before the top of the tree, the part resting on the opposite bank, finally gave way. Eight soldiers didn't make it to the other side.

When the tree gave way, it rolled to the right, throwing the soldiers into the river. One soldier was killed outright when he hit his head on the tree trunk. Two others were screaming, carried off by the crocodiles seconds after they hit the water. Two went under and failed to reappear, and the remaining three were last seen being carried away south, by the swift flowing current of the river.

Lieutenant Nakamura was stunned by the sudden turn of events. He had just lost almost half of his men and not a single one of them was lost due to combat.

~ ~ ~

Lieutenant Watanabe was on the march again. He was heading back along the same path where he found the torn clothing hanging from the thorn bush. *I lost the trail somewhere near that piece of cloth. I think that thorn bush is where I'll start the search from.* This time, though, he sent Sergeant Takagi up on the ridge first to make sure their elusive visitors, if they were still in the area, didn't climb over the ridge to escape. Because of the height of the ridge, he would have a better view of the jungle floor where the jungle allowed it.

Their march from the supply-base to the rise overlooking the beach took about forty-minutes. Pausing to get his bearings, Lieutenant Watanabe stared at what he was about to enter and shook his head. Then he gave the order to move down the hill into the interior of the jungle. He could see his previous tracks leading out of the jungle, so he followed his own trail until he came to the thorn bush. The torn piece of clothing was still stuck to the spiny bush.

Halting his squad, he searched the ground for tracks other than his own. He soon discovered a print, but instead of a full boot print, he noticed that it was just a soft outline of what could be a boot print. It was heading towards the beach.

Still following the soft outline of the prints, he was surprised when they abruptly ended. Now he was puzzled. As hard as he looked, he was unable to find anymore prints beyond where they stopped, so, deep in thought, he began to search the area around the trail. *Maybe they jumped into the jungle to the left or right of the trail. No, had they done that, they would have definitely left the foliage disturbed, or at the very least, some really deep boot tracks.* The mystery was a puzzle to him, so he kept searching the ground for more tracks, anything that would give him an idea of where the unknown visitors went. *How could they have just disappeared into thin air like – that.* Then he noticed a low hanging branch.

Moving to the low hanging branch, he spotted something else as well. A crushed plant directly below the branch. He kept looking up to the branch and then back down at the crushed plant until a smile formed on his face. It was not a humorous smile. Grunting from his exertion, he jumped up and grabbed the branch. Pulling himself up and onto the branch, he quickly looked around, trying to figure out where to go from where he was perched. The only way he could go to get down off the trail was to his right. In less than a minute, he was staring down at a set of deep, softly outlined boot tracks that were facing north. He had found what he was looking for.

When Lieutenant Watanabe found the tracks on the other side of the tree, the time was around 1200 hours. About twenty-five minutes later, he was looking at a wall of vines and thorns. Here the tracks ended. Turning, he grabbed a bayonet from one of his men and parted the vines and thorns. He stood still for a moment somewhat shocked at the reality of what he was staring at.

The area was just large enough to hide four or five men, and in this small area, he discovered there had indeed been someone inside. Several someone's in fact. Doubt was now beginning to enter his mind as to the real identity of the pursued. Looking around the inside of the hideout, he shook his head, puzzled. However puzzled he was, he knew how the unidentified intruders had eluded him. His next step was to figure out where they went from the hideout. Not long after he discovered his enemy's hideout, he found his answer. His uninvited ship-wrecked survivors were heading back to the north.

Watanabe waited for his platoon sergeant to climb down from the ridge before they headed north. The trail they were now following took them close to the same marsh one of his men fell into, but just before they entered a boggy area, the trail turned east. Every now and then, Sergeant Takagi would find a really deep print where the ground was extra soggy, strengthening the lieutenant's determination to press onward.

Sergeant Takagi was a farmer and a hunter before the war, just like the rest of his men in the small detachment. They all knew how to hunt and stalk their prey, and live off what the land yielded. The men had to in order to survive: as a result, hunting was not new to them. But tracking down and stalking men through a jungle was something totally different. It was a whole new experience, a whole different kind of game. Their prey was the most dangerous creature on the planet, not to mention, they were also U.S. Marines. But Lieutenant Watanabe had no idea he was trailing the best jungle fighters Uncle Sam had to offer.

The tracks the platoon sergeant was following were somewhat hard to find, except for the occasional boot heel that was missed by those who were trying to hide their tracks. In the terrain everyone was traveling through, it was hard to cover their trail completely. After another two hours, the Japanese detachment finally reached the far eastern edge of the marsh.

The beach, if you could call it that, was only about twenty-feet deep, and was littered with all kinds of sea vegetation and dead crabs. The odor was not pleasant to smell.

Lieutenant Watanabe was absentmindedly staring

down at the tangled mess littering the beach, when he noticed some softly outlined tracks amongst freshly broken crap shells. Bending down, he studied the tracks until he heard the dull drone of an airplane, and then he stood upright. It was a Mitsubishi F1M recon floatplane, what the Americans called a "Pete." It was flying up and down the east coast of the island. The enemy detachment waved at the airplane and received a return response from the pilot. A few minutes later, the floatplane turned north and left the area.

After their short break was over, they began following after the Marines again, with Lieutenant Watanabe in the lead. The trail led north a couple of hundred-yards along the beach before it turned west into the jungle. Shortly after turning west, the enemy discovered that tracking the elusive runners was becoming more and more difficult. The ground wasn't as soggy deeper into the jungle, so it was a little easier for the pursued to hide their trail. By the end of the day, however, the Japanese were only six hours behind the four Americans, and they had a new direction. The four intruders were heading north again.

~ ~ ~

Gunny was shaking his head, absolutely perplexed. *This is beginning to look like our last mission. We've only been on this island for two days and we already have the Japanese chasing after us.*

The Marines had found a small stream and were following it north through the rocky ridges that seemed to cover the whole southern end of the island. They were able to fill up their canteens from the fast flowing stream, but they had to use one of their socks to strain out the sand and silt. Whatever else was in the water was ignored for the time being, due to the intense circumstances. They didn't have the time to boil their water, pure, and their purification tabs were resting on the ocean floor, almost a mile below the surface.

One of the scouts had managed to kill a brown and white opossum looking critter. He had no idea what it was, but it tasted pretty good once it was cooked. With their bellies satisfied, heads began to droop, so the man in charge decided to take a two-hour break before continuing on through the night. That two-hour rest turned into three hours before they were on the move again.

As it turned out, the stream the Marines were following was a small tributary of the same river that Fox and Choctaw had crossed earlier. After following the stream for another couple of hours, Gunny decided to call a halt for the night; then it started raining. As tired as the Marines were, the steady sounds of the falling rain was all they needed to lull them to sleep quickly. The soft symphony of rainfall worked too well.

Gunny was shaken awake sometime around 0400 hours. PFC Bonito's expression told him all he needed to know, he let the scout fill him in on the rest.

"Gunny, there's a squad of Japs about a hundred-yards south of us. They're heading right for us."

Gunny was now instantly wide awake. "Get everybody up, Geronimo."

Quickly, the two Marines woke everyone up, and in seconds, they were on the move again.

"How did they find us so quickly?"

"I don't know, Gunny. Maybe the Japs just followed the river like we did."

Sergeant Stamper didn't like running from a fight: it bristled his neck hairs. Now he was being forced to run again. "Roger, are you getting cranky? You know what they say about that, don't you?"

"Yes, Al, but when I look at you, I breathe a sigh of relief. I look nothing like you, so I can't be getting old."

"Head west, Roger. Get us away from this river."

"Aye, aye, Gunny." whispered Sergeant Stamper.

The sergeant from Idaho was now on point with PFC Bonito bringing up the rear. Gunny wanted the scout to keep an eye on the Japanese coming up behind them. It was a logical move, and past history proved that the Japanese always underestimated Gunny's ability to evade capture. But on this night, it was the Gunny's turn to underestimate his enemy.

The Marines were only about a hundred-yards west of the river; when they were unexpectedly surprised and overwhelmed by over a dozen Japanese soldiers. The men had been creeping through a somewhat small clearing and suddenly found themselves surrounded. Over a dozen rifles were pointed at them, and there was nothing they could do about it.

Gunny was standing behind Sergeant Stamper and noticed his friend's grip on his .45 had tightened, and his thumb was pulling back the hammer. Looking at all the rifles pointing their way, he tapped Sergeant Stamper on the shoulder. "No, Roger, not a good idea. The Japs are too close. You might miss one."

Turning to face his friend, the urge to attack was in his eyes and in his posture, until Gunny shook his head. "Not this time, sir. Wait. We still have three aces out there. Remember?"

Turning back to face his adversary, Sergeant Stamper lowered the hammer on his .45, and then grabbed his pistol by the barrel and held it out towards his enemy. When the enemy commander reached for the weapon, Roger Stamper released his grip, and with his eyes, followed the falling weapon down until it landed, half buried in the jungle muck. Looking back up at the man in charge, he smiled, and received a rifle butt to the stomach for his rude display. Patting his friend on the back, Gunny said; "Good surrender, Roger. Well handled."

PFC Bonito heard the commotion about fifty, sixty-feet away. He also heard the Japanese shouting, and knew the four Marines had been discovered. Startled by two quick shots, he ducked low to the ground, and heard a third shot, but no bullets came his way. Still under cover, he heard Gunny shouting above the enemy's shouting. "Damn, Geronimo. That hurt. Just stop it and leave us alone." Even from fifty, sixty-feet away, Bonito heard the rifle butt smack into Gunny's face.

Because the Japanese had nothing to tie their captive's hands with, they used Marine Corp bootlaces, which did the job nicely. With their hands tied, the Marines were roughly pushed back towards the river.

Walking through the jungle was really tough for the Americans, especially without the use of their hands and no bootlaces. The Japanese constantly had to help them back onto their feet after they had fallen. This extra duty angered the enemy, and in turn, resulted in a rifle butt to the body of the hapless Marine who had fallen.

Watanabe's troops were also angry for all the trouble the Marines had put them through. The fact that they had to travel in this rain soaked, insect infested jungle didn't help matters at all, and their anger showed in the way they treated the Marines. After a twenty-minute struggle, tramping through the jungle, all were back at the river. Much to Gunny's surprise, there was another dozen or so enemy soldiers waiting for them by the river.

"Very good, Sergeant Takagi. Your idea worked well."

Sergeant Takagi bowed to his platoon leader. "These Americans are stupid. They blunder through the jungle like lost children."

Only the Japanese were laughing at the comment. Gunny figured they were laughing at him, and he was somewhat right. The enemy, however, was laughing at all the captured Marines, especially Corporal Kirby. When he tried translating what was said, he received a rifle butt to the stomach for his efforts.

Gunny's smile wasn't humorous or joyful. "Hey, rice ball. Get your hits in now while you can because pretty soon you'll be dead." His outburst earned him a well-placed rifle butt to the stomach, and he immediately doubled over and started retching from the blow. *Great*, he thought. *We've been captured by another bunch of jungle skunks. Just like on our last mission. Maybe we ought to quit going on these kinds of missions, and do something different.*

The yap of a coyote stopped their laughing. Despite his retching, when Gunny heard the coyote call, it brought a weak smile to his face.

Yep. You're in trouble now.

~ ~ ~

PFC Bonito had moved north about sixty-yards, keeping just out of his enemy's line of march. He stood, gritting his teeth, forced to watch the Japanese mistreat his friends, and there was nothing he could do about it at the moment. He had no weapons to speak of, other than his K-bar. A lot of good that would do him; he was up against about a dozen Japanese soldiers. When the procession of enemy troops stopped at the river, his heart sank even lower. Now there were over twenty Japs. It was one thing trying to take on a dozen men at night, but now there were over twenty. The odds were not very good at all.

PFC Bonito was raging inside. He saw what the Japanese did to Gunny. A rifle butt to the stomach was a lot worse than getting hit in the stomach by a fist. Shaking his head at his inability to change the situation, he moved deeper into the jungle and then let go a coyote yap. It was his way of letting Gunny know that he was still around. It stopped the Japanese from laughing, but that was about all it did. Moving closer to the Japanese camp to keep an eye on the captured Marines, Bonito settled in for a long wait to sunrise.

~ ~ ~

The two enemy squads prepared to move out about an hour after the sun came up, but they were unexpectedly brought under fire. The shooting came from the opposite side of the river. For about four-minutes, the firing was hot and heavy, but then Lieutenant Watanabe heard someone shouting out orders in Japanese, so he ordered his men to cease their firing. Immediately following his shouted cease fire order, he turned and shouted across the river. After a few seconds, the firing from that side also stopped. Stepping out from behind a tree, a man wearing a Japanese officer's top-cover walked into plain view.

The two lieutenants, after shouting at each other for a few minutes, had their two forces come out from under cover. Shortly after both units left cover, Lieutenant Watanabe was ordered by Lieutenant Nakamura to hand the captured Marines over to him. Another argument ensued, and the two lieutenants looked as if they were going to come to blows. But after another few minutes of verbal exchange, Lieutenant Watanabe was forced to follow the senior lieutenant's orders. He was Lieutenant Nakamura's junior by five months. Another problem the two lieutenants faced was there was no place close by that the two forces could cross the river, except where Lieutenant Nakamura had crossed, using the tree for a bridge. However; the senior lieutenant wasn't about to go through that disaster again.

The tree bridge was still stretched across the river, but it was no longer resting on the top of the opposite bank. It stopped at the edge of the river, twenty feet below the top-edge of the embankment. Neither man wanted to cross the tree bridge, so they both agreed to head south. The junior lieutenant won the next argument by suggesting to Nakamura that they look for a crossing, closer to headquarters. "Let's follow the river south until we find a safer crossing, then I will merge with you."

Lieutenant Nakamura had no idea that the river even existed until his two prisoners had escaped, and he was forced to go after them. The two men who had escaped, were also heading south, he could see the big man's tracks. The little Marine's trail, however, was much more difficult to ascertain. His tracks were almost none-existent. *This is going to work out just fine*, he thought. *Captain Matsui will be very pleased indeed. Not only will I bring back the two escaped Marines, but I will also be handing him a bonus ... four more Marines.*

Chapter 11

Both men heard the screams from their enemy when the tree bridge gave way. They stared back towards the nature-made crossing, looked at each other, and for a short few seconds, their excitement rose. Gazing back in the direction of the scream, the chief was the first to speak his thoughts. "I wonder how many bought it. I sure hope it was all of them."

The big Marine didn't know what to say at first. He looked back towards the crossing for a moment or two, then he shook his head, exasperated. "I don't know, little man. With the way our luck's been running, I think a wish would be a wasted effort."

Then PFC Fox thought of something else, so he looked over at PFC Choctaw and said. "Let's head east, deeper into the jungle and let the Japs get in front of us. Once they get in front of us, we can follow them all the way to their base."

The big man stared at Fox for a few seconds before he turned to look at their backtrail again, contemplating. "I like the way you think." Turning back to face the scout again, a smile interrupted his previous expression and he winked and said; "Little man my ass. My face still remembers what you did to it. You lead on; I'll follow." An hour later, the enemy passed by Fox and Choctaw and never looked back.

The two Americans were about sixty-yards to the east of the Japanese when they passed by the two men. The scout gave his enemy a ten-minute head start, and then the two of them proceeded to follow their enemy until Lieutenant Nakamura finally called a halt. With nothing more to do, the two Marines found a comfortable spot about eighty yards from the enemy camp, and settled down for the night.

The sun was an hour below the horizon when, out of the blue, PFC Fox remembered hearing a crow caw. *Well what do you know. He made it. I wonder if anyone else did. If the call was from Jose, then he's well south of where I first heard the crow.*

Just the thought of the crow caw brought a smile to the little man's face. He thought several times about looking for the scout, but in the end, he decided on his first choice. *First I get my knife back, and then I go looking for Geronimo.*

~ ~ ~

Everything was peaceful and quiet until about an hour after sunrise: then the jungle exploded with the sounds of battle. The two Marines were forced to duck from the hail of bullets that were zinging over their heads. At first, they thought they had been discovered, but then that thought quickly disappeared when they saw their enemy firing towards the opposite bank.

Several minutes went by before the firing stopped. From where the two men were crouching, it was hard to see what the Japanese were shooting at. Then the chief spotted enemy troops moving around on the opposite bank, and let out a sigh of disappointment. A couple of minutes later, the two Marines watched while one enemy soldier bent over and jerked someone to his feet. That someone was Corporal Kirby. Then they watched helplessly while Gunny, Sergeant Stamper, and Sergeant Thomas were all jerked to their feet.

So, they got Gunny and the guys. Then another thought entered his mind. *Where is Jose?* Staring a hole through his adversary, the chief continued to watch the four Marines being jerked around like animals on a leash. Frustrated at his inability to alter the situation had him deep in thought. His devious plotting, however, was interrupted by PFC Choctaw's whispered question.

"Where's PFC Geronimo?"

The scout looked over at Choctaw and had to smile at what the big man said. *PFC Geronimo. Now that's a new one. Even the Ox is calling Bonito, Geronimo.* Still, the whispered question aroused the little man's curiosity. Where was PFC Bonito?

Fifteen-minutes went by before the enemy troops on both sides of the river, began heading south. After a few minutes of waiting, the two men followed their enemy, cautiously moving from shadow to shadow, but always keeping their adversary in sight.

After two hours of walking south, the river began to narrow down a bit, and as luck would have it, they found a crossing. The two Japanese forces met on the east bank of the river. It was Lieutenant Watanabe's turn to cross the river by using a tree bridge. After his last experience, Lieutenant Nakamura wasn't about to try his luck again.

Lieutenant Watanabe was the first to make the crossing, and he immediately went on the attack. "Lieutenant Nakamura, my orders were to capture or kill these Americans. I have captured them. General Sasaki has ordered me to bring them to *him* for interrogation. Are you going to dispute the general's orders?"

Lieutenant Nakamura smiled and then replied. "Not at all, Lieutenant Watanabe. I am merely saving General Sasaki the trouble of having to send the Americans back to Captain Matsui. You will take the Americans to your general, and he will, in-turn, send them to us. If you wish, you may use our radio to contact General Sasaki and tell him what has happened. I am sure he will agree to my decision."

"And if he does not agree to your decision?"

Again Lieutenant Nakamura smiled before he replied. "Then you will have lost only one day. You and your men will have full stomachs when you leave, and I will give you the use of one of our trucks to transport you and your men back to your headquarters."

Lieutenant Watanabe didn't like the decision, and he didn't like Lieutenant Nakamura, but he had to follow his orders. With a sigh of resignation, Lieutenant Watanabe bowed to the senior lieutenant's wishes.

His next thought put a smile to his face. *General Sasaki will eat him for breakfast when he hears about what happened.*

~ ~ ~

"What do we do now, little man? There's over thirty of the little monkeys. We can't get our guys out of this mess, not with that many Japs around."

PFC Fox just smiled and said; "You let me worry about that, Ox. You just be ready when the time comes." Pausing for a moment to search the area, he continued. "First we see where they take Gunny, and then we go find Geronimo."

"Why do you call PFC Bonito, Geronimo?" the big man asked.

The scout's reply came with a devious expression attached to it. "Because he hates it. He doesn't hate the name, Geronimo. He just hates *me* calling him Geronimo."

~ ~ ~

The sun was on its way down when the Japanese finally made it to the east coast road. It wasn't exactly a road. It was a ten-foot wide path cut along the eastern edge of the jungle, separating the beach from the jungle. The dirt path stretched from Captain Matsui's encampment on the southeastern tip of the island all the way up the east coast, to the top of the island, 250 miles to the north. The lane worked out okay for vehicular traffic as long as it didn't rain for very long.

Two hours after reaching the east coast road, the two lieutenants, their men, and their four captives, arrived at their encampment. The Japanese troops were tired and hungry, but their hunger and rest would have to wait. They had four Yankee dogs to take care of first.

~ ~ ~

Fox and Choctaw were just inside the jungle, watching to see where the Japanese put the Marines. Gunny didn't look so good, and neither did the rest of the squad. The enemy had done a bang up job of beating on the four men.

"Damn those Japs," whispered PFC Fox. "I wish I had my carbine. I'd shoot them all right where they stand."

PFC Choctaw looked worried. "Now what, little man?"

For a few seconds, the chief was hard-pressed to keep his emotions under control, then a devious expression appeared on his face. "You wait here. I'm going after my knife. If anything happens to me, you get Gunny and the guys out of there. I'll be back in a couple of hours."

PFC Choctaw was about to argue, but the scout cut him off.

"I'm not doing anything else without my knife. You wait here two hours. If I'm not back by then, it's up to you to free Gunny and the guys."

Again the big man tried to argue. "But Fox."

"That's an order, Ox. I'm senior enlisted, so you have to follow my orders. Two hours, Ox. Then we can get Gunny and the boys away from the Japs."

Just before he left, the chief hooted the owl twice, hoping Bonito would hear it and be able to figure out where they were. Then he turned, smiled at the Ox, and disappeared into the shadows. For the first time since being a Marine, PFC Choctaw shuddered at the thought of being alone in the jungle.

~ ~ ~

The captured Marines were put into the same bamboo hut Fox and Choctaw had been held in, but this time, there was a guard inside and outside of the hut. When the Marines had been secured, the two lieutenants went and paid a visit to Captain Matsui.

The captain's eyes lit up when he heard the news, but his smile didn't last long. Lieutenant Watanabe reminded the senior officer what General Sasaki's orders were. Captain Matsui, knowing General Sasaki like he did, decided to concede to the junior lieutenant's request. The fact that Takeo Sasaki was Watanabe's uncle contributed greatly to that decision.

~ ~ ~

PFC Bonito was about 300 yards south of the chief's position when he heard the two hoots, so he sent a return signal, but there was no response from the little man. *Maybe he's too close to the Japs to answer.* Seconds after his deduction he was moving north, hoping to find a long-lost, Cherokee scout, but he wasn't about to let *anyone* know he was happy the chief was still alive.

~ ~ ~

The area where the small Japanese base was situated on was flat and grassy, and had plenty of coconut trees to provide a little shade for the 250 or so Japanese troops based there. The beach east of the small encampment was white sand and beautiful Pacific green water. It would have been the perfect Pacific paradise hideaway if not for the war. The debris littered beach and the broken freighter was the perfect contrast to the peaceful, Pacific scene. Its rusting, holed, and cracking hulk was lying partway on its port side. At high tide, the water came up almost to the freighter's portside railing. The beach around the freighter was littered with pieces of the dead ship, torn from the hulk by the rising tides, and the many storms that ravaged the island. PFC Fox was hiding in one of those torn off pieces. It was the upper part from one of the dead ship's stacks.

The little scout was waiting for the activity in the camp to die down, so he could go after his knife. Captain Matsui was the last person he saw with it, so he located the captain's quarters, then sat back to pass the time away, contemplating until the captain's lights went out, indicating he was going to bed. *Once the lights go out, it'll probably take him maybe thirty minutes to fall asleep. Plenty of time to take out the rear sentry. Once he's gone, I'll just sneak in and grab my knife, and be gone before he knows I'm there.*

Sometime around 2230 hours, the lights in Captain Matsui's quarters abruptly went out. Because he was so tired, it took the scout a few seconds to realize the lights had been turned off. When he did realize they were out, his expression changed from excited anticipation to one of intense focus. No humor accompanied his next thought. *Well what do you know. He does go to sleep.* Even before his thought was finished, he was silently moving towards the enemy commander's quarters.

Because Fox and Choctaw were still on the loose, Captain Matsui had guards stationed all around the small base, including around his sleeping quarters. The two guards watching his digs were walking parallel to each other, along the front and back of the bamboo structure, but walking in opposite directions. The building itself was rectangular in shape, about twenty feet wide and just over forty-feet long.

Every once in a while, both men ended up at the same end of the structure, at the same time. Fox was waiting for them to end up at opposite ends of the bamboo quarters before he acted.

As silent as a hunting wolf, Fox lay in the tall grass about twenty-yards east of the hut. The only weapon he had was a piece of the freighter's railing about sixteen inches long, with one end, the broken end, forming a jagged point. Not his weapon of choice, but it would have to do.

The big man's ordered wait time was thirty-minutes into the past, so the chief had to make this idea of his work quickly, or the possibility of him getting his knife back would be gone when the Ox tried to free, Gunny and the guys. Ten-minutes went by before the situation he had been waiting for finally happened. The guards were now at opposite ends of the captain's quarters. The chief didn't hesitate.

When the guard walking at the rear of the quarters started walking west, away from Fox, the scout started crawling towards the sentry. When he was out of the man's line of peripheral vision, he rose up, and silently sprinted to the back of the structure, sliding between the ground and the two-foot crawl space under the floor of the bamboo structure. There, he waited for the guard to return. When the man passed by where Fox was waiting, the little scout silently slid out from under the building and quickly attacked him from behind. Within seconds, the short skirmish was over. Now came the hard part: getting into the building without being heard.

~ ~ ~

PFC Choctaw didn't know how to tell time at night without his watch. The Japanese had taken it when he was captured, but that fact wouldn't have made any difference anyway because the saltwater of the Pacific had ruined his watch long before the Japanese could collect it from him. The watch was still lying on the beach where a disgusted Japanese soldier tossed it after he discovered it didn't work anymore. The big man also had no idea how long PFC Fox had been gone, but when the lights started going off around the base, he figured it had been at least two hours since the little man left. *What do I do now?* he wondered.

He could see the hut his buddies were being kept in, about sixty-yards from where he was hiding. When he had escaped with Fox, he had gone out through the back of the hut, but where he was hiding now, he could see both the front and the back of the hut, and the sentry guarding the entrance.

120

The big man watched the Japanese put their four captives into the hut. Four of the enemy had escorted the Marines into their new digs. But when the Japanese came back out, only three were seen leaving the hut. *Sneaky little bastards. They left one inside. Taking the guard out front shouldn't be too hard.* What bothered the big man the most was the guard inside. He figured to have a problem with that one.

He was preparing to try his luck with the outside guard, when, out of the blue, the outside sentry started looking around, as if trying to find something.

Looking for the source of the strange chittering, the soldier started walking around, behind the hut. The bruiser from Louisiana was hunkered down, frozen in place, watching his enemy act strangely, and he was puzzled. Seconds elapsed until, astonished, the big Marine noticed a shadow detach itself from the rear corner of the hut, just as the enemy guard passed that same corner. The shadow turned into a shape, and the shape turned in Bonito. *SSHICK*, and seconds later, Bonito was rolling the dead Jap under the hut. Then faintly, he heard the chittering and chirping of Bonito's animal calls.

The inside guard finally heard the chittering and chirping, but he didn't know what it was. Going outside to investigate, he discovered that his friend was gone, but he did see his friend's rifle leaning up against a coconut tree, about ten-feet from the hut. *Maybe he had to pee. Hmm.*

Moving towards the back corner of the hut, the enemy sentry called softly to his friend. Again the shadow struck, but this time, the deadly silhouette emerged from under the front corner of the hut and closed in on the unsuspecting guard, and seconds later, Bonito was rolling the second guard under the hut.

Choctaw quickly left his hiding place, running bent over towards the hut when he saw the second man go down.

Bonito heard the thumping of the big man's steps and turned to face the new threat, his K-Bar ready for throwing. Then he paused. "Damn, he's too big to be a Jap." Almost immediately after his whispered words, he recognized who it was.

"Come on, PFC," whispered Bonito. "We have to get the guys out. Where's PFC Fox?"

"I don't know," whispered Choctaw. "He went to get his knife back, but that was over two hours ago. I was going to try and spring the guys when I saw you."

Bonito looked around to make sure they hadn't been spotted and then looked back at Choctaw. "Never mind about Fox. Let's get the guys out."

Moving to the back of the hut, Bonito paused to listen for a moment. Not hearing anything inside the hut, he cut his way through the bindings holding the bamboo wall together. In seconds, they were inside the dimly lit hut, with the four captives. Gunny looked pretty badly beaten and so did Kirby, but the other two looked all right compared to Gunny and the corporal. Only seconds went by before the six Marines were heading out through the back of the hut. Gunny had to be carried, but the other three were able to move under their own power.

"Get them out of here, Ox. I'll go find Fox. Follow the river for about an hour and then head west. We'll catch up to you when we can. Find a place to hide out and stay there."

The big man nodded and took off for the river with Gunnery Sergeant Baker slung over his shoulder. Nobody was concerned about rank at that time, especially Sergeant Stamper. *Isn't this fun? Now the scouts are in charge!* Sergeant Stamper felt the same as Gunny when it came to the scouts. Absolute trust.

While Sergeant Stamper was leading the escapees to the river, PFC Bonito was shaking his head. *Damn that Cherokee. Why the hell does he want that knife back?*

Moving from hut to hut, Bonito searched for his friend. He was about seventy-yards from a rectangular shaped hut when all hell broke loose. The Apache scout stood flat-footed and amazed while he watched a bloody headed Japanese captain, run through the camp, screaming at the top of his voice. Lights immediately popped on, one after another, all over the small base. The west side machine gun towers had their search lights on, and were searching the grounds, as were the north and south towers, but the two east towers were still dark: their search lights hadn't come on yet. Bonito shook his head and then let the big cat, scream. Shortly after the echoes of the call died out, he heard a howl. *Little man my ass. Big trouble in a little bottle is more like it.* He had found David Little Fox.

~ ~ ~

Twenty-minutes after their escape, the five Marines found the river, and stopped for a much needed break. Gunny had regained consciousness about halfway to the river and stormed his argument upon Sergeant Stamper's ears, but to no avail. The big man, under Sergeant Stamper's orders, refused to let him down. After a twenty-minute breather, the Marines were on the move again. This time, however, Gunny was on his feet and raring to fight anybody if they tried carrying him again. Sergeant Stamper was smiling. He was betting on the gunny, and of course, he had no takers. Nobody wanted to tangle with the gunnery sergeant from Oklahoma, even as beat up as he was. After a few rough-shod words between the two sergeants, the Marines headed north, with Gunny under his own power.

"Where we headed, Roger?"

"Back to where the Japs left our boots, Al. We don't have any socks, so we'll probably get blistered because of it, but at least our feet won't get cut up anymore."

"Okay Roger, you take the lead." Gunny then turned to PFC Choctaw. "Where're Bonito and Fox?"

123

"I don't know, Gunny. Right after we snatched you guys out, Bonito said he was going after Fox. He told us to follow the river north for about an hour, and then head west. He told me to find a place to hide and wait for them there. I think it was only a couple of minutes after we split up that I heard the drunken Cougar. I also heard the howl, so I believe they found each other."

Gunny stared at the big man, and for a moment, couldn't think of anything to say. Then he shook his head, amused at the comment. "A drunken Cougar?"

Choctaw had a somewhat puzzled expression on his face when he continued. "Well, that's what PFC Fox thinks the call sounds like. He says Geronimo's call sounds like a drunken Cougar to him. I can't tell the difference one way or the other. The calls sound real to me."

They all heard Kirby's laugh. "That's what the chief thinks all right. He told me that the first time we heard it when you were on top of Flat Head waiting for us."

Shaking his head, the gunnery sergeant was definitely cracking a smile when he spoke his thought out loud. "Huh, a drunken Cougar? I'll have to remember that one."

The Marines had been moving north, following the river for almost two hours. When they arrived at the spot of the shoot-out, they found their boondockers patiently waiting. Only Sergeant Stamper thought about saving some of the laces, but he had only enough lacing to tie the top two eye holes on their boots. At least, it would keep their boots from falling off their feet. Anything was better than nothing.

After a short break, the stranded Americans began moving west, into the rocky terrain that occupied the southern portion of the island. They still didn't know what island they were on, and now, thanks to the enemy, they didn't even have their canteens or any of their weapons.

The five marooned escapees continued moving west until they noticed through the jungle canopy, the night sky was beginning to lighten. The beginning of sunrise was also the signal to start looking for someplace to hide. They found a small cave on the side of the ridge they were on and decided to stay there and rest. The condition their feet were in wouldn't allow them to go any further. They were beaten bloody and exhausted from running, but they were free for the moment.

Chapter 12

He was knocked unconscious in his quarters while his back was turned, but now he was fully awake, and Captain Matsui was furious. He was being forced to sit while a little Yankee Marine shaved the left side of his head with a hunting knife. The enraged captain could feel the blood running down the left side of his face, but he was powerless to do anything about it.

Captain Matsui was tied to a chair with a sock jammed in his mouth, and one of his monogrammed handkerchiefs tied around the outside of his mouth so he couldn't spit out the sock. The little Yankee dog had already cut off the right side of his mustache, leaving the captain's lip torn and bloody. Now the skinny American was scalping the left side of his enemy's head. At least, that's what he called it, and he was smiling. PFC Fox also left a small reminder on the captain's forehead just in case he forgot who the culprit was. The little reminders were the letters L F for Little Fox, his hidden name.

Five-minutes after David Little Fox left the captain, still tied to the chair, the enemy camp abruptly came to life. The chief was just entering the jungle, about a hundred-yards east of the captain's hut when he heard the scream of a big cat. He immediately cracked a smile, then he let the wolf, howl. Instantly, gunshots followed the howl and he started laughing. *I guess he got loose.* After twenty-minutes of searching, the two scouts finally found each other.

Geronimo's look of surprise was priceless. Then he started laughing and said; "You'd better not let Gunny see that. He's liable to shoot you for it." Bonito had never seen a real live, Indian taken, scalp before.

Fox, however, was not concerned with Gunny at the moment. He was struggling hard to keep his excitement contained. "It'll be worth it just to see the expression on his face when he sees it."

Still laughing, Bonito's reply was slow to come out. "Just wait until I get behind Gunny before you show him. I don't want to be in his line of fire by mistake."

The humorous reunion was short because an excited enemy was storming about. As quickly as it erupted, the reunion was over, and the two scouts were moving west. It was time to get away from an enraged foe.

The two scouts headed west for another half an hour before they changed direction and turned north. They traveled north for another hour and then stopped for the night. "We'd better stop here until it's light enough to see," said Bonito. "We don't want to cross Gunny's trail during the night and miss it. I told Ox to follow the river north for an hour and then head west, so they should be west of our line of march by the time the sun comes up." Widening his smile, the Apache scout winked. "Let me see that thing again."

~ ~ ~

The sun was just climbing above the horizon when the two lieutenants formed their men up in front of command headquarters. Their orders were to hunt down the Yankees and capture them, especially the little Yankee. Captain Matsui had something special planned for him. Lieutenant Nakamura was to cover the east side of the river, while Lieutenant Watanabe covered the west bank. Captain Matsui stood in front of the two formations, his head bandaged, and his mustache shaved. And he was greatly agitated.

Staring at the troops standing in formation, he shouted; "These Yankee Marine dogs have landed on our island, and they have humiliated His Majesty the Emperor and his troops. We will hunt down these Yankee cowards and bring them back here, no matter how long it takes. No matter the cost. The only way to remove this humiliation is to capture them and take off their heads. The Emperor's honor demands this be done. Banzai! Banzai! Banzai!"

Captain Matsui saluted his troops, gave out his orders, and then headed for the front of Lieutenant Nakamura's detachment. The hunt was about to begin.

While Captain Matsui was searching north along the east bank of the river, Lieutenant Watanabe, with his two squads, went north, following Sergeant Takagi, who was twenty-yards out in front, and looking for tracks along the west bank of the river. The trail of the escaped Marines wasn't all that hard to follow once they located it. The little smears of blood from their torn and bloodied feet was the marker, and it was bold enough to follow at a fast walk. It was like following the yellow brick road from the book, *The Wizard of Oz.*

Lieutenant Watanabe immediately called his radioman to the head of the squad, and when the call went through, he reported his discovery to his superior. "Captain Matsui, we have found their trail. They are on the west side of the river."

The sound in the captain's voice revealed his hidden thoughts, and his reply was not pleasing to the ear. "Wait where you are. We will come to you."

Definitely not what Lieutenant Watanabe wanted to hear. Now, he was forced to stop and wait at least an hour for Captain Matsui to catch up to him. He had seen the methods the captain used to extract information out of his captives, but he didn't approve of those methods. Now, because of the way he had treated the American captives, his head was bandaged, and the prisoners had escaped...again. Lieutenant Watanabe had a strange feeling that this hunt was going to end badly for him and his men.

To hell with Captain Matsui.

~ ~ ~

The sun was about thirty-minutes away from poking its head above the horizon. The two scouts had been awake for twenty-minutes, carrying on a whispered conversation, and PFC Fox was smiling. He was as happy as a jaybird eating pie now that he had his knife back.

"What's so important about that knife that you had to risk getting captured again just to get it back?"

PFC Fox thought about the question for a moment before he answered. "My grandfather gave me this knife. It has been in my family since the late 1700's. I was told it was taken from a white man one of my great ancestors killed in battle. That's why I went back after it. Besides, this is the second time someone has taken it away from me, and that really pissed me off, so I took it back. I'll die before that happens again."

Geronimo's reply was slow in coming because he was laughing. "You should have thought about that before you got captured."

"I didn't have a choice. I was unconscious and on the beach when the Japs found me. There really wasn't much I could do about it, now was there? All I remember was walking towards the conning tower when this big shadow came out of nowhere and rammed the sub. The next thing I know, the Japs are dragging me and the Ox up the beach. What was I supposed to do? Hey you, gimme back my knife so I can kill you guys. I'm sure the Japs would have loved that one."

PFC Bonito snorted through his nose and a smile appeared before he spoke. "Well, the sun's up, so we might as well get going. I'm sure the Japs are out hunting for Gunny right now. The boys were in pretty bad shape when we got them out. The Japs threw their boots away, so they're out in the jungle, walking barefoot."

"Those jungle skunks." hissed Fox. "Maybe we should go on the warpath against these goons. Show them what's what."

"Let's find Gunny first," said Bonito. "Then we can go on the warpath. Besides, we've already been on the warpath. We've been at war with the Japs ever since they bombed Pearl Harbor. Remember?"

The smile didn't remain long on the chief's face. He looked over at Bonito and his expression turned hostile. "Yeah, but I don't think the Japs take us seriously enough. Maybe it's time they did."

Geronimo stared at his friend for a long few seconds, and he was thinking the same thoughts, but now was not the time. They needed to heal first before they could fight back. Shaking his head at his ending thoughts, he replied. "You lead. We need to catch up with the guys."

The two scouts were traveling north, about a half a mile northwest of the nearest enemy troops, Lieutenant Watanabe and his two squads. The Japanese were just starting out on their hunt for the Baker Boys.

~ ~ ~

Nobody had any water because the Japanese took everything they had, including their canteens. Their feet were a bloody mess, and because the Marines had no water, they were unable to clean their wounded feet. Gunny shook his head, exasperated. *This has to be the worst situation we've ever been in. No water. No food. No socks. And we can't walk anymore. Surely it can't get any worse than this.* Then he shook his head with greater emphasis. *No. I suppose being dead would be a little worse than this. Well. Maybe.* Afterward, he turned his attention to the big man.

"Ox, you're going to have to be our go-for on this trip. We can't walk until our feet heal, so you're going to have to go for water and food. Don't head east to the river because the Japs will be expecting us to do that. You'll have to go either north or west to find any water. Be careful out there, PFC. Try not to leave any tracks."

Looking at the bloody mess his feet were in, Gunny was worried. He knew they would have to stay hidden for at least a week in order to give their feet a chance to heal. They needed the water to clean out their injured feet so the wounds wouldn't go septic on them. The jungle rot they had been walking on was squished into their wounds, so the men could end up dying from blood poisoning or possibly gangrene. Not a very pleasant situation to be in.

The cave the Baker Boys found was barely big enough for the five of them. They could sit up, or they could crawl around on all fours, which was all they could do anyway because of the condition of their feet. The roof of the cave wouldn't allow them to stand. The cave was hot, humid, and dirty, but it was a roof over their heads, and a place to lie low and heal.

Gunny looked at his watch to see what time it was and ended up shaking his head, instead. *Hmm, it seems the Japs took everything but the kitchen sink.* Looking around the cave, he smiled. *Yep, there's no kitchen sink in here, so they must have taken it too.*

Corporal Kirby was in bad shape. Besides his feet being torn up, his face was all battered and bruised, as well as his chest and rib area. The fact that he had made it this far without passing out really amazed Gunny. *It's good he's out, cold, he needs the rest.* The man in charge was also concerned about PFC Choctaw. The big man had gone out looking for water three hours earlier and hadn't returned yet.

~ ~ ~

Sergeant Takagi found where the Marines had stopped for a short break. He also found the boot tracks PFC Choctaw had left behind. He had heard the story about Captain Matsui's two prisoners escaping, yet the captain was saying nothing about his wounds. It obvious something happened to him; it was too difficult to hide stark white bandages seeping blood. Sergeant Takagi smiled for first time since he ran into Lieutenant Nakamura, and it was a satisfying smile. *These tracks must be from one of the Americans.*

About forty-minutes into his wait, the veteran sergeant spotted Captain Matsui approaching from the south, with Lieutenant Nakamura following. Not more than a minute after spotting Captain Matsui, Lieutenant Watanabe came into view from the southwest, trailing about thirty-yards behind Nakamura's men. When Sergeant Takagi spotted his platoon leader, he immediately, out of a war created habit, started walking towards his platoon leader to give his report. Sergeant Takagi didn't walk very far before his ears were abruptly assaulted by a shouting and extremely agitated captain. "You report your findings to me, Sergeant! Not to Lieutenant Watanabe! I am in command here, not him!"

"Hai." replied Sergeant Takagi.

Captain Matsui was still angry. "Now! What did you find?"

"Sir, the blood trail ends here. This is the spot where we removed their boots. The boot tracks lead west from here."

Captain Matsui's eyes were on fire, but the fire from his anger was not going out until all the Americans were lying dead and headless at his feet. "Why didn't you throw their boots into the river, you fool? We could have caught them in a couple hours, but no, you had to be stupid and leave their boots here for them to find!"

Sergeant Takagi knew what would happen to him if he spoke out, but he had his say anyway. "They escaped from your custody, Captain, not ours! That is why they wear their boots. Not because we left them here."

The enraged captain reached for his sword. "I should cut off your head as a reward for your stupidity and insolence!" But Lieutenant Watanabe stuck up for his sergeant.

"Captain Matsui, Sergeant Takagi is our best tracker. If you kill him, we will never find the Americans. I know this to be true. We didn't find the Americans by luck. We found them because of Sergeant Takagi's tracking skills and smart thinking."

Captain Matsui was still very angry and wanted *so much* to kill the arrogant sergeant, but the thought of losing the skinny American because he killed his only decent tracker, planted the seed of reason back in Captain Matsui's head.

"Then you had better teach this idiot some manners, Lieutenant. He won't be so lucky the next time."

The captain had pulled his sword out several inches before Lieutenant Watanabe could stop him. There was a loud, audible, snap, when it slid back into place.

"Start tracking you idiot." The captain's head and lip were burning from the salt of his sweat because of the shave the chief gave him.

~ ~ ~

The sun was five hours old when Bonito discovered the trail of the escaping Marines. He was somewhat surprised that they had to walk an hour longer than anticipated. *Where did they get the boots from?* Turning to Fox, he whispered. "The guys are wearing boondockers now. Look at the tracks. The Japs must have left them, and somebody remembered where they were. I bet it was Gunny or maybe Sergeant Stamper. That man has one hell of memory."

"Well," replied Fox. "Let's go find them. You want me to lead this time?"

"Yeah, you lead and I'll follow. Besides, I don't want to take a chance on you trying to scalp me. Our ancestors

134

didn't get along once. Remember?"

Fox looked at PFC Bonito indignantly. "That's not true. We never went to war against the Apache back then."

Bonito paused for a few seconds until his smile widened, and then he spoke. "Maybe so, but your scalp happy now, and I don't want to be the first Apache to fall to a Cherokee blade."

Smiling, the chief had no idea what to say in return; he was speechless for the count of twenty, then; "I saved your bacon once, remember? You owe me your life. So why would I want to kill you when you owe me one? With you dead, I can't collect what you owe me."

Laughing, Bonito took a second or two to reply. "I pulled your fat out of the fire once too. Do you remember that incident?"

"Don't remind me." whispered Fox.

"You're a fat-head." whispered Bonito. "Why would we kill each other when each one of us owes the other? If you kill me, you would still owe me one. If I killed you, I would still owe you one. It makes no sense to kill each other, so why even talk about it?"

"You started this conversation, not me."

Bonito shook his head and said. "You damn, Cherokee. Are you going to start tracking, or are you going to just talk?"

"Damn Apache," muttered Fox. "Your cougar call sounds drunk."

"Damn Cherokee," whispered Bonito. "Your wolf howl sounds like a sick puppy."

The bantering between friends had been long in hiding until time and circumstances finally permitted it. The two scouts were whispering and carrying on until they couldn't stand it anymore, and then the seriousness of the situation got the better of them. With Fox leading the way, the two scouts began following the trail left by their buddies, and the snickers continued. "Gunny is going to love your explanation. Damn, wolf-man. Slow down!"

After tromping three hours through the jungle's snares, the two scouts were crouched down, watching a lone man struggle with a pair of boots. It was PFC Choctaw. He was carrying the boots as if they were made of egg shells. Confused, the two scouts looked at each other, each speaking their thoughts out loud at the same time, "What is he doing?"

They watched the big man for about ten-minutes until he disappeared from sight. The two scouts waited a couple minutes. When he didn't reappear again, they looked at each other. "You go down where we last saw him, and I'll cover you from here."

Bonito looked at Fox. "What are you going to cover me with? Your knife?"

Smiling, the chief reached into his back pocket and pulled out a Japanese type 94, Nambu, 8mm pistol.

"Where did you pick that up from?" asked Bonito.

"I took it away from that Jap officer last night. I figured I needed it more than he did. Besides, he took my knife, so I figured to return the favor by taking his pistol."

"You're a good Marine, Fox. Just make sure you don't shoot me with that thing."

"Don't tempt me, Jose. Now get going."

He watched Bonito's progress as he started down the ridge. It took the Apache scout about fifteen-minutes to reach the spot where they last saw PFC Choctaw. A couple of minutes later, Bonito signaled for Fox to come on down, so he did.

Back at the cave, the reunion was a happy one, but it was short. Kirby was not looking so hot. He was also running a fever, which was never good, especially in the jungles of the Pacific.

"What are we going to do, Gunny?"

"I don't know, chief. We don't have any medical supplies, and we only have the one canteen PFC Bonito has on him." Gunny then looked at Fox. "The only place I know of to get any medical supplies is that Jap base."

PFC Fox didn't hesitate. "I'll go. Corporal Kirby's my friend, Gunny, and he needs help. He's always been there for us. Now we have a chance to return the favor."

Smiling, the little Marine continued. "You remember all that food I took from the Japs on our first mission, don't you? This should be a cinch grabbing their medical supplies. I'll be back in about two or three days."

Gunny looked at Fox. "You be careful, chief."

Always happy to be of service, the scout replied. "Aye, aye, Gunny." Then he turned serious. "Gunny, would you be mad if I took a small scalp? You know, nothing big, just a little one?" Fox pinched his thumb and forefinger together until they were barely apart. Gunny just stared at the chief, his eyes narrowing a little. After a few seconds, the little man started fidgeting a bit.

Gunny continued his stare, watching PFC Fox squirm. "Are you asking me before you do it, or after you did it? Never mind, I don't want to know. Now get outa here."

PFC Fox turned to leave, but then he stopped and turned back to Gunny. He looked like a kid confessing to a cookie theft. "After I did it, Gunny." The chief then handed Gunny the type 94 pistol. "You might need this. I took it off that Jap officer that beat me and the Ox. I didn't think he was going to need it anymore."

"Did you kill him?"

Hesitating for a second or two, he replied. "No Gunny. I shaved off half his mustache and the left side of his head with my knife. I went a little too deep, and ended up taking off part of his scalp. I didn't mean for that to happen. It's just that I never used my knife to shave a man's head before. Honestly, Gunny. I didn't set out to scalp the man. It was

137

just an accident. I figured shaving his head was kind of like payback for beating on the Ox and me."

"An accident? How do you accidently scalp a person?" Gunny was still staring at Fox. "Go on. Get out of here, chief. We'll talk about this matter when you get back. Now get."

The little scout could tell Gunny was agitated, just by the expression on his face, but the tone of his voice made that assessment a definite yes.

"Aye, aye, Gunny." Immediately, the chief turned around and headed for the Japanese base.

PFC Bonito heard Fox confess his sin to Gunny and was happy to see that the scout had waited for him to get behind Gunny before he handed him the pistol. He knew Gunny wouldn't shoot the Cherokee, but it never hurts to be extra careful. Why tempt fate?

Gunny turned towards Sergeant Stamper and said; "He probably should have killed that Jap instead of letting him live. Now we'll be hounded until he either captures us again or we kill him. If it's that captain that was beating on us, then we're definitely in for a tough time. He looked to me like he was a stubborn cuss, with no quit in him. A good hater."

Sergeant Stamper's expression was somewhat neutral when he replied. "What are you going to do about the scalp?"

Gunny just looked at Sergeant Stamper. "I don't know, Roger. I've never dealt with a scalping Indian before. I guess the best thing for us to do is to keep our steel pots strapped to our heads."

Sergeant Stamper shook his and replied. "Really? Then I guess we better hide from the chief because our steel pots are rusting on the bottom of Zdp;pmon Sea!"

Chapter 13

PFC Bonito, with PFC Choctaw's help, managed to move the four wounded another half a mile further northwest to a vine-encrusted ridge. The ledge they were now resting on was completely hidden by vines that stretched about forty feet down from the crest of the cliff. The ledge itself, was only about fifteen-feet below the ridgeline.

PFC Bonito had found the shelf by following a game trail, which led straight to the concealed hideaway. He found all kinds of nests made by the small creatures that inhabited the rocky terrain, indicating a possible source of food close to their new digs. He had also discovered a small rock basin that contained fresh water, about forty-yards from the ledge the Baker Boys were now hiding on.

~ ~ ~

The sun was on its way down, just into the late hours of the afternoon. Sergeant Takagi walked several steps past the last boot print before he realized there were no more. Abruptly he stopped and made a quick eye-search of the area, then let out a frustrated sigh.

The under-strength, enemy platoon, about thirty-five men, had been moving steadily westward for the last four hours, following Sergeant Takagi, who in turn, was following the trail the Marines had left behind. But now, after a thorough twenty-minute search, he was convinced that the tracks had indeed ended. Now, he waited for the onslaught of anger that was sure to come from Captain Matsui once he found out there was no longer a trail to follow. Sure enough. The veteran sergeant was correct. He hit the nail, dead on the head.

~ ~ ~

PFC Bonito was sitting in a tree about twenty-yards off the trail, watching his enemy, and smiling at the scene. The Japanese were now about thirty-minutes from the cave the Marines had just recently vacated. The tree was as far as Geronimo was able to go before running into the enemy. He was trying to cover up the tracks the squad had left behind. Judging by the frustrated look on the enemy tracker's face, and the screaming tirade of the bandaged officer, the job was nicely done. Immediately upon realization, the scout's face lit up. *This must be that Jap officer Fox scalped.* He almost broke out laughing. *Ho, is that man disturbed*!

~ ~ ~

PFC Fox was half way to the Japanese base when Sergeant Takagi lost the trail. The chief wasn't too concerned about running into the enemy where he was because he was hours away from the nearest pursuing Japanese troops, but he didn't abandon all caution, either. And that little bit of alertness saved his life. It was during one of his instinctual stop-to-listen sessions. Had he continued moving instead of stopping, he would have blundered right into a five-man Japanese patrol.

He was crouched down listening to the jungle sounds when he saw a blur of movement. The blur was there and gone so quickly that, at first, he wasn't sure he saw the movement. But his past experiences told him to hold fast, so he did. And there it was again. The little man smiled, but it wasn't a pleasant smile. It was an *I've got you now* kind of smile. Twenty-minutes into his wait, a five-man patrol broke cover, ending their rest break, and started moving south with the Marine scout following them. The five-man patrol was heading back to their base.

Around 1430 hours, the jungle began to grow dark. A bruiser of a storm was moving in from the west, and the clouds were black and ominous; it promised to be one hell of a first rate storm. The enemy patrol had also noticed the jungle growing darker and knew what that meant. They kept glancing towards the west, hoping to reach their barracks before the storm hit them, but it didn't look like they were going to make it in time. No one liked the idea of moving through the jungle carrying steel lightning rods. War was hazardous enough without the heavens interfering.

Watching the enemy patrol, "little man" noticed the anxiety the coming storm was causing his adversary, and an idea began to form. He moved about a hundred-yards to the east before he started moving south. The five-man patrol was walking fast, so the scout was running as fast as the jungle would allow him, racing to get in front of his enemy. When he had run for about fifteen-minutes, he stopped to catch his breath. He knew he was somewhere ahead of the Japanese, but he wanted enough time to slow down his breathing before he struck. He could hear the thunder booming from the west, and it was moving straight toward him, fast.

Immediately after the thunder boomer, PFC Fox squatted down on his heels and waited silently, urging the storm to hit before the Japanese came into view. He needed the darkness *and* the rain to hide his movements and add eeriness to the conditions in order to unnerve his enemy. The adrenaline was coursing through his body, and the excitement of imminent contact with his adversary had him shaking and alert, ready to do damage to those who had killed and ruined so many of his friends. Gunny be damned. This was his time to exact his revenge, his time to wreak havoc on his enemies, and to show his enemies whom they were up against: They were up against David Little Fox, United States Marine Corps.

~ ~ ~

PFC Bonito sat on his perch in the tree watching the bandaged officer go through his tirade. He was both amused and excited at the demonstration the wounded man was giving. On the one hand, it was comical. On the other hand, he saw the anger of the damaged captain as an advantage. A fighter who allows his anger to control his thoughts is easier to defeat than a fighter who keeps his anger under control during a fight. And this raving commander was by no means calm.

While he was watching his enemy mill about, something else struck him as comical: he was stuck in the damn tree until the Japanese left the area. *I wouldn't run a war this way if I had my choice. Sitting in a tree is for birds*. Again he shook his head at the situation. Before his thoughts were finished, the thunderous roar of a new tantrum erupted from the wounded captain, and a fresh smile appeared on the scout's face. *He sure is an entertaining cuss*.

~ ~ ~

The rain was coming down so hard the jungle canopy was unable to hold it back. The thunder struck like the sounds of artillery going off, and the lightning was popping and crackling enough to scare hell into submission. The sizzling bolts were coming so close to the two enemies that it was causing the hair on everyone to stand up despite the rain. Of course, PFC Fox was smiling at the worsening conditions. His smile, though, was only an expression of what he had planned. It was always there when he was about to attack his prey. Oddly enough, the chief was unaware that he was smiling when he was stalking his enemies. Only the dead knew that fact, but they weren't about to spill the beans.

~ ~ ~

The little scout had already dispatched one of his adversaries, and the other four were still none the wiser. The small enemy patrol was moving quickly through the jungle in single file, and were only interested in getting back to headquarters as quickly as they could. All of the lightning, thunder, and rain gave the jungle a spooky, eerie, appearance, something they wanted to get out of.

~ ~ ~

The chief was crouched down in the shadows, unmoving, when the enemy hurriedly passed by him. They were still moving in single file, with about a five or six-foot gap between each man. Several hours were still left before the sun went down, but with the storm clouds and the rain, the jungle scene almost looked as if the sun had already dropped below the horizon.

The enemy was feeling the creepy eeriness of the eroding conditions, and that mood immediately put them on edge. Out of nowhere, there was a startled gasp from the rear of the four-man column, followed by choking sounds. Surprised, the Japanese column stopped, and as one, they all turned, and then, stood frozen in-place like stone statues, their mouths' wide open. Shocked was an understatement. Where two men were supposed to be bringing up the rear, there were none. The two privates covering the rear were not where they should be.

The sergeant in charge of the five-man squad was the first to come to his senses. Acting quickly, he moved his men into the jungle, off the small footpath they were on. He then took stock of the situation and found he was down two men, but he didn't know why. His next step was to move his men north. Following the footpath, but about ten-yards to the west of the path, they started backtracking their steps to find out what happened to their two missing soldiers.

Not knowing what to expect, they were moving cautiously through the jungle, carefully searching the jungle with their eyes. With their weapons at the ready, the sergeant led them north. This time however, they were close together, almost stepping on each other as they headed north, paralleling the footpath.

A couple of minutes into their search, the enemy patrol began to hear strange animal sounds coming from the jungle. The sounds were coming from their left. They heard soft chittering sounds, followed by soft snarls, and then the hoot of an owl. Whatever was making those sounds seemed to be keeping pace with them. The strangeness of the animal calls were beginning to effect the sergeant and his men. Each step they took brought them closer to those sounds and a feeling of dread washed over the enemy patrol like a smothering fog.

The Japanese had been on the island and had been patrolling the interior of the jungle for over a year, yet the only animal sounds they recognized were the owl hoots. The other sounds were something new to them. A peculiar, uncomfortable feeling began to erode what confidence remained, and their nerves began to twitch. After the owl hoot, there was silence for a minute or two, but that didn't last long. The silence of the jungle was interrupted once again by chittering sounds and then by soft snarls. What really drained the blood from their faces, however, was the howl. It caused them to shudder involuntarily, uncontrollably, and the howl was close by.

Stopping immediately, they were casting nervous glances into the jungle to their left, wondering what was going to happen to them. The two junior enlisted men were looking at their sergeant, hoping he would call off the search and head back to base, but it didn't appear as though their silent prayers were going to be answered.

Sergeant Takasu was a seasoned veteran of Southeast Asia and its predators, so this part of the world wasn't new to him, but what was happening to them was. If his men were killed by predators of the jungle, then his two missing men would have surely screamed out in pain and fear. But they didn't. The eeriness and strangeness of the situation had everyone on edge, including Sergeant Takasu. He was casting nervous glances into the jungle just like his men. Also; whatever was making those sounds, appeared to be stalking them.

~ ~ ~

PFC Fox moved silently through the rain and shadows about thirty or forty-yards to the left of his worried enemy. He could see the men were nervous and on edge, so now his only problem was how to kill them without getting killed himself. His only weapon was his knife, a close in, eyeball to eyeball, combat weapon. The Japanese were moving too close together for him to use his knife effectively without getting shot by at least one of them. Not the situation he wanted.

He continued moving along his enemy's flank, toying with their minds with his animal calls, hoping they would give him an opportunity to strike again without exposing himself.

A few minutes into their search, the enemy patrol found the last man PFC Fox had killed. He was leaning up against a tree, just off the footpath, his rifle lying across his lap. Now the chief had their undivided attention. No animal would leave their comrade unmolested like he was. If not for the blood the rain hadn't washed away yet, they would have thought their pal was taking a nap.

Sergeant Takasu looked around, but there wasn't much to see with the rain coming down so hard. Turning to his remaining men, he ordered them to pick up the dead soldier. "We are carrying him back to headquarters."

Then Fox had another idea. *That sergeant's a tough cookie. What will they do without their sergeant around?* From what he could see, the enemy sergeant was doing a pretty fair job keeping his men calm, so he started thinking. It was a long shot. It was also a very dangerous idea. If he followed through with his idea, and it didn't work, he would be weaponless against at least two armed men, possibly a third. But the idea wouldn't leave him alone. The more he thought about it, the more it appealed to him.

~ ~ ~

Sergeant Takasu was moving along the footpath leading his men south, his rifle at the ready. His men were following behind, carrying their dead comrade on a makeshift stretcher, using their rifles as the carrying poles, and their shirts, with their rifles pushed through the sleeves, for the body to rest on. The two stretcher-bearers were nervous, but with Sergeant Takasu leading the way, they felt somewhat secure. They hadn't heard any of the animal sounds for almost twenty minutes, so their hope was that whatever it was killing them had decided to leave them alone.

From out of nowhere, the anxious warriors heard a low vicious snarl. Before another breath could be taken, a shadow moved about fifteen, twenty-feet ahead of them and off to their right. Immediately grabbing their attention was a strange flapping noise, somewhat like a bird flapping its wings. Then, *Shhick.* All movement stopped. The two stretcher-bearers were frozen in-place, immobilized with fear; staring at their patrol leader. A couple of seconds of sudden quiet followed, then Sergeant Takasu crumpled to the ground, dead. Immediately following the sergeant's death, the two frightened stretcher-bearers heard a second howl.

The two men were in a panic now. Without their rifles, they were defenseless except for their bayonets. Seeing Sergeant Takasu lying on the path with a bone handle knife sticking out of his chest, had the desired effect. The two-terror stricken men started running down the path, casting frightened glances everywhere, trying to outrun whatever was after them. They ran fast and furious for about fifteen-minutes before their lack of wind forced them to stop.

The two frightened warriors were leaning up against a

tree, sucking in great gasps of air when PFC Fox finally spotted them. Moving east through the jungle, he circled around to get out in front of the two men. When he was in position, he stopped and waited for his two remaining enemies to appear. Ten-minutes into his wait, the chief spotted his enemy walking slowly down the footpath, looking all around, alert. Their only weapons, their bayonets, were clinched tightly in both hands. The two men had been forced to remove their bayonets from their rifles when they made the make-shift stretcher, and when they took off running, they were too panic stricken to remember to retrieve their rifles.

The chief took a deep breath, laid his sights on the first man, using Sergeant Takasu's rifle, and slowly exhaled. *Crack!* The lead soldier's head snapped back as the bullet hit him in the forehead, causing him to fall back into his buddy. Private Toda stumbled backwards from the impact of his friend hitting him, but in less than a moment, he too, was lying on the ground, dead.

The chief slung Sergeant Takasu's rifle across his back and climbed down the tree. When he reached the ground, he tossed the sergeant's rifle into the jungle and then headed for the Japanese base. He had a job to do and friends to save; it was time he got on with it.

Chapter 14

PFC Bonito was still stuck in a tree when the storm hit. Of course, the Japanese troops were also ill-equipped for the storm, especially for Captain Matsui's raging tempest. All the scout could do was sit on his perch and hope the Japanese didn't spot him. The only consolation for him was the wounded officer; he was constantly haranguing his men. Watching him kept the scout entertained and smiling throughout his time of discomfort. An hour after the deluge stopped, Captain Matsui gave the order to continue moving west. The tracks they had been following were going west, so that was the direction he chose. Twenty-minutes after the enemy had moved out of sight, Geronimo, wet and sore, left his perch and started following the ill-tempered captain.

~ ~ ~

Late in the evening, sometime around 2130 hours, PFC Fox found the Japanese infirmary. He had been searching for the medical aid station for over an hour. Three orderlies were on duty at the time, but there wasn't a whole lot for them to do. With only two bedridden privates in the make-shift field hospital, there wasn't much to do except mill about, bored.

Two hours into his wait, the last lights in the sickbay were finally turned off, leaving a small desk lamp lit at the far end of the infirmary where the only orderly still awake sat. All the beds in the infirmary were now covered in darkness.

About sixty-minutes after the lights went out, PFC Fox was on his way back to the cave, carrying two backpacks full of medical supplies. Smiling, he thought, *Hopefully I got the right stuff. Too bad Lance is laid up, I could've used him to tell me what to take.* After a short pause, he cracked an ear to ear smile, proudly gloating over his latest feat. *Wait until the Japs find their orderly tied up, and most of their medical supplies gone. That ought to really get their goat.* Humming to himself, the scout from North Carolina continued heading northwest towards the ridge where he and Bonito had spotted the Ox from.

~ ~ ~

PFC Bonito was only twenty-yards outside the circle of light given off by the fire. The night, as usual, was hot and muggy, and the insects were out in force, but the Apache scout seemed oblivious to the little monsters. He was more concerned about not being spotted by the enemy. The Japanese, however, were having fits of their own, trying to combat the swarms of insects that bombarded them relentlessly. He was also thinking seriously about whittling down their numbers, and making his enemy's life entirely miserable, much more than what the insects were doing.

The night was perfect for raising hell and pissing off an adversary. The jungle was soaked, and with the steady drip, drip, plop, plop, of the rainwater, his movements would be masked. All he had to do was wait for somebody to leave the fire to take a leak, and then, *his* fun would begin.

Bonito had to laugh to himself. *A drunken cougar, he says. That damn Cherokee needs to feed that weak, sick, puppy he calls a wolf howl. Then maybe it might do him some good!* After a short pause to search his surroundings he continued his wistful thinking. *Damn. I wish that Cherokee was here, now. Together we could do some serious damage to these rice balls.* A finger snap later, his attention sharpened. One of the enemy warriors was moving towards the edge of the firelight. A smile spread slowly across the scout's face. *This guy's gonna be blind when he leaves the light of the fire. He spent too much time looking directly into it. Now, his eyes won't be worth a damn when he steps out from camp.* The Apache scout sat where he was, watching; waiting. A silent warrior biding his time and itching to attack.

The soldier stopped at the edge of the firelight, waiting for his eyes to adjust to the jungle darkness, but he didn't stay there long. Nature was very insistent that he do now what he had set out to do. Looking back, he hesitated for a moment or two, as if he wanted someone to go with him. Then the reluctant soldier shook his head at his childish behavior and moved cautiously off into the darkness.

The Japanese encampment was set up as two separate camps, with the two fires being the center of the camps. Lieutenant Watanabe and his men were sleeping in one camp, about forty-yards south of Lieutenant Nakamura's camp. The soldier that left the camp was one of Nakamura's men. The Japanese had guards posted, but they were all on the west side of the camp perimeters. The men they were chasing were heading west. No one was expecting anything to happen because the fugitives were unarmed.

Captain Matsui was deep in conversation with Lieutenant Nakamura at the far southeastern edge of the camp. The time was around 0230 hours, and still, the jungle was stifling. The enemy private who had left the camp to fulfill nature's call had not been noticed leaving the camp, so no one was looking in that direction. Without warning, the quiet stillness of the jungle was rudely interrupted, and both camps heard the vicious, heart stopping snarl of a *big* cat, followed almost immediately afterwards by a terrified scream from one of their men that was abruptly cut off. Both camps stood frozen in-place, alert, searching the jungle for the nightmare that just emerged. *What the hell was that?* they all thought unanimously.

~ ~ ~

PFC Bonito moved slowly through the jungle, parallel

151

to his opponent. When they were about twenty-yards from the northernmost camp, he closed in for the kill. While he was closing in on his adversary, his enemy stopped by a large eucalyptus tree to relieve himself, but never got the chance. He never even started. The man had just finished slinging his rifle across his back when he saw a shadow separate from the eucalyptus tree at the same time he heard a vicious snarl. His only reaction was his scream of terror. It was his last act.

Bonito quickly moved about thirty-yards southeast of his dead foe, and again, belted-out the call of his big cat. Whatever the Japanese had planned immediately ceased when they heard the snarling scream. Some of the Japanese troops had heard the large cats of Southeast Asia before, but this one was different. It sounded like an inhuman scream followed by a vicious snarl. This one sent shudders of fear through their bodies. Everyone knew there were no tigers on this island. In fact, what they heard didn't even sound like a tiger. When they heard the scream again, it was due east of them.

Captain Matsui took control of the situation and ordered his men to fire into the jungle, hoping to chase away or kill whatever animal was making that fearful scream. Firing into the jungle also helped alleviate some of the fear and anxiety some of his men were experiencing. No one wanted to go traipsing around the jungle at night, looking for what killed one of their men. It was too dark and close-quartered to be chasing after something sounding that ferocious.

PFC Bonito was crouching behind a rather large vine-encrusted tree when Japanese bullets started whizzing by. *Wow, they must really be spooked.* For two or three-minutes, the enemy continued firing into the jungle until a heated shout called for a cease-fire. When the last of the shooting had stopped, the jungle fell into an eerie silence.

With the high humidity and no wind, the lack of movement from the fog and stench of smokeless powder enhanced the eeriness of an already dangerous night and the jungle an un-earthly, unreal appearance. It also had his adversary on edge.

Forming his men into a skirmish line, Captain Matsui issued the order to advance. As each man moved forward, the slowly thickening fog swirled around them like tiny twisters, following the men as they reluctantly pressed forward. The fog wasn't terribly thick, but it was thick enough that vision was just barely enough to get by.

Bonito watched his enemy cautiously move forward. The men he was stalking were dark silhouettes outlined by the firelight, so he had no problem avoiding them and circling to the north. When he was facing his enemy's left flank, he moved behind a tree and then let his coyote call, yip and bark. Lieutenant Watanabe and his men had heard this animal before, right after his men captured the four Marines, but at that time, the call held no meaning. It didn't seem to pose a threat, so it was ignored. This call, however, definitely had the lieutenant's attention because it was followed by a vicious snarl, the same snarl he heard just before one of their men died, screaming in terror.

Geronimo stayed behind a tree, waiting for the Japanese to open fire again. When the shooting failed to happen, he cautiously moved west, keeping some of his enemy still outlined against the fire's light.

Before they began their search, the Japanese had piled a bunch of wood onto the fire in Lieutenant Nakamuras camp to increase the circle of firelight. The hope was to catch a reflection from the eyes of the animal that had killed one of their men, but now, their only light was receding fast.

The enemy was moving north, trying to keep their lines formed, but the nighttime and the jungle terrain made it almost impossible to do. There were stragglers on the left flank, and those stragglers were still somewhat outlined by the light of the fire.

Bonito began closing in on the stragglers, always keeping his foes silhouetted against the light. He was using the trees and shadows to remain invisible to the Japanese, and he was doing a ghost of a job. Ten-minutes into their northern move, the enemy again heard the yip and bark of a coyote, followed by the shouts of one of their men. As they moved in that general direction, they unexpectedly heard a high-pitched scream of terror cut short, at the same time they heard another hideous cat scream. And just as abruptly, the jungle night was ripped apart by a thunderous roar of gunfire.

Screams and shouts could be heard above the din of chaos. Panicked soldiers were firing at anything that moved, including their own men. Shadows of movement, real or imagined, were brought under immediate gunfire. The troops thought they were under attack by some hideous creature that killed them at will, so they tried to fight back the best they could. It didn't matter that they were killing their own men. Captain Matsui's troops were becoming unnerved. Panic was setting in, and the enemy commanders were losing control of their soldiers.

Panic, however, was interrupted, and Japanese heads turned south, catching the final echoes of a wolf's howl off in the distance. It was a lonesome, mournful, chilling sound, and it came from behind them. A few seconds went by, then the enemy heard another howl. Slowly, the shooting sporadically died out, as the nervous soldiers reluctantly turned in the direction of the howl. By the time the third howl ended, the shooting had stopped altogether. Now the officers could take control of their men again, and they did.

~ ~ ~

PFC Fox was about forty-minutes away from where

they had spotted the Ox when he heard the first terrified scream. It was faint, but it was definitely a scream. He was still too far away to hear Bonito's cougar, but he heard the sudden eruption of gunfire. It was coming from the northwest. The Marines had no weapons to fight back with, except for an 8mm popgun. *What is all the shooting about?*

Immediately, the chief started running as fast as the two backpacks full of medical supplies and the jungle darkness would allow. *Something major's going on up north. Somebody's doing a lot of shooting, but who is doing the shooting?*' Then a sudden thought brought his running to a halt. *Geronimo? That's definitely not the guys firing. Maybe Jose has the Japanese spooked. That has to be it. It sounds like only the Japs are shooting.* Immediately, a smile appeared on the Marine scout's face.

After another twenty-minute run, Fox stopped to take a breather. He was crouching down, sucking air when he heard a real faint yipping, much like a coyote, but he wasn't sure if that was what he heard. Out of nowhere, the jungle erupted with gunfire for the second time, and now, there was no doubt in his mind about what was happening. "It is Jose," he whispered to himself. Three times the wolf howled, and the excitement of the moment had him laughing out loud. *Save some for me, Geronimo.*

~ ~ ~

PFC Choctaw was on watch just below the crest of the ridge when he heard a faint, high-pitched scream of terror. Without the two scouts, he was watching out for the wounded pretty much on his own. During the day, Gunny stood watch, while PFC Choctaw slept. The night, however, belonged to the Ox. All of it. When the big man heard the scream, he moved back down below the ridge-crest and onto the vine covered ledge the wounded Marines were resting on. Gunny met him at the edge of the vines.

"Was that someone screaming?"

155

"I think so, Gunny. It sure sounded like it."

The two Marines stood just inside the vines, talking and trying to figure out what was happening. A few minutes went by before the two men heard another faint scream, but this one didn't sound human. Immediately following the scream, the two men heard the first round of gunfire. *Damn that Geronimo.* Gunny then went deeper onto the ledge to wake everyone up, but it was unnecessary. The sound of gunfire had everybody stirring by the time Gunny reached his sleeping Marines. Corporal Kirby was the only man still lying down. His face was pale and gaunt, and his ragged breathing was worse than before.

Gunny pulled the type 94 pistol out of his back pocket, ejected the magazine, and counted the rounds. Six bullets were in the magazine. He slid the magazine back into the magazine well and shook his head. "Six rounds. Not a good way to run a war." A few minutes later, the squad heard the second round of shooting.

~ ~ ~

PFC Bonito was about forty-yards west of the enemy camp, silently cursing his luck for not having anything to hit back at the Japanese, with. *Now would be the time to hit these bastards. Now, while they're still close to panic, before the sun rises, and their courage rise with it. But all I have is this damn Ka-Bar. Where is that damn Cherokee anyway? I sure could use him right about now.*

Geronimo knew he had to keep the Japanese on edge. He had to keep them awake for the next four hours, deprive them of sleep so that when night fell again, they would be too tired to remain focused. Moving a little closer to the enemy camp, he was about to yip the coyote, but stopped midway through a deep breath. *Was that a howl?* Seconds later, he heard it again and smiled. Immediately following the howl, Bonito sounded his owl hoot and then an owl screech, letting the chief know the enemy was close.

~ ~ ~

After the officers regained control of their men, Captain Matsui decided to move them back to camp and wait for daylight. There was nothing else they could do right now. They couldn't see what was out in the jungle, and they were killing their own men faster than that creature was ... if it was an animal. When they arrived back at camp, the fire was built back up and then a head count was taken. Captain Matsui found that he was nine men short. Almost one-third of his men were missing, and he didn't even know what was killing them. Whatever it was would be easier to spot in the daylight.

Looking at his watch, he noticed there was still a little over four hours left before sunrise. It was going to be a very long four hours. Then he heard the hoot of an owl. Before a second breath could be taken, the hoot was followed by an owl screech resonating from the same area. Captain Matsui smiled for the first time in two days. *Finally we will have good luck.* To the enemy captain, hearing an owl was a good omen. Two hours later, that new found hope began to dwindle.

Chapter 15

Colonel Thomas Travis sat waiting in the outer office, listening to the clicking of over thirty typewriters, all clacking at almost the same time. Concentrating on the rhythm of the typewriters kept his mind off the bad news he had just received. He was waiting for Lieutenant General Clayton Swift to finish up with his meeting with Brigadier General Maxwell Strong and his staff. Something was in the air, and, as usual, no one was talking about it. This was the third meeting in as many days. Something was definitely in the wind. For two hours he sat waiting for the meeting to end, listening to the typewriters and the subdued voices in the background. Ten-minutes after the meeting was over, he was sitting across from General Swift.

"You don't look happy, Tom. Is it bad news?"

"Yes, General. I'm afraid it is." He then handed General Swift a folder. The man in charge began reading the report, paper-clipped to the inside of the folder, occasionally glancing at the accompanying photos. The photos were somewhat blurry, but what he was looking at was easily recognizable. When he was finished, he closed the folder and looked up at Colonel Travis.

"Are these intercepts accurate? Do you think it was your boys, Tom?"

Colonel Travis nodded his head to the first question and answered the second question. "Could be, General. I just don't know. They would've been in that area around the time this was reported to have happened. We tried contacting the *Green Jack* as soon as we obtained the report, but we haven't received a response yet. We took the *sub's* course and speed and the time she left port and calculated the distance she would travel from the time she left port to the time she was reported sunk, and those calculations put her within the area of this oil slick. You can see in the photos, the bits of debris floating in and around the oil slick. Something was definitely sunk there. We just don't know what it was. We'll know more in a couple days."

"Well, Tom, keep me posted. Hopefully we'll find out it was just a Dutch freighter the Japanese sank. Just for good measure, Tom, I'll keep my fingers crossed."

"Thank you, General. As soon as I hear anything, I'll bring it to you. Goodnight, General."

"Goodnight, Tom."

After leaving command headquarters, the colonel glanced at his watch and immediately nodded his head. *Yes, sir. Plenty of time left to tie on a good one.*

~ ~ ~

The Japanese were unable to get any sleep thanks to PFC Bonito. About an hour before the sun came up, PFC Fox joined in on the fun. The jungle shadows, however, were beginning to disappear, so the two Marines pulled back about a hundred-yards from the enemy camp to discuss what they were going to do next. After discussing the situation over for a couple of minutes, the two scouts decided to move again, but now they were heading for the ledge. Corporal Kirby needed the medical supplies, and it was time to find another hiding place. The Japanese were now only a half a mile from the ledge and moving in that direction. The two scouts had no doubt the enemy would find the ledge and their wounded buddies. The game trail was too well used to be able to hide it, so the time to leave was now.

PFC Choctaw was on watch. He was listening for any movement and searching the shadows for any tell-tale sign of the enemy. One minute he was calm and confident, and the next, he was feeling the icy cold fingers of fear in the pit of his stomach. Two figures appeared out of nowhere at the same time. One on his left and one on his right. The big man never heard a sound. Then the Ox heard a soft snicker, followed by a soft whisper. "You'd better get your ears cleaned out. We made enough noise to wake the dead."

The big bruiser from Louisiana let out a sigh of relief the men on the ledge could have heard, had they been awake.

"Come on, Ox. We have to get the guys up. The Japs are about thirty-minutes away from here."

Gunny met them at the edge of the vines.

"Gunny, we gotta move. The Japs are getting too close for comfort. They'll be here in about thirty-minutes."

Gunny looked at PFC Fox for a second before shifting his gaze to Bonito and Choctaw. Turning his gaze back to Fox again, he nodded. "Okay, chief, you take the lead. Geronimo, you cover the rear."

PFC Choctaw had already hoisted Corporal Kirby on to his shoulder. "I'm ready, Gunny."

A quick last look around, and they were heading out the back door towards the basin of water. Fox had picked up four extra canteens, so they stopped at the basin for fresh water. No telling when they would come across more. After a short stop to fill canteens they were cautiously struggling down the ridge.

The climb down from the ledge was about ninety-feet to the next ledge they were aiming for. The going was tough for the most part, but they were able to reach the lower pathway just as the sun was coming up.

Gunny now had a decision to make. He had several choices. He could follow the ledge southeast until they eventually ran into the jungle, but that would put them back in the area they started out from. Heading in that direction would also put them dangerously close to the Japanese base they had just escaped from. Or they could continue to move west. Moving west, however, would mean a long, hard, climb down the rock-infested mountain. From where they were, the climb down would be at least a six-hundred-foot decent, probably more. Not only would the exertion be hard on the Marines, their chances were good that one or more of them would wind-up seriously injured in the process.

Staring down at the long descent, Gunny was shaking his head. "Long way down, chief. I don't think we can make it. Move northeast along this trail and find us a soft climb back up the ridge. We can then circle around the Japs, and head for the deep interior of the jungle, locate the river, and then hole-up to rest and recuperate."

"Aye, aye, Gunny. Give me a moment to lay some false trails. Jose, create a trail leading back towards that Jap base. You guys go ahead, we'll catch up when we're finished, here."

"Aye, aye, little squirrel."

Startled, the chief paused for a second. *That wasn't Jose.* Looking towards the voice, the only person the little man spotted was Gunny, and his expressionless pose had the chief stumped. *What is he up to?* Then he gulped. *Oh boy. What did I do now?*

After finishing up with their false trails, the chief led the way northeast. Sure enough, approximately two-hundred-yards from where they began their northeastern move, the little scout found a switchback game-trail that wound upwards towards the top of the ridge. After ascending the dusty, back and forth, trail for about thirty-minutes, he reached the top of the ridge, followed by the rest of the squad, less than a minute later. Moving beside a large, dried-out clump of kunai grass, the chief paused to search the area until all of a sudden he froze, statue-still. He was staring at the enemy. They had discovered the game-trail leading to the ledge.

The Japanese were on top of the same ridge the

Marines were on, but about two-hundred-yards south of where the Americans were standing. Slowly, very slowly, the men lowered themselves to the ground. The enemy was on the game trail about fifteen-feet above the ledge the Marines had vacated about an hour before.

Matsui's men were tired. They hadn't slept in over thirty-hours thanks to Fox and Bonito, so their alertness had diminished considerably. Had they been more alert, they probably would have spotted the Marines. It was a good thing they didn't spot them. Because of the bad shape their feet were in, they could have been easily recaptured.

Gunny waited until the enemy had descended below the crest of the ridge before he gave the order to move out again. If the Japanese continued along the same path the Marines took, then they would be an hour away from the ridge-crest the wounded men were now leaving behind. Plenty of time for the two scouts to eliminate as much of the squad's tracks as possible. If they were lucky, they might be able to make a clean getaway.

~ ~ ~

Sergeant Takagi was standing on top of the ridge following the game trail with his eyes until his gaze was stopped by loosely hanging vines trailing well below the ledge. While his eyes followed the game trail down, he caught a movement out of the corner of his eye. Stopping, he looked along the top of the ridge to his right, searching the crest for movement. Not seeing anything, he continued to scan the top of the ridgeline until, shaking his head, he finally gave up. *Maybe I just imagined I saw something.* A minute or so after his imagined sighting, the rest of the under-strength platoon, now roughly 29 men, thanks to Bonito, reached the top of the ridge.

"Sergeant Takagi, why have we stopped here?"

"Captain Matsui, I believe this is where the Americans were staying after they escaped. We must be close to them.

Look, over by the cliff wall. See the dirty bandages? If they were not in a hurry, I'm quite sure they wouldn't have left them there for us to find. I believe they were rushed when they left, which means we are now very close to them."

"Then why are we still standing here, Sergeant? Why are we not following after them right now?"

"Captain Matsui, you gave me orders to report everything to you. I am doing that. In order for me to report to you, I am forced to stop and wait for you to catch up. That slows us down considerably."

"Why you arrogant fool..." Captain Matsui was so agitated, he couldn't finish his thought, and the hesitation infuriated him even more. He was starting to lose control with every word he said. He was so agitated spit was flying everywhere when he spoke. Again he reached for his sword, and again Lieutenant Watanabe came to his sergeant's rescue.

"Captain Matsui, we are very close to the Americans. If you kill Koji, the Americans will escape from us, and we will never find them."

The captain was in a lot of pain from where part of his scalp was missing and from the stinging caused by the salt of his sweat. His lip was also burning because of the knife burns caused by the chief shaving off half his mustache, and then there was the heat and humidity, which aided and abetted his discomfort even more. Add to that the insult to his honor and the humiliating experience he was forced to endure at the hands of his enemy, and you have an extremely short fused Japanese captain, a captain who didn't care if he had to kill his own men to get the results he was looking for. But once again, the seed of reason sprouted forth, overruling his overwhelming desire for satisfaction.

Captain Matsui looked at Sergeant Takagi and spoke viciously to him. "From now on, Sergeant, you will remain within three meters of this detachment, or I will shoot you where you stand. Do you understand this order?"

Sergeant Takagi stood facing Captain Matsui with a blank expression on his face and answered. "Hai, I understand your order."

"Very good, Sergeant. Now lead us to those Yankee dogs."

Sergeant Takagi bowed, and then searched the ground for tell-tale signs of which direction the Marines had gone. The chore took a couple of minutes, but he found what he was looking for. A partial boot print facing west. The only way west from where the he was standing was straight down from the ledge. He could see the trail the Marines left behind as they struggled and slid down the side of the cliff. Without saying a word or even looking at the captain, he headed down to the ledge directly below. Thirty-minutes of scrambling and sliding went by before the enemy finally made it to the lower ledge. Now they had to figure out which direction the Marines took from there.

A hint of a trail led down from the lower ledge, and it stopped Sergeant Takagi only for a moment, just long enough for him to sort out the situation. *My enemy's feet are in bad shape, and it's a long descent down to the bottom. No. They did not go this way. They are too wounded, and the climb down is too treacherous.* Staring off in the direction of headquarters, he again thought things out. *To go southeast would put the Americans closer to our base, so they probably didn't go southeast either.* Even though there were tracks indicating the Marines went that way, Sergeant Takagi's belief was that his enemy went northeast, so he told his thoughts to Captain Matsui, and then waited for the captain to give the order. That order wasn't long in coming, but the order Sergeant Takagi received was a big surprise.

"Sergeant Takagi, you will take Lieutenant Watanabe and his men down this ridge and search the bottom for the

American dogs. Lieutenant Nakamura and I will follow the tracks northeast..."

Lieutenant Watanabe's platoon sergeant was stunned.

After Sergeant Takagi explained his theory, Captain Matsui started thinking. *When we find the American Marines, Lieutenant Watanabe will insist they be taken to General Sasaki for interrogation. If that happens, then I will not be able to teach these swine what happens when they insult the honor of an Imperial Japanese officer. I would have to kill Sergeant Takagi, his lieutenant, and all of his men. That might be a little hard to explain, but without him and his arrogant sergeant around, I will then be free to do as I please with the Americans. If anyone asks what happened to the Americans, I can always say they refused to surrender, and preferred to die fighting. Lieutenant Nakamura and his men will say nothing, and Lieutenant Watanabe and his men will not be around to dispute what I have said because they will be searching for the Americans at the base of the mountain.* With his thoughts formulated into a plan, his devious plot was put on hold, while he issued out his order.

"Lieutenant Watanabe, you will follow Sergeant Takagi down the mountain and search the bottom area. If you find nothing, then you will return to this ledge and search southeast. If you do not find the Americans there, then you are free to catch up with us. Lieutenant Nakamura, you will follow the tracks along this ledge, northeast. If we catch up to the Americans, we will fire three shots. Those shots, Lieutenant Watanabe, will be your signal to return to base. We will meet you there. Do you understand these orders, Lieutenant Watanabe?"

The junior lieutenant bowed to Captain Matsui. "Hai. I understand your orders."

"Good! You may carry them out now."

Again, he bowed. With nothing left to do but follow

Captain Matsui's orders, Sergeant Takagi started down the mountain, followed by Lieutenant Watanabe and his men, leaving the wounded captain smiling in anticipation of his impending meeting with the Yankee Marines.

Lieutenant Watanabe was seething inside. He knew what the captain was up to, but there was absolutely nothing he could do about it. If he disobeyed a direct order, then Captain Matsui would just have him shot. Then he thought of something else. *If he fails to find the Americans, then it will be his fault...and his head.* The junior lieutenant smiled at the thought of Captain Matsui losing his head. *It would serve the arrogant bastard right.* Disgusted, he shook his head and followed Sergeant Takagi down the mountain.

~ ~ ~

PFC Bonito was watching the Japanese from the top of the ridge and was mildly surprised when he saw half the Japanese force heading down the mountain. What didn't surprise him was the force moving northeast along the ledge. It was being led by the wounded officer. *That damn Cherokee must have really pissed off ole bandage-head something fierce. That rice ball doesn't know when to quit. At least there's only a squad coming after us instead of a platoon.* Moving deeper into cover, he quickly retreated back to the squad.

It didn't take him long to catch up with Gunny. As slowly as they were moving, even a turtle could have outrun them. Gunny stood leaning up against a tree, listening to Bonito give his report. Then he interrupted. "Call in the chief, PFC. We need to figure out what to do."

"Aye, aye, Gunny."

Five-minutes after the call-in, Gunny was talking to his two scouts.

"We've got six, maybe seven hours of daylight left. Those rice balls have been chasing us for almost three days now, and two of those days they haven't slept a wink. You two get back there and try to slow them down some, but don't get yourselves killed. I don't think your mother's will be very happy with me if that happens. You'll have to be the judge on how much time you've gained for us. If you feel you've slowed them down enough, then you get the hell out of there and catch up with us. Don't take any stupid chances. I don't want to have to kick your asses after I get to hell. Do you hear me, PFC?"

"Yes, Gunny, I hear you." Then Gunny got into the little man's face. "And no more scalps, chief. You got it?"

PFC Fox gulped and smiled weakly. "Yeah, Gunny. I got it."

"Good, " replied Gunny. "Now get the hell on back there...and be careful."

Chapter 16

"The report has been confirmed, General. The *USS Green Jack* has been sunk with all hands, sir. It looks like operation Night Hawk is dead and buried, General."

"I'm sorry to hear that, Tom. Gunnery Sergeant Baker and his boys were the best intelligence gatherers I've ever had under my command. We are sorely going to miss their special talents. Are you absolutely sure they are gone?"

"Not absolutely, sir. According to the Japanese intercepts, there might be three or four survivors on this island ... here. The intercepts say the survivors are sailors. Until we can confirm this intel, we have to go with what the intercepts say. I thought about sending some recon flights over the island, General, but they will be flying into the strongest concentration of Japanese air power in that part of the Pacific."

"Tell you what, Tom. Why don't you send a couple of recon flights over the island around dawn and then a couple more around dusk just to see what you can come up with. In the meantime, let's start putting together another team. I've had feelers out for men with special talents and received quite a few candidates, some of which I think you might be interested in. Why don't you get back with me next week? I should be done with all the staff meetings by Friday, so...let's say Monday. Maybe about 1300. In the mean-time, see what those recon flights can come up with."

"That sounds good, General. I'll see you Monday at 1300 hours."

Immediately after Colonel Travis left the general's office, he headed for the airfield to schedule the recon flights the man in charge okayed. *Hopefully the recon fights can come up with some answers. It's a long shot, but if Gunny and his men are still alive, then maybe we can send in another team to get them out. Maybe it's time we had a little luck on our side for a change.* Minutes after he arrived at the airfield, the recon flights were scheduled and he was on his way back to night operation headquarters.

Colonel Thomas Travis was a diehard Marine. After his first encounter with Gunnery Sergeant Baker, he fell head over heels for special night operations and what it entails, and he found Gunnery Sergeant Al Baker to be the perfect, head-screwed-on-tight, kind of Marine needed to run this type of operation in the field. He let the gunny pick his own cadre. That decision worked out better than the colonel imagined.

The possibility of Gunny and his men reported missing in action and presumed dead put a cold knot in the pit of his stomach. The Baker Boys were on their sixth mission when the shit hit the fan, and that event didn't set well with Colonel Travis. It hit him hard to realize the reality of what could happen, that he could be sending his men to their deaths. However, if you asked Gunnery Sergeant Baker his opinion on the matter, his answer would probably be along the lines of, "I'm a Marine. It's my job. Dying is a hazard we face every day. A United States Marine fights to win, or he dies trying, taking a bunch of his enemies with him. At the gates of hell, even the devil shudders when he sees a United States Marine."

General Clayton Swift on the other hand, is a United States Army, general. Although special night infiltration wasn't his cup of tea, he was given this command and found out that he excelled in the clandestine operations' command he was given. He put out feelers for staff officers to form up his operation's staff and was told by the higher ups that Colonel Thomas Travis was to be his first candidate. "What the hell are you assigning me a Marine for? This is an Army operation. I don't want a Marine on my staff." That thought changed almost overnight.

Not only was Colonel Travis the perfect man for the job, he also had the perfect men for the job. Now Colonel Travis had a leash tied around his neck. That way, nobody could steal him away from the general. If someone tried, the power behind the three stars on his epaulette would simply declare war on the unfortunate soul. It would be a short, swift war, with the victor being General Swift.

Currently, however, the general was worried. He might have just lost his best team on their way to their latest mission, code named Night Hawk. Gunny and his Marines were to land on Mindanao and meet up with a band of Philipino guerilla fighters, who in turn, were to help the Marines gather intel on Japanese troop strengths and where the best possible landing site might be for a proposed invasion of the Philippine Islands. Now those plans had to be scraped because there were no other units available that were capable of completing that kind of mission in the time allotted. *Damn this war anyway. Too many good men are dying because of some crackpot emperor. Somebody ought to shoot that bastard and end this stupid war in the Pacific. Then we can go fight the Germans and finish this war altogether.*

The first of two PBY flying boats took off from the airfield at about 0230 hours, with the second PBY taking off about thirty-minutes later. Their mission was extremely dangerous. The probability of them coming back home bullet riddled was high. The odds against them coming back at all were a lot higher, but it was a chance that had to be taken, a chance General Swift was willing to take.

~ ~ ~

The roots of the trees resembled octopus tentacles, and with a little added mud-work from the Marines, the roots proved to be an adequate, but temporary place to hide from the Japanese. The men were scattered about, hiding under the tentacle-like roots of three different trees, hoping to fool the enemy. PFC Fox and PFC Bonito were out and on the hunt, distracting the Japanese from their mission of recapturing the wounded men. Already the two scouts had whittled the fifteen-man detachment down to thirteen rifles, but now it was time to sit and wait out the enemy. All indications pointed to the end of a day for the tired Matsui warriors. They were setting up camp.

The Japanese were frustrated at not being able to find the Marines. Captain Matsui could see where the trail ended, but was completely baffled as to where their enemy disappeared to. They checked every likely spot they could think of, including looking among the roots of the trees. But they found nothing. It looked to the captain as if their elusive foe had disappeared into thin air. *Where could they have gone?*

The day was in the closing stages of late afternoon when Captain Matsui finally called off the search. It was time to set up camp. Lieutenant Nakamura's theory was that the escapees were still in the area, they were just well hidden. "Keep a sharp lookout. And no talking. Sergeant Takagi, set up a watch. Make sure your men stay alert." Turning away from his men, he stared off at nothing, puzzled over the disappearance of his wounded enemy.

Captain Matsui was worried. He was beginning to regret his decision of splitting up his forces. Over the course of the day, he had lost three men. Three men he could ill afford to lose. *Where could the Americans have gone? Four of the Yankees were wounded, their feet torn from traveling barefoot in the jungle. So how could they have escaped capture so easily? We have the advantage, so why haven't we found them yet?* These questions, so far, remained unanswered.

The camp was quiet and dark. The enemy was tired and in no mood to talk. Because he assumed the Marines were close by, Captain Matsui ordered that no fire was to be lit. Four of his men were on guard duty, while the other men slept. It was the first chance they had to sleep in almost three days, so it didn't take long for those not on guard duty to slip into wishful dreaming. Because of the length of time his troops had been without sleep, he decided to relieve his men on guard duty every two hours.

About fifteen-minutes before the first guards were due to be relieved, Captain Matsui woke up his sleeping men and started them doing exercises in order to get the blood pumping and the juices flowing, and to remove the last vestige of sleep before they relieved the men on duty. The time was around 1730 hours when the first relief took over the guard duty.

The sentries were awake and alert, but they were still very tired. Two hours' sleep were not a lot considering the length of time they had been without it. The guards were due to be relieved in two hours, which really wasn't that bad. All the sentries were looking forward to their first relief because when they returned to their pallets, they would have four hours of sleep instead of just two. Extra sleep was always something to look forward to. An hour into their watch, heads were beginning to nod, and alertness was dropping as well as their heads.

~ ~ ~

Gunny was completely covered with mud, but he was smiling. He was the only Marine besides Bonito and Fox not hiding in among the tree roots. Alistair Baker was a fighter, all the way down to his dirty fingernails. He preferred to fight standing up. If he was going to die, then he was going to die on his own terms, fighting in the open and fighting for what he believed in. He was a United States Marine fighting for his country.

Gunny was smiling because he wasn't going to die this day. None of his Marines were. They had foiled their enemy's plans, and now their adversary was setting up camp for the night. The time was ripe for the scouts to harass their opponent.

Gunnery Sergeant Baker was sitting with PFC Fox and PFC Bonito about a hundred-yards north of the Japanese camp, his arms aching. He had been buried up to his face against the side of the ten-foot tall riverbank by Fox and Bonito. He looked as if he was standing against the riverbank and a giant hand shoved him into it while he was still standing, and then covered his face with mud and vines. The sergeant from Lawton, Oklahoma had been forced to stay there in a standing position, hanging on to one of the roots to keep from sliding down the bank for over five hours while the enemy searched in vain for him and his troops. At one point, two privates had stood just three feet above him, while he lay buried against the riverbank. Now it was time for his two scouts to retrieve the four remaining, root-bound mud-Marines.

Shortly after the recall, all seven were back together again, smiling and smelling ripe. Age old sweat and jungle rot, mixed with muck, what a nose burning experience it was, and still, the Baker Boys were smiling. In fact, they were itching to take the fight to the Japanese as quickly as possible. They were tired of running.

The Marines were on the west side of the river, about one-hundred-yards north of the enemy camp, right where Fox and Bonito had left Gunny when the two scouts went after the root-bound Marines.

The Japanese had taken the bolts from the rifles of their dead, so the escapees were still unarmed except for the 8mm pistol Gunny was carrying. Those circumstances, however, were about to change. The time had at last arrived for the two scouts to remedy the unarmed situation they were in. "Chief, you and Geronimo go scrounge us up some weapons, but do it quietly. Don't let the Japs know you're there; then get back here pronto."

The two men arrived at the enemy camp just in time to see the first relief take over the watch.

Sometime around 1745 hours, the two scouts split up. The chief headed for the west side of the enemy camp, while Geronimo turned and moved south. When the two scouts were in position, they both hunkered down for a much needed nap. With PFC Fox west of the camp, Gunny to the north, and PFC Bonito to the south, the Japanese were pinned in with their backs to the river. If the Marines had been armed, then the enemy would have been in dire straits for sure. But the only firearm they had was the 8mm pistol with only six rounds in it.

~ ~ ~

The sun was almost down when PFC Fox woke up with a start. He'd been asleep for almost two hours. What woke him up was the Japanese tromping around their camp, trying to knock the sleep out of their system. It was almost time for the enemy to change guards. There were two soldiers standing a watch, with two more walking the outside perimeter, checking up on the stationary sentries about every fifteen-minutes. Out of nowhere, the caw of a crow broke the stillness of the jungle night, followed shortly after by the soft sound of a whippoorwill. Gunny heard the two birdcalls and nodded knowingly.

"I'll bet you ten dollars that was the chief and Geronimo. Any takers?" whispered Gunny.

Sergeant Stamper shook his head, but didn't say anything. Sergeant Thomas knew better than to bet against the Oklahoma gunnery sergeant, but he accepted the bet anyway.

"I'll take that bet, Gunny." It was in the spirit of the moment that he took the bet. He knew it was the two scouts. The demo man was beginning to feel like he was finally a part of the squad. One of the Baker Boys. Gunny's Baker Boys. That was why he took the bet even though he knew better.

"Hey, Sarge," whispered Corporal Kirby. "You're gonna lose that bet you know. Never bet against the gunny or Sergeant Stamper. They always win."

The master of blast chuckled softly and said. "What makes you think we'll still be alive to pay up on that bet? We're out numbered fourteen to one. The Japs have fourteen guns to our one popgun, and that's not counting all the bullets they have on-hand. There's not a snow-ball's chance in hell we'll survive this one."

Quiet snickers erupted from of everyone, for they knew that with the chief and Geronimo, there was always a shot at surviving.

Sergeant Stamper was nodding his head, proud as hell. Nobody was down because of the predicament they were in. Morale was still good. *Hell, look at 'em*, he thought. *They're mud caked, battered, and bruised, and they move around on bloodied feet, yet the boys are still smiling and joking with each other. Hell, even Kirby's smiling now.*

They stank of jungle rot and ancient sweat, yet the will to fight, the desire to fight, was still strong in their hearts. They just lacked the weapons to fight back with.

~ ~ ~

Out of the stillness of the evening, a lone crow caw resonated through the jungle, disturbing the enemy's conference. Looking up and around, some were a bit surprised that a crow would be out at night. The majority, however, were thinking about the ancient belief that the crow symbolized divine intervention, and a small few just didn't care.

The two scouts came up with a series of signals using their animal calls. The screech of an owl told the squad of imminent danger, and to seek cover. The hoot of an owl was used for rallying, and as an all-clear signal. The crow and the whippoorwill were used to identify the scouts, and to give the squad their location. Those two calls were also used to call for a confab between the two scouts, and to occasionally signal the start of hostilities. The rest of their calls were used to unhinge their enemies.

Matsui's troops were tired, hungry, dirty, and frustrated. A few minutes after they heard the crow, strange animal calls gradually caught their attention. Odd chittering and clicking noises, sounds the Japanese had never heard before. Within a few minutes, the strange animal calls were distracting the enemy guards, causing them to lose focus, and slowly lose their will to stay awake. Then one of the roving guards heard a soft grunt, followed by a rustling of foliage. Not wanting to wake up the sleeping camp in case it was nothing, the curious guard moved to where he thought he heard the rustling. Out of nowhere, a shape emerged from the shadows of a vine-cluttered tree.

Bonito was busy moving the man he had just killed deeper into the jungle when he heard the roving guard approaching. Moving into the shadows of a large tree, Bonito waited. The first sentry had been easy to dispatch. He had been leaning up against a tree, half asleep when the Apache scout struck. The only sound that escaped the dying man was a soft grunt.

Geronimo had just moved out of the shadows of a tree he was hiding beside, to attack the oncoming guard; however, he was stopped short when he saw a hand come out of another shadow and clamp down hard on the sentry's mouth from behind. He heard a *shhick* and the man went limp, but he didn't fall to the ground. A soft whisper reached the scout's ears. "Kind of nice of the Japs to share their weapons with us, don't you think?"

"Thanks for the backup. Let's get these weapons back to the guys." Then a short pause. "What the hell are you smiling about?"

"We're armed, Jose. Now we can fight back," whispered the chief.

The remaining Japanese in the camp, secure in the thought that they were safe, woke up to find that six of their men were missing. They seemed to have just disappeared into the night. Those left in camp were now wide awake. No one knew what happened to the missing men, and it was still too dark to see anything.

What happened to the men who were on guard duty? Where did they go? Captain Matsui was stunned. In less than thirty hours, he had lost over half of his troops, and had no idea how this happened. He was now down to seven men, not counting Lieutenant Nakamura and himself. *Did the Americans do this?* he wondered. Now, instead of chasing six men, some of them wounded, all of them unarmed, he might be chasing six Yankee Marines armed with Japanese rifles. The situation had indeed changed. Another thought hit the enemy captain, and it hit him hard. He now had to try and link up with Lieutenant Watanabe to gain more men. To admit this kind of defeat, especially against supposedly unarmed men, was humiliating enough. What worsened the matter was the enraged captain would have to admit his defeat in front of that arrogant Sergeant Takagi.

Just minutes after breaking camp, the enemy was struggling through the dark jungle, heading west. They were moving toward the ledge where Lieutenant Watanabe had started down the mountain.

Chapter 17

A lone PBY was closing in on the southern end of the island the Marines were stranded on, flying at an altitude of 20,000 feet. The plane was trying to hide in the clouds, out of sight until it was time to make its recon run; then, once below the clouds, it would be extremely vulnerable to fighter intercepts.

No allied planes had flown over the island in quite a while, so the hope was that the recon flights could swoop in and swoop back out before being detected. The plan was daring and dangerous, but some questions needed answering. The recon photos may turn up something that might lead to those answers.

The first plane had it somewhat easy. The odds of it escaping without being shot down were somewhat good. However; the second plane, coming in about thirty-minutes later, might not be so lucky. As it was, both planes made it in and out without any problems.

On the sixth recon foray, the dusk scout planes ran into trouble. They were flying at about 20,000 feet, thirty-minutes apart. The first plane noticed a reflection from one of the mountaintops and swooped in to investigate. A couple of minutes into their circling, they spotted a series of flashes coming from the same mountaintop. The plane then dropped down to 8,000 feet to get a closer look. Sure enough, the flashes were manmade. A minute or so later, the co-pilot realized that the flashes were in Morse code, so they continued to circle. It wasn't a message that was being flashed; it appeared to be just two words. After the two words had been flashed for the fourth time, the PBY ran into trouble in the form of four Kawasaki Ki-61fighters, what the allies called a "Tony."

Thinking that the message, or words being flashed was important, the pilot ordered the radioman to relay the message to the trailing PBY. In the meantime, the lead flying boat tried to make it back up into the clouds before the Japanese fighters could shoot it down, but it didn't make it. Just before the floatplane was hit, the radioman received a confirmation of receipt from the trailing plane. A frantic radio message was then sent to the following recon flight. "We are under attack, head back to Charlie-six-two." Within seconds, the wounded PBY went spiraling down out of control until it crashed into the waters of the Pacific and exploded. Meanwhile, the trailing plane, having been ordered to head back to base, turned south and flew back to the airfield at Charlie-six-two. With a bit of luck, the message meant something; hopefully something important enough to warrant losing a PBY and its eight-man crew.

During the heat of the action, the flying boat did manage to damage one of its attackers prior to getting shot down. The wounded pilot immediately turned and made for the beach, landing almost perfectly until the right wheel-strut gave-way, and the right-side landing gear collapsed. The starboard wing dipped and then dug into the soft beach sand, flat-spinning the Ki-61fighter across the terrain like a skipping-stone until it was violently stopped by the thickness of the almost pure white sand, still in one piece, but facing the opposite direction. Twenty-minutes after the sudden stop, the pilot died from a shattered liver, ruined by a 30-caliber machine gun bullet sent his way, courtesy of the dying PBY.

~ ~ ~

Colonel Travis was waiting for the surviving PBY when it landed, the same as he did with all the previous recon flights. All the Catalina pilots were under strict orders: "No radio transmissions just in case the Japanese are listening in. Bring home what you find." The plane took a few minutes to taxi up the ramp onto dry land, but the wait was worth it. The pilot walked up to Colonel Travis and handed him a piece of paper. "I hope this is good news, sir. We lost Oscar-one-six getting it." Written on that piece of paper were two words, and those two words set the colonel's hair to standing straight up.

Colonel Travis took his eyes off the two words and looked at the pilot. "Captain. Your downed crew might have just found the Baker Boys. Damn, Captain. I knew it!"

Everyone within earshot heard the colonel's shout. He kept repeating over and over again, "I knew it! I knew it!" He was smiling so big it didn't matter that his driver had fallen asleep. "Move over Dennis. I'll drive." As soon as Lieutenant Hagan vacated the driver's side, Colonel Travis hopped in his jeep and sped back to headquarters and General Swift. He didn't even wait for the orderly to announce his arrival; he just barged right on into the general's office. He even forgot the general was a general. When he came rushing into his commander's office, General Swift was with his planning staff, bent over a map table, planning their next mission.

"Clayton, they're alive!"

The man in charge straightened up and turned to face a very excited colonel. "What the devil are you shouting about, Tom? Who's alive?"

It was then that Colonel Travis realized what he had just done.

General Swift had never seen Colonel Travis lose his composure before. Even under the most strenuous of times, the man had always maintained strict military discipline. He's a Marine colonel. Hell, they never lose it. Still, a person just doesn't barge into a general's office unannounced, and they damn sure don't call the general by his first name, unless more stars adorn the interrupter's collar. Colonel

Travis had just committed a serious breach of military protocol, but all the general could do at the time was laugh. He didn't even flinch at the infraction. He reacted as if they were just a couple of friends sitting at home, listening to the radio, and the colonel's favorite football team had just kicked the game winning field goal.

General Swift looked at his planning staff and nodded his head towards the door, indicating for the planning staff to leave. "Gentlemen, meet me back here at 1830 hours." With that done, he turned towards Colonel Travis.

"Now, Tom, what was so important that you would risk losing your job, by barging into my office unannounced like that?"

"Sorry, General. I guess I lost my head for a second. I should have knocked first. I'm sorry, it won't happen again, sir."

General Swift shook his head, somewhat annoyed at his subordinate, but also somewhat like an uncle having to scold his sixteen-year-old nephew for the first time.

"Well, Tom. Make damn sure it doesn't happen again, or you'll force me to do something about it."

By this time, Colonel Travis had regained control of his excitement. "Yes sir, General. I promise it won't happen again, sir."

"Good! I don't want to have to take you to the woodshed for something like this. Now what the hell stung you?"

Colonel Travis handed the general the piece of paper and waited for him to react. General Swift read the two words and then looked up at Colonel Travis with a *you barged in on me in the middle of a planning session for this*, expression on his face, but that expression changed half way through the deep breath he was taking. That deep breath was meant to fuel the sudden storm that was about to hit Colonel Travis' ears. However; that storm never broke. It died out as quickly as his intake of air. On the piece of paper were two words ... Night Hawk!

~ ~ ~

The Marines were slinking quietly to the west, heading back for the ridges. The move was one Gunny figured the Japs wouldn't expect. The Baker Boys had done some damage to the enemy following them, and they had also managed to arm themselves with the rifles of the dead. Now it was time to get out of the neighborhood with a whole skin, and find a place to hole-up and heal. There would be plenty of time later, after they healed up, to start hitting the enemy as hard as they could. All appearances indicated that they were going to be stuck on this island for the duration, so why not make the most of it?

"What do you have for me, chief?"

"Nothing, Gunny. I haven't found any place safe enough to hide us all yet. It doesn't look good from what I've seen so far."

"Well, keep looking, chief. There's got to be some place around here we can use as a hideout."

The Marines could see the treeless ridge about forty-yards from where they were. Gunny was standing about three-feet from a large and imposing tree. When he stepped between two of its roots, his foot sank down about six-inches. When his next step hit the ground, the jungle floor between the twin tentacle-like roots immediately gave way, and Gunnery Sergeant Baker disappeared .... *Sheeeeit*! Pandemonium immediately broke out. Everybody was running around, trying to figure out what to do. They could hear Gunny swearing, but the words were faint, and then there was silence.

PFC Fox was the first one to go into the hole after Gunny. After finding a vine stout enough to use as a rope, and being that he was the lightest of the Marines, Sergeant Stamper volunteered him to go after Gunny. It was comical to watch the chief try to worm his way out of his appointed rescue mission. He hated small, cramped, spaces, and that hole looked to be uninvitingly cramped. Poor PFC Fox was in a panic, his fear of cramped spaces was written all over his face, and his facial contortions were changing constantly.

"Come on you guys, you're not gonna really make me go down there, are you?"

"Let's go, chief. You're the only person small enough and light enough to fit down that hole."

It was hilarious to see him squirming around, scared to death of a little hole. The scene was all the more side-splitting because the little man was fearless in battle, he wasn't afraid to close with his enemy, or fight somebody twice his size, but he was scared to death of a little hole.

"Come on you guys. You know I can't stand small places like that. What about PFC Bonito? Why not him? He'll fit through there."

"No use arguing, chief. You're going, and that's that. It's also an order."

"But Sergeant Stamper?"

Sergeant Stamper, however, wasn't backing down. He hardly ever backed down. The only person he backed down to was Gunny, but only when the gunny was right.

"Get going you little squirrel. Gunny might be hurt."

PFC Fox could see he'd lost his fight. Sergeant Stamper wasn't backing down, and the man looked as though he was having fun with the situation. *Oh brother. Why do I keep getting into these situations? I'm always volunteering, or getting volunteered, and it's always for something stupid and dangerous. Man. I can't seem to win at anything these days!* Finished with his silent commenting, the chief shimmied his way down the vine into the dank, dark, nasty smelling hole. Without warning, his foot touched ground, and just as abruptly, he lost his footing and his grip on the vine, and away he went.

Craaaaaaaa!!!! Then the Marines up top heard the soft drone of an airplane.

"Quick," whispered Sergeant Stamper, "hug a tree. Geronimo, see if you can identify that airplane."

"What about Gunny and PFC Fox?"

"You let me worry about Gunny and the chief. You find out if that airplane is friendly or not."

"Aye, aye, Sergeant Stamper."

Quickly, PFC Bonito moved to the edge of the jungle and peered up into the sky. Instantly, he dropped the ground. The plane was descending right for the very ridge he was on. Astonished, he all of a sudden recognized the airplane, and the stars on the wings. *What is a PBY doing flying over here*? Then a thought hit him. *Are they looking for us*? His heart skipped a beat. *Why else would they be flying over a Jap infested island*? As soon as that hypothesis was concluded, he stood up waving his arms, almost ready to shout, but then something caught his eye. Immediately he turned and stopped, still as a statue. *Japs*!

Crouching down and moving cautiously back into the jungle, PFC Bonito laid-in a course straight to Sergeant Stamper to report his finding.

"The Japs are on the ridge, about a hundred-yards south of us. I don't think they saw me, but I can't be sure. I think they were looking up at the PBY. Sarge, I think that PBY is looking for us. Why else would they be sending a slow footed elephant to this island. That flying tub has really long legs, that's got to be the reason."

The news hit Sergeant Stamper hard. "How did the Japs find us so fast? How many did you see, Geronimo?"

"Forget the Japs, I was talking about a PBY, Sarge."

"Forget the PBY, Geronimo, what about the Japs? There is nothing we can do about that damn airplane, but there is something we can do about the Japs."

Shaking his head, PFC Bonito answered with just a hint of disappointment in his voice. "There were about twenty Japs, but I don't think they know we're here. I watched the Japs split up earlier and this is the other half. There was only a squad chasing us before we headed west. I think these guys have no idea what happened to their buddies."

Sergeant Stamper made a quick decision. "Geronimo, you stay topside and try to hide this hole. The rest of you guys start climbing down."

Sergeant Stamper then looked back at PFC Bonito. "Good luck, Jose. When it's clear, come back and get us."

"Aye, aye, Sarge."

Just as Sergeant Stamper began his climb down the vine, he heard all kinds and varieties of swearing that quickly faded into just noise. Seeing nothing but darkness, he began to worry. *What am I in for now?*

~ ~ ~

Gunny was soaked to the skin and slightly agitated. He had several bleeding cuts on his face from the Japanese rifle banging into his forehead several times on his way down the hole. *What the hell just happened?* He was still trying to figure out that puzzle a few minutes later when he heard a loud, child like yell, just before he was assaulted by the chief's feet. The two Marines collided hard, banging heads and rifles together, and landing in the same pool of water the gunnery sergeant had just climbed out of.

"Who the hell just hit me." he shouted.

"Are you all right, Gunny?"

"I was until you ran into me. Hell of a ride, wasn't it? Where's everyone at, chief?"

"They're still up top, Gunny. They volunteered me to come after you."

Gunny hadn't expected the answer he received from PFC Fox. "They volunteered you to come after me?"

186

"Yep, they surely did."

The man in charge could only shake his head and start laughing, and because he was laughing, PFC Fox started laughing. Both men had bloodied faces from their heads colliding and the Japanese rifles banging into them. Both men were in pain, and both men were laughing hysterically over what had just happened. Then they were unexpectedly assaulted by four additional pairs of feet, one right after the other. All six were now soaked to the skin, and all six were sitting in the same pool of water Gunny had just climbed out of several minutes before. *What a hell of way to wage war.*

Almost a week passed before the Marines, still hiding in the cave they accidentally slid into, finally got the chance to signal to the plane flying recon over the island. At first, Gunny didn't think the plane saw his flashes, but when the airplane started circling overhead, he knew his flashes had been spotted.

At last. We just might make it off this island after all. He didn't know there was another flight thirty-minutes behind the plane he was looking at, so when the Japanese fighters started attacking the lightly armed PBY, Gunny thought their chances of getting off the island had died along with the spiraling airplane.

Chapter 18

The allies had gone on with their plans without Gunny and his boys, and had caught the enemy by the nape and they weren't letting go. The enemy was now on the defensive, everywhere in the Pacific. Their once powerful fleets had been pounded into the abyss of darkness, and lay scattered along the bottom of the Pacific Ocean. However; despite the naval victories, there were still a lot of Japanese held islands that had to be either taken, or neutralized, so the Allies continued with their planning; pounding their enemy hard every chance they got.

The once impregnable area of Japanese held islands, where their mighty airpower held sway over the Pacific had been bypassed, left to whither on the vine. With their airpower now greatly diminished in that area, the Japanese were vulnerable to invasion. But that wasn't the plan.

In bayonet strength, the enemy still commanded over 300,000 troops in that island area. A lot of American lives would be lost trying to take those islands away from the Japanese, more lives than the allied commanders were willing to lose. Bypassing and cutting off those islands, allowed the allies to keep those 300,000 plus Japanese soldiers from entering the battle, thus saving countless more American lives. Nevertheless, there were still seven Americans stranded on one of those islands. Seven U.S. Marines at last count. Gunny and his men had been stranded on their island since August of 1944. General Swift decided that now was the time to rescue his stranded Marines, if they were still alive. "Go get our boys and bring them home, Colonel."

~ ~ ~

The *USS Longfin* was slowly cruising along the surface of the Pacific, her diesel engines pushing the sub through the water at about 4 knots. They were closing in on the area where the *USS Green Jack* was sunk, just six months earlier. The crew and her captain were on edge, feeling a little spooked at having to sail into the graveyard of the sunken sub and her crew. Shortly after 0130 hours, the *Longfin* arrived at their first destination.

The mission was to drop off three men on the southwestern side of the island. Their assignment was to find the Baker Boys and guide them back to the sub. The sub would then take the stranded men home. They had earned their ride home the hard way, a free ticket back to the States, and a hero's welcome. There would be no more missions for these seven Marines. Seven damn good Marines.

Captain Jared Rogers had been the *Longfin's* skipper since the start of the war. So far, his boat had sunk ten merchant ships, three destroyers, and three cruisers. He had also put his stinger into the hulls of a dozen other ships that were later sunk by other boats. Now, his boat was relegated to secret missions, under the cover of darkness. Intelligence-gathering missions. Assignments that had no glamour. No zing. No glory. His boat was an older class boat. The newer class boats had taken over his job of sinking the Japanese navy and merchant ships. But he was still proud as hell of his boat and his crew. Both had done an outstanding job in the early days of the war. If sneaking around gathering intel is what the Navy wanted him to do, then he would do nothing less than an outstanding job of being a ghost in the enemy's backyard.

It was also fitting that his boat was chosen to bring Gunny and his Marines home because it was his boat, the *USS Longfin*, that transported the Baker Boys to their first mission. Now, his boat would be taking the boys on their last mission. They were going home.

"Skipper, we've arrived at the location, sir. Lookout's are in place."

Captain Rogers looked up at his executive officer. "Thanks, Rick. Assemble the crew topside."

"Aye, aye, Skipper."

Captain Rogers waited for his XO to leave before he reached down and opened his sea chest.

As soon as Captain Rogers found out he was going to be in the area where the *USS Green Jack* was sunk, he thought of one last errand. Just before he left Pearl, he went out and bought a Lei. Now he was going to pay tribute to the *USS Green Jack* and her crew. When Captain Rogers reached the conning tower, he looked out at the crew lining the side-rails, and his eyes began to tear up. Every member of the crew manning the side-rails had a Lei in his hand.

As soon as the quick memorial service was over, the sub submerged and got underway, silently moving towards the southwestern corner of the island. Captain Roger's three passengers were standing by, ready to disembark when the sub surfaced, but the wait was an hour longer than anticipated. Still, the delay was a boon, the later the better. Late night eyes were less apt to be alert.

The *USS Longfin* finally surfaced sometime around 2250 hours, about two-hundred-yards from the shoreline. From previous experiences unloading the Baker Boys, the boat's crew had no problem getting the three rafts inflated and quickly into the water. Loading them up with supplies and men was even faster, and off they went.

Paddling against the wind was brutal, but they managed to hit the beach about forty-minutes after disembarking the sub. Immediately after hitting the beach, three men – a Marine sergeant, an Army Ranger, and an Army scout – were busy hiding the three rafts under the jungle vegetation.

~ ~ ~

"Corporal Jackson, get out front and keep us from running into the Japs. We'll be about forty-yards behind you. And remember, Corporal, the Japs are real sneaky little bastards. They're not like the Germans. These guys don't give up until *after* they're dead."

Corporal Timothy Jackson looked back at Sergeant Daniels. "Nuts, Sarge. Nothing to it." Corporal Jackson, however, was nervous. He had heard stories about fighting the Japanese. Nervous or not, the matter was stoically resolved. He couldn't care less about who he was fighting. The enemy was the enemy no matter what country they came from. His job was to kill the enemy and the Japanese were his country's enemy.

Moving silently through the hot, steamy jungle, Corporal Jackson was amazed at the scene unfolding before him. He had never been in terrain like this before. He had seen pictures of jungles before, but that was the African and South American jungles, not the jungles of the Pacific Islands. Beautiful, and deadly, it set his taste buds for exploration zinging. He was looking at a whole new land to explore, new trails to blaze. At least they were new trails to him.

The destination of the three men was the tallest mountain on the southern end of the island. Somewhere on the southwest side of that mountain was where the shipwrecked castaways might be found. That location was also where the flashes of Morse code came from. The occasional recon flights hadn't spotted any flashes from the stranded Marines in almost a month, so if they weren't there, at least it would be a good place to start.

The small river the three Americans were to eventually follow north roughly ran from the base of the mountain, southeast for about eight to ten miles, before it turned east with a small tributary meandering southwest. When the three Americans reached the southern tip of the tributary, they planned on following the small stream to the north, which in turn, would run them into the river that flowed near the base of the mountain they would have to climb. If the three rescuers could average three to five miles a day, it should take them about a week and a half to reach the mountain, and return to the sub. That is, if things went according to plan. But in war, plans never seemed to survive past first contact.

The two men following Corporal Jackson were carrying a crate that was loaded with seven M1 carbines, a handful of grenades, extra essentials, and about a thousand rounds of carbine ammunition. They carried this crate on a sling stretcher for easier handling. The backpacks weighed about eighty pounds each, and they were loaded with extra uniforms, socks, boots, shaving kits, and their own extra ammo and food rations. All in all, the two men were roughly carrying close to three hundred fifty pounds of munitions and supplies. Nothing to it for Uncle Sam's boys.

Short, quick barks brought the two stretcher bearers to a halt. Quickly, the two men slid out of the straps, hid the stretcher under some vines, then hit the ground, and waited. The two ammo carriers couldn't hear or see anything yet, so they didn't quite know what to expect, but they did know Corporal Jackson's warning call, the bark of a prairie dog. It was something he came up with during their training for this mission.

Marine Sergeant Aaron Daniels had fought on many of the islands the Marines had invaded. He had fought the Japanese on Guadalcanal, Rendova, New Georgia, and Bougainville and was wounded on Saipan. He spent the next six months recovering from his wounds and was told his island hopping days were over.

Army Ranger, Corporal David Logan had many battles under his belt as well. His most recent encounter with the enemy was June 6, 1944, on the beaches of Normandy. He was wounded shortly after D-Day and had spent three months in England recuperating from his wounds. When he left England for Europe, he arrived in France and found that too many of his buddies were dead and gone; the news hit him hard. When he rejoined his old unit, the luster was no longer present; only strangers were there to greet him. Not liking his current situation, he asked for transfer to the Pacific theater. Corporal Logan left his Ranger unit and was reassigned to fight the Japanese in the Pacific, but he was Army and didn't quite fit into the Marine Corp's scheme of things. Corporal Logan was shuffled off to the side until this mission came up. He was highly recommended to General Swift, as well as was Marine Sergeant Daniels.

Corporal Jackson had not suffered any physical wounds. He started his war fighting the Germans in North Africa, and ended the European part of his war shortly after the Ardennes battle. His best friend, Samuel Lemons, was killed during their last fight with the Germans, and his other friend, Charles Baker was transferred to intelligence. His mentor, Sergeant Alfred Brooks was wounded and sent back to the states, minus one leg.

No one he knew remained with his old unit; wounded or otherwise. All because of the Nazis. He was done fighting in Europe. He'd lost many friends, just like everyone else fighting in the war. However, because of what he had done for Sergeant Brooks and the squad during their escape from the Germans, he was promoted to corporal, and was given his choice of what he wanted to do. "Do you want to go home, son?"

"No sir, General. I want to go to the Pacific and fight the Japs." Jackson's name was at the top of General Swift's list, and now he was in the Pacific about to fight the Japanese.

~ ~ ~

"Sarge!"

Sergeant Daniels nearly jumped out of his skin. Jackson's whisper caught him by surprise, plus it scared the hell out of him. He never heard the little army brat coming up on him. He caught Corporal Logan by surprise too.

"Don't do that again, Jackson or by the lord Harry, I will shoot you dead." Sergeant Daniels couldn't see that Jackson was smiling because it was still too dark to see past their noses.

"Sarge, there's a Jap patrol up ahead of us. I think we should wait here and let them pass."

"Are you sure they're Japs and not the men we're looking for? You've never seen a Jap before."

Jackson was still smiling although no one could see it. His reply was a soft whisper. "They're not speaking German, and they're too short to be Marines. Even you're taller than they are, Sarge"

Sergeant Daniels shook his head in disgust. "Which direction are they moving in?"

Squatting down on his haunches, he replied. "The Japs are coming at our right, straight across our line of march, Sarge."

Sergeant Daniels looked in the direction where Jackson's voice was coming from. "I can see you're going to be a pain in my ass, Corporal Jackson, so listen up. If you ever sneak up on me like that again, I will beat the begeezus out of you. Am I clear on that, Corporal?"

"Yeah, Sarge, crystal clear. But maybe you should get a hearing test or something. I thought I was making enough noise that even the Japs could hear me."

Sergeant Daniels took a sudden intake of air, ready to blast out at Corporal Jackson, but a quiet snort from Corporal Logan stopped him.

"What the hell's so funny, Corporal Logan?

"Nothing, Sergeant Daniels. Nothing."

195

"Then why were you laughing?"

"He's good Sarge. He scared the hell out of both of us. You've got to admit it, Sarge, neither one of us heard him coming. Now, here we are on this Jap island and nothing has changed. If you remember Sarge, he did this to us during training. Like I said, nothing has changed."

Sergeant Daniels was still a bit agitated. His anger hadn't run its course yet, and that fired him up even more, so he turned back to Jackson."Listen, you little army brat. We do things differently in the Marine Corps, sonny. If you ever pull that stunt again, I will bust you down to private in a heartbeat. Do you understand me, Corporal?"

Sergeant Daniels didn't get an immediate response from Jackson, so he waited for the scout to answer back. After waiting a few more seconds for a reply, he shook his head, realizing that Jackson was no longer with them. "Now where in the hell did that kid get off to?" His whisper was to no one in general, but Corporal Logan replied anyway.

"I heard some stories about what that kid did. He can hear things nobody else hears. He's got eyes that see things most people have to use field glasses for. And he's as quiet as a ghost when he's in the woods. I heard rumors that while he was in North Africa, on his first mission, he snuck up on a German machine gun position in the middle of the desert and captured the machine gun crew without firing a shot. Captured the whole crew. I also heard he's a clown. He likes to play jokes on his friends. Some say he's a holy terror in a fight."

Out of the blue, the early morning jungle was energetically awakened by the outraged yelling and swearing of many agitated Japanese soldiers, followed quickly by the sound of gunfire. A minute or so later, the firing stopped. The two men could still hear the enemy yelling, but the angered voices seemed to be moving east and growing fainter. Then the shouting died out altogether.

Both men were thinking the same thought. *What the hell was that all about*? Ten-minutes went by before the two men both heard a whisper. "This way, quickly."

Sergeant Daniels and Corporal Logan both jumped at the whispered command. Sergeant Daniels was a little irritated at the sudden order, but Corporal Logan was smiling. *This is going to be fun.*

It had been a long time since Corporal Logan had actually enjoyed being in the field. He had watched Corporal Jackson during their training, and at first, thought the kid was a hotdog, a cocky eighteen-year-old prankster. He thought the kid wasn't taking the training seriously enough. After all, they would be going into enemy infested territory together, and he wanted to make sure this youngster didn't get them all killed. He didn't know that Corporal Jackson already had over a year's worth of serious combat experience under his belt, before their mission training even began. However, by the time their training was finished, Corporal Logan was beginning to think differently about Corporal Jackson. Now that he was seeing firsthand how the Army scout handled himself in a real combat situation, his first opinion of Jackson changed dramatically.

Both men reacted quickly. Slipping the slings over their shoulders, within seconds, they were moving rapidly along the riverbed, following Jackson. By the time the sun broke the horizon, they were a mile and a half from where they had previously dropped to the ground.

An hour after taking a breather, they were on the move again. Jackson was now on stretcher detail with Corporal Logan, while Sergeant Daniels led the way. The switch lasted for another hour before Sergeant Daniels was back on stretcher duty with Jackson, and Corporal Logan was leading the way. They kept this routine up hour after hour until they reached their first landmark. Shortly after arriving at their dot on the map, they began their long break in earnest, too exhausted to eat. They were now about five hours from the base of the mountain.

~ ~ ~

For the 100,000 or so enemy troops on the island, their war had pretty much ended. Now the Japanese were in a different kind of fight. A fight for survival. They had received no new supplies in almost four months, and were now forced to fend for themselves. They were forced to hunt for the food they ate, and sometimes fight the inhabitants for what food they possessed. The enemy had no way of getting off the island short of swimming, and those who did try swimming to escape the island, were eaten by the many sharks that swam in the warm Pacific waters.

However; on the southern end of the island, there was a private war going on between an under strength company of Japanese soldiers, and seven United States Marines under the command of one Gunnery Sergeant Alistair Baker. It was a lopsided affair with the Japanese holding the much higher odds. Bad odds, however, didn't mean a damn thing to the gunnery sergeant from Oklahoma. He and his men were stuck on this island, so they figured to make the most of it. The United States was at war with the Empire of Japan. A handful of the enemy was right in front of them, so why not try and kill them all? The Baker Boys had nothing to lose. The Marines also had no idea there was a mission underway to get them off the island.

Time had no meaning to them anymore. Hell, they had no idea how long they'd been on the island; it seemed like they'd been stranded on their jungle-infested rock forever. The Marines were also in a fight for survival. The clothes they wore were tattered. Their Marine Corps uniforms had long since disappeared and were replaced by what was left of the Navy stuff they salvaged when they first hit the island. Their hair was down below their necks, and they were sporting beards. The Baker Boys no longer looked like Marines, but they damn well fought like Marines.

They were pure mean, lean, and eager to pounce on their enemy. The squad gave no quarter and expected none from their enemy. The victor would be the last one standing after the last enemy soldier was killed. The Baker Boys were working hard to be the victors.

Chapter 19

Captain Matsui was still in charge of the pint-sized company, but they were cut off, and isolated from the rest of the world. All communication with the northern units ceased altogether thanks to the allied air attacks. The last working radio Captain Matsui had was destroyed over a month prior, during one of those air attacks. Lieutenant Watanabe was also in dire straits as well. He had been ordered by General Sasaki to aid Captain Matsui in recapturing the Americans.

Besides crippling radio communication and killing the enemy, the Allied air attacks also put a halt to all vehicular traffic going up and down the east coast, so the junior lieutenant was unable to get in touch with his superiors to seek permission to leave that raving lunatic. He was forced to remain with Captain Matsui's forces until he heard otherwise. His problem at this point was pretty much unsolvable because General Sasaki was killed in a naval bombardment on the northern installations, almost a month before.

Even if he had been able to contact any of his superiors, they probably would have let the general's order stand because of the situation with the Marines in the south. Every major Japanese installation on the east coast was getting bombed or bombarded, and every commander on the island was keeping a tight grip on their men. They had their own defenses to man. No more reinforcements were going south.

Every now and then, a supply sub slipped past the blockading allied forces and off loaded the supplies it was carrying. But that unexpected surprise happened rarely, and most of the supplies the Japanese did manage to off load were generally not what was needed. "What are we supposed to do with spare airplane parts? We have no airplanes to repair!" As for Captain Matsui, only his insane desire to kill the Marines kept him going. Several times he had come close to killing the Yankee dogs, but somehow, they always manage to slip away. Then there was this other problem. The Japanese were running low on ammo. Once out of ammo, they would be forced to fight with clubs and spears.

~ ~ ~

"Lieutenant Nakamura, gather all of our supplies together, I want to see what we have left."

An hour later, Captain Matsui was taking inventory on what supplies his unit had on-hand. The company had no food rations, so he didn't have to worry about that. The men would just have to continue hunting for their food, no big deal. A lot of little monkeys were on the southern end of the island.

He also discovered a disheartening fact; the company possessed only two serviceable type 99 light machine guns with about five-hundred rounds between the two, and six-thousand rounds of rifle ammo. Now six-thousand bullets sound like a lot of ammo, but when it was divvied out to about 110 soldiers, it came to a little over fifty rounds each. Not a lot of ammo for a long, sustained campaign.

"Lieutenant Nakamura, form up the company. We are going on a hunt for Yankee pigs."

From call-to-arms to fully assembled took less than three minutes. What was left of the company, 110, strong, including officers, stood in formation under the coconut trees, waiting for orders.

The company was divided into two platoons. Lieutenant Nakamura commanded one platoon, and Lieutenant Watanabe commanded the other platoon. The senior lieutenant was completely loyal to Captain Matsui, but that wasn't the case with Lieutenant Watanabe.

General Sasaki's nephew hated Captain Matsui and his pet lieutenant. On several occasions the junior lieutenant almost ordered his men to open fire on the captain and his watchdog, but he held back. Now he was regretting that decision to hold off. He started out with over twenty soldiers, only nine were still with him, including Sergeant Takagi. The rest of the men under his command were loyal to Captain Matsui. He would only be committing suicide if he ordered his men to open fire on the captain now.

Without warning, there was a shout from one of the soldiers standing in formation. "Look, Captain Matsui, reinforcements."

Captain Matsui turned to his right and was completely unprepared for what he saw. He had an unobstructed view of the bomb cratered dirt road, and trudging south towards the company compound, about one-hundred-yards down the road, was a long column of Japanese soldiers marching single file, right towards him. He was dumbfounded. All he could do was stand and stare at the column of soldiers moving down the road, while everyone else was pointing and smiling at the approaching troops. Captain Matsui turned to Lieutenant Nakamura and said, "Lieutenant, take charge of the company and make sure they're ready to move out."

Lieutenant Nakamura bowed to his captain and then faced his men to issue out his orders. In the meantime, the captain started walking towards the column of troops and met them half way up the road. "Ah, Major Mikawa, this is an unexpected surprise. What brings you here?"

Major Hiroshi Mikawa returned the captain's salute before he answered. "General Sasaki has ordered me to come down here with a reinforced company and take over command of your units. He is displeased with your lack of progress in recapturing the Yankee Marines. Our bases in the north have been hit hard, and it seems that the Americans might have cut us off from our supplies for now. But we are still strong, and we will still win this war despite our setbacks. Stand down your men and come with me. We have a lot to talk about."

Captain Matsui was stunned. *Displeased with my results? Maybe the general should try his hand at capturing the Americans. No. He wouldn't dare venture out into the jungle; he'd get his shiny new boots all muddy.*

The two officers headed towards the only structure that had yet to be hit from the air attacks. A long, rectangular building made of bamboo, it was nestled up against the edge of the jungle, situated well back from the rest of the structures and well camouflaged. It used to be the supply building, but now it served a dual purpose. It was Captain Matsui's sleeping quarters, and it served as the company's new headquarters' building.

The major was still unaware that General Sasaki had been killed during a naval bombardment. He had left the far northern base a couple of days prior to that event, so all that happened after he left was unknown to him.

He began his march with five trucks, six mules, over 250 troops, and enough supplies to last for quite a while. The trucks and mules were carrying all of their supplies. After weeks of damaging air attacks he was down to just three mules and no trucks. During their three-week march, south, his troop strength had also been considerably reduced, resulting in a serious loss of manpower. When he arrived at Matsui's encampment, he had just a little over fifty men. And the "enough supplies to last quite a while" was now down to just several day's worth. The allied flyboys had done their jobs with a great deal of gusto.

Captain Matsui was put in command of the company, with Lieutenant Nakamura his executive officer. However;

instead of being his own boss, he now took his orders from Major Mikawa. The men were divided up into three platoons of fifty men each. Lieutenant Watanabe was in command of one platoon, Lieutenant Jinichi Hashimoto was in command of the second platoon, and Lieutenant Takeo Ishida was in command of the third platoon. The total compliment of serviceable troops available to Major Mikawa was 165 men, but he decided to take fifteen men from his order of battle and form them into a company headquarters unit to provide security for the base.

With the company reorganized, the captain and the major discussed what to do about the Yankee Marines in Major Mikawa's new headquarters. Captain Matsui was relegated to sleeping on a flimsy cot in the headquarters' section of the building, while the major slept in the captain's old quarters, on his nice, comfortable bed.

A six-foot-long rectangular table had been set up along the wall at the far end of the headquarters' section. The two officers were bent over that table studying all the lines of march penciled in on the map by Captain Matsui. The X's marked on the map were places where he had encountered the American Marines. There were a lot of X's decorating the map.

While the captain and the major were studying the map, the new arrivals were busy building their bamboo sleeping huts. They were small huts, which made them easier to camouflage. In addition, the materials the Japanese needed to build larger huts was scarce, thus the main reason for the small sleeping quarters. Because the huts were small, it took no time at all to rebuild them after they were damaged by air attacks. The location where they were forced to build their little huts left them exposed to the unexpected air attacks. The air attacks directed against Captain Matsui's compound were mostly harassing attacks, hoping to catch the Japanese napping, killing a few more of the enemy in the process. The Allied main effort was in the north where the Japanese had their greatest troop strengths.

Captain Matsui's men were helping the new arrivals build their huts. Because of the excitement caused by the newly arriving troops, no one thought to post lookouts in the jungle, so the attack came sudden and unexpected. Three volleys were fired from the jungle, and then there was silence. The Japanese were caught with their pants down. Six soldiers were hit, two of them were dead. Captain Matsui knew any effort to find those responsible for the attack would be futile; they had already disappeared. Staring off into the jungle, his frustration was apparent the second he kicked at the ground. *Damn! They are attacking again. One of these days they will make a mistake, and I will have them. One of these days. Yes.* And while his thoughts raged on, his fists were clenched so tightly that his knuckles turned white.

~ ~ ~

"Did you hear that?"

Both men jerked at the sudden and unexpected whisper, causing the crate to topple off the stretcher onto the ground.

"Damn you, Jackson." hissed Sergeant Daniels. "I'm gonna rip your head off your shoulders and pour dirt down the hole if you don't quit sneaking up on us like that."

"But Sarge, didn't you hear that gunfire a second ago?"

"What gunfire?" Sergeant Daniels was looking at Corporal Jackson like he wasn't quite sure of what Jackson had said. Puzzled, his anger at the scout was forgotten. Looking over at Corporal Logan he asked, "Did you hear any gunfire?"

"No, I didn't. But that doesn't mean the kid didn't hear it. What direction did it come from?"

Jackson pointed behind Corporal Logan. "I think it

came from the east, Lo."

Jackson had started calling Corporal Logan "Lo" when they were in the last stages of their mission training because it was quick and easy to say. Corporal Logan didn't mind for he had taken a liking to Jackson and had started addressing him as "the kid" or just kid, which didn't bother the scout in the least. The two Army brats had fought in the same mud and against the same enemy, so that in a way, those experiences they shared had begun melding into a bond of friendship. On the other hand, Sergeant Daniels was a Marine, and he didn't care to make friends with his two army brats.

Corporal Jackson had an eager "let's go" expression on his face. "What do we do, Sarge?"

"What do you mean what do we do? We continue on with our mission; that's what we do."

Sergeant Daniels looked at Jackson, but the scout's expression didn't change, and immediately, the sergeant's irritation at him flamed brighter. "Did you hear what I said?"

"Yeah, Sarge, I heard you. But what if it's the guys were looking for? If they're in a fight, they could probably use our help."

Sergeant Daniels stood up taller, looked at Corporal Jackson, and then smiled somewhat menacingly.

"Maybe the great, wise *Captain* Jackson can explain to us peons how we're supposed to cross those two ridges in time to help whoever is doing the shooting? Tell us that, oh great *captain*. Tell us how to cross those ridges in time to help."

The scout's expression and smile slowly drained from his face. "Geeze, Sarge. You're supposed to already know that. You're a Marine, aren't you?"

Sergeant Daniels was speechless. Stunned, he tried to say something many times, but he ended up failing. All he could do was shake his head as he stared back at Jackson. His expression was a cross between absolute astonishment, and *is this kid for real*, with just a little bit of *I don't believe this kid just said that* mixed in. Again, he tried to say something to the Army scout, and again he ended up just shaking his head, still speechless. Finally, he just threw his hands up in the air, waded into the middle of the small stream and sat down, chest deep in the water. He was still shaking his head.

Both corporals looked at each other, surprised at the sergeant's actions. *What did I do* was written all over Jackson's face. However; before anything else could happen, the scout jerked his head towards the east, and just as quickly, Sergeant Daniels stood up and faced in the same direction, water cascading off his uniform.

"All right Ma..." The pause was extremely short. "Damn you, Jackson! You two army brats grab a couple of carbines and some ammo. Hide the rest in the vines."

Sergeant Daniel's face was turning red for almost calling his two army brats Marines. "Well, what the hell are you waiting for, a presidential citation?"

The two corporals looked at each other and then quickly pried off the lid on the crate and snatched out of the crate, three carbines, and two bandoliers of ammo for each weapon. In less time than it took to hide the crate, the three men were on the move.

Thirty minutes of hard climbing brought them to the end of their immediate goal; the crest of the first ridge. Then their hearts sank. It wasn't two ridges they had to cross over; it was three. Staring out at the next two ridges, Sergeant Daniels winced, knowing they had a tough chore ahead of them; another sweat-squirting experience to endure.

"Damn you, Jackson," muttered Daniels. "I'm gonna beat the crap outa you when this mission is over."

He was looking at Jackson's back, but he could still hear Jackson's snicker and then his reply. "Oh, come on, Sarge. You're a Marine. This should be easy for you. A piece of cake."

It would have been a piece of cake for Sergeant Daniels except for the fact that he had a large chunk of his right butt muscle missing, and because of that missing chunk, he was having a difficult time climbing up the ridge.

Damn. Those docs were right. I should be behind a desk sharpening pencils instead of busting through the jungle like this. His thoughts, however, also had him smiling.

"What the hell," he whispered to himself. "You're a Marine. Suck it up and quit your complaining."

The second ridge took forty minutes longer to crest. Winded, the three men waited to catch their breath before they continued on. Sergeant Daniels was hurting from his butt wound, but there was no way in hell he was going to let these two army brats get the better of him. It just wasn't going to happen.

They could hear the weapons' fire a little clearer now that they were on top of the second ridge. The gunfire was currently a little northeast of the ridge the three men were on: a few quick shots, followed by a large volume of fire, and then silence. A couple of minutes of quiet would abound, then the shooting would start all over again. The firing always began from a different location, but it invariably ended up coming from the northwest, moving deeper into the jungle with each new episode. It sounded like someone was leading the larger group on.

The three men were moving northwest, scurrying along, just below the crest of the second ridgeline, until it made a curve to the northeast and then dipped down into a small valley. When the three men reached the valley floor, they turned due north and started running towards a small rocky hill about a half a mile away. Once the three men reached the top of the small rock pile, they could look down into the jungle and perhaps see who was chasing whom. It was a long shot, but worth the effort. They just might be able to spot someone. The three Americans would also be in a position to hit the chasing party in the rear of their left flank if the chasing party turned out to be the enemy.

The sun was below the tallest mountain when the three-man team finally reached the top of the rocky mound. They could see the intermittent flashes of gunfire through the jungle canopy, but now the shadows were hiding whoever was doing the shooting. They watched the area where they last saw the gun flashes, but nothing was happening at the moment. The shooting had stopped, and its lack left the jungle eerily quiet. Almost ten-minutes went by before the jungle abruptly erupted with gunfire again; this time, however, the gunfire came from the northwest. The return fire was intense for a few seconds, and then it died out.

The three men could see the pursuers advancing towards the northwest, firing as they moved. The larger group appeared to be winning the contest because their opponents were giving up ground from the concentrated attack. Then, for some reason, the enemy fire shifted to their rear and immediately intensified for a brief minute; the following explosion was horrendous.

Without warning, sudden, violent death struck again. A huge fireball erupted from the position of the larger group. It went blossoming up through the jungle canopy, followed a second later by a tremendous explosion that rumbled the ground the three men were standing on. Almost one-hundred-feet of jungle where the explosion had occurred was leveled and on fire. Men were running and screaming in all directions through the tangled terrain, their clothes fiercely on fire. Then the shooting began again.

Within a few minutes, the shooting and the screaming stopped, and the jungle was quiet again. "Damn, that was intense. What do you think caused that?" asked Jackson.

Corporal Logan was showing off his pearly-whites when he answered, "An explosion. Boom!"

Chapter 20

The sudden attack from the jungle caught the Matsui detachment completely by surprise. Six men were already down before anyone could grab his weapon. As quickly as it started, the attack ended. The captain already knew who the perpetrators were, and he also knew they would be long gone before he could organize any real pursuit. But Major Mikawa didn't share that opinion. He was sent down south to kill the Yankee Marines and he was determined to do just that.

"Lieutenant Ishida, form up your platoon. Take as much ammunition from these men as you need and start hunting down those raving lunatics. As soon as I can, I will have Lieutenant Hashimoto follow with his platoon and extra ammunition. I'm afraid we don't have enough food supplies to go around, so be prepared to live off the jungle."

Lieutenant Ishida bowed to Major Mikawa, and within a few minutes, he was leading his platoon into the jungle, in pursuit of the hated Marines.

Captain Matsui was seething inside. His insane desire for revenge had erased all thoughts of honor and glory for the Empire of Japan, and the fact that the Empire was now in a desperate fight for its very existence. His only thought was to kill the Yankee swine. *They are mine to kill, mine alone. No arrogant boot kisser is going to interfere with my plans to kill these dogs. I will be the one who kills them, and I will do it slowly, painfully. But first, the major must die!*

~ ~ ~

Gunny was waiting, watching the Japanese as they moved past his position. The plan was to give the Japanese a fifteen-minute lead, and then start following them. The ambush site was perfect. The area was somewhat open, but it still had enough foliage to hide the five-gallon can of aviation fuel and the ten sticks of dynamite wired to it. This was Sergeant Thomas' idea. Lure the Japanese into the kill zone and set off the dynamite. What the dynamite didn't kill, the aviation fuel was sure to finish off. The squad's last count put the Japanese numbers at 110.

"Okay, chief. You three get moving. We'll wait for you to get the ball rolling. After your third attack, we'll come up and hit them from behind. Be careful out there and keep your heads down. Remember: don't get careless. Just stick to the plan."

After a ten-minute scurry, the three men had caught up with the left flank of their enemy, undetected. They were about seventy-yards out from their nearest foe, and they were nervous and scared to death. The fear was real, and it was deep-seated. For the moment, however, that dread was sitting on the back burner while intense focus and unwavering determination took its place. It was time to start the ball rolling.

When the enemy platoon passed his position, Gunny waited about fifteen minutes, and then he started following after the Japanese. He had with him, Sergeant Stamper, Sergeant Thomas, and PFC Choctaw. Corporal Kirby went with Fox and Bonito. The actions of those three would set the plan in motion.

PFC Fox managed to confiscate a double armload of dynamite the Japanese had been using to blast out tree stumps. Now that their task was done, they had no more use for the surplus dynamite, so he kind of borrowed some on one of his scrounging runs. The enemy noticed the disappearance of their explosive sticks and wondered what happened to them. The Japanese were also surprised when they ran out of supplies a lot sooner than they expected, again, thanks to PFC Fox. They had no idea the little scout was dipping into their supplies. The aviation fuel came from a downed Ki-61 fighter that crash-landed on the southwest beach. They found the pilot dead in the cockpit from a bullet wound, courtesy of the dying PBY.

Corporal Kirby was nervous, and tried to hide it when he whispered. "Do they have any flankers out?"

"I don't see any," replied the chief. "Geronimo, do you see any?"

Picking up Corporal Kirby's new habit, PFC Bonito was stone-faced when he replied. "No, little squirrel."

"Very funny, Jose. I suppose you'll be calling me squirrel from now on, won't you?"

The whispered reply was as expected. "You bet, you little squirrel."

"Can it you guys. We got a job to do, so let's get on with it."

The chief looked over at Corporal Kirby for a second, then shook his head and said, "Damn, Lance. Now you're really scaring me. You said that just like Gunny."

The three Marines positioned themselves behind some large trees about thirty-yards from the Japanese flank. Bonito cawed the crow, and all hell broke loose. The first three shots immediately took out three of the enemy, all of whom were caught flat-footed. They immediately hit the ground and opened fire in the direction of the three men. Just like PFC Fox said they would. With bullets flying all around, the time for an escape had arrived, so they hugged the ground and low-crawled to their next position.

The three Marines fired several more shots to convince the Japanese they were still under attack, and then they low-crawled northeast, to their new location. The enemy continued firing, not realizing they were no longer under fire. Just as PFC Fox said they would.

"Remember Lance (Corporal Kirbys' first name),"

whispered PFC Fox. "The Japanese will most likely hit the ground and then return fire. That will give us a chance to crawl away before they can think to advance. Once the Japs figure out we're no longer shooting at them, they will stop firing and start moving forward again. By then we should be close to our next position and ready to do it all over again."

So far, the plan was moving along exactly the way Fox thought it would. The three men were almost to their new digs when Lieutenant Ishida realized that his soldiers were the only ones firing.

"Cease fire!" he shouted. "Cease fire!"

In less than a minute, the jungle went quiet again. Quickly, Lieutenant Ishida spread his men out, dividing them up into three squads. One squad covered the right flank, one squad watched the left flank, and the third squad was the point squad.

The flanking squads were in a loose right and left oblique formation, with the point squad in a loose wedge formation. The sun was going down, so it was becoming harder to see into the shadows. Without warning, firing erupted again, but this time, it hit the right side of the point squad, and two more of the enemy were killed. This firing didn't last long. Each Marine only had enough time to fire two rounds before he had to skedaddle on out of there. The Japanese were a bit more prepared for this attack.

The point squad tried to keep the shooters engaged while the right flank closed in on the perpetrators, but the right flank was a little slow in its maneuver. The left flank was moving straight up to block that avenue of escape, but being a bit slow, as well, gave the three Marines time to sneak around their left.

With the point squad and the right flank still searching northeast, the left flank was exposed and separated from the other two squads by about sixty to seventy-yards. The three Marines quickly opened fire on the left flank, killing three soldiers in the opening volley. The enemy's cohesiveness was beginning to unravel, and they were beginning to waver.

The other two squads, seeing that their left flank was under fire, rapidly closed on the left to help them out. The firing abruptly ended, leaving four more Japanese dead. With their numbers dwindling, Lieutenant Ishida decided to keep his forces closer together for a much heavier concentration of firepower. Before he could get his men reorganized, however, they were suddenly brought under fire from the rear. Lieutenant Ishida was really flustered, now. Ordering his men to open fire, he faced them towards the shooters and ordered his men to advance, hoping to force the Americans to expose themselves and die for their efforts.

The enemy had moved into a somewhat large open area that looked as though it had been cleared out for a small base-camp at one time. A slight movement caught the lieutenant's eye, and when he turned, he spotted two men running and disappearing into the cover of the jungle. "There they are! Kill them!" Immediately, thirty-eight screaming and enraged, Japanese soldiers took off running after the two Marines. Within reach was their quarry, their prey. The Japanese had seen their enemy, and now they were hungry for the kill. Banzai!

Lieutenant Ishida's men had almost made it to the other end of the open area when their world abruptly exploded in flames and body parts. Those that weren't killed instantly, were lying on the ground broken and burning. Some managed to escape being killed by the explosion, but they didn't escape the burning aviation fuel. Within minutes, not a single man in Lieutenant Ishida's platoon remained alive. The very few who did escape the explosion and the burning fuel were hunted down and killed. All in all, it was a devastatingly successful ambush.

The Americans had no idea Lieutenant Ishida was being followed by another platoon, so they didn't immediately leave the area. Having no weapons of their own, the Marines scoured the area for any serviceable weapons and ammo. The firearms they were using had been taken from the Japanese dead, so the Baker Boys were looking over the ambush site for more. Leave nothing useful behind.

Startled for some reason, the two scouts stopped what they were doing and looked towards the south, alert. Something was not right, they could feel it. The jungle was too quiet. For the second time, Gunny had underestimated his enemy.

The men were spread out in the now semi-darkened jungle, looking for more weapons and ammo. Sergeant Thomas was the only Marine starkly visible in the open area, where the fires from the burning fuel and the moonlight lit up the surreal scene. Without warning, as sudden as violent death can happen, the jungle erupted once again with the sounds of gunfire and screaming Japanese. Sergeant Thomas was hit in the chest many times; he was dead before he hit the ground. Gunny took a bullet through his right hand, and another bullet grazed his hip, just below the wound he received on a previous mission. All hell immediately broke loose.

Within seconds, the Marines were running through the darkened jungle, trying to escape the bullets that were zinging, hissing, and buzzing all around them. They had been so spread out looking for weapons and ammo, that when the shooting started, they all took off in different directions, not knowing if anyone had been hit.

~ ~ ~

Corporal Kirby was panic stricken and unsure of what to do. His first thought was to keep running. But to keep running was to keep on making noise. *If they can hear you, they can get you.* Out of nowhere, Kirby remembered what PFC Fox told him.

"Lance. Remember. If you get separated from your unit, don't panic. Look for the deepest, darkest shadow and hide there. The best place to hide is by a vine-covered tree. It's very deceiving hiding in the vines on the trees. Slow down your breathing so they can't hear you, and don't panic. Chances are they'll move right on by you."

Corporal Kirby had no idea in which direction he was heading. When the shooting erupted, he took off into the jungle, running for his life. He was about one-hundred-yards from the blast area when he recalled what PFC Fox told him.

Everything around him appeared spooky and unsettling. The sun had set shortly after the ambush ended, and the jungle where Kirby was standing was bathed in total darkness. He could barely see his hand six inches in front of his face. He stood where he was, looking for the shadows PFC Fox told him to hunt for, but all he saw was total darkness. Slowly, a smile spread across his face. *How do I find a shadow in all this darkness*?

~ ~ ~

Gunny went down when a Japanese bullet carved a groove across his hip, but he didn't stay there. Sergeant Stamper saw him fall and immediately went to his friend's aid. By the time he reached the gunny, he was already back on his feet and heading for the jungle darkness. Using the trees to help block the bullets, the two Marines scurried deeper into the jungle, cursing the Japanese for sneaking up on them undetected and the war in general. The unexpected hoot of an owl brought the two men to an abrupt halt. It caught both men by surprise and also scared a number of strange noises out of the two Marines. The hoot came from their right, about ten-feet away.

"Gunny, it's me, PFC Bonito."

"Damn you, Geronimo, I almost dumped a load. I oughta shoot you right where you stand. You just scared the skin off our bones. Did everybody get away okay?"

"I don't know, Gunny. I know PFC Fox got away. I saw him grab the Ox by his shirt, and they both disappeared into the jungle. I don't know where the rest are. I think they got Sergeant Thomas."

"Damn." swore Gunny. "He was a good Marine. Are you hit anywhere?"

Before PFC Bonito could answer him, a shot sounded from the burning battlefield, and a loud, dull thwack was heard, followed immediately by the whistling of a ricochet bullet, and Sergeant Stamper limply collapsed to the ground. "Roger, where are you hit?"

Dazed, he was slow to answer. "I don't know, Al. I feel like I got hit on the head by a baseball bat."

Smiling, Gunny shook his head and said, "Huh! Must not have been a strong bat, you're still talking. That head of yours is so hard, not even common sense can penetrate it. You'll be okay until morning."

When Gunny received a rude response, he knew his friend would be fine. "You'll probably carry a headache around with you for a while, Roger, but it looks like you'll live." Turning back to PFC Bonito he said; "Let the chief know where we are. We'll stay here for a while to let Sergeant Stamper catch his breath."

In less than a minute, another owl hoot was heard. Four heartbeats after the second hoot, a response was heard; another owl hoot, and it originated somewhere east of Gunny's position. Everyone within earshot heard the hoots. Corporal Kirby smiled and began walking towards the first hoot. PFC Fox heard the hoot and answered with his own hoot. Immediately following his action, he and Choctaw began moving towards the first hoot. The Japanese heard the two hoots and thought nothing of it. To them it was a good sign. Three other men heard the two hoots, and one of them whispered.

"I didn't know desert owls lived in the jungle!"

~ ~ ~

With Jackson on point, they were on their way down the ridge as the last of the shooting was dying out. The climb down was tough, and it took them almost an hour to reach the base of the rocky hump. They could still see the glow of the aviation fuel induced, jungle fire reflecting off the clouds. It gave the darkened sky the appearance that it was on fire. By the time they were three-hundred-yards from where the explosion occurred, the sun had finally closed its eyes to sleep, leaving the jungle in complete darkness. Even the moon was of no help to them.

While the three men struggled cautiously through the jungle towards the fire, shooting abruptly broke out in the jungle once again. A lot of shouting and yelling could be heard through the din of gunfire. Some of it sounded a lot like it came from the Japanese. Then above all the shouting and the noise of battle, they heard what sounded like orders being shouted out. The same phrase was shouted out over and over again until the chaos of the battle died down to just the occasional shot, and then the shooting died out all together.

Crouched down at the base of a vine entangled tree, the three men waited, listening to what was going on up ahead. They had been traveling in single file, almost stepping on each other's heels because it was too dark to travel any other way. Someone might get lost in the darkness.

"Jackson!"

There was a pause. Sergeant Daniels waited for an answer, but he didn't get one.

"Jackson?"

Again there was a pause, and again Sergeant Daniels

didn't receive an answer. There was no answer because Jackson was no longer with the two men. All Sergeant Daniels could do was shake his head in anger.

"Damn that Jackson, I'm gonna fry him up for breakfast in the morning, and to hell with the Japs."

All the two men could do now was stay where they were and wait for Jackson to return. *Shhick*! What came next was smothered choking. They had heard that sound many times before. Startled by the suddenness of the noise, both men prepared for battle.

"Corporal, you hear that? Listen." A few seconds went by, and nothing. Before another breath could be taken, however, they heard a soft rustling of the foliage, followed closely by the bark of a prairie dog. A few tense minutes went by before the two Americans heard a low whisper. "Don't shoot, Sarge. It's me."

Sergeant Daniels had a smile on his face. "That kid's not as dumb as I thought he was."

Chapter 21

Corporal Kirby was stumbling through the jungle towards the sound of the last hoot. He knew it was either the chief or Geronimo, but he couldn't tell one from the other. Every nerve in his body was on edge. His heart was pounding hard enough to beat hell to death, and his hands were shaking from the adrenaline rush. *Come on, you guys, hoot that owl again so I can get my bearings.* He kept thinking this thought over and over again all the while sweating and shaking from the anxiety of his situation. *Come on, guys, just one more hoot. That's all I need.* But he didn't hear the owl hoot again. What he did hear, though, was a soft, ominous, growl, and it sounded like he was heading right for it. *Oh, Damn! Please, don't let it be hungry.*

Taking a tighter grip on his rifle, he cautiously moved towards the growl. *Please, let it be Fox. Please, please let it be, Fox.* He remembered what the little scout did to him on their third mission when he was so tired he could hardly keep his eyes open. *This is nuts! It has to be Fox. It's just too damn dark to see anything, and I don't like surprise pain.*

He was closing in on what he thought was the location of the growl, taking extremely short steps and gripping the rifle so hard his hands were hurting. He had even forgotten to breathe. Looking up and all around, his eyes wide open, he continued to advance until he heard the growl again. This time, though, the growl was much closer, so close he could almost feel its breath.

BOO! Corporal Kirby jumped back so fast that he lost his footing and his rifle, and landed hard against a tree, knocking the air out of him.

"Damn you, Fox!" was all he could say. Immediately after his words, he was sucking for air on his hands and knees. Despite the presence of the Japanese nearby, Fox and Choctaw were rolling on the ground laughing so hard their sides were hurting.

Still struggling to catch his wind, Kirby managed to whisper a few words between gasps for air. "Damn you. You scared the hell out of me."

"Shh, quiet, Corporal. You'll let the Japs know where we are."

"I don't care if the Japs know where we are. Hell, your laughing alone probably let the Japs in on that secret, chief, so why worry about it? I almost pissed my pants because of you. Damn, bone-headed idiot."

PFC Fox couldn't stop laughing.

~ ~ ~

Two enemy squads were thirty-yards apart, spread out in a loose skirmish line. They were moving northwest, towards the sound of laughter, and they were greatly agitated. An entire platoon had just been wiped-out by those Yankee dogs, and they were laughing about it. The deed was done in a most devious and horrendous way and they wanted payback. The fact of the matter was completely ignored; Japan was at war with America. Also ignored was the reality of war; that the enemy was killed anyway they could be, and with any and all means available. The Japanese were out for blood, and not just any enemy's blood; American blood. Yankee Marine blood to be precise.

The laughing had set them off. It didn't matter why the Yankees were carrying on, so. The enemy thought the Americans were laughing because of what they had done to them. Nothing anyone could say or do would dissuade them from their mindset. They were craving revenge. Banzai!

Sergeant Kiyoshi Mitsuo was a veteran of the Chinese

and Southeast Asian campaigns. He was a worthy warrior, a samurai of old fighting in a modern war. The men serving under him mirrored their sergeant. They had also fought and won many battles against their enemies. He knew how to fight in the jungles of the Pacific, and so did his men, and they all were determined that these Americans would not leave the island alive. In fact, Sergeant Mitsuo was fiercely determined that the Americans would fill the bellies of the carrion eaters and never leave the island at all.

After forty-minutes of trying to fulfill that wanton desire, Sergeant Mitsuo finally gave up the hunt, and started back to the open area. His stubbornness refused to allow him to quit, but his commonsense and reasoning told him it was fruitless to try and find the Americans in the darkness. This battle between stubbornness and commonsense finally came to a close forty-minutes into their search, with commonsense winning the struggle. After a quick, final eye-search of the area, he and his men were on their way back to the explosion site.

When Sergeant Mitsuo arrived back at the scene of the ambush, he ordered his men to help with the burial detail, then he went to Lieutenant Hashimoto to give his report. After he gave his report, the two men moved off into the jungle to discuss what to do next. A few minutes into the discussion, a runner was sent south, back to company headquarters.

The sun was poking its head above the horizon by the time the burial detail had finished their grizzly task for the moment. The enemy still had to search the jungle for what they missed during the night, and no one was looking forward to that final search. When they finally laid to rest the last of their comrades the sun was almost straight-up, noon. The need for vengeance was also on the rise, and with it, rose the lust and determination to put an end to those Yankees forever.

~ ~ ~

No one moved. No one said a word. In fact, no one was breathing. The Japanese were so close to the three Marines that if they had taken a breath, they would have been heard. They were in agony. Their lungs were on fire, screaming for that one breath of air that would release them from their pain, but they dare not breathe that one breath of air for it would surely mean their deaths. One Japanese soldier was so close to the chief that he could have reached out about six inches and tied the man's bootlace. Then there were whispered words, and the enemy slowly, silently, withdrew, moving back in the direction they came from.

When PFC Fox could no longer hear the Japanese, he tapped his two companions on the shoulder and they were immediately gasping for air. The little scout waited another ten-minutes before he felt it safe enough to move out. They ran into Gunny, about an hour later.

"The Japs got Sergeant Thomas, Gunny. They got him clean."

Gunny shook his head and let out a big sigh. "Yeah, chief, I heard."

Expressionless, the man in charge looked around the jungle at nothing in particular, contemplating on their recent dose of bad luck. Turning to look at his men, he nodded his head as if coming to a conclusion. "It's obvious we're not getting off this island anytime soon, and we damn sure can't go back to the ambush sight, so we might as well head back to the cave."

"Gunny?"

"Yeah, chief, what is it?"

"These Japs are good. I mean, they snuck up on us so quietly that they almost got us. They knew we were there, but they just couldn't see us. The Japs were so close to us, I could've untied their boot laces."

"Yeah," muttered Corporal Kirby. "If you two hadn't

been laughing so hard, they probably would've never found us."

Gunny shook his head, amazed. "You were laughing? Never mind. I don't think I want to know. Geronimo, keep our rear, clear. Chief, get us back to the cave. Somebody give me a hand with Sergeant Stamper."

"No, Gunny, I'm all right, I can walk."

"Shut up, Roger. It's your turn to be carried."

"But what about you, Gunny? You were hit too, you know."

Shaking his head, he replied with his usual stone-faced, expression. "I'm fine, Roger. You're the one that's brain damaged; not me."

~ ~ ~

With Jackson back in-hand, the Marine sergeant's anger began to brew-up towards boiling mad again.

"What the hell was that all about, Jackson?" whispered Daniels.

"That Jap was starting to get too close to us, Sarge. I thought I'd better take care of him before he stumbled on to us. You didn't hear him?"

Sergeant Daniels shook his head. "No. I didn't hear him. How do you hear things we don't?" Before he received an answer from Jackson, he heard a snort. "What the hell are you laughing at Corporal Logan? You think it's funny? This is the second time you've interrupted me. Don't make interrupting me a habit, Corporal. I break habits with a vengeance."

Gazing at his corporal, he noticed the look on his face. "Okay, Corporal. Your expression tells me you have something else to say."

"Yeah, Sarge. I do. The kid's good. Maybe you should quit thinking he's Army and use his talents like we used them against the Germans. He's damn good at what he does." Turning a bit more serious, Logan continued. "You know, I ran into a colonel once in Saint Lo. This colonel was recruiting men for a special operation he was heading up. He couldn't tell me what it was about, but the he did tell me he was looking for men with special skills. He was hitting the Rangers pretty hard for some of those men."

Pausing as if gathering his thoughts, he continued. "Do you know what he was using for his staff car? He was using a German halftrack the kid, here, took off the Germans in North Africa. He not only took the halftrack, he captured the officer and the four men who owned it. The kid snuck right up to the track, captured the guard, and then captured the rest of the Germans while they were sleeping."

Sergeant Daniels was somewhat surprised at the added information. *There was nothing in the kid's file about his skills other than he was part Apache and had good ears. Hm, army brats, who needs them?* The sergeant in charge still had his doubts, but now they were fewer. He also had a better understanding of the skill-set the Army scout possessed.

"Jackson, do you think you can sneak up on the Japs and see what they're up to without getting caught?"

The former beanpole from Arizona stood tall and issued out his best western drawl. "Does a bear hibernate?"

The man in charge shook his head in disgust. "Just shut up and answer the question."

It was still too dark to see anything, but Sergeant Daniels could feel the scout was having fun. "Yeah, Sarge. I can sneak up on the Japs without getting caught."

Jackson was back with the other two men about an hour and a half later. "Sarge, if those were our guys that did all that damage, they surely did a number on those Japs. There must be at least thirty or forty dead getting buried back there. I watched a couple of squads come in from the north, so maybe our guys headed north."

Sergeant Daniels thought the situation over for a

moment, and then answered. "Get us around these Japs and find us a place to hole-up until daylight. Do you think you can track our guys down?"

"Yeah, Sarge, I think I can find their trail."

Corporal Timothy Jackson was excited. Really excited. Sneaking about always stirred his juices for adventure. What he loved to do the most, though, was about to begin.

Jackson volunteered for the Pacific to try and get away from the memories of his lost friends. He missed Sam the most. But he also missed the freedom he had serving with Sergeant Brooks. He missed the games he played, sneaking up on Sergeant Brooks and the rest of the guys. He just missed his army buddies tremendously.

At first, he didn't want to make new friends when he volunteered for the Pacific. He didn't want to make new friends only to see them die. During his mission training he began to realize that he needed new friends to hide the bad memories, and to keep in his heart, the good times he shared with his lost buddies. For the first time since volunteering to fight in the Pacific, he felt almost like his old self. The happy go lucky joker, the prankster, the smile inducer. *If only Sergeant Daniels would loosen up a bit. This mission just might turn out to be fun.*

The three Americans were approximately one-hundred-yards west of the ambush site when they stopped earlier that night. They were about three-hundred-yards north of the open area when Sergeant Daniels' called a halt; his butt muscle was hurting. He used the excuse of sending Jackson back to check up on the Japanese to justify the halt.

"Hurting?"

The question caught Sergeant Daniels by surprise. The sun was about to make its appearance, but that wouldn't be for another half an hour or so. Enough predawn light was filtering in through the trees that the two men could somewhat see each other.

"Now why would you think I was hurting?"

Corporal Logan smiled, and then replied. "Because, Sergeant Daniels, I can see you trying to hide your limp. You should have waited until you were fully healed before you tried to get back into the swing of things. Now look at you. You're limping along like a busted wheel."

"Don't worry about me, Corporal Logan. I promise you. I'll be the last one standing in this contest. Besides, if I had waited to fully heal, they'd have stuck me behind a desk instead of letting me be out here in this tropical paradise with the likes of you two. I'd be missing all the fun. You guys are very entertaining on a hot night. Watching you two is almost as entertaining as watching a movie."

Bowing slightly, the corporal replied. "I'm glad you're enjoying the entertainment. I'll make sure your stay at the Waldorf is a pleasurable one. Would you like for me to call room service?"

Both men were on the verge of laughing. For a couple of minutes, they forgot who they were and where they were. The sudden barking of a prairie dog brought them back down to reality.

"Don't shoot, Sarge. It's me."

Both men turned towards Jackson's hail. "You really got that kid spooked, Daniels. He thinks you're really gonna shoot him if he doesn't announce himself first."

"That's the idea, Corporal. I'm tired of my heart skipping a beat every time he sneaks up on me. I think he gets some sort of pleasure out of seeing me jump."

"Shh. I can hear you two talking a mile away."

Both men jumped at about the same time, leaving their skin lying on the ground.

"Damn you, Jackson. I told you not to sneak up on me like that!"

"But, Sarge," he whispered sternly. "What if I was the enemy? You'd be dead right now, wouldn't you? You know,

Sarge, you really need to learn how to separate nature's noise from man-made sounds. That knowledge might save your life someday." Corporal Jackson paused for a moment, struggling with his thoughts. Still preoccupied, he shook his head and whispered; "Come on, you guys. We need to get out of here. It's starting to get light, and I'm sure the Japanese are already on their way here."

The scout had barely taken three steps before he stopped and turned around to face the two men. Neither man had moved, and this lack of action killed the last of his patience. Frustrated and disappointed, he shook his head and voiced his thoughts. "You know, I really miss Sergeant Brooks. At least, he knew the value of silence. He didn't mind me sneaking up on him because it kept him on his toes. You don't like it because you feel it makes you look stupid. I'm not trying to make you look stupid. I do it to try and teach you the difference between jungle noise and human noise. If you can hear me coming up on you, then you can hear the Japanese trying to do the same thing. Bust me down to nothing if it'll make you feel any better, but if you don't start paying attention soon, I'll be the only one leaving this island alive."

For only the second time in his military life, Jackson ignored the fact that he was talking back to a superior NCO as if *he* were in charge. His words captured the sergeant's attention, and Daniels smiled to himself. *I didn't know the kid had it in him.*

"Okay, junior," whispered Daniels. "Why don't you lead us away from the bad guys and get us to the Promised Land. You think you can do that?"

Again, the reply was laced with western drawl. "Does a skunk stink?"

"I think I'm still going to beat you senseless when we're through with this mission."

"He's just a kid, Sarge."

"Yeah, Corporal, and just as irritating."

By 0900 hours, Jackson had located a sign that the Marines had been there. He couldn't tell how long ago because somebody had tried to hide the trail. He spent the next hour and a half looking for more sign, going this way and that, his eyes focused on the task at hand.

Sergeant Daniels and Corporal Logan stood off about twenty-feet from where Jackson first found signs of the Marines. The two men were forbidden to leave their spot under threat of losing their hair, so they leaned up against a tree and watched the show.

The scout was moving around, searching, and occasionally moving away branches or small leaves of the ground plants to check under them, but he never broke them. When he was certain he had thoroughly covered a section, he expanded his search. The two men stood where they were, never thinking to sit down. They were amazed that an eighteen-year-old jumping bean had the patience to look for more sign. All seemed normal until they heard a strange chittering sound. After a pause they heard what sounded like a squirrel.

"Maybe we should see if Jackson found something."

Corporal Logan shook his head before he replied. "You know, Sarge, I think maybe we should wait and let the kid tell us he found something. I don't know about you, but I kind of like my scalp where it is."

"What's the matter? You guys didn't hear me calling you? I found it. They're heading for our mountain."

Neither man had been surprised this time because they saw Jackson walking towards them. "Can we move without you scalping us?"

Jackson nodded and a smile appeared, then he answered. "Yeah, Lo. You can move now."

The trail wound through the jungle like a snake crawling along the ground, always changing direction.

Sometimes the trail would lead north for a half a mile before disappearing, only to re-appear heading east, and then it would switch back to a northwesterly direction. But no matter how many times the trail changed direction, its course always ended up northwest. Right for the backside of the mountain the three men were heading for when they first landed on the island.

"Yeah, Sarge. They're definitely heading towards our mountain."

Staring off towards their final destination, Sergeant Daniels rubbed his chin while he pondered over the situation. Less than a minute passed before he turned back to look at his two corporals. "If that's the case, why don't we just make a beeline straight for the mountain? We know where they're headed, so why not? A straight shot to the mountain would definitely save us a lot of time."

Jackson looked at Sergeant Daniels, half expecting the Marine to stop him before he could say more than a couple of words. "We could do that, but I think it would be better if we headed south for about an hour, turn north, and then cross south below the mountain. We could then climb up the west side of the mountain until we find where they're sending the signals from. By doing that, we have a much better chance of throwing off any pursuit the Japanese might have, planned."

"Hmm. Nice plan, kid." Nodding his head, Logan looked over at Sergeant Daniels. "I have to agree with the kid's idea. It makes a lot of sense."

"What do you two think this is, a democracy? You two are attached to the Marine Corps, so you'll do it my way, or you can find your own way off this rock. Got it?"

Jackson and Logan both looked at Sergeant Daniels somewhat disappointed in him.

"Yeah, we get it, Sarge." replied Logan.

Sergeant Daniels looked at both men then nodded his

head and said, "We might as well get moving. Jackson, you lead the way."

The scout started leading them north and had taken about four steps when… "Where the hell are you going, Jackson?"

Looking back at Sergeant Daniels, he had a confused look on his face. "You told us we had to do it your way, so I'm going north."

"That's the wrong direction, Corporal. We need to head south for about an hour before we head north. That way we can cross below the mountain and head up the mountainside from the west. What's the matter, don't know how to follow your own game plan?"

"But, Sarge?"

"But, Sarge, hell. Move out now, Jackson."

"Yes sir, Sergeant…"

"Don't call me, sir, Corporal. I ain't your daddy."

Shaking his head, the former beanpole from Arizona started moving south, still kind of confused. Corporal Logan on the other hand was smiling. "There's still hope for you yet, Sergeant Daniels."

"Shut up, Corporal, and start walking."

Chapter 22

The sun was on its way down when the runner finally reached company headquarters. Only a couple of minutes passed by before he was talking with Major Mikawa. He was pointing out on the map where the ambush occurred and what plans Lieutenant Hashimoto had made. The major was stunned by the report on the ambush and, for the moment, was unsure of what to do next. *A whole platoon destroyed in one fell swoop? How could that happen? How could just five Americans do that?*

"Major, why don't you let me lead Lieutenant Watanabe's platoon to reinforce Lieutenant Hashimoto's platoon? I know exactly where the ambush site is. It was one of my earlier base-camps." He was hoping that Major Mikawa would allow him to lead the platoon. It was a malicious hope, filled with diabolical thoughts. *Who knows? If the major goes along, maybe a stray bullet will accidently kill him, or if we get into a skirmish with the Yankees, maybe I could remove the major from the playing field myself. That would be enjoyable.* But what happened next was definitely not to his liking.

"No, Captain. I alone will be going with Lieutenant Watanabe's platoon, but just to keep an eye on the situation. Lieutenant Hashimoto and his men are very good at what they do. They've turned our enemy's flank from the jungle, many times in many battles, so he will lead. I want no interference from you."

"I understand, Major Mikawa. What am I supposed to do in the mean time?"

"You will stay here with the headquarters unit and guard our base in case the Americans decide to double back and attack here."

~ ~ ~

Lieutenant Hashimoto was not about to wait for reinforcements to arrive. To do so would be a great waste of time, precious time he could ill afford to lose. He knew if he waited for his reinforcements to arrive, the Americans would have plenty of time to make good their escape. Not what he wanted. *We must go after them now, while they are still scattered. Kiyoshi said he was close enough to the Americans that he could almost smell their fear. Maybe it's time we saw their fear.*

"Sergeant Mitsuo, lead us to the Americans."

Lieutenant Hashimoto again reorganized his troops. This time, however, instead of three sixteen-man squads, he now had four twelve-man squads. Not as heavy a concentration of firepower as the sixteen-man squad, he now had three maneuver and one reserve force.

While they were leaving the smoldering death trap, Lieutenant Hashimoto was off by himself taking one last look at the graves they were leaving behind. Tears welled up as he looked at his buried comrades. These Japanese dead were his friends, his comrades in arms. Most of them had fought together with him in China, Malaya, Singapore, Shanghai, and several other spectacular victories. It saddened him to know that he would never hear their laughter again. Staring down at the graves, he whispered a silent prayer and said his last farewells to his lost companions, and then he softly spoke his thoughts.

"You will be avenged, my brothers."

Hashimoto's force left the ambush site around 1245 hours. The platoon took over an hour to reach the location where Sergeant Mitsuo finally called off his search. He had left his bayonet stuck in a tree, to mark the location, so they had to find the bayonet to begin their search for the Yankees. The enemy also found the rifle Corporal Kirby lost when Fox scared the hell out of him. It was standing straight up, butt to the ground, partially visible in the middle of a large bush. The three Marines were searching blindly on the ground, not in the foliage.

The platoon sergeant could see the broken bushes and trampled terrain where the Marines had hidden from him. His bayonet was stuck in a tree only six feet from where the Yankees cowered in fear. He pointed down to the ground, just to the left of where he was standing.

"Look, Lieutenant. You can see how close we were to the cowardly dogs last night. Like I said, I could almost smell their fear."

Lieutenant Hashimoto looked down at the disturbed foliage and scuffed-up ground, and for a moment, said nothing. His expression was neutral while he studied the confusing mess of tracks his enemy left behind. Turning to look at his platoon sergeant, his expression changed and his mood turned dark, vengeful. He was eager to retaliate and impatient for the hunt to begin. "We will wait here while you figure out the direction they took."

The chore took the platoon sergeant about an hour and a half, but he found what he was looking for, then a direction. "They are heading south, sir. I think they are the same Americans who cowered in the bushes by the trail last night."

"Very good, Sergeant Mitsuo. You have done well. The time has come to track these dogs down and kill them. I want to present their heads to Major Mikawa by the end of the week. Is that understood?"

Sergeant Mitsuo bowed at the same time he replied. "Hai!"

Again, the platoon was formed up as before, and then they marched south. Keeping their formation in the jungle was tough, but this unit could handle it. These troops were old pros, veteran warriors. There were no shouts of close up your ranks, or watch your spacing, or keep your formation. They didn't say a word. The head movements their leaders gave them, and their squad leader's arm signals told the troops what needed to be done. They were as silent as a ghost. All metal objects had been rapped with cloth to avoid any rattling or squeaking. Not even the occasional swearing was heard.

The troops cursed out the jungle, their officers, the insects that were bombarding them, and the heat and humidity that was torturing them, but all in their minds. Silence was their main weapon, and they used it well. Their opponents feared them so much because they were one of the best jungle fighting armies in the world during WWII.

The Japanese had been moving south for about an hour when Sergeant Mitsuo came across the first of many booby traps. He had been caught napping. Only his quick reflexes saved his life. He felt an un-natural tug on his right foot, and instantly he fell backwards to the ground, hearing the woosh of a pointed stick as it skimmed across his stomach, ripping his shirt. "Chikusho. That was close." His whispered words were a nervous reaction to an almost violent ending; the shakes came next.

Hand signals went up, and the entire platoon halted in place. A long time had passed since he last encountered this kind of booby trap. *I wonder where the Americans learned about it. Now we have to slow down our pace and be on the lookout for more of these traps. These Americans are smart. No one got hurt this time, but that fact doesn't matter. We are being slowed down because of this delaying tactic, and while we are looking for more traps, the Americans are gaining more time to escape.*

~ ~ ~

Corporal Jackson was watching the Japanese from his perch, about thirty-feet up in a tree that overlooked the false trail he had purposely made and the booby trap he had laid.

With all the excitement going on down on the ground, he didn't think the Japanese would bother to look up into the trees. He was right; they didn't. The enemy was more concerned about what was going on down on the ground, than they were about the clamoring birds above their heads. He was a little disappointed in the outcome of his little trap, but at least his traps were slowing down the enemy.

The Army scout waited about twenty-minutes after his adversary disappeared from sight before he climbed down from the tree. The jungle was already growing dark despite being mid-afternoon; a storm was brewing up dark and nasty, and it was moving in from the east.

~ ~ ~

Sergeant Daniels and Corporal Logan were already on their way north. After their hour of moving south, Jackson was sent back to keep an eye on the progress of the Japanese. Corporal Logan had the scout's backpack, so Jackson had nothing to eat. He started thinking about his stomach, and snare-traps entered his mind, but then he came up with an idea. Viola ... booby traps. He was excited; he had a new idea to play with.

The storm hit around 1630 hours. It was a huge bang and pop storm that lasted about fifteen-minutes, and then it was gone. It had come and gone so fast that the rain hadn't had a chance to properly soak through the forest canopy yet. But now, the water left by the storm was slithering its way through the trees, worsening already bad conditions, and making it extremely difficult for both forces to hear anything.

~ ~ ~

"All right Corporal, it's time to take a break. We need to give Jackson time to catch up with us. We've been going at it for two hours now, and it's suffocating in this damn jungle."

"How long do you figure to wait, Sarge?"

Looking along their backtrail, the sergeant paused to take a deep breath before he replied. "I figure about thirty-minutes, and then we'll move out again. Hopefully, that'll give Jackson time enough to catch up with us before we get to the mountain."

"What if he doesn't show up when we reach the mountain?"

"Well then, Corporal Logan. We'll head up the mountain without him. Speaking of heading up, it's time to move out again. We only have a couple hours of daylight left, so we'd better make the most of it. I'll lead; you keep an eye on our rear."

Tapping his right wrist with his left index finger, the corporal responded. "Hmm. Interesting watch you carry around. Does it gain ten-minutes every other minute? Maybe you should send it to a shop and get it repaired. We've only been here a few minutes. What gives?"

Sergeant Daniels looked back at Corporal Logan and mockingly said. "Aw, come on Corporal. You're supposed to an Army Ranger. This should be easy for you. A piece of cake."

Looking at Sergeant Daniels as straight faced as he could, the corporal replied. "Very funny, Sarge. Very funny. Don't you worry about me, Sergeant Daniels. I promise you. I'll be the last one standing in this contest." Then they both broke-out laughing until someone struggled through the laughter and whispered; "Lead on, Macbeth."

Ten-minutes into their trek the two men stumbled onto a bog and found themselves struggling through ankle deep muck; then the storm hit. Shortly after the deluge began, they ran into a small, barely trickling stream. By the smell of their surroundings, they had blundered their way into a marsh.

Corporal Logan grimaced. "Whew, this place smells worse than our latrines. We'd better turn around and head back until we're clear of the marsh, and then go around it. No telling how far this stink goes."

"No, Corporal. We'll continue on in this direction. We'll just swing a little west. We'll waste too much time backtracking. I'm sure if we swing to the west, we'll clear the marsh in no time."

That *no time* lasted forty minutes and found both men standing at the base of a ridge. Looking up at the obstacle before them, they stood in-place contemplating the scene for a moment or two. When the moments were over, they looked at each other, nodded, and then dropped to the ground exhausted. The climb could wait. It was time to take a real breather.

The break lasted for over an hour before they started up the ridge. After a lot of slipping and sliding, the two men finally reached the top of the ridge just in time to be greeted by an almost setting sun. Through the remaining light, they could see the mountain they were aiming for off in the distance. From where the two men stood, it looked as though the mountain was being hit by the same storm that just dumped a torrential rain on them about an hour before.

~ ~ ~

Corporal Jackson was crouched in the shadows of a large tree, surrounded by vines and other plant life, watching his enemy set up camp. His plan was to wait until the Japanese were settled in for the night, and then try to decrease their population, starting with those on watch.

What should have taken the enemy about an hour to accomplish, stretched into almost two hours. They were only 200 yards from where Sergeant Daniels and Corporal Logan had started their trek up north. Thanks to Jackson's snare traps, the enemy platoon had lost an hour, plus two men dead. As much as he wanted to continue with his little inconveniences, he knew it was time to head up north and meet up with the rest of his team.

241

Something else was pushing him on. Time was getting tight for everyone. In less than 24 hours, the sub would be at the rendezvous point. If the Americans missed their meeting with the boat, then it would be another week before the sub could rendezvous for another attempted pickup. If they missed the boat, the delay would not only give the Japanese another crack at finding the Americans, they would also have enough time to finish the job once and for all.

~ ~ ~

Sergeant Daniels chose a flat spot about twenty feet below the crest of the ridge to make camp. The spot he chose was located on the west side of the ridge. It was very unlikely that the enemy would stumble upon their camp, so he built a small fire to boil some coffee. He hadn't had any coffee since the mission started, and he was dying for a strong, hot, cup.

Although the enemy couldn't see or smell the fire, someone else did. With the breeze blowing northwest, picking up the aroma of freshly brewing coffee wasn't hard.

"Gunny. Someone's got a fire going, and they're making coffee."

"Are you sure, Geronimo?"

"Yeah, Gunny. I'm sure. You want me to go check it out?"

"Yeah. Why don't you and the chief go find out what's going on."

"Aye, aye Gunny. Who's in charge?"

Stone-faced as usual, he looked at both of his scouts and said. "Just so there's no confusion as to who's in charge of this little scouting expedition, I'm appointing me to be in command. Any questions?"

Neither scout said a word.

"Good. Now get out of here before I change my mind and have you two digging latrines for the rest of **my** stay on this island."

A sudden snort erupted from Sergeant Stamper and his head shook with great emphasis. "Damn, Gunny. Those poor boys will be old and gray before you kick the bucket. That's a long time to be digging latrines."

By the time Sergeant Stamper was finished talking, the two scouts had disappeared from sight.

"You seem to have put the fear of you into their hearts. I do believe they took your comment seriously, Al."

"You know, Roger, you may be right. I think that's the fastest I've seen those two disappear since we first landed on this island." Turning to face the departing scouts, he stood staring at nothing and wondering.

~ ~ ~

Sergeant Mitsuo had a strange feeling they were being watched. He couldn't explain why he felt that way, he just did. Yet, there was nothing to indicate someone was watching, given that he hadn't seen or heard anything. The situation had him puzzled.

He was still puzzling over this feeling he had as he raised his canteen for a drink...and abruptly stopped. His expression turned cold when he realized what was bothering him. *I don't hear anything because the normal jungle sounds of the night have stopped. Something or someone is out there lurking about. I wonder if it's one of the Americans.* His hesitation lasted only long enough not to be noticed, and then he took a swallow of water. After his second tilt of the canteen, he walked up to one of his squad leaders and whispered softly to him.

"Corporal Kagawa, pick two men and wait here for me."

Walking over to another of his squad leaders, he whispered his order. "Corporal Takahashi, pick two men and wait for me over by Corporal Kagawa. I will be with you shortly."

Corporal Takahashi did what he was told, and after he had picked his two men, the three warriors went over and stood with Corporal Kagawa and his men.

While his men were congregating around Corporal Kagawa's pallet, Sergeant Mitsuo walked over to speak with his platoon leader. "I believe one of the Americans is somewhere out in the jungle watching us. I have Corporal Takahashi and Corporal Kagawa standing by with two men each. I want to go hunting for whoever is out there spying on us. Do I have your permission?"

The lieutenant knew his sergeant well. If he said there was someone out in the jungle watching, then something needed to be done about it.

"Do you need more men?"

"No, sir. The men I have picked out will be enough. Any more might give our intentions away." Sergeant Matsuo smiled deviously. "No, sir. I have all the men I need."

"Then don't let me keep you waiting, Sergeant Matsuo. I will inform the men to hold their fire until they hear from me."

The platoon sergeant bowed, and walked over to where the six men were waiting. After a brief conversation, they checked their weapons and prepared to move out. This would be a stalk and kill mission, something these men were very familiar with.

Chapter 23

The enemy camp was set up, facing north. Corporal Jackson was at the three o-clock position, about twenty-yards due east of the camp. The Japanese didn't have a fire going so as not to give away their position, and to keep their numbers hidden. The only talking that was done was done in hushed whispers that couldn't be heard from more than three or four feet away.

Spying on the camp, the Army scout noticed his enemy was placing their guards all to the north and west of their camp. He had already spotted six men moving west through the jungle about a minute apart. *This is going to be easy. I'll just start on the left and work my way across to the right.* His expression was determined, with a little bit of fear and anxiety mixed in.

Every nerve inside of him was twitching relentlessly, driven by the closeness of imminent contact with his enemy. He never fully relaxed. Corporal Timothy Jackson was like a permanently wound up toy; a very deadly and dangerous wind-up toy.

Settling back deeper into the shadows, he waited for his time to attack. His breathing was slow, quiet, and even, and not a muscle on his body, moved. He was as still as a stone statue. Slowly, the jungle nightlife relaxed and began to stir again. All was quiet and peaceful for about fifteen minutes, until a strange feeling washed over him. Something was not right. Something was out there, and it was freezing the jungle nightlife in its tracks. *An animal maybe? What are the predators like in this neck of the woods?* The situation had him stumped.

Instantly, icy fingers of fear grabbed at his stomach

and he cocked his head. *What was that?* Holding his breath, he waited, listening to the jungle sounds, trying to sort out what was man-made. A couple of seconds went by before he slowly, quietly exhaled; nothing. Smiling to himself, he thought, *It must be my imagination. Maybe not being used to the jungle is playing tricks on my mind.* Then he heard it again. The soft sound of clothing brushing up against a plant. *Someone **is** out there! Do they know I'm here?* The sudden urge to run hit the Army scout hard, but the impulse died almost as quickly as it appeared. *To run is what the rabbit would do to escape the wolf. But I am not the rabbit. I am the wolf.*

~ ~ ~

Sergeant Matsuo was moving silently around the northern end of the camp. He was alone. Corporal Kagawa and his men were slowly moving around the southern perimeter of the camp, while Corporal Takahashi and his men were following about thirty-yards behind Sergeant Mitsuo.

The idea was to try and force who ever it was watching them into the center of the triangle formed by Mitsuo and his men, once they were in position. The sergeant had used this plan before with good results, but with a much larger force. He didn't need a large force for what he had in mind. He believed only one or two Americans were watching the camp, so he felt he had the correct number of troops to do the job. He was afraid that if he used a larger force, then whoever it was in the jungle would know something was up and maybe leave. He didn't want who ever it was to leave, he wanted to capture them.

Corporal Takahashi's squad was all ready in position to block the unknown infiltrators from the north. Corporal Kagawa had just moved into his position, but he wasn't set yet, and Sergeant Mitsuo was still moving further north to close the lid on the three-corner trap. His position was about sixty-yards due east of the camp. His goal was to drive who ever the culprit was, towards his men. If someone was spying on the camp, they were probably less than twenty-yards away.

While Sergeant Mitsuo was waiting to hear from his men, he tried to visualize again what he had seen of the Americans. Their uniforms were torn and ragged, and they were unkempt in their appearance. Their hair was long, falling almost below their shoulders, and they wore beards. They certainly didn't give the impression of being soldiers by their look. They appeared more like what they were reported as, survivors of a sunken sub. What was there to worry about?

The sergeant's head jerked up when he heard the high-pitched call of a Kingfisher coming from the southeast. A couple of minutes later, he heard the same call from the north. *The men are in position, good. Time to start herding the Americans into the trap and to their deaths.* The sergeant was anxious to spring his trap.

~ ~ ~

Corporal Jackson hadn't moved from his hidden position yet. He was waiting to see what he was up against. So far, it sounded as though maybe one person was out there, but he wasn't positive. One thing he was sure about: whoever it was, they were moving very quietly through the jungle. Then another thought occurred to him. *Could it be the island's inhabitants?* He remembered reading a book about the tribes of lower Africa. *Maybe that's what I'm hearing. One of the islanders sneaking around.* Then a different thought entered his mind. *Is it the Japanese? Could they be sneaking around the jungle this quietly?* Instantly, he recalled what Sergeant Daniels told him. "The Japs are sneaky little bastards, Corporal. One minute all is quiet, and the next minute, you're fighting for your life, wondering where the little rice balls came from."

Jackson sat in the shadows waiting, but he heard nothing else. Everything seemed to have quieted down in the last couple of minutes, but he wasn't about to move. Then, out of nowhere, somewhere off to his left, he heard a high-pitched bird call. *What was that? Was that some kind of bird?*

A couple of minutes went by before he heard the same call again, but this call was almost directly in front of him, and it had him wondering. *Hmm. That didn't sound natural. Someone is definitely out there and is probably doing exactly what I'm doing. Listening, waiting for someone to make a mistake. Could those calls be some sort of signal?* A couple of seconds into his thought, his smile turned cold. Tight-lipped. *Why not? That's what my ancestors did.* A slight noise caught his attention, and again, he heard the soft sound of a plant rubbing up against clothing. The chill he had felt earlier re-emerged, sharpening his focus. Whoever was out there was coming up behind him.

His carbine was leaning up against the tree he was crouching beside, but to grab for it now, would only give his position away. He knew, the minute he touched it, something on it would rattle. *I'll just have to use my knife. Crap on the ground!*

Not the ideal situation to be in. He was only twenty-yards from the enemy camp, and someone was coming up behind him. Startled, his sudden thought had him wondering. *Are they looking for me?* The realization that he was their target was a jolt that sent chills down his back, and immediately seized his full attention. Interrupting his attention, something else caught his interest, the soft crunch from a foot crushing a leaf, and it was only a few feet away. Very slowly the scout reached up to release the thong holding his knife in its scabbard.

~ ~ ~

While Corporal Jackson was getting set to strike at the Japanese, Sergeant Daniels and Corporal Logan were enjoying their freshly brewed coffee. It wasn't the best coffee in the world, but it was hot and strong. Good Marine Corps coffee. The only thing they had to brew the coffee in was a canteen, so he just dumped half a handful of coffee into the canteen of water, and a few minutes after it started boiling, it was done. At least to Sergeant Daniels' satisfaction.

The Marine sergeant watched as Corporal Logan took a swallow of the freshly brewed coffee. Then he noticed the corporal looking into his canteen cup.

"What's the matter? Something land in your coffee?"

Looking up, the corporal struggled hard to remain expressionless, but to no avail. He was slowly losing the battle. "No, I was looking to see if there were any ships floating around in my cup. This coffee's so strong, I believe the U.S. Navy would have no problem sailing in it." Still, he fought the losing cause. The coffee tasted terrible, and he didn't want to start a ruckus by saying something.

"Good. I guess it turned out okay. I was afraid it was weak. I didn't want to give you the wrong impression of the Marine Corps with weak coffee."

"Oh, I don't think that's going to be an issue, Sarge. Your coffee stands Marine Corps proud. Robust enough to float the world's Navy."

The fire was put out right after the coffee was brewed, so the two men were sitting in the dark. Sitting on the side of the ridge where they were, what stars were out, enabled the two men to dimly see each other, at least enough for Sergeant Daniels to see Corporal Logan looking into his cup. Sergeant Daniels was first to notice the quietness of the night. It was too quiet.

"There's something out there, Corporal. Secure your weapon."

"Yeah. I noticed that too."

A few minutes went by before the two warriors heard a soft snicker from their left, and whispered words from their right. "You know, it's rude not to invite your friends for coffee. Don't you think so, Geronimo?"

"Yeah, especially when we haven't had any coffee since we got stranded on this damn island. What are you two doing here?"

Sergeant Daniels was stunned scared when he heard the chief's voice just a few yards away, so his smile was forced when he replied. "We're looking for you. We're here to bring you home."

Absolute silence followed the statement. The two scouts could have been knocked over by a whispered breath had there been one. Still lying prone from their recent deployment, the two men looked up at the scouts for a couple of moments before they stood up. "Hi. I'm Aaron Daniels; he's just an Army brat who goes by the name of David Logan." Reaching down to retrieve his canteen cup, Sergeant Daniels was smiling when he handed the cup to Fox. "Here, this ought to get your juices flowing strong. We got your message, but we were a little busy and couldn't get here any sooner. Sorry for the delay. Are there any more of you?"

The chief stared at the two men while he tried to comprehend what he heard. He remembered the night their world collided with a Japanese Destroyer, and all the events leading to this point. He was still uncertain if all he was seeing and hearing was real, so he reached out and tapped Sergeant Daniels on the shoulder just to make sure. "Wow, this is better than Christmas. Yeah, they're in a cave on that mountain over there. Come on, pack up, you gotta meet the rest of the guys."

When no one moved, the chief cocked his head a little to the right and said; "What are you waiting for? Let's go!"

The little man from Swain County was really excited. When the PBY went down, so went their hopes of ever getting off the island.

"Come on, Sarge, get a move on. Gunny is sure gonna be happy to see you guys."

Sergeant Daniels was looking at the two scouts. "Are you two, Marines? You're wearing navy stuff, so I can't tell. Don't you have a razor?"

"Sarge. We don't have anything left but what we're wearing. Hell, we're even carrying Jap weapons."

Smiling, Corporal Logan came to the rescue. "Throw those antiques away boys; the cavalry is here."

Corporal Logan reached down and picked up two, M1 carbines and handed them to the two scouts, along with a couple of bandoliers of ammo for each man.

"Feel better now?"

Both scouts were beaming as bright as the stars. "Wow," whispered Fox. "This *is* better than Christmas. Come on Sarge, you're wasting time. We have to get back to Gunny."

"Who are you?"

"Oh, sorry, Sarge. I'm PFC David Fox, and he's PFC Jose Bonito, and yeah Sarge, we're Marines."

After the introductions were made, the chief continued his quest to motivate the two men into leaving for the cave. "Come on, Sergeant Daniels, we really need to get moving."

"We can't leave yet, PFC. I still have one man out. We have to wait for him to catch up with us."

"Where is he?" asked Geronimo.

"I don't know, PFC Bonito. He should have already been back."

Corporal Logan was smiling when his whispered words sprang forth. "I wouldn't worry about Corporal Jackson. He knows what he's doing."

"Yeah," whispered Sergeant Daniels. "He says he's one part American and three parts Chicacowa."

Somewhat confused, both scouts looked at Sergeant Daniels. "What's a Chicacowa?" asked the chief. "Is it good to eat? Maybe it's a bean, Jose."

Corporal Logan quietly laughed at the expressions on their faces. "He's part Apache."

Immediately, PFC Bonito understood what the sergeant was trying to say. "Chiricahua, Sergeant Daniels, not whatever you said."

"Sorry," replied Sergeant Daniels. "I knew it was something cahua. I don't know which end is up when it comes to Indians. I only know the Marine Corps. I also know that Corporal Jackson is one sneaky son of a bitch. Sometimes that boy scares me, he's so quiet."

Fox looked over at Bonito and said; "Hey, Jose. Why don't you go back and let Gunny know what's going on. I'll wait here with these guys."

PFC Bonito shook his head and laughed softly before he replied. "Not on your life, little squirrel. I'll wait here while you go tell Gunny. I'm not about to leave an Apache at the mercy of a damn Cherokee."

Both scouts were excited. Anyone could tell by the soft bantering that the two scouts were good friends, despite the insults they threw at each other. But this hadn't always been the case.

When they met for the first time, it was like two male wolves competing for the same female. Hackles raised and fur flew. It even came down to the last man standing, but that little skirmish ended up in a draw and a severe butt chewing from Gunny. After the butt chewing, things settled down somewhat on the outside. The two scouts started working together instead of competing against each other. During their confrontation with a Japanese sergeant, the two Marines started to develop a strong friendship. By the end of their third mission together, the two had become good friends, but neither man would admit it out loud. *That damn Apache. That damn Cherokee.* And now, they were almost inseparable.

Sergeant Daniels stared at the two scouts for a long few seconds until an idea came to mind. "To make it fair, short end of the stick goes back to your cave. Give me a minute to find some twigs." A moment later, he found what he was looking for. "Okay, PFC Bonito. You're closest, so you choose first."

PFC Bonito pulled a twig out of the sergeant's hand and swore. "Damn, it looks like I got the short end of the stick this time."

"Ha! Who's the short one now?"

"You better watch what you say, little squirrel, I'm armed and loaded."

"Oh, I don't think I need to worry about your shooting. You'll aim at me and hit Sergeant Daniels. You can't hit anything unless you have the bore resting up against your target." Turning to face the two newcomers, the chief spewed forth new words of wisdom. "Don't worry guys. Hide behind me and he'll miss all of us."

"You pint-sized shit. I had to show you which end to point down range when we first met." Then the Apache scout turned serious. "Watch your back little fox. Remember. These guys are rookies. Look after them."

Just before he left, Corporal Logan gave the scout the extra carbine Jackson had been carrying, plus the last two bandoliers of ammo. "Hand this to your sergeant, I'm sure he'll appreciate it."

Geronimo walked over to the corporal, stopped beside the man, and put a hand on his shoulder. Leaning in close, the scout spread *his* words of wisdom. "Being that you're army and not a Marine, I figure to give you fair warning. He's a Gunnery Sergeant, and he doesn't like to be called sergeant. Call him Gunny or he'll chew you a new one. He's a tough one, but there's nobody else I'd rather serve with."

Corporal Logan nodded. "It wouldn't be the first time I've been chewed out, but thanks for the warning. Gunny it is."

The Apache scout nodded, produced a lazy two-fingered salute, and then headed north for the mountain hideaway. *Man is Gunny going to be surprised.*

Both scouts had forgotten about the coffee, so when they finally did take a swallow, it was cold, but it sure tasted good to them.

Handing Bonito's cup back to its owner, the chief sat down with the two men and the debriefing began. The session was not the normal military style debrief, it was three men exchanging information, and getting caught up with all that had happened.

"That was quite a show you put on back there, said Corporal Logan. "According to what Corporal Jackson told us, you wiped out almost an entire platoon with your little fireworks demonstration. He said the Japanese were burying around thirty or forty dead. Whose idea was it, and what did you use?"

"Dynamite and airplane fuel. Sergeant Thomas thought up the idea."

"Sounds like an interesting man. Is he at your cave? I'd like to meet him."

Almost as stone-faced as Gunny, the little man had a tight grip on his emotions. "He's dead, Corporal. The Japs caught us by surprise a few minutes after we ambushed one of their units. We were searching the dead for more ammo when they hit us."

"Sorry to hear that."

"Did you hear us when we approached your dead, ash-bed?" The interruption caught both men by surprise. Sergeant Daniels was first to reply. "No. We didn't hear your approach. What caught our attention was the absence of nature's voice. Nothing was stirring around."

"If we had been the Japs, you would have been dead before you had a chance to think anything. We were standing twenty-feet away, right over there, before we split up and came in from the east to make contact. These Japs are pros, Sergeant Daniels. Don't ever let your guard down. If you do, they will chop you to pieces."

Sergeant Daniels stood up, and the chief stood up with him. The two men stared at each other for a long few seconds until Sergeant Daniels shook his head and sat back down. "Damn! Another Jackson!"

"Who's Jackson?" asked the chief.

Smiling carelessly, Corporal Logan responded. "Army scout. Fought in Europe for a while until he decided to come over here to fight Japs. All I know about him is that he is dangerous to the enemy. Can't hear him until it's too late."

"Where is he, now?"

"Just head due south for a little while and then east. Eventually you'll run into the Japanese or Corporal Jackson. Be careful PFC. He won't be expecting any help."

Chapter 24

Corporal Jackson could feel the closeness of his enemy. He couldn't see anyone yet, but he knew his enemy was standing just a few feet away, waiting for him to move. "The kid," however, had no intention of moving. To move now would only get him killed. Again he heard the soft sound of clothing rubbing against a plant. A few seconds went by before he heard someone breathing off to his left. *That Jap is close! Really close!*

A short moment went by, then he watched a shadow moved forward a couple of feet, and then stop. *Man, this guy is good. I can barely hear him moving. Hopefully, he can't smell my sweat.*

The Army scout had smeared the sap of a small, brutally smelling plant on his uniform, hoping the overpowering fragrance of the plant would cover the stench of his sweat. He could hear his adversary sniffing around, and for a minute or so, he waited tensely until he heard the man snort. Very quickly after the snort, the searching enemy quietly moved away from the scout's position. From the sound of his withdraw, he was moving back towards his camp.

Listening intently, the former beanpole from Arizona heard another high pitched call, followed a few seconds later by two such calls. One from the southeast, the other two followed a few seconds later. The first call came from his right. Fifteen-minutes went by before he noticed the nighttime jungle was breathing again; the enemy had stopped moving.

Jackson slowly rose to his feet and grabbed his carbine, wrapping his hand around the bolt. Gently, he picked it up and then headed east about a hundred-yards before he circled around to the north. *Whew, that was close. These Japs are good. No wonder we're having such a hard time beating these guys.*

After another twenty-minutes of slinking about, he was looking at the Japanese camp from the north. There wasn't much to see in the darkness, but the whole camp appeared to be asleep. A sudden movement caught his eye and he spotted a shadow moving off to his right, partially silhouetted against the broken, jungle canopy. Then two more shadows appeared. Like an unexpected fist to the chin, his grasp of the situation was a shock; he was being stalked by his enemies.

Jackson had never been stalked by this enemy before, and the notion almost unnerved him. He had been hunted before, but nothing like this. The Germans were clumsy compared to the Japanese. The Germans blundered their way through the woods, but these Japanese warriors seemed to know what they were doing. Again he was forced to remain absolutely quiet.

For what seemed like an eternity, but it was only about fifteen-minutes, Jackson didn't move a muscle. He waited until he was absolutely sure the shadows had left before he moved north, but he only scurried about thirty or forty-yards to the north. He was irritated at himself for almost getting caught by the enemy, and for his clumsiness in figuring out what his enemy was up to. Also added to all of his displeasure was the aromatic fragrance adhered to his uniform.

Hoping to pick up the shadows again, he cautiously moved towards the west. As much as he didn't want to, he leaned his carbine up against a tree and continued on with just his knife. In this situation, the rifle was too unwieldy, too cumbersome, and too noisy. He needed stealth and quickness to succeed. Pausing for a moment, he got to thinking; *I should catch up with Sergeant Daniels and Corporal Logan. I found the enemy, so why am I still here?* He kept asking that question over and over in his mind, all the while, stalking the shadows he spotted earlier, and sub-consciously thinking: *how good **are** these guys?*

During his cautious move west, he stopped every few feet to listen, hoping to catch some indication that his enemy was near. During one of his listening breaks he heard what sounded like breathing, and then a soft whisper, coming from just a few feet away. Moving to his right, and crouching down, he tried to put his enemy into the little bit of starlight filtering through the trees. After he had moved six or seven feet to his right, he was unexpectedly rewarded with the silhouette of a man. The enemy warrior looked as though he was crouching down, waiting for something. The Army scout smiled knowingly. *I'll bet it's me you're looking for. Well here I come.*

Jackson gripped the handle of his knife with the blade flat against, and under his forearm, with the business edge of the blade facing away from his body. Ever so slowly, he inched his way towards the unsuspecting enemy. He couldn't tell which direction his enemy was looking, so he moved a little more to his right until he saw a reflection from the man's eyes. His adversary was looking up at the stars.

Studying the silhouette, for a moment or two, the Yankee scout nodded his head, thinking to himself; *you won't be able to see me when you look me in the eye. You shouldn't have been looking at the stars.* Out of nowhere, there was an odd sound as Jackson's knife sliced forcefully through the air, followed immediately by another strange sound when his knife struck his enemy at the base his neck, all but decapitating the man. Only the soft sound of air escaping lungs that no longer served a purpose could be heard. The dead man crumpled to the ground almost without making a sound; almost. The fingers on his right hand convulsed one last time and the jungle exploded with the sound of a rifle shot.

Crap on the ground (Jackson's version of intense swearing). He didn't wait around to see what would happen next. He took off running straight for the tree he had leaned his carbine against. He didn't get very far before the jungle erupted with gunfire. The firing started with just a few shots, but within seconds, it sounded as though the whole Japanese army was shooting at him. Bullets were zinging past him like a bunch of angry bees, cutting and shredding the trees and foliage, and at the same time, raining down debris on the scurrying scout.

Jackson made it to the tree his carbine was leaning up against and immediately grabbed for his rifle. He barely had a grip on it, when it was violently knocked out of his hand, the shoulder stock holed by several bullets. *Crap on the ground!*

Still hugging Mother Earth, Jackson felt around for his carbine, found it, and then started low-crawling east as quickly as he could without giving away his position. The firing continued for a few more minutes before it slowly died out. He could still hear the Japanese shouting back and forth, until the yelling died-out altogether. All was quiet for a couple of minutes until the enemy discovered their dead comrade. Immediately, the shouting erupted all over again.

The time to get the hell out of Dodge had arrived. Jackson stood up and immediately felt woozy. Surprised, he discovered he'd been hit several times. Nothing serious, but he was bleeding. *Crap on the ground!*

Searching the jungle around him, his scrutiny didn't stop until he was satisfied the enemy was nowhere near him. When he was convinced of his safety, he hastily looked to himself to see how bad he was hit. That chore didn't take long at all. He just pushed where it hurt the most and viola.

He had a small chunk of meat missing from his calf, which he quickly dressed with part of his shirt, tying off the dressing with some of the string he always carried with him. He never went anywhere without a wad of string somewhere on his person. He was also burned twice on his right hip. *Crap on the ground! I need to find, Lo!*

Within a couple of minutes, he was back on the move again. This time he was heading due north. When he had traveled for about twenty-minutes, he took a break to check on his wounds, and to look at his damaged stock. His wounds had pretty much quit bleeding, but he wasn't sure how long that would last. With all the moving around he had been doing, it was a wonder the bleeding had stopped at all.

His rifle stock was still serviceable, but he had three holes punched through it. *Man was I lucky.* After a ten-minute breather, the beanpole from Arizona was on the move again, heading away from his enemy. He had about three hours left before the sun came up, so he quickly scampered northwest to get clear of that neck of the woods, first, before he made a run for the mountain. The odds were greatly in favor that the enemy was all ready out looking for him. That assumption turned into an accurate assessment, and boy were they mightily disturbed.

Jackson was about two-hundred-yards north of the Japanese camp when he stopped again to check on his wounds. After traveling for almost another hour, he found himself about five-hundred-yards west of the enemy camp and he was beginning to drag his feet. He was slowing down. His wounds had started bleeding again, and they were hurting like the dickens. *Crap on the ground, I need to find a place to hole-up.*

He was ten-minutes into his breather when he suddenly had a feeling he was no longer alone. *Japs? How in the world did they track me here in all this darkness?*

Cautiously, painfully, the Army scout rose to his feet, and then melted into the shadows, waiting. The jungle had gone quiet again; breath-holding quiet. He didn't know if it was because *he* moved, or if it was because someone else was out there. Either way didn't matter to him. He felt as long as he stayed quiet, he should be all right. At least, until the sun came up. Then he would be in some serious trouble.

~ ~ ~

Jackson woke up with a start. He had no idea where he was. Everywhere he looked he saw total darkness. Shaking his head, he realized he must have passed out. He didn't notice the man sitting in the shadows just a couple of feet away. Without an introduction, the shadow spoke. "It's a good thing you don't snore because the Japs were so close they could have pissed all over us and scored a direct hit. So you're the Chicacowa I've been hearing so much about. What happened?"

Jackson stared at the man in the shadows for a minute or so before he spoke. "It's Chiricahua, you feather-head."

The man in the shadow snickered before he replied. "You got that right, but I'm a Cherokee feather-head. What happened? What did you do to piss off the Japanese so much?"

"I killed one of them." replied Jackson. "I guess they didn't like that. Who are you, anyway?"

The man in the shadows hesitated before he answered. "I am PFC David Fox, United States Marine Corps. I'm one of the Marines you came to rescue."

"A leather-head. That explains it."

"It's leatherneck you feather-head. So you killed one of them. It's a wonder your still alive. I heard you stumbling around a mile away. How did you get away from the Japs without getting caught?"

Jackson didn't care too much for Fox at the moment, so he shrugged his shoulders and paused before he replied.

"Lucky, I guess."

"So you're Corporal Jackson. Sergeant Daniels told me about you. He said you were real sneaky for an army brat."

"Yeah, I'm Corporal Tim Jackson, United States Army. I thought the Marines bludgeoned their way through everything and anybody. Why are there Japs still on the island? I would've thought you would have killed them all by now."

PFC Fox stared back at Corporal Jackson. "You kill one Jap, and now you're the know-it-all, man? We've been on this island fighting these bums from day, one. We chase them, and they chase us. But we've managed to whittle them down some."

A smile was forming at the same time the corporal nodded his head. "Yeah, that little fireworks display was great. I saw what was left of them. They were all dead and planted. I must admit, you did a jim-dandy job on those guys."

"You saw them burying their dead?"

"Yeah. I was about ten-yards from the clearing. You really pissed those guys off when you killed all their buddies like that. I tried to decrease their population, but I was only able to get one of them before the bottom fell out. These boys are good in the jungle."

PFC Fox shook his head, remembering the night before. "Yeah, tell me about it. We almost got skewered by a couple of Japs. They were so close to us that night that I could've reached out and shaved them all."

Now that the two men had something in common, their animosity towards each other began to subside.

Jackson shook his head, confused. "You said the Japs were so close to us that they could piss on us and be sure of a hit. How long was I out?"

Smiling, PFC Fox replied. "About five hours."

"Five hours! Then why is it still dark outside?"

"It's not. The sun's been up for almost two hours. We're in a small cave covered with vines. Are you ready to head back to the ridge now?"

"Yeah, I think so." replied Jackson.

After a twenty-minute delay, the two men were on their way to the ridge where Sergeant Daniels and Corporal Logan were still waiting.

PFC Fox was tickled pink. He had an M1 carbine and two bandoliers of ammo. What more could a man want. To be off this damn island. That's what else a man could want. He was like a kid ready to go to the movies, but had to wait for his mother. "Come on Mom. It's time to go."

Jackson, on the other hand, was lost in his new world, the jungle. Everything was so much different than what he was used to. The whole situation was new to him. The jungle, his enemies, his new-found friend.

The chief wanted to know where the enemy was so the two scouts made a detour to the southwest. They found out very quickly where the Japanese were. They were about an hour away from the ridge the little man vacated in his search for the former beanpole from Arizona. Sergeant Daniels and Corporal Logan had left plenty of tracks for the Japanese to follow.

The two men reached the ridge about forty-minutes ahead of the Japanese, only to find no one there. But the little scout did find a trail marker PFC Bonito left behind. Pointing to the clue, he explained to Corporal Jackson how to read the trail markers in case they got separated.

Fox and Jackson arrived by the side entrance to the cave, the hole Gunny had accidently discovered, sometime around 1430 hours. The chief showed him this entrance, just in case, but they didn't use it. Instead, they climbed down the side of the mountain until they reached a tiny hole that was the actual cave entrance.

When PFC Fox entered the cave, he stopped dead in

his tracks, absolutely floored. Everybody was in clean uniforms, but him. Hell, they were even clean shaven, and some of the men had even trimmed their hair. "Little man's" expression was entertaining to everyone.

Bonito arrived shortly after the other two scouts. Even he had on a clean uniform and was clean-shaven, although his hair was still down to his shoulders.

"Gunny, we have a problem. The Japs are on the ridge. If we try to climb down this mountain now, they'll spot us for sure."

"Damn. We need to leave now in order to meet up with that sub tonight. Gentlemen, it looks as though we're stuck on this island for another week. At least, we're wearing Marine Corps uniforms now." Turning his attention to PFC Fox he said; "Chief, what the hell are you doing out of uniform? You need to get yourself squared away."

Chapter 25

Captain Matsui was furious at having to stay behind. Standing at the edge of the jungle, he watched Major Mikawa disappear from sight, and he was a bundle of raging anger, staring a hateful, burning hole in the major's back. *Chikusho*! *Who does that Major think he is coming in here and ruining my plans*?

Lieutenant Nakamura was watching his captain silently fight for control over his barely concealed fury. Standing behind Captain Matsui, he could see the death grip his commander had on his sword, and the whiteness of his finger tips as a result. His left hand had all ready unbuttoned the flap on his holster, yet, he didn't pull his pistol out. He just stood in-place, still as a statue, glaring at the departing troops. Knowing his captain as well as he did, he knew that Captain Matsui wouldn't remain behind for long ... and he was right.

An hour after the major left with Lieutenant Watanabe's platoon, Captain Matsui ordered the headquarters unit to grab what supplies and ammo were left behind and be ready to move out in thirty-minutes. He told the men that Major Mikawa and the platoon were in danger of being destroyed by the Americans, just like Lieutenant Ishida's platoon was destroyed two days prior. "We must quickly catch up to Major Mikawa and warn him of this danger."

"How do you know this?" asked Sergeant Adachi.

Captain Matsui stared at Sergeant Adachi for a moment or two while he swallowed down the urge to draw his sidearm. When the urge had passed, he smiled tightly and said; "You must trust my judgment on this, Sergeant. I have fought against these Yankee dogs for almost six months now. I know how they think. They have already wiped out one platoon, and now they will try to do the same with Lieutenant Watanabe's platoon."

Still not convinced, Sergeant Adachi protested the captain's orders. That was a big mistake. Thirty-minutes after the call to arms, the sixteen-man detachment, including the two officers, left the Japanese base, one man short. Sergeant Adachi was left behind, lying on the ground, dead, a bullet through his forehead. As calmly as a windless night, the captain strode over to Sergeant Adachi, drew his sidearm, and shot him dead while the sergeant was standing at his post, in formation. Nobody in the headquarters unit objected because they were too afraid the same thing would happen to them. Captain Matsui had won the men over with fear and a lie.

~ ~ ~

Watanabe's platoon was not all that hard to follow. For one thing, the major wasn't worried about being followed, so he wasn't concerned about hiding his trail. Their enemy was somewhere out in front of them. In addition, he never dreamed that Captain Matsui would deliberately disobey his orders. What Major Mikawa didn't realize, however, was that Captain Matsui was no longer the proud, Imperial Japanese soldier he had once been ... thanks to PFC Fox.

The man had lost his mind. His insane longing for revenge had overridden his sense of duty to Japan and his emperor. He no longer cared about anything, except the overwhelming desire to kill, to butcher, those Yankee dogs. Even Lieutenant Nakamura was beginning to have doubts about his captain, but that didn't stop him from carrying out his captain's orders.

Before the war, Corporal Hitoshi Aoki was a skilled hunter and a fair tracker. He was a somewhat good soldier, but a little afraid of Captain Matsui. When the captain asked who could track, he let his presence be known. He didn't want to take the chance of not saying anything and then have someone suddenly remember that he could track. He didn't want to end up like Sergeant Adachi, dead.

"Get out front, Corporal, and keep us on track. You report only to me. Is that understood?"

Corporal Aoki bowed. "Yes, Captain."

The corporal was about twenty to thirty-yards in front of the detachment. He could see the trail left by the platoon without any problem, but that wasn't what was bothering him. He was more concerned about being shot in the back by that insane captain. *He has to be a lunatic to disobey a direct order from a superior officer, especially Major Mikawa.* The corporal was also having thoughts of running into the jungle, just to get away from Captain Matsui, but he didn't have the guts to take off into the jungle alone, so he resigned himself to whatever fate his gods handed him.

During their march, Captain Matsui kept thinking about how he was going to eliminate the major without bringing suspicion on himself. A difficult task at best, but necessary in order to achieve his greatest desire; watching American heads hit the ground before their bodies. *How do I get away with murder*? *How do I succeed*? He had been thinking so hard in trying to hatch a foolproof plan that he failed to notice that Corporal Aoki had stopped. Captain Matsui was irritated at the interruption of his thoughts.

"What is it, Corporal? Why have we stopped?"

"Major Mikawa stopped here for a short break, sir. I think we are gaining on him. Do you want me to continue on?"

The captain's irritation showed in the way he answered the corporal. "Yes, you fool. When I want to stop, I'll tell you. Now get out there and do what you are told, or you'll end up like that fool of a sergeant."

Corporal Aoki immediately did what he was told.

Forty-minutes into their quest, the corporal came across another one of the major's rest stops, and again he told Captain Matsui about it. This time, though, he didn't linger; he started following the trail again, right after he gave his report. *This man is insane!* Out of nowhere, a feeling of doom settled over him. He had a sudden notion that he didn't have long to live.

It came as no surprise to Captain Matsui that the major was stopping about every thirty or forty-minutes. *Major Mikawa is soft. He has spent too much time parading around in his polished boots and not enough time going out into the field. He is fat and lazy, out of shape. Of course, he is. He spent all his time kissing General Sasaki's boots.*

Captain Matsui reluctantly called a halt for the night just as the sun was setting. It was getting too dark to see the tracks, and he didn't want that fool of a corporal to lose the major's trail.

His fury contained for the moment, the captain was still trying to figure out how to eliminate Major Mikawa, and take over command. No fire was lit in case the major was closer than expected, however, even that precaution couldn't assuage his concern about being discovered accidentally, before he could carry out his task. To convince his troops that all was not well, he told his men that the enemy was close by, and he didn't want to give away their position.

Sitting in his tent, alone in the darkness, Captain Matsui still hadn't come up with a plan to get rid of Major Mikawa. He was racking his brain, deep in thought, when Lieutenant Nakamura interrupted him.

"What is it, Lieutenant? I thought I told you I didn't want to be disturbed."

Lieutenant Nakamura noticed for the first time the malicious tone in his captain's voice. "Yes, sir. You did tell me that, but I think I spotted the major's fire, Captain. It's about one-hundred-yards north of us."

Captain Matsui's head came up sharply. "You think you have spotted the major's fire?"

"Yes, Captain. Come, I will show you."

An idea began forming in Captain Matsui's mind. "Does anyone else know about this? Has anyone else seen this fire?"

Lieutenant Nakamura had a strange, uneasy feeling come over him, but he shrugged it off as being tired. "No, Captain, not that I'm aware of. At least, no one has brought it to my attention, yet."

"Good! Let's keep this between you and me. Understood, Lieutenant? Only you and I are to know about this."

Captain Matsui followed Lieutenant Nakamura out into the jungle for about thirty-yards and then stopped. The lieutenant pointed off to the northwest, but Captain Matsui was unable to see the fire. It wasn't until he moved a couple of feet to his right that he finally saw the fire through the jungle foliage. For some reason, which he couldn't figure out, he was suddenly excited. Then it hit him. The perfect plan. Smiling to himself, the two commanders headed back to camp. *At last, I have thought of a way. Tonight, Major. You will die!*

~ ~ ~

Slipping quietly away from camp, Captain Matsui moved cautiously through the jungle, looking to locate the major's tent. His intent was to come back later and kill the officer in his sleep. The captain's envisioned scenario had him itching for the kill. *In all the excitement, I could say I saw the Americans running from the major's camp after they shot and killed him. Yes, yes, this will work. And if someone questions why I was out in the jungle at that particular time I could tell them I was out relieving myself when the Americans killed the major. No one will doubt my word. Why would a captain of His Imperial Majesty's troops kill a fellow officer?*

The more he thought about the situation, the more excited he became. He was almost giddy over the imagined results. His only uncertainty was Sergeant Takagi. The sergeant was a festering thorn of doubt that wouldn't leave him alone. While he was brooding over that dilemma the captain's thoughts turned even darker. *Maybe I should kill him, as well.* Pausing to consider the addition to his scheme, he stared off towards the major's camp until he smiled and nodded his head. *Hmm, not a bad idea.*

An hour after his scout, Captain Matsui was back in his tent, staring down at his pallet where Sergeant Adachi's rifle was patiently waiting. Then he smiled. *It's a good thing I grabbed Sergeant Adachi's rifle. After I kill the major and Sergeant Takagi, I can throw the rifle to the ground, and maybe, just maybe, Lieutenant Watanabe's men will think the Americans dropped it in their haste to make good their escape.* Immediately, his smile left his face. *No, the men saw me leave the compound with Sergeant Adachis' rifle. If I throw it away, how will I explain it being gone?* Once again, he was deep in thought.

By 2330 hours, Captain Matsui's camp was sound asleep. Just a little past 0045 hours, he was sneaking his way past the sentries and on his way back to the major's encampment. He found out on his first trip exactly where the major's tent was, so all he had to do now, was figure out a way to kill him quietly inside his tent. Or better yet, lure him outside the tent and then shoot him dead.

His slithering journey to the major's camp took him forty-minutes. Staring out of the shadows, he crouched down, about ten-yards from Major Mikawa's tent.

As he was reaching for his knife, the captain abruptly stopped and stared at a new, and unexpected danger. His eyes narrowed, and for a moment, he almost lost control of his anger. There was Sergeant Takagi, standing on the far side of the camp. Immediately, all thoughts of his original idea, disappeared, and his smile turned malicious. Moving quietly to his right, he reached for his rifle that was leaning against a tree, and then he moved back another ten-yards before he took a bead on Sergeant Takagi.

While he was aiming at Sergeant Takagi, he decided to move back, another ten to fifteen-yards, just to give himself a little more distance from the camp. His sudden change of position also gave him a better chance of escaping without being seen. When he was in position, with a clear line of sight, he drew in a deep breath and slowly exhaled. His malicious smile of satisfaction was growing larger, as he slowly squeezed the trigger.

Crack!

The shot rang out sharp and loud in the quietness of the jungle night, and Sergeant Takagi was slammed to the ground from the impact of the bullet. Those who were sleeping immediately rose up from their pallets with their weapons ready for battle. Chaos was in command of the base-camp for the moment, so the encampment was rowdy with shouting soldiers. "Sergeant Takagi has been shot! Quick, he needs help!"

Major Mikawa came rushing out of his tent, demanding to know what was going on, and at the same time, Captain Matsui took aim.

Crack! Another shot rang out, and Major Mikawa slumped to the ground. Several more shots rang out, and immediately, everyone in the camp hit the ground, and then there was silence. One of the soldiers heard what sounded like someone running, just north of the camp and gave a shout to arms. The crashing sound was actually Captain Matsui's rather large stick hitting the ground north of the camp. It was meant to throw off any pursuit in his direction.

Panic and chaos left the Japanese reacting instead of thinking.

While Mikawa's men were focusing their attention to the north, Captain Matsui's escape to the south went unobserved and unhindered, so he made it close enough back to his camp for his alibi to work. He had barely finished reloading when he heard someone running towards him. Quickly, he started firing into the jungle. Crack! Crack! Crack!

The running man turned out to be Lieutenant Nakamura. The two officers were about twenty-yards from their camp, and of course, the entire encampment was awake and shouting.

Lieutenant Nakamura could see the excitement in his captain's eyes. "What are you shooting at, Captain?"

Captain Matsui was somewhat out of breath. "Lieutenant, did you see three men running by here? I think they were the Americans, and I think they just shot at the major's camp!"

"No, Captain, I didn't see anybody. Are you all right?"

"Yes, Lieutenant, I am fine. At least, I was able to get off some shots at them, but I don't think I hit any of them."

The two officers could hear the shouting going on in the other camp. Something had definitely happened over there.

"Calm the men down, Lieutenant Nakamura, and get them ready for battle. We will wait here until we hear from Major Mikawa."

Lieutenant Nakamura looked at Captain Matsui for a second or two and then he went back to camp to settle the men down. The troops of the fifteen-man detachment were part of, what remained of, Major Mikawa's battalion.

The battalion had lost over two thirds of their strength due to air attacks. The same thing had happened to 3rd company while they were marching to the southern base.

All that was left of the battalion, one reinforced platoon, was out in the jungle, looking for the Americans. And now this attack. It was a definite shock to the fifteen-man detachment. Their battalion commander, Major Mikawa, had just been attacked, and they were a bit concerned. The men wanted to know what had happened, but with the threat of an attack imminent, they settled down quickly and prepared for battle.

Lieutenant Nakamura was watching his captain a little more closely now. It seemed just a little odd that he appeared to be coming from the direction of the major's camp, right after the shots were fired. The senior lieutenant did not question his captain's story, but it still seemed a bit strange that his captain would be out in the jungle at that particular time, relieving himself.

Captain Matsui was jumping for joy inside, but on the outside he was stone-faced and quiet. The deed was done. He had accomplished what he set out to do. He had removed Major Mikawa from the playing field, and at the same time, he had removed the threat of exposure when he killed Sergeant Takagi. *All is done. I will wait until I hear word that Major Mikawa is dead before I assume command. I don't want to appear to be too eager to take over. I must appear somewhat reluctant.* His next thought was of Sergeant Takagi, and it was festering into deep concern the second it came to mind. *Why was he in Major Mikawa's camp?*

The thought never entered his mind that the sergeant was actually where he should have been; with Lieutenant Watanabe's platoon. His hatred for the sergeant was like a raging fever burning through his mind, and all coherent thought left in its wake.

Before the sun was an hour up, both camps had merged as one. The burial detail was just putting the finishing touches on Major Mikawa's grave, and Captain

Matsui was watching Sergeant Takagi out of the corner of his eye. The sergeant's left arm was bandaged tightly against his chest, and his left shoulder was also bandaged tightly. The bullet had missed its mark by several inches, a testament to the marksmanship of the Japanese military of the time. But not all Japanese were lousy shots. Thousands of dead Marines could attest to that fact. A brutal and bloody fact.

Most of the men in the platoon were Lieutenant Nakamura's men, so there would be no problem taking over command. If there was a problem, then it would come from Lieutenant Watanabe and the few men he had left. The fact that Sergeant Takagi was still alive irritated Captain Matsui to no end. He was completely loyal to Lieutenant Watanabe; so therefore, the veteran sergeant needed to be watched closely.

Sergeant Takagi was relieved of his scout duties, and Corporal Aoki was put in his place. The corporal was a bit more manageable than Sergeant Takagi was. Besides, the sergeant was wounded. He didn't need to be further burdened with the strenuous duties of being a scout. And with Sergeant Takagi no longer out in front, he was much easier to keep an eye on. One other adjustment occurred after Captain Matsui took over command of the platoon. Lieutenant Watanabe was relieved of his command and was replaced by Lieutenant Nakamura. Why keep in positions of power, those who oppose?

~ ~ ~

Lieutenant Hashimoto's platoon was a little more than a day and a half ahead of Captain Matsui's detachment. Hashimoto's forces had reached the ridge Sergeant Daniels' brewed his coffee on, just a little after sunrise, but he kept his men below the crest, on the reverse-side of the ridge, hidden, until his platoon sergeant had a chance to scout out the area.

Sergeant Mitsuo was crouching in the same flat spot where Sergeant Daniels and Corporal Logan had been. He was studying the ground, somewhat confused. The Japanese had been chasing three men all through the day before, but the tracks where he was crouching were showing that only two men were on the ridge the night before. *Where is the other American?* He wondered.

Sergeant Mitsuo stood up and slowly inched his way north along the top of the ridge, searching the ground for answers until he noticed that the two Americans were now four in number. While he was bent over, studying the new set of tracks, something kept nagging at him. Something he should be seeing, but was not, and his ignorance had him shaking his head, greatly annoyed. *What am I not seeing? What is not registering in my mind?* This perplexing problem he was trying to solve was raging through his mind without letup. *What is it I don't see?*

Angry at himself for being so foolish, he stood up and paced back and forth, not once looking down at the tracks. His pacing lasted only a couple of minutes before he couldn't stand it anymore. Throwing his hands in the air, he returned to stare at the tracks again. His frustration and the bewildering dilemma continued to bother him for another ten-minutes before he finally shook his head in disgust. Something was bothering him about the tracks, but he just couldn't put a finger on it. Exasperated, he climbed back down to where Lieutenant Hashimoto was waiting for him.

"Lieutenant Hashimoto, we are now chasing four Americans instead of three. Their tracks show they are heading towards the mountain that is due north of us. But there is something about their tracks that has me confused, and I haven't been able to figure out the puzzle yet."

Smiling, Lieutenant Hashimoto said; "Don't worry Sergeant Mitsuo, you'll solve your dilemma. You may take a while, but in the end, you'll figure it out. You always do."

Sergeant Mitsuo could only shake his head. "Your confidence in me is reassuring. I am ready to go if you are."

Instead of silhouetting themselves on the top of the ridge, for all to see, Lieutenant Hashimoto decided to keep his men hidden below the ridge, until they were eventually forced by the terrain to come out into the open. By that time, the Japanese would be on the south side of the mountain at its base.

Corporal Takahashi was having trouble with his boots. They were hurting his feet. Stupidly, he decided to requisition new boots just before his unit marched south with Major Mikawa. He was still paying for that mistake. He should have kept his old boots to march around in, so he could slowly break in his new boots until they were ready to wear full time.

Laughing, Sergeant Mitsuo watched his corporal massage a sore foot during one of their breaks and said; "Hiraku, you should know better than to wear new boots on an extended march like this one. Maybe next time you won't be so..." Sergeant Mitsuo stopped mid-sentence and stared intently at his corporal's foot for a stunned moment before shouting; That's it! How could I be so stupid!"

Immediately, he walked over to his platoon leader. "Lieutenant Hashimoto. I have cleared the confusion from my mind. There are four Americans and four separate pairs of tracks. Two pairs show worn out soles. The other two pairs of tracks show much newer soles. I believe, Lieutenant, that the Americans have landed more men on the island, and they are somewhere on that mountain."

The veteran platoon sergeant immediately had his platoon leader's complete attention. "Are you sure, Kiyoshi?"

"Lieutenant, the only other explanation I can think of would be an air supply drop. But surely the allies wouldn't be dropping boots down to the Americans. It would be more efficient to drop freshly supplied troops. No, Lieutenant. I believe strongly that the Americans have put more men on the island."

Lieutenant Hashimoto looked at his sergeant. "You may be right, Kiyoshi. That might explain how the Americans came up with the explosives that killed Takeo and his platoon. Hmm. I wonder ... How many Americans do you remember seeing at the ambush site?"

The platoon sergeant thought about the question for a minute or so before he answered. "I think I saw five, counting the one we killed."

"Did they look like soldiers to you?"

"No, Lieutenant. They looked more like shipwreck survivors. Everything about them looked worn and ragged. Even their boots looked worn out."

Lieutenant Hashimoto smiled at his sergeant. "Then how were they able to receive a supply drop? Worn and ragged tells me the Americans are alone, with no outside help, or they would be better equipped. I believe your assessment of the situation is correct, Kiyoshi. The Americans have landed more men on the island."

~ ~ ~

PFC Fox and Corporal Jackson were standing in the middle of the cave, listening to the rest of guys laugh at the chief's indescribable expression. The fun lasted less than a minute because Sergeant Stamper was handing the chief the last of the fresh uniforms. Gunny was the first to break up the laughter when he turned to the little scout and said; "Get cleaned up and shaved. Come back looking like a Marine, or don't come back at all."

An hour passed, and Fox was back in the main cave, his face bleeding from the many nicks he gave himself from shaving, and looking more or less like a Marine in serious need of a haircut.

Staring at each other, the men of Baker squad were chomping at the bit to get moving down the mountain. A new excitement was taking over the squad, and it was festering fast. Just hours away was their freedom, their ride home. Yet, before they could leave the island behind forever, they had one last military ritual to perform, a long standing military tradition; they had to *hurry up and wait* for the sun to go down.

While the cave dwellers were waiting for the sun to go down, mutiny broke out. PFC Fox was refusing to leave the cave by using the back entrance on the grounds that his bright, shiny, new uniform would get all muddy.

"I've only been wearing the thing for a couple minutes, Gunny. If I go out the back entrance, it'll get muddy."

Gunny, being the compassionate gunnery sergeant that he was, gave PFC Fox an extra ten-minutes to enjoy his fresh uniform ... And as he said; "If you're not heading out of the back door, one second after the ten-minute bell, I promise you, I will bury you up to your neck in the foulest smelling muck I can find."

Smiling, Corporal Logan thought the gunnery sergeant was joking around, so he immediately provided some important intel on the subject. Not being around Gunny for very long, the corporal wasn't aware that "Deadeye" didn't bluff. When he said he was going to do something, it happened; no matter how rank the smell was.

"Gunny, I do believe I know exactly where to find that foul smelling muck. It's about a half a mile southeast of the ridge we were on last night. That marsh would put a week old latrine to shame."

PFC Fox shook his head. "Thanks a lot Corporal." Disgusted, the little scout from the Carolinas turned around and headed for the back end of the cave, followed by Corporal Jackson and PFC Bonito.

"Might as well get this over with," he said. "At least it was clean for a little while."

Chapter 26

Lieutenant Hashimoto positioned his men just below the crest, at the northern most point of the ridge, overlooking the mountain. An immensely imposing chunk of real-estate, it looked even more so from where they were standing. The Mountain stood over 5,000 feet high, and its long axis stretched for over fifteen miles.

The southwestern corner of the mountain was not a peak. It was actually a thick, jungle-infested plateau, with the tangled terrain ending about 300 feet from its western edge. The distance was a little over 600 feet from the base of the mountain to the top of the plateau. The long axis of the plateau was about two and a half miles, with the short axis just a little over a mile and a half deep. Fifty feet, directly below the western edge, about midway across the long axis of the plateau, was a small ledge extending out about four feet. Less than a yard above this ledge was a small hole, barely wide enough for a 160lb man to skinny through. The hole was the west side entrance to the cave. A person had to be directly facing the hole in order to see it. From where the Japanese were standing, it was completely hidden from view.

The back entrance to the cave was about thirty-yards inside the jungle, hidden between two large tentacle-like roots. The hole itself was covered by vines. In fact, the whole tree, roots and all, was covered by vines, making it look like solid ground. Gunny didn't know there was a hole where he was stepping until it was much too late.

The hole dropped twenty-feet before it started curving like a very lazy J for about a hundred-feet, and leveling out, a few feet in front of the pool of water. The walls and floor of the hole were constantly in a mud-state. If anyone fell into the hole, the chance of breaking any bones was very minimal. A few bumps and bruises along the way, but nothing serious. Getting back up through the hole was a different story altogether. That's where the thirty-feet of vine came in. Without it, getting out that way was impossible.

The climb out of the back entrance took the three scouts almost thirty-minutes to accomplish. When they emerged from the hole, they resembled three huge mud-cycles; the chief's fresh uniform was no longer OD green, and he was gazing at Corporal Jackson, somewhat bewildered.

About one-hundred-feet north of the hole was a stone basin with enough water in it to rinse themselves off. This basin was their first source of fresh water until they discovered a smaller version in one of the side tunnels. The larger stone basin on top of the plateau spilled over after hard rains and ran along a trough cut through the jungle straight into the hole, where it flowed through the cave and out through a small hole; the west side cave entrance.

So far the Marines had not experienced the same rush of water through the cave they had experienced on their third mission. During that particular episode, the water roared through their cave so hard, they were almost washed out and dumped thirty feet below onto some rocks.

The back entrance to the cave was well hidden, but it definitely had a drawback, the mud they had to climb through to get out of the hole. It wasn't so bad for the men, but it was pure murder on their weapons. Once they made it out of the hole, they had to field-strip and clean their weapons and wipe down their ammo, necessary tasks that took some time to do. Still, from start to finish, going out through the hole was faster and safer than climbing up the west side of the mountain, despite having to stop and clean their weapons.

After another thirty-minute cleaning session, the three scouts were on their way south. Their mission was to locate the Japanese, see what they were up to, and report back to Gunny what they had found out. Their orders were explicit. "Do not engage. Just do what you're told and get back to the cave."

"Corporal Jackson, you're in charge. Make sure they follow my orders to the letter."

"Yes, sir, Gunny. I will, sir."

Everyone could hear Fox and Bonito snickering as they moved towards the rear of the cave. They were waiting for the massive thunder storm they thought was about to hit Corporal Jackson for calling Gunny, "Sir." When the thunder storm failed to happen, the two Marine scouts stopped their snickering, but they could still be heard whispering, even as far back in the cave as they were.

"Geez, Gunny must be getting soft. Corporal, I can't believe you're still walking. Don't ever call him sir. Never!"

"Yeah," whispered Bonito. "He's a hard-ass when it comes to addressing rank."

"I heard that, you two," said Gunny.

The two Marine scouts looked at each other for a moment while Jackson started up the vine first. "Damn, Jose. There's nothing wrong with *his* hearing. I bet he heard every word we said."

"I think you're right, little squirrel. Now shimmy on up, so I can get out of here. This place stinks."

~ ~ ~

Sergeant Mitsuo, and two of his three corporals were out searching the west side of the ridge, looking for a trail to follow. The platoon sergeant lost the enemy's trail about a third of the way down the ridge. Now, they had no idea where their enemy went from there. The search was an exhausting one, climbing up and down the ridge, exhausting, and also frustrating to the enemy scouts, but they didn't quit. Their search continued until the setting sun forced them to stop. Still, nothing had been found.

Lieutenant Hashimoto had set up camp on the east side of the ridge, at its base, about two-hundred-feet from its most northern point. The location was a good place to set up camp because the reflection of the fire couldn't be seen from the west except from the top of the ridge. As far as the Japanese were aware, their enemy was west of them.

The three, exhausted, scouts made it back to camp just as the sun dipped below the horizon. They immediately reported to Lieutenant Hashimoto their failure to find any tracks and shortly after, were leaning up against a tree sound asleep, and dreaming of better places.

Lieutenant Hashimoto had a decision to make. *Do I continue with the search, possibly wasting more time, or do I head across the mountain in hopes of finding the enemy?*

Returning to base was eliminated right off the bat. He was not about to call off the search. The American dogs they were chasing were responsible for putting Lieutenant Ishida and his platoon six feet under. The avenging lieutenant had no doubt in his mind that the Yankees were going to pay with their lives. Only time could throw a wrench into his plans, now. All he had to do was figure out which of the first two options he was going to choose.

~ ~ ~

Captain Matsui was now only a little more than a half a day behind Lieutenant Hashimoto. After Lieutenant Watanabe had been relieved of his command, the junior lieutenant saw no sense in remaining at the head of the platoon, so now he was walking at the rear of the formation. The position he now found himself in was not one he desired, but at least he didn't have to worry about getting shot in the back by a raving captain.

Like Lieutenant Nakamura, he thought it strange that Captain Matsui would be in the jungle at the same time Major Mikawa's camp was attacked. He also thought it strange that both the major and Sergeant Takagi had been shot. *Why wasn't anyone else shot? Why were they the only men targeted?* General Sasaki's nephew was baffled only because he didn't know the truth. He did, however have his own theory, and coincidence didn't belong in his puzzle. Major Mikawa and Sergeant Takagi both had run-ins with Captain Matsui, and both had been shot. Sergeant Takagi had been lucky, but Major Mikawa was dead. Now Captain Matsui was back in command of the unit. A stroke of luck? Fate? Lieutenant Watanabe didn't think so. More like designed scheme in his eyes.

~ ~ ~

The three scouts had no idea there was another enemy platoon closing in on them. The Americans only knew of Lieutenant Hashimoto's platoon, so that was the platoon the three scouts were looking for. Gunny didn't want to leave the cave until he knew where the Japanese were. The man in charge didn't want to take the chance of being spotted by the enemy while his men were climbing down the mountain. If they were spotted, then the squad would really be in trouble. They would be forced to fight an enemy that held the high, high ground.

Corporal Jackson smelled the smoke first. The three scouts were crouched down in the jungle, trying to discover which direction it was coming from. PFC Fox decided to climb a tree to see if he could spot some smoke. His venture up the tree didn't help in that regard, but he did see a faint glow off to the northwest, so off they went. A couple of hours of sneaking quietly through the jungle rewarded the scouts with the discovery of Lieutenant Hashimoto's camp. The time was around 1930 hours when they found the enemy camp. Once they were satisfied that the Japanese were staying the night, they headed back to the cave. Their silent scamper back to the cave took the three scouts a few hours, but they finally gave their report to Gunny sometime around 0240 hours.

"Are you sure they're done for the night?"

"Yeah, Gunny. They have guards posted, and the rest were snoring a six-part harmony."

"What do you think, Sergeant Stamper? We missed our first appointment because the Japs had us pinned down in this damn cave. They're sound asleep, now, and the sun won't be up for at least, another four hours. If we leave now, we could be halfway down before sunup. By the time they're up and moving about, there's a chance we could be so far down the mountain they won't see us. I don't like the odds, but I think we can make it."

"Tell me, Al. You plan on leading the Japs to the sub? I don't think there's enough room for them and us."

For a moment the Oklahoma gunnery sergeant stood stone-faced and silent, staring at his friend; devoid of all thought. Still gazing intently at his friend, he finally replied. "Roger, I think I'm going to leave your words of wisdom with you, the rest of us are leaving now. Why don't you stay behind and apologize to the Japanese for not having enough room on the sub to take them along?"

Turning to face the squad, the man dubbed "Deadeye" was having a difficult time maintaining a straight facial expression. "All right gentlemen, Army, pack it up and let's get off this mountain."

After a five-minute rush to gather equipment and essentials, the men were shoving their stuff out through the small cave entrance. When the final equipment check was completed, they took a deep breath and moved off, down the mountain.

The going was tough enough with the sun shining, but in the dead of night it was even worse. The Americans were slipping and sliding almost uncontrollably. If not for the trees and vines, they would have made the six-hundred-foot descent in less than a minute.

The Baker Boys were only halfway down the mountain when the sun started poking its head above the horizon.

"Gunny, there's movement on top of the ridge."

Gunny turned to stare up at the top of the ridge from the small ledge they were resting on. After about a minute or so, he turned his gaze back to Corporal Jackson. All he could do was shake his head. *I must be going blind. I can barely see this kid, so how does he expect me to see movement on the ridge?*

"Hey, Roger. Am I getting old?"

Sergeant Stamper never passed up an opportunity to twist his friend's tail. "Al, you're so old you make old look young."

Laughing, Gunny shook his head before replying. "I should have known better that to ask a smartass a dumb question." Then he turned back to Corporal Jackson. "Are you sure you saw movement on that ridge?"

"Yes, sir, Gunny. I saw a silhouette of something man size. Then it was gone. Do they have bears on this island?"

Gunny looked at Corporal Jackson for a moment, somewhat incredulous, and no longer stone-faced. *Bears? Is this kid for real?* Still shaking his head, he turned to his lead scout. "Chief, take the kid here and head back up the hill. Find out what the Japs are up to. We'll meet you at the bottom."

PFC Fox was stunned. "Back up the hill? You've got to be kidding me! This is no hill, it's a damn mountain!" The expression on his face was hard to see in the dark, but it was still visible. The chief's eyes were wide, and his mouth was open. "You've got to be kidding me!"

Gunny just stared at the little scout, not saying a word, but his eyes said, "Move it Marine!"

Shaking his head, PFC Fox let out a groan and started up the mountain. The two scouts had barely climbed sixty-feet when they heard Gunny whisper. "Hey chief. Why don't you take a twenty-minute break? Who knows? Maybe the Japs will meet you halfway, so you won't have to climb so far. You're not tired, are you? My grandmother moves faster than you."

Even at that distance, PFC Fox could see the grin on Gunny's face. Both men looked down at the man in charge and shook their heads. Disgusted, the chief waved Gunny off, and then they continued their climb. Twenty-minutes into their climb, the two men were unexpectedly brought under fire. The ridge was loaded with Japanese, and they could see the two scouts plainly. The sun was up and at the enemy's back.

After spending a couple of minutes dodging bullets, PFC Fox decided he had seen enough. "Yep, the shooters are definitely Japs. Time to head back. Let's go, Corporal. We're moving down hill." *Boy am I in trouble. Gunny's not going to believe this is not my fault.*

Past experience told a startling story. Every time the Japanese started shooting it was because PFC Fox did something to rile them up. Gunny carried that thought. Sergeant Stamper had that theory, as well. Hell, everyone in the squad nourished that same notion. Most of the time the run-in was accidental, but the fact remained that when the Japanese started shooting, bets could be placed with no takers, that the enemy was shooting at PFC Fox.

Not again.. That kid can't do anything without getting shot at? "Damn, Roger. The Japs seem drawn to him like a magnet. Maybe we should leave him at home when we go on our next mission." *Our next mission? Hell, we have to get out of this mess first.* Gunny was still shaking his head when they started down the mountain again.

~ ~ ~

At the speed the two men were running down the mountain, they could have caught up to Gunny in only a couple of minutes. The Japanese were still firing, but they were firing blindly. Half were on the ridge-top firing into the jungle while the rest were climbing down the mountain pursuing the Marines. The shooters didn't hit anything, but the added fire support sure felt good to those climbing down the mountain. Within a few minutes, however, the squad on top of the ridge quit firing, and they too, were climbing down, chasing after the fleeing Americans.

The two scouts were running neck and neck, and PFC Fox was excited. There was something about running in the woods that really started his heart pumping. Back in the States, he couldn't get enough of it, but out here in the Pacific, he was getting all he could handle, and more. He was amazed at how fast they were running *down a mountain*. When that thought entered his brain for the second time his excitement soared and overruled his concentration, and bam, down he went, chest first.

Corporal Jackson saw the little scout flying through the air and started laughing, so hard his concentration was distracted as well. His flight to Earth was a little harsher. The chief found him after a quick, five-minute search. Corporal Jackson was spread-eagle on the ground, face first, out cold. He looked ... dead.

PFC Fox was bending over to check if Jackson was still breathing. He was worried because the man really looked ... dead. Just as he turned Jackson onto his back, the former beanpole from Arizona immediately came to life and shouted, "*BOO!*" The chief sprang backwards so fast that he would have put a started cat's reaction to shame. He was surprised, shocked, and then angry.

He was surprised that Corporal Jackson even thought of pulling off a gag in their present situation. He was also shocked that the corporal was actually successful in his endeavor, and *the-fox* was blowing out steam, greatly agitated because he didn't think of it first.

Finally paying attention to what was going on around them, the two scouts heard the Japanese blundering down the mountain. That's the only way to describe the climb down. That's how the Baker Boys did it.

"You done wasting time? Your little stunt allowed the Japs to close the distance on us."

Corporal Jackson was grinning when he painfully grasped some of the little man's hair between his two fingers and said; "Yeah, but look at the gray hair I just put on your head."

Jackson's grin was huge. *This is almost like old times back in Europe.* Then the bullets started ripping through the jungle growth.

"Let's go. Follow me." Immediately, PFC Fox took off heading northwest. The chief's sudden plan was to draw off as many Japanese troops as he could, and then lose them somewhere on the other side of the mountain. His aim was to buy Gunny the time he needed to reach the weapons' cache. A re-armed Marine was a power to behold. A re-armed Baker squad was dangerously more so.

The two men moved about sixty-yards north of their previous position, and then quite unexpectedly, PFC Fox stood up tall and started firing. Immediately, everything in the jungle started snapping, crackling, and popping from the enemy return fire. Corporal Jackson looked at PFC Fox. "What are you doing? We're supposed to kill the enemy, not get killed by them. Are you nuts?"

Ducking and snickering, PFC Fox replied; "I'm drawing them away from Gunny to give him time to reach the weapons. Do you think you can out flank the Japs? Hit them from a different direction?" Corporal Jackson's grin gave the chief his silent answer. But first, the two scouts had to convince their enemy to chase them, so they opened fire.

Within seconds, the Japanese troops responded to the invitation by laying down a hot and heavy fire, aimed directly at the two scouts.

Everything growing four-feet above the jungle floor was getting shredded, and the debris was raining down on the two scouts. For the first thirty seconds, the shooting was intense, only lessening slightly when the two scouts stopped firing. The Japanese, however, didn't stop. They continued shooting for about a minute or so before their platoon leader realized no one was shooting at them anymore. Hell had been raised by the two scouts, but hell was still waiting for its payment of death; and hell's payment wasn't long in coming.

The time the enemy wasted shooting at nothing allowed the two men time to move to a new position, and continue the draw-on. Slowly the Japanese were turning their attention towards PFC Fox and Corporal Jackson. The immediate threat to their rear couldn't be ignored.

The enemy was losing men. They had to go after the two Americans now, or by the time they did catch up to Gunny, there would be none of them left. Sergeant Mitsuo understood this fact, and so did Lieutenant Hashimoto, so the order was given; "Kill these Yankees first, and then hunt down and kill the rest."

The Japanese had to kill the two Americans first; they could not leave an enemy at their rear. If they ignored that threat and continued their chase, they were at risk of being destroyed; by just two Americans.

Chapter 27

Twice, Lieutenant Hashimoto had tried to break-off from the fight and go after Gunny, but both times the scouts were in a position that forced him to stop his maneuver and fight back. Along with the nasty jungle terrain the men had to contend with, the mid-day sun was also being a bully, sapping everyone's strength to press on. Yet, for hours, the Japanese leaders kept maneuvering their men through the stifling heat and humidity, trying to catch their enemy in a crossfire. Still, the two Americans were not caught yet, and Lieutenant Hashimoto had another dangerous decision to make.

"Corporal Takahashi, you will take your squad and kill the two Yankees. I will take the rest of the platoon and hunt down the other Americans."

The weapons and equipment check lasted for about two minutes, the farewells and splitting-up of forces took a minute longer. After last minute goodbyes, the two forces wished each other luck, then both went their separate ways.

Corporal Takahashi knew what kind of mission he was about to go on. He was facing two very dangerous adversaries. He knew he would lose men. His men knew this as well, and they had all, readily accepted their fate. His squad had been handed an extremely important and dangerous assignment, and they were all determined to succeed or die trying. The corporal's secondary mission was to still be alive when the last American lay dead on the ground.

~ ~ ~

Smiling, Corporal Jackson whispered his inspiration to Fox, hoping to entice the chief into thinking his way.

Nodding his head in agreement with himself, he tossed out his first morsel. "They're splitting up. Do you want to sneak around these guys and hit the main force from the rear?"

The scout looked at Jackson as if he was seeing him for the first time. He was amazed. "Wow. My thought exactly." They looked at each other, nodded, and immediately started formulating a plan of action.

The two scouts had managed to hold three squads at bay, so to them, an end-run around their enemy's left flank should be a piece of cake. However; their end-run had to be done without giving away their intent. As much as he wanted to be on point, Jackson knew that in order to live long enough to learn the lessons he was being taught, in and about the jungle, he had to follow and learn from the experienced—PFC Fox.

Fighting in the jungles of the Pacific islands was a different kind of war than the one being fought in Europe. The European theater wasn't as hate filled as the Russian or Pacific theaters.

The German, Russian conflict still raised the black flag on both sides, but surrenders did occur. Many surrenders. Not so with the Japanese. The war in the Pacific was about as brutal as any war could get. The Japanese were willing to give up a life to take as many of the enemy with them as they could. To surrender was worse than death. In turn, the Americans fighting in the Pacific were forced to kill their enemy twice, to make sure they were dead before they approached enemy bodies. The Japanese rarely surrendered. They were dangerous, crafty, and very deadly warriors. Banzai!

The two Americans moved due west for about ten-minutes, before they changed direction, and headed due south. About fifteen-minutes after their turn south, they found themselves behind the enemy squad, cautiously coming up behind the two left flankers.

The Japanese were spread out, moving in a staggered skirmish line in order to cover more ground in their search. Although the sun was shining brightly, in the jungle, there were still shadows to hide in, and the scouts blended in perfectly.

Slowly, cautiously, the Japanese warriors inched their way through the jungle towards their enemy's last known position. They had no idea that they themselves were being stalked. The corporal in charge was under the impression that he was the hunter and not the hunted.

From out of nowhere, the enemy heard a howl that brought his men to a staggering halt. As soon as they heard the howl, they turned to look back and started tripping over the jungle's snares. They tried to regain their footing, but for the moment, they were unable to do so because they were still staring back in the direction of the howl, not where they should be placing their feet.

Abruptly, a soldier on the extreme right dropped to the ground. With all the trouble the enemy troops were having trying to keep their footing, the squad leader thought his warrior just lost his balance. The short distraction allowed the enemy to regain their footing. But something was up. Their comrade in arms was still on the ground; he hadn't stood up yet.

Spreading out, rifles at the ready, the Takahashi detachment cautiously advanced towards their fallen friend. While they were advancing, another howl was heard. It came from their rear. The second howl immediately grabbed their undivided attention, and their alertness sharpened. Every shadow or twitch from the foliage was investigated until they were certain the cause of their suspicion was not their enemy.

While Takahashi's men was looking in the direction of the howl, his men were hearing rustling noises coming from the same general direction. With their attention now completely focused on the howl, and the rustling noises, they missed what happened to one of their own; the man they positioned behind the skirmish line to watch their rear.

Again, Corporal Takahashi ordered an advance towards the sound of the howl. The men had barely taken ten steps when they heard an anguished groan coming from their rear, followed by the thump of a body hitting the ground. Signaling his men to continue on, the corporal turned to see what caused the groan, and discovered one of his privates lying face down on the jungle floor, with one of their own bayonets sticking out of his back. While the corporal stood staring down at his dead comrade, another wolf howl broke the tense quietness of the jungle. The howl came from the north, and it sounded very close.

Cautiously searching the jungle with his eyes, the thought of being deliberately hunted crept its way into the corporal's mind. He had never fought a battle like this before, where he was the prey instead of the predator. Not like this. When he had fought his enemies, he was the hunter, herding his enemy to their deaths. Unsettling as the situation was to him, the real chill-raiser was they have yet to see who was killing them. Only the brightness of two separate muzzle flashes greeted the corporal and his men when they entered into a short skirmish with the Americans.

The enemy squad was now facing to the north. With the realization that they had become the hunted, Corporal Takahashi had to change his strategy. He wasn't rattled, or unnerved by the quickly changing circumstances, but he was concerned that this little skirmish might turn into a fight to the death, a last man standing kind of fight.

Corporal Takahashi was a soldier in His Majesty's Imperial Japanese Army. He was prepared to do or die, but was not prepared to do or die, at least the last part, against just two guns. Not with the numbers he had.

Forming up his men into three short-squads, of three men each, he ordered them to advance north. The three squads were about ten-yards apart, with the flanking squads in a left and right oblique. Every man in his detachment was given a certain area of concern, to keep an eye on in order to spot the Americans before they could kill again. So far, every idea he had come up with had failed. Shaking his head, he wondered if his new idea was doomed to failure as well.

As the day wore on, his plan appeared to be working. Every time his men came under fire, they quickly formed into a skirmish line and laid some hot fire in the direction from where the shooting came. The concentrated fire forced the Americans to retreat farther away from their friends. He was pushing his enemy back. That part of the plan was working out fine. However; the sun was on its last leg down, and the part of his plan that *had* to succeed was not; the Americans were still alive.

~ ~ ~

At the last minute, PFC Fox had a change of mind. As much as he agreed with Corporal Jackson's idea of hitting the main force from the rear, he didn't like the idea of having an enemy force behind him at the same time, so he decided to lead his antagonists farther north until he was absolutely certain that any immediate help for either enemy unit was impossible. Then, when night fell, the little scout planned to kill them all. Once the enemy was removed from their back, the two scouts were then free to carry out their plans without any interference.

Both men had bullet burns and wood splinters on the upper half of their bodies from all of the near miss, tree hits. They were tired. They were bleeding, and now, they were agitated to the point of doing something about ending the situation.

Corporal Jackson had not said a word at all during

their retreat north. He knew they were moving away from the rest of the guys, but he didn't know why. Startled, he realized Fox had changed direction again, and he had failed to notice the change; they were heading east, back towards the ridge.

Twenty-minutes into their eastward trek, the two scouts came across a small trickle of water seeping out of the side of the mountain. With a sweep of his arm, PFC Fox moved the vines the water was trickling down, and revealed a small, stone basin with just enough water in it to fill two canteens. *Hmm. Hidden watering holes. Just like back home, only green.* The former beanpole from Arizona studied the chief for a moment before he shook his head, awed at the little scout's ability to find what was needed when the need was critical.

"Do the Japanese know about this seep?"

Shaking his head, the chief smiled and said; "I doubt it. I just found it this morning on our way down the mountain."

After drinking their fill, Fox smiled and looked at Jackson. "Let's go, Corporal. We have some work to do."

The two Americans arrived within striking distance of where they last saw their enemy, just before the sun made its final dive below the horizon. After a few minutes of scouting the area, they discovered that their enemy was not where they left them. "You think the Japs might be on their way down the mountain to rejoin their unit?"

"Maybe," said Fox, "but I don't think so. They're probably waiting for one of us to do something stupid so they can locate us and kill us. What do you want to do, Corporal?"

"Too dark to see any tracks. Let's wait here and just listen for a few minutes." PFC Fox glanced to his right, and from out of the blue, he felt a chill. The shudder was slight. No one standing beside him would have noticed, but he sure

298

felt it. The lack of sound from the insects stopped him cold, and the jungle went deathly quiet.

When the chief looked to his left to get Jackson's attention, he discovered that the corporal had quietly slipped away somewhere. He made several quick glances around the area, but no Jackson. Not a trace of the man appeared anywhere.

A slight sound caught his attention, then he heard the sound again; something soft scrapping across clothing. Cautiously, PFC Fox moved deeper into the shadow of the huge tree he was crouching beside, and then stood up, his back against the tree, deep in the tree's shadow. He had already been surprised by his enemy several times during their chase, so he had a healthy respect for his enemy's jungle fighting skills. The chief didn't mind, though. He was in their element during the day, but the situation had changed. Night had arrived; the little scout's favorite time to wage war.

The rasping from the enemy's movement was getting closer. The little scout from Swain County, closed his eyes and concentrated, tuning out the jungle's voice, and only focusing on the unnatural sounds, manmade sounds. Like bushes rubbing against cloth.

After a few seconds, he realized there were two, maybe three men heading towards his tree. They were moving quietly through the jungle, an action the Carolina scout wasn't familiar with. One or two Japs had given him trouble, but as a whole, he usually heard them easily enough. The men he was engaged in mortal combat against were different. These men were a very dangerous adversary. An enemy who seemed at home fighting in the jungles of the Pacific.

The enemy split up to go around the tree. Two went around the chief's left while the third soldier went around his right. Fox was all set, waiting to attack the lone man coming around on his right. He was ready to go, eager for his enemy to take one more step. Out of nowhere, an arm shot out of the shadows and wrapped itself around the surprised soldier's neck, followed immediately by another arm, striking down across the man's chest, and that short struggle was over.

Crack! Crack! Crack! Then all hell broke loose. Enemy bullets flew towards the shadow that had just killed their friend. The enemy troops engaged were some of the best jungle fighters in the Japanese army. They had just lost another friend to their enemy, and they were determined to avenge his death. With this thought in mind, the two enemy soldiers went after what they saw, but what they saw was another three or four feet past the tree where PFC Fox was hiding. Tunnel vision. The two enemy warriors didn't notice a little Marine scout standing in the shadow of a tree.

Because of the position they were in at the start of the fight, the two men on the chief's left were forced to move in single file until they had moved past the tree, and they were moving quickly. Without warning, the trailing warrior was jerked off his feet by an arm that was wrapped around his neck, and then the soldier was slammed down to the ground, flat on his back. The impact knocked the soldier senseless long enough for Fox to drive his knife into the man's heart. The leading trooper heard the commotion and began his turn-around, but that was as far as he got. All this happened very quickly, including the response from Corporal Takahashi and the rest of his squad.

~ ~ ~

Twenty minutes after the shooting ended, PFC Fox was behind Takahashi's squad, trying to figure out what happened. A trap had been set by his enemy, but for some reason, the ambush fell apart. That much he was sure of. *They were looking for us at night and almost got us.* After his thought, a small prick appeared in the little scout's pride bucket.

Still trying to figure things out, he went over the sequence of what happened. He remembered turning away from Jackson for about four or five-seconds, and when he turned back, Jackson was gone. The chief was somewhat surprised. Not even Bonito could sneak away that quietly.

~ ~ ~

Fox was in the shadows, watching the Japanese settle down for the night. His enemy looked a little short on men, so he thought some of them were out on watch, hidden somewhere. *We couldn't have killed **that** many?* He was still watching the Japanese from the shadows when he heard a short, bark. Stumped, he shook his head, trying to remember. He had heard that bark before. Then he heard it again, and so did the Japanese. In a finger-snap, the entire camp was melting into the jungle.

Quickly, silently, Fox melted back deeper into thicker cover, moving about forty-yards north before he turned west.

The Swain County scout lost his brand new carbine thanks to the Japanese, so now he was in a payback frame of mind. He spent close to two hours trying to locate the Japanese. During all that time, he had the uneasy feeling he was not alone in his hunt. He had no idea where Jackson was, and at the moment, he didn't care. *That man left me hanging in the breeze.* At least that's what he thought.

A howl came out of nowhere, startling the Japanese. After a slight hesitation, the Japanese were quietly moving towards the howl. They knew it was one of the Americans doing the howling so it didn't bother them anymore. What the howl did do was tell them where their enemy was. A couple of minutes into their pursuit, they heard the howl again, but this time it was off to their left...and it was close by. Very cautiously, they converged on the area they thought the howl came from. About twenty-yards to their right, Takahashi's men heard a single shot, then silence. There were no rustling sounds, so whoever fired the shot had not left yet. Takahashi's men just quietly turned and headed that way. The young corporal had an idea on what they would find.

~ ~ ~

The climb down the mountain was an all day affair. The sun was about thirty-minutes from setting when the men of Baker squad, at last, reached the flatland after their stumbling 600 foot descent down the treacherous incline. All through the day, Gunny could hear the shooting. His concerns were obvious only to Sergeant Stamper. They grew up together in the Corps, so Sergeant Stamper knew the gunnery sergeant almost as well as the gunny knew himself.

Roger was on point, and just happened to glance back and catch Gunny shaking his head. *Is he arguing with himself?* The strange episode occurred shortly after the start of the second round of firing, before the Japanese split up. Sergeant Stamper looked at Gunny for a few seconds and immediately began to worry. *Is he losing it?* It was an important concern to Sergeant Stamper because, at the moment, Gunny was only partly a Marine. If an attack occurred while the gunny was distracted, Sergeant Stamper feared that his friend would be the first to get hit. Then for almost three hours, the Oklahoma gunnery sergeant heard nothing from his two scouts still on the side of the mountain. This really drove Gunny, wild.

"Hey, Geronimo. Take a break and head back up the hill. We need to find out what the Japs are up to."

PFC Bonito stared at Gunny for a moment hoping his imagination had just kicked-in, but the scout knew he wasn't dreaming, so, with a smile of resignation on his face, he headed up Gunny's *hill.*

Bonito found the main Japanese force forty-minutes

into his scout. The Japanese had placed, about thirty-yards out, one man on point and one man on each flank. When he had all the info he needed, he headed back down the mountain, after Gunny. After two hours of searching and dodging the enemy, he found the gunnery sergeant and the rest of the guys standing beside an empty weapons' crate, and they were smiling. The Baker Boys were back in business.

Sergeant Matsuo wasn't with the Japanese force when PFC Bonito found them. He was making the rounds, checking-in with his scouts, and so far, nothing was happening on the left. He was heading towards the point when he noticed the right-side flanker was not where he should have been, then he saw some movement.

At first, he thought something was wrong, so he started moving towards the right flank. But then his scout stepped out from behind a tree, and once again, was moving parallel with the main force. With his suspicion alleviated somewhat, Sergeant Matsuo turned and headed towards the point man. Thirty-minutes went by before the sergeant discovered that he was right the first time. When he went looking for his right-side flanker, he found his scout's bloody shirt and helmet, along with his rifle, lying on the jungle floor. A couple of minutes into his search, he found his shirtless scout, and the man was dead.

Chapter 28

When the Hashimoto detachment arrived at the base of the mountain, they set up camp. The encampment was dark because an enemy was near. No fires and no smoking were the whispered orders; "The Yankee dogs are close by."

While camp was being set up, Lieutenant Hashimoto was standing off, talking to Sergeant Mitsuo. Their conversation lasted only a few minutes before the platoon sergeant received *his* orders; "Find them and report back to me. We will attack at first light. Good luck Kiyoshi."

Sergeant Mitsuo smiled and said; "Luck has nothing to do with it Jinichi. I will see you soon." Then he was gone.

The jungle area the Japanese were in was actually a long, narrow, valley, stretching from the base of the mountain, west, northwest for almost a half a mile. The vale was about eighty-yards-wide at its widest point, and was saturated with chest-high clumps of kunai grass, with a few trees sprinkled about. Lit-up only by the stars, the valley took on a ghost-like appearance, and shadows were everywhere. It was spooky, and it was hard to tell manmade shadows from nature-made shadows.

Sergeant Mitsuo and his two privates were only halfway across the length of the valley when a slight breeze sprang up from out of nowhere. A couple of minutes later that slight breeze had some strength behind it. A storm was moving in. With the dark clouds rolling in, the stars began to disappear, and then the rain started in. It wasn't bad at first, but after a few minutes, the storm clouds opened up and let loose a pouring rain, and seconds later, PFC Bonito was soaked to the skin.

The Apache scout was trailing about thirty-yards behind three Japanese soldiers. When the lightning started popping, it caught both sides by surprise. Bonito was in route to another position when the lightning struck. Sergeant Mitsuo just happened to be looking to his rear at that same time. Both men saw each other, but Sergeant Mitsuo was just a shade faster on his reaction.

Crack!

Bonito was hammered back hard by the impact of the bullet, and quickly disappeared in the kunai grass when he was knocked off his feet by the blow. Then the valley went dark and a breath-holding tension followed. Only two eye-blinks passed before the valley was lit up again by the flash of lightning, which was followed almost immediately by a tremendous blast of thunder.

Sergeant Mitsuo had seen his enemy get knocked off his feet by the bullet, but he did not believe, not even for a second, that he had killed the American. He also felt that his wounded enemy was still able to fight back, so he didn't rush headlong to where he had fallen. Instead, he spread his men out and moved to encircle the wounded American, or at least try.

The going was slow because they had to make sure the injured man didn't slip past them. The storm didn't help either. The rain had dropped visibility down to about twenty-feet, and the wind was whipping everything into frenzied movement. Everywhere the three men looked, the kunai grass was being wildly blown about by the wind. It was hard to tell if anyone was moving through it, so the three Japanese warriors had to be extra careful.

Without warning, Sergeant Mitsuo tripped and came crashing down, face first, onto the rain soaked ground. He hit the ground hard and was momentarily stunned. He could feel his legs moving, but he couldn't understand why. Then the fog in his head began to recede. Quickly he grabbed his rifle and got back to his feet, his heart pounding in his chest. *I tripped over the American and he is still alive!*

Yes, sir. Poor Bonito was wounded, but he wasn't thinking about that situation at the moment. He was more concerned with the consequences of his capture. *Oh brother, not again! That Cherokee will never let this be!*

When he tried to sit up he immediately started retching. The bullet had clipped the side of his head knocking him senseless for a few minutes. Sergeant Mitsuo's tripping over him brought him out his painless dreaming. Something he was strongly regretting. He didn't feel a thing when he was out cold. Now his head was just pounding.

It took Sergeant Mitsuo a few minutes to stop the bleeding, and again, the rain was no help at all. There was a three-inch long gouge cut along the right side of Bonito's head, just above the ear. He didn't want the American to bleed to death, so he did what he could to stop the bleeding, just in case his platoon leader had something special planned for the wounded Marine.

~ ~ ~

Gunny heard the shot and immediately figured something was up. PFC Bonito rarely put himself in a position to get shot at when he was on the scout, so Gunny gathered up his men and headed towards the sound of the shooting. Besides, Gunnery Sergeant Baker was tired of running. It was time to take the fight to the enemy. Re-armed, the gunnery sergeant from Lawton Oklahoma was a force to be reckoned with, all by himself.

The squad was waiting for Bonito to report back, just inside the jungle, about fifty-feet from the kunai grass clearing. When the gunfire erupted, it took everyone by surprise. Gunny needed Bonito to find out everything he could on the Japanese so he could formulate a plan of action. The squad was about two or three-hundred-yards from where the shot was fired.

~ ~ ~

Cautiously, the Baker Boys moved east along the northern perimeter of the kunai grass, only stopping every now and then to listen, but the squad stumbled onto a lost cause. The rain was coming down so hard they had to yell to be heard. Yet, despite the worsening conditions, their slinking through the grass only took them about ten-minutes to reach the area of the shots. However; when the Marines arrived at their destination, they found nothing. Then Gunny spotted something shadowy about forty-yards out. "Sergeant Stamper, your eight-o-clock. What is that?"

With the wind coming in at their backs, Gunny had an idea. Without warning, and not waiting for Sergeant Stamper to answer, Gunny let out a shrill whistle. Nothing happened. Then he let the whistle shrill louder, above the collateral sounds of the storm, and immediately, what appeared to be windblown waves of rain, turned to face the whistler ... they were Japanese. Gunny didn't need the lightning to recognize his enemy. The shape of their helmets and the fixed bayonets on their weapons was all the evidence he needed.

Gunnery Sergeant Alistair David Baker stood where he was, staring at this enemy like a father staring at the person who just brutally hurt his son. No one messes with Gunny's boys unless they were prepared to meet the deadly consequences.

While the man from Oklahoma was staring at his adversary, his enemy turned and took off running and yelling. Surprised for a second, Gunny quickly realized what might have happened. "If the Japs had Bonito, then he bolted, and that's why they took off running. Let's go."

The Japanese weren't afraid of the Americans. The fact that they were standing only forty-yards from their enemy told Gunny all he needed to know about who he was facing. These Japanese troops were jungle fighters. Marine nasty, jungle fighters. It was pouring down rain, with a gusting wind...and the Japanese were standing in the same mud facing their enemy, unflinching. No, the Japanese were not afraid of the Americans.

Gunny didn't hesitate. Right at this moment he had his enemy outnumbered, but that could change very quickly. As soon as the Japanese warriors disappeared from sight, Gunny moved southeast towards the southern perimeter of the valley. His enemy already knew where he had been...now they would have to guess where he had disappeared to.

The delay lengthened the chase a little bit, but now the enemy had no idea where Gunny was. The enemy scouts knew he was coming, but that was all.

Gunny took Corporal Kirby and PFC Choctaw with him while Sergeant Stamper had Marine Sergeant Daniels and Army brat Corporal Logan. Gunny was in the lead, followed by Kirby and then Choctaw. The other three men were following several meters behind the Ox. If the trouble they ran into was more than they could handle, their orders were to split up and disappear into the jungle ... just in case. But Gunny had no intention of letting that *just in case* happen.

From out of the blue, Gunny heard a hoot. The call sounded a little slurred as if the caller was drunk, and it had Gunny shaking his head and smiling. *Well, at least Geronimo's still alive*! Unbidden, and without warning, the memory of what the chief thought of Bonito's cougar call came to mind, and he struggled desperately not to laugh.

Abruptly, another hoot was heard, and it sent chills through the body of the man dubbed "Deadeye." *Damn! I'm glad those boys are on our side!'*

~ ~ ~

Corporal Jackson was cursing himself out for being so stupid. He wasn't using the usual words you hear the Navy or Marine boys using. He had his own words and phrases. *Crap on the ground* was the phrase he used most often. In the minute or so after he realized he was surrounded, he had thought to himself those very words over two dozen times ... and then a slow smile spread across his face. The enemy had no idea he was there. The Japanese were about to walk right past him.

Slowly, quietly, Jackson slid in behind the last enemy soldier to pass by him. Two steps later, the unsuspecting soldier's right foot was just striking the ground when Corporal Jackson sprang into action.

As the enemy's right foot struck the ground, Jackson kicked him behind his left knee, forcing his knee forward, buckling it, causing the man to collapse back-first to the ground. Grabbing the man from behind, Jackson clamped his hand down hard over the man's nose and mouth, and at the same time, he slammed the man's head down on the ground as hard as he could, helping his enemy reach Mother Earth a little faster. Jackson's knife entered the man's heart just seconds after he hit the ground, stunned. It happened so quickly, the disoriented enemy never had the chance to call out.

Quickly, Jackson melted into the deeper shadows and waited...nothing happened. After few minutes had passed, he was on the move again. Only a few minutes had elapsed before the scout found his enemy again. It was really easy thanks to PFC Fox; his howls kept the Arizona scout informed on the Japanese whereabouts.

The Japanese had no idea Jackson was around until Corporal Takahashi discovered he had only three men left. He didn't like it one bit. *There is someone behind us!* The corporal shook his head, frustrated at the situation. He had lost two men in the last twenty minutes, and he was just now discovering that fact. He cursed himself for a fool; *All that howling was nothing more than a distraction while the real threat has been behind us the whole time.* So the corporal changed his strategy once again; he was going after their enemy hiding in the shadows.

Jackson was about twenty-yards behind the Japanese when Fox let out another howl. He was expecting the Japanese to head towards the howl, but this time, they didn't. A couple of minutes passed by before the enemy finally started creeping towards the west, so the former beanpole from Arizona started followed the Japanese. While he was following his enemy, he was struck with an idea. His endeavor took him about forty-minutes to complete, and then he stood back to admire his handy work. Another forty-minutes passed before he finally relocated the Japanese again.

~ ~ ~

PFC Fox was having a heck of a time trying to rattle his enemy. The Japanese just weren't cooperating. Then he saw some movement. *It's about time!*

He was beginning to think the Japanese had given up on him. He hadn't seen or heard a Jap in almost twenty minutes. Then he saw the movement again...and he smiled. Slowly and ever so quietly, PFC Fox moved to his right, trying to get in front of whoever was moving about. Earlier, he had gone back to the tree to retrieve his carbine, but his carbine was gone. *Damn those jungle skunks, they took my carbine.*

While he was moving slowly through the jungle, he turned to slip behind a tree and came face to face with his enemy. Literally. The chief took a step towards the tree, heard something crack, looked down to see what it was, and then he was knocked off his feet by the body of a dead Jap. All the chief could do for the moment was lie on his back, and stare at the dead soldier swinging around in slow circles. The vines tied under the dead soldier's arms kept him just inches off the ground. Without warning, laughter erupted, and it was coming from Corporal Jackson.

"Shut up you idiot or you'll bring the Japs down on us," said Fox.

After hearing the chief's words, Corporal Jackson only stopped laughing long enough to whisper; "They're all dead."

Even after a few seconds, the words still hadn't sunk in. "Who's all dead?"

"The Japs. While you were keeping them occupied with your howls, I was sneaking up behind them, killing them one by one. That corporal was a mean one. I think even you would have had a hard time with him."

Fox stared at Corporal Jackson for a few seconds before he said; "You left me flapping in the breeze, Corporal."

"No I didn't," replied Jackson. "I only moved a couple of feet to your right, into the shadows. I figured I'd cover your flank so you could take care of your right. I didn't expect them to split the way they did, but I never left your side."

Then it dawned on the chief what Corporal Jackson told him. "You killed them all?"

Corporal Jackson chuckled and said; "Only five were left. You got most of them. I was just the clean-up crew."

Still staring at Jackson, the chief asked; "Where were you while I was doing all the work?"

Both men looked to the southwest and then at each other. The strange sounding hoot stopped all conversation. "That was Jose!" The chief immediately snickered and said; "Has he been drinking? Wow. That call sounded worse than his cougar!"

Corporal Jackson had no idea what Fox was talking about. He was only three feet away when Fox let his owl hoot, and it startled the bejesus out of him. "Hey, warn a guy beforehand. I damn near dropped a load!"

Still grinning, the chief said; "Aw shut up and quit complaining. You should have been paying attention. Are all Apaches like you and Jose? Come on Corporal, we have to find Gunny."

Quickly, Fox moved off, leaving Corporal Jackson bewildered ... and following.

~ ~ ~

Gunny heard the return hoot and knew that at least PFC Fox was on his way back. If the chief had been unable to do so, the hoot would have been a screech instead. Gunny knew his scouts well. His thoughts, however, were interrupted by a tap on his shoulder, it was Sergeant Stamper.

"We have Japs on our left. Do you want to hit them there, or someplace else?"

Gunny called a brief halt, so everyone crouched down to listen. "We're gonna keep going. Roger, I want you on point. Don't run us into an ambush. Corporal Logan, you take the flank. Don't let those rice balls get near you. If you see they're after you, kill 'em where you stand. We'll just start the war from there. Once we're done here, we'll go back for Geronimo. If he can run, he can hide, so he should be all right until we're done here. All right, let's move out"

Cautiously, the squad began moving east again.

The Japanese on the American's left happened to be Sergeant Mitsuo and his men. The sergeant had decided to head back and try to find the wounded American. The three Japanese soldiers were on their way back to where Bonito took off when Sergeant Stamper spotted them. The rain was still coming down hard, and the wind was still blowing just as hard, but the thunder and lightning had moved off to the back-side of the mountain.

The Americans were soaked to the skin. There were

little rivers of water running off of just about every part of their bodies. Yet not a single man thought about it. They were about to fight a battle with a very worthy opponent, and the only help they had was somewhere up on the side of the mountain. This was an *on your own* kind of fight. Something the Marines were now quite used to.

~ ~ ~

PFC Bonito was really hurting bad. When he took off running, his head started hurting so mercilessly that he barely ran ten-yards before he passed out cold. His passing out saved his life. The Japanese almost stepped on him in their haste to find him, but they didn't see him lying there, so they ran right past him.

Fifteen-minutes passed before PFC Bonito regained his senses. He had to let Gunny know where he was, so he tried to hoot the owl, but his first attempt ended up sticking in his throat. Raising his face to the rain, he opened his mouth. "*Oh wow!*" A few seconds later, he managed a hoot, but it was wavy sounding, and it brought a smile to his face. *Fox will love that one!* When he heard the return hoot, his smile widened. *Watch out Japs, here we come.* Then he passed out again.

~ ~ ~

The time was 0200 hours when Sergeant Stamper finally reported back to Gunny; he had found the Japanese main force. "The Japs are set up in a box formation with their strength facing north and south. If they have machine guns, they'll probably position them on the corners. I counted ten manning the perimeter. I couldn't get a count on the sleepers, but my guess is maybe twenty to twenty-five total, counting the Japs we saw earlier. They've got us outnumbered, Al."

Sergeant Stamper saw the grin forming on Gunnys' face, and was already shaking his head before his friend issued-out his words of wisdom; "Just wait till the bastards surround us, Roger. Then they'll really be in trouble."

Sergeant Stamper was still shaking his head when he said; "You know, Al. Bob Hope on his worst day puts you to shame with no effort, so why don't you quit with the jokes while you're still alive. I certainly don't want to hear them after we're dead. Besides, your face is beginning to crack from the effort."

Gunny was trying to come up with a response, but the response never materialized. Out of nowhere, the northern flank of the Japanese camp erupted with gunfire. Bullets were ripping through the kunai grass, forcing the two shooters to duck and scramble back for the protection of the jungle.

Fox! Now it was Gunny's turn to shake his head. "It never fails, Roger. Damn! We better go bail the chief out." At least Gunny knew where his lead scout was.

The firing went on for about thirty seconds, and then it ended. It was Fox's intention to hit the Japanese from the rear, but the two scouts had to contend with Corporal Takahashi and his men first. That fight had ended, so now the chief was hitting the Japs from what he thought was their rear. However; instead of receiving a slowly advancing volume of fire as the Japanese woke up and joined the fray. The two scouts received immediate machine gun and rifle fire. *Damn, the Japs were waiting for us. Did they know we were coming?* The Swain County scout immediately realized that he might have bitten off more than he could chew. *These Japs are good*!

In less than a minute, the volume of fire directed at the two scouts quickly intensified, as more riflemen entered the fight. The grass was getting ripped apart and the two scouts were unable to do anything more than just hug the ground. It didn't take them long to get out of the neighborhood. "Crap on the ground, Fox. What was that?"

Jackson stared at PFC Fox, and he had absolutely no

idea about what to say next. All he could do was shake his head at the chief while he watched an unbelievable scene take place. The adrenalin, the fear, and the excitement of the moment; everything had control of "little man" and he couldn't keep a handle on it. He was rolling on the ground laughing so hard he could barely breathe. Corporal Jackson, on the other hand, was sweating profusely despite the downpour, and he wasn't laughing. He had forgotten what it felt like to be under the intense fire of an enraged enemy. He was reminded very quickly of what it was like.

Cautiously, the scouts moved west. The rain had let up some, but now fog was beginning to move into the valley. The two scouts also had another problem. Any tracks the squad might have made would be washed out by morning, so they were going to have to trust to their skills.

People have said that Jackson can track a fly in a snow storm. Well, that point was never proven because the flies tended to die very quickly in the zero degree cold, so the flies never got the chance to leave any tracks. But he is good at what he does ... *very good*!

When the shooting stopped, Gunny sent Sergeant Stamper out to see what the Japs were up to. After Sergeant Stamper's quick scout, Gunny and squad were back in the kunai grass, couching down, about twenty-yards from their enemy's southern flank, and the gunny was smiling.

The Japanese, so far, had not made many mistakes, but now they were making a *big* one; their southern flankers were showing themselves to their enemy. They were standing up at their positions, looking north, talking excitedly about the shooting. Lieutenant Hashimoto was screaming at his men to settle down and focus, but they were too excited about the short battle and didn't pay attention to their commanding officer. In the blink of an eye, their world was abruptly torn apart by death and chaos.

Without warning, the four flankers went down under

a hail of fire coming from only twenty-feet away. The Japanese southern line didn't know their enemy was there. The southern force never stood a chance. Yet, the gunny from Oklahoma didn't stop there. The attack had taken the Japanese by surprise and now he was pushing it to the limit. "Let's get 'em Marines," and immediately, the six Americans stood up and advanced on the Japanese camp, firing from the hip while they moved.

There was a lot of lead zinging through the air, mowing down the grass and the Japanese. The enemy, however, was by no means out of the fight yet. They could have melted into the jungle, regrouped, and probably laid a good whuppen on the Americans, but it didn't turn out that way.

Lieutenant Hashimoto was screaming at his men, trying to get them back into the fight, but his efforts to rally his men ended when he took a bullet in the throat, and down he went. Now the Japanese were leaderless, and they were quickly losing their cohesiveness as a unit. Lieutenant Hashimoto was dead and their platoon sergeant, Sergeant Mitsuo, was a little over 150 yards to the west. Shortly after the Japanese lieutenant fell, the battle ended. The battle itself only took about two or three minutes from start to finish. The Baker Boys counted twenty-three Japanese dead, not counting Lieutenant Hashimoto.

Gunny forgot there were still three Japs out on the loose until Sergeant Stamper reminded him of the situation. "Gunny, we still have three Japs running around somewhere, do you want to go after them?"

A howl interrupted the gunny before he could answer back. Looking in the direction of the howl, a satisfied smile appeared on his face, and he said; "No, Roger, I think we're done hunting for the day. We'll wait here for our little sneakers to return. In the mean time, gather up what weapons and ammo we can use and then get ready to move out. We'll leave as soon as the chief gets here."

~ ~ ~

PFC Bonito was not having a good day. His head was pounding, his equilibrium was off, and he was puking. Not a pleasant situation to be in for the Apache scout. He could hear his enemy trying to locate him, but there was nothing he could do about it. He lost his carbine when he got hit, so the only weapon he had on him was his Ka-Bar. He didn't pull it out because he was afraid he'd stab himself when he fell.

When he tried to walk he resembled a blind, staggering, drunk. He couldn't maintain his balance for more than two or three steps. It was step, step, splat. Then he was on the ground. It would have been hilarious to see if the circumstances weren't so serious. The situation he was facing also had him shaking his head, frustrated that he was unable to fight back, due to his injury.

Searching his surroundings, he found a clump of grass strong enough to lean up against, and there he waited for his enemy. He could hear the battle going on to the east and whispered; "Go get 'em Gunny," and then; "Hmm. I guess this is it." His only regret was not meeting his enemy on equal terms. Immediately, a smile broke through his frustration and he whispered; "What the hell, I'm a Marine. There's nothing equal about us. We're all meaner than the next!" Then he had another sobering thought. *Who will know where I am? Where I died?*' With that thought in mind, he let the cougar scream. Halfway through his attempt, the scream died out; he was out cold again.

The scream caught the attention of the Japanese, Gunny, and PFC Fox. To PFC Fox, it sounded like Geronimo was in some kind of trouble. The two scouts were on their way back to the Japanese encampment when the scream erupted. They had heard the firing break out and started back for the enemy camp, but by the time they got halfway there, the firing had stopped, so the two scouts turned, and headed back, towards the scream.

Sergeant Mitsuo thought the Marines were the men dying until he realized that the last few shots fired were not from a Japanese weapon. He was stunned. The thought that his platoon had been completely wiped out by the Americans stopped him cold, then he heard a scream. "The wounded American! He is close by!"

All that was on Sergeant Mitsuos' mind, at the moment, now, was to kill the wounded American; cut him to pieces and let his gods take care of the identification. However; before he could move towards his wounded enemy, he heard a howl.

The howl sounded so close that he felt he could turn around and touch it. This time, though, he was chilled to the bone by that sound. The last time he had heard the howl, it was coming from somewhere on the mountain, almost a mile away. The fact that the howl was so close, told him that his friend, Hiraku, along with his men, were also dead. This revelation saddened the enemy platoon sergeant deeply.

The rain was still coming down, but the squall was about over. The strength of the storm was now beyond the mountain, so the men on the ground were getting the last it had. The wind was still blowing east, but it too, was starting to die out. And slowly, as the wind and the rain departed, the fog started creeping in.

The two scouts were moving slowly through the grass, with visibility rising to about twenty-yards, after the rain had slackened up some. They had only moved fifty, maybe sixty-yards from where they first heard the botched scream when they heard someone yelling. It was Bonito. Shortly after the shouting, they heard cursing, and the chief was shaking his head. *Maybe Geronimo tripped.* He was about to call out to let PFC Bonito know they were coming in, but froze on the inhale; he could hear his enemy whispering. Quickly, he looked over at Corporal Jackson, threw out a few hand signals, and the two scouts split up.

PFC Fox was circling around to the south to come at the Japanese from the east. Corporal Jackson moved a few feet to his right and then stopped, which put the three enemy warriors at the point of an intersecting crossfire. Then the deadly fun began.

The chief figured he was about thirty or so yards from the Japanese, so he started playing his usual games. It didn't take long for the Japanese to start shooting in his direction. Abruptly, the little scout heard a single crack from a carbine, and then silence. Almost immediately following the lone shot, he heard two quick shots, and then, again, silence reigned supreme.

The little scout had no idea what just happened, but before he could move on to find out, he heard that stupid little bark and stopped dead in his tracks. He finally remembered the bark. It was the bark of a prairie dog. Here he was, in the middle of a kunai grass filled valley, with the enemy, in spitting distance, and he was celebrating his recollection.

"Hey Fox, I think I got all of them. Don't shoot, I'm coming your way."

PFC Fox whispered back. "Thanks for the warning, Corporal. I'll just wait until I can see you before I start shooting."

"Hey. Remember? If it wasn't for me you wouldn't have your weapon back."

PFC Fox started chuckling. By that time, however, the two scouts were standing together, looking down at the three dead Japanese. PFC Fox bent down to check their pockets, and was surprised to see that all three of the enemy were hit in the head. The chief looked up at Corporal Jackson, somewhat surprised. The only shooting light came from what stars the rain clouds couldn't hide.

"Did you see what you were shooting at, or did you just

close your eyes and pull the trigger?"

"Yeah, I think he just closed his eyes and pulled the trigger." And there fell PFC Bonito, grinning bright enough to chase the blues away.

PFC Fox was stunned. "Where did you come from?" Then he started laughing and said; "What have you been drinking?"

The bantering was not new to Jackson. He remembered bantering around with his friends in Europe, but the people doing it here were new to the Arizona scout, so he moved back, giving the two friends a chance to unwind...among friends. Jackson was just there to keep watch.

Ten-minutes went by before Gunny and squad came crashing through the kunai grass grinning from ear to ear ... until he saw PFC Fox. Then his grin disappeared rather quickly.

PFC Fox could see Gunny's mad forming up like an ominous storm, so he launched a preemptive argument. "Gunny, it wasn't my fault. They shot at me first. What do you want me to do? I had to defend myself!"

Gunny's mad was almost at the boiling point when he said; "What the hell took you so long to get down off that mountain, chief. I send you on a simple little scout and you're gone all day and half the night. What's Army going to think about us Marines if you get to roam around free. I should have brought my leash!"

Sergeant Stamper was bent over trying to quiet his snickering. Corporal Kirby and PFC Choctaw just burst out laughing. Sergeant Daniels and Corporal Logan started laughing because everyone else was...which left Gunny and Jackson the only men not laughing at the expression on the chief's face. That soon changed. The laughter was genuine. But it was also the laughter of relief. The Baker Boys had made it through another fight, and they were all, still in one piece.

Chapter 29

Captain Matsui was soaked to the skin, but at least he was alive. He was now down to just eighteen men, not counting himself. Part of the mountain-side bordering the northwest corner of the plateau came pouring down and hit the Matsui warriors before they had a chance to react.

The platoon heard a rumble, felt the ground shift, and then it was over. About forty-six men disappeared underneath the mudslide. Only nineteen of the sixty-five men in his detachment, managed to survive the slide. It was a miracle any survived at all. To Captain Matsui's way of thinking, it was a good omen. He felt he had been kept alive for the sole purpose of killing the Americans. He just had fewer men to do it with.

Corporal Aoki had been Captain Matsui's scout, but when he lost the American's trail, he was relieved of his duties...permanently. Now Sergeant Takagi was back on point and he did not like it there. His back crawled all the time just knowing he was in the captain's crosshairs. He felt like a million bugs were constantly crawling up and down his back.

Lieutenant Watanabe was in the same boat. He was now walking with Sergeant Takagi, on point. This was his choice. If he was going to die, he wanted to die in the company of his only remaining friend, Sergeant Takagi. The two had already resigned themselves to the fact they were going to die on this mission. Either the Americans were going to kill them, or Captain Matsui was. It was just a feeling the two men shared. The fact that they were disarmed by Lieutenant Nakamura, contributed greatly to their feeling of doom.

"Get down on your knees when you address me, you insolent dog."

He is insane! Sergeant Takagi knew he was about to die. He could see it in the captain's eyes. Then Lieutenant Nakamura whispered something to his raving lunatic.

"Captain Matsui, why don't you have Takagi report directly to me? I could then report his findings directly to you, so you don't have to deal with his insolent behavior."

Captain Matsui looked at Lieutenant Nakamura as if he was seeing him for the first time. "Ah. Kenji. It is good to see you." Then he smiled and said; "Yes, Kenji. I think you are right." Then, through the falling rain, Captain Matsui saw the flashes of gunfire off in the distance.

The Matsui warriors were on the plateau, facing west, when the gunfire erupted. The weapons' fire was just little speckles of flashes, but somebody was definitely shooting at someone. Captain Matsui's eyes lit up instantly at the sight.

By the time the sounds of the firing reached the Japanese on the plateau, the little skirmish, had by then, come to a close, and Captain Matsui was already on his way down the mountain, followed by what remained of his men. They were still trying to reach the ledge, just below the west-side cave entrance, when shooting erupted again.

~ ~ ~

PFC Bonito was happy to be alive. He couldn't walk on his own yet, but he was still alive. That, however, was not his thoughts thirty-minutes earlier. Bonito knew he was going to die. It wasn't until he heard Fox taunting the Japanese, that it dawned on him that he just might live to fight another day. The Japanese were standing only ten feet away when Jackson intervened.

It took the squad until sunrise, to get deep into the jungle, before Gunny felt comfortable enough to take a break. PFC Bonito was still having trouble walking on his own, so Gunny put the Ox in charge of the human crutch detail. At first, that didn't work so well. PFC Bonito was only five-foot-eight if he stood on his tip toes. PFC Choctaw, however, stood over six-feet tall. To remedy the situation, Choctaw grabbed a hold of the back of Bonito's shirt. When the Apache scout lost his balance, PFC Choctaw would just raise his arm and lift the scout off the ground a couple of inches, and then set him upright on his feet again. The Marine Corps training wheels were working out nicely for the Apache scout.

~ ~ ~

It was noon by the time the Matsui warriors reached the base of the mountain. Captain Matsui also discovered the Japanese dead. It took his men the rest of the day to bury their dead. By the time they were finished with their grisly task, they were an exhausted group of warriors. They just dropped to the ground, completely worn out. Twenty-minutes after their grisly chore was finished, the snore-saws were running all out.

~ ~ ~

The Marines were starting to enter familiar territory, well, somewhat familiar territory. They were about a mile away from the horseshoe shaped ridge they had to climb over when they first fell on the island. They still didn't know what island they were on, and no one thought to ask. The rescuers didn't think about volunteering that information because they were too busy fighting for their lives.

Gunny was worried. He had not forgotten about the captain PFC Fox had scalped. The two enemies had seen each other off and on during their many skirmishes in the jungle, so Gunny somewhat knew how the man fought. The enemy captain had a crazed look in his eyes, and Gunny could tell the man was not right by the way he treated his men. The man was a brutal leader.

That worrying thought had Gunny deeply concerned. *Where is that captain now?* The gunnery sergeant from

Oklahoma didn't think he'd seen the last of the enemy captain just yet. So, and because of that gut feeling, PFC Fox and Corporal Jackson were sent back to the kunai grass clearing to keep an eye on their backtrail. They arrived at the far western end of the valley just as the sun was dropping below the horizon.

The next morning, the two scouts split up. PFC Fox was skirting around the northern perimeter of the valley while Corporal Jackson was moving along the southern edge. The plan was to meet at the far eastern end of the valley. If the two scouts didn't find any Japanese, they were to find a place to hole-up until the next day. If there was still no sign of the enemy by 1300 hours the next day, they were to head back to Gunny. Simple enough, but PFC Fox wasn't thinking about that. He was thinking about the last of the conversation he had with Gunny. The man looked really pissed.

Gunny looked Fox straight in the eyes. "If Geronimo wasn't so addle brained, he'd be going out instead of you. You need a break, chief. You look like hell."

Then Gunny turned his cold, hard, stare towards Jackson, looking the former beanpole from Arizona dead in the eye.

"Corporal, I'm holding you personally responsible for the chief's well being. Nothing happens to him ... you understand? And you." Gunny was now staring back at PFC Fox. "*Stay out of trouble!*" Then, he turned and walked away.

Both scouts were floored. Jackson had very little experience with Gunny. He took Gunny for a hardass, but ... wow! Fox on the other hand has had plenty of experience with the gunnery sergeant, both the good side and the bad side. The chief could only remember one other time Gunny was like this. That thought made him shudder involuntarily. So, with his mind on the conversation instead of what he was supposed to be doing, PFC Fox walked straight into darkness. The hit on the head put him there.

Jackson heard a commotion off to his left and quickly hit the ground. Listening for a few seconds, he heard really faint whispering. At first he wasn't sure he was hearing it, but then the whispering excitedly turned heated. *Japs!* He didn't know what to do at first. *Where's PFC Fox?*

Cautiously, he moved back to the edge of the jungle, and then, very slowly, he stood up. He was hoping he was hidden in the background. When he could see what was going on, he froze, statue-still. He didn't like what he saw. The Japanese had Fox, and they were none too gentle with him. A couple of minutes went by then his heart sank even further. Five more of the enemy had just made their appearance, and one of them was carrying a sword. Now he was really stumped. *Do I try to help Fox, or do I go back for help?*

There was only forty-yards of kunai grass separating Jackson, from his enemy, yet they couldn't see him. He was well blended into the jungle background, and he was not moving. Movement catches the eye.

Without warning, the sword wielder screamed, and then raised his sword as if he was going to strike at Fox. "*Nope!*" Jackson didn't hesitate.

Everything happened at once. Captain Matsui raised his sword to relieve Fox of his head, Jackson raised his rifle to kill the captain, and three enemy soldiers jumped at Captain Matsui to keep him from killing PFC Fox. The Japanese and the bullet arrived at almost the same time. The bullet meant for Captain Matsui hit Corporal Isaki instead. Then everybody disappeared from sight.

Jackson quickly took the hint. Crouching over, he started moving west along the edge of the jungle. A couple of minutes later, he headed into the kunai grass. His thought was to see things from a different angle. Maybe then he could come up with a plan to free PFC Fox. He really didn't know what else to do other than follow the Japanese. Ten-minutes later, Jackson was crouching down about twenty-feet from the northern edge of the valley. He could hear the Japanese whispering excitedly, but the whispering was receding fast. It sounded as though they were moving deeper into the jungle. Then he had an idea.

Jackson had been with the stranded Marines going on five days now. The two Marine scouts were good. They had their own signals when danger was near, and when the two scouts had to talk, they had their own meeting calls.

Jackson couldn't imitate those calls, but he did have his own calls. He could growl like a bear, but that was only good for about two or three attempts, his throat couldn't handle any more than that. Besides, it couldn't carry the distance needed, so that call wasn't going to work. He also had the bark of a prairie dog, but that call was only good for short distances as well. He didn't like his only remaining option. The only call he had left was the screech of an eagle, and he hadn't tried that one since before he went to war. But still, he had to do something. *Maybe Gunny will come running, thinking something's up when he hears the call.* It was a long shot.

Jackson couldn't leave Fox to go after Gunny because he was the chief's only protection. He felt like a little kid going on stage to perform in his first play, embarrassed and almost too afraid to try. Attempting the eagle call was really bothering him. And like the little kid in his first play. If he screwed this up, his friends would never let it drift quietly into obscurity.

The Japanese were barely sixty-yards inside the jungle when they heard a shrill, screeching noise. It was loud and it hurt their ears. It sounded almost like chalk protesting loudly on a dry chalkboard. The call was piercing to the ear. Then the Japanese heard coughing and immediately started laughing. *Was that one of the Americans making that hideous noise?* Not one enemy soldier could keep a straight face. Captain Matsui was the only exception. "Shut up you fools, you'll tell the Yankee dogs where we are." Quickly, the laughter stopped.

The Japanese had Fox tied up with his own boot laces and walking barefoot. The deranged captain smiled at the chief while he cut up his captive's boots. He remembered the episode by the river, and wasn't about to leave a perfectly good pair of boots lying around for the Americans to reuse. His expression was malicious and venomous. *This little one won't have to worry too much longer about being barefoot in the jungle.*

Captain Matsui didn't care about the other Marines anymore. Why should he? He had PFC Fox in his hands. And now, Captain Matsui felt he could die a happy man ... after he was finished with that insolent Yankee. *I will skin him alive, and then I will hang him out to dry!*

During all this time, PFC Fox had not said a word, but he was seething with hatred. His eyes never stopped looking for a way out, and when he looked at Captain Matsui, he had murder and mayhem in his eyes. Oh how he hated that Jap captain. He had the little man's knife again, and the fact burned the PFC up to no end.

When Fox heard a screech, he stared in the direction it came from, trying to figure out what it was, then he heard the coughing as well. *Was that Jackson?* Even Fox started laughing. When the order to shut up was given, the little scout stopped laughing, but he still had a grin on his face. He was looking straight at Captain Matsui when he started shouting; "*Hey cowboy, we're...*" Then the lights went out.

~ ~ ~

Gunny and PFC Bonito both looked towards the east at the same time, and then they looked at each other. PFC Bonito was grinning because Gunny was shaking his head.

What the squad heard was Jackson shooting at Captain Matsui. However; Fox's storied history made Gunny's misunderstanding more than just a possibility.

"Damn that kid. The chief must have found some Japs." Then he looked at Sergeant Stamper and said; "Roger, we're going to have to scrub that kid down when we get off this island. Maybe run some magnets across his body to degauss him. He's like a magnet to the Japs. Why is it always the chief?"

While the two sergeants were discussing Fox's polarity, PFC Bonito was smiling. It sounded stupid, but he was glad to hear Gunny's voice again. Then the Apache scout stiffened, and cocked his head a little to the right.

"*Shut up!*"

But the warning wasn't necessary. Gunny caught Bonito's stiffening out of the corner of his eye, and was already turning towards his scout when Geronimo unexpectedly jumped to his feet.

Once again Bonito apologized to Gunny for telling him to shut up, but for some reason, the man in charge wasn't angry with the scout. In fact, his eyes had humor crinkles around them, and the sight had Bonito worried, but at least Gunny wasn't mad. Instead, he had a, *good boy, keep it up*, look on his face. The gunny's expression kind of surprised Bonito. In fact, he forgot about what brought him to his feet, and for a minute or so, continued to stare at Gunny's expression, waiting for him to say something, but the man in charge didn't say a word, he just continued to look at PFC Bonito. Another minute went by ... *This is getting bizarre.* "What?"

It wasn't long before the rest of the squad noticed the staring contest between the two Marines.

Bonito was still looking somewhat confused. "Hey, Gunny, what's going on?"

Gunny was stone-faced when he turned to face

Sergeant Stamper and said; "See. I told you. You owe me ten dollars, Roger. Geronimo has been on his feet for two-minutes and he hasn't fallen down yet ... so pay up!"

Everyone was floored, including PFC Bonito. "You placed a bet on me?"

"Deadeye" was grinning when he replied. "You bet! Now what did you hear?"

The question brought a grin to Bonito's face before he answered; "I think that Cherokee was trying to sound like an eagle, but this one sounded like it was in a lot of pain."

Gunny looked at his scout, somewhat surprised. "Is that what I heard?"

Everyone was grinning at the description Bonito made of the attempted call, until Gunny abruptly took a deep breath and stiffened. "That wasn't PFC Fox, so it had to be Jackson. The chief doesn't deviate from the arranged signals. They must be in trouble. Pack it up, boys, we're heading east." They didn't have to be told twice. Within seconds, they were moving east, towards the northern edge of the kunai grass clearing.

Their journey to reach the western end of the valley took them about three hours. When they arrived, Gunny called for a short break while PFC Bonito went out to scout around. While they were on route to the far eastern edge of the valley, the Apache scout was begging Gunny to give him the lead. "Come on, Gunny, please. Put me on point. I'm the only who knows how to find that Cherokee. Just put me out front and I'll find him."

So there he was, out on point, looking for his friend. *Come on you damn Cherokee, leave me a sign.* He had no doubt that if Fox was able to, he would leave sign. All he had to do was find it.

A few minutes into his scout, he found where Jackson had crouched down when he attempted his call. From there, Bonito could see a faint trail leading off to the northeast, so he started moving in that direction, following Corporal Jackson. He had barely walked twenty-yards when he, all of a sudden, remembered Gunny. *Damn, not a good idea! Get halfway to hell and have to turn around because I forgot about Gunny. Man, that would really piss him off.* So he ushered-out a crow caw. A couple of minutes later, Bonito was in discussion with Gunny.

"Are you sure you can handle this? I can send Sergeant Stamper out if you..."

"Gunny, I'm okay. The bullet only hit the right side of my head. The left side is still working just fine."

Gunny stared at PFC Bonito for a few seconds, and then he shook his head, not happy with his decision.

"Okay, Geronimo. Let's go find our boy."

Those last seven words were all he was waiting for. Seconds after permission was granted, the squad was heading into the jungle, trying to keep the Apache scout in sight for as long as they could. Gunny could only shake his head. *Damn! To have his skills in this body. Damn I'm glad they're on our side.*

Twenty minutes into their journey, Gunny found Bonito standing beside a tree, and he was smiling and shaking his head when he said; "Jackson is leaving us a trail." Having said that, the scout turned northeast again, following Jackson's bread crumbs.

As the squad passed by the tree Bonito was leaning against, Sergeant Stamper happened to glance at the tree, and instantly burst out laughing. Pointing at the tree he said; "Hey, Al. Come take a look at this."

When Gunny saw what Sergeant Stamper was looking at, he too, burst out laughing. Yeah. Jackson was leaving sign all right. *This way,* and an arrow pointing northeast was carved into the tree. Gunny winked at Roger and said; "He must think we're just a bunch of Boy Scouts!"

~ ~ ~

The Japanese were only two hours ahead of Gunny when Captain Matsui called a halt. He had found what he was looking for, a defensible position with only one-way in ... or out. It was exactly what the captain was looking for.

The enemy warriors were standing in the aftermath of an age-old rockslide. One minute they were struggling through the hot, steamy, jungle. And then bam, everything changed. They noticed the rocks right away. The whole area for almost a hundred-yards in either direction, all the way to the ridge, was nothing but creeping broad leaf vines, an occasional tree, and rocks ... big rocks ... and lots of vines. The vines owned that whole area of ground. They covered everything; the trees, the rocks ... and the bigger rocks.

The position put Captain Matsui's men butt-up against the ridge, but that's what brought on the smile. *We can't be taken from the rear without an awfully hard climb.* It wasn't perfect, but with a little work, their position could become deadly to the attacker. *Heh, heh, heh*! Captain Matsui's chuckle sounded...not quite human.

The Japanese had a good field of fire with the absence of the main jungle vegetation; all the other jungle crap that didn't grow there for some reason or another. While everyone was shoring up the position, Captain Matsui was off by himself, with his back leaning up against the face of the ridge. He was dreaming up ways of inflicting a lot of pain, for a very long time. The recipient being PFC Fox. All of a sudden, Captain Matsui turned and stumbled back several steps. It sounded as though something was crawling towards him, through the vines. His first thought sent chills through his body; he hated snakes.

He stood looking into the vines, trying to spot what he thought was crawling towards him, but he didn't see anything. Hesitantly, he moved forward a couple of steps, then he saw a glint. Drawing his pistol, he moved closer, and heard again, what he had heard earlier, but it wasn't something live crawling through the vines, it was a real small trickle of water, dribbling through the vines. *Where is the water going? It's certainly not ending up on the ground. At least, not where I'm standing. So where is it going?*

He continued to study the puzzle in front of him, while he absentmindedly moved to his left. When his third step touched ground, he stopped. It was an abrupt stop. He looked at the ridge for a couple of seconds, and then, very cautiously, he pushed his hand through the vines, and instantly, his eyes grew wide. He was feeling nothing, only a soft, cool, breeze. Quickly, he put his arm deeper into the vines, all the way up to his shoulder, and still, all he felt was a soft, cool, breeze. Quickly glancing back at his men to see if anyone was watching him, he immediately had a thought. *Is this a split in the ridge? A way to get to the other side without having to climb over?* The accidental discovery definitely had an impact on his thinking. PFC Fox was no longer at the forefront of Captain Matsui's thinking at the moment.

Chapter 30

Jackson was slowly, slithering his way closer to the Japanese, rock by rock. He was half expecting to get shot every time he moved from one rock to the next, but so far, his enemy didn't seem to be paying much attention to their front. He was still about sixty-yards out from the Japanese position when they proved him wrong.

Quickly, he dove back behind the rock he just left, but now he was somewhat pinned behind that rock. *How much ammo do the Japs have left*? He was on his third recon of the enemy position when they spotted him.

The Japanese had him pinned, so Lieutenant Nakamura sent three men out to get him. The Japanese kept up an intermittent fire just to let the corporal know he hadn't been forgotten. Meanwhile, the three men climbed over the makeshift wall and began moving on his position.

The closest rock to the Army scout was a little over thirty-feet from his present position. With the vines as thick as they were, running fast was out of the question. Then he began to grin. Out of the blue, he recalled the expression on a German officer's face when the officer suddenly realized he had just surrendered his twenty men to just *one*, pint-sized, American. *I'd like to be grinning into that Jap officer's face when I drive my knife into his heart.* Then his grin widened. *Maybe Fox might like to collect the rest of his scalp. Wouldn't that be something?*

Jackson could hear the Japanese coming for him. The enemy had him pinned, so he wasn't going anywhere, so why be quiet? He had two magazines left plus the mag in his carbine. He was still smiling, still remembering. *That Marine sure went apes when he was asked to trade his carbine for a Thompson.*

Jackson was issued a Thompson .45 submachine gun when he volunteered to fight the Japanese. The Thompson was one brush busting SOB, but Jackson preferred the M-1 carbine, like PFC Fox. The carbine was perfect for what he did. It was light, compact, and very easy to handle. Its only drawback was its knock-down power. Still; even the biggest man will sink with enough lead in him.

Jackson could hear the Japanese, clearly now. Listening to the amount of noise the enemy was making, he deduced that two were coming up on his right, while the other one was coming up on his left. This was not a fight he thought he could win, but he did know one thing. The two on his right were going with him no matter what followed, and if he had time, turn back to his left and kill the other one ... If he had time.

~ ~ ~

One, two ... Jackson didn't get to three. Without warning, the two Japs on his right were hit hard by what sounded like a carbine. Crack! Crack! Crack! Crack! Crack! The former beanpole from Arizona didn't hesitate; he took off running towards the shooter.

Jackson's knees were coming up so high because of the thickness of the vines, he looked like a Majorette running across a football field. Those legs of his were pumping so hard, and his knees were coming up so high, it looked as though he was hitting himself in the face with each stride he took. It was hilarious. Jackson could hear Bonito laughing at him from forty-feet away. Of course, because PFC Bonito was laughing, he wasn't hitting anything, so the third Jap made it back to the wall still in one piece.

The Japanese were not asleep while all this was happening. As soon as Jackson took off running, they opened up on him. Bullets were chewing up everything but the running scout. There were almost twenty Japanese soldiers firing at Jackson, and yet, not a single bullet hit him.

~ ~ ~

Gunny was about twenty-minutes behind PFC Bonito when the shooting first started. He recognized the crack of a carbine and then the Japanese rifles. Out of nowhere, a sudden pang of fear shot through him ... "Fox! Did the Japs just shoot him? Roger, get the hell out of the way and follow me."

Gunny didn't need Sergeant Stamper to keep them on track anymore, thanks to the shooting. He turned a little to his left, and then laid in a course straight to the weapons' fire.

Gunny was not stupid in the woods. In fact, he was pretty damn good when he had to be. But the men doing the scouting were born to it. That's why they were out in front, sniffing out the ambushes instead of Gunny.

Sergeant Stamper just kind of fell face first in the mud, and after following Staff Sergeant Baker around for ten years, he rinsed himself off and knew what he was doing. But now Gunny was in the lead, and the jungle shook from it.

Gunny had lost thirty pounds since the Marines fell on the island. What was left was all muscle, sinew, and 150 lbs of pissed off Marine. And Gunny was greatly agitated.

"Get out of the way, Roger!"

"No, Gunny. You don't know how many Japs are out there. Slow down. Let's figure this out."

"Get out of my way Roger, before I rip your head off."

Without warning, Sergeant Stamper exploded. "You never saw the day you could hit me in the face, let alone rip my head off, you overgrown loudspeaker!"

The whispering was harsh. The two Marines sounded as though they were about to tangle. However; that confrontation didn't occur because Gunny stopped in mid-sentence. Something caught his attention. Immediately, his arm went up, and everyone hit the ground ... and then the squad heard snickering.

"You can stand up now. The Japs heard you guys whispering, so they know where you are."

Gunny stood up shaking his head. Nobody said a word. They were stunned. The two Marines, who seconds before were about to come to blows with each other, were grinning at each other. "What was all the shooting about, Geronimo? Did you see PFC Fox?" Then the grins turned sour.

"No, Gunny. We couldn't get close enough. We stick out like a sore thumb when we try crossing that stuff in daylight. They spot us every time we try. We'll just have to wait for the sun to go down."

There was a hint of malice in Bonito's smile. Sunset was just about an hour away, so he took off, leading the way to the Japanese position. Out of the blue, Corporal Jackson took off to the right and quickly disappeared.

The journey to the enemy position only took the squad about twenty-minutes to make. When they arrived at the scene, they stood at the edge of the vine covered clearing, staring out at their enemy. Twilight was just starting to set in, and so were the shadows.

Gunny divided his men into two really short squads. Sergeant Stamper had Sergeant Daniels and Corporal Logan again, while Gunny kept Corporal Kirby and PFC Choctaw with him. Sergeant Stamper moved about forty-yards to his left, which put him at the center of the Japanese position while Gunny moved to a position on the Japanese left. The two scouts were quietly slithering unseen for the Japanese right.

As the shadows started moving in over the vine covered clearing, so did the Americans start moving towards the Japanese position. The Baker Boys were all in position before darkness was in full swing, so the Japanese knew where they were. Sergeant Stamper could see his enemy looking at him, and was baffled as to why they weren't shooting at him. *Could they be low on ammo like we are?* He smiled to himself. *Wouldn't that be nice?*

Now that everybody was in position, the squad had to wait for the two scouts to start the ball rolling; they didn't have to wait long. Without warning, the Japanese right erupted with weapons' fire, followed seconds later by the explosions from hand grenades.

Along with the carbines in the crate, there was a handful of grenades ... nine to be exact. Until now, Gunny hadn't seen the need to use them. Besides, Gunny and his boys never carried them, so he didn't think to use them until now.

The power of the attack on the right took the Japanese by surprise. They were expecting the attack to come at their center or on their left because they saw Gunny and Sergeant Stamper moving into their positions. The Japanese didn't see the two scouts moving up on their right.

Two of the three enemy warriors manning the right were killed at the start of the attack. When the two grenades went off, the explosions killed three more. Two more grenades went off, and all the work the Japanese put in on the right side of their position, just disappeared. Two blinks later, the Japanese left came under fire, followed seconds later by the center. The attack on the left was just as shocking, and just as powerful as the attack on the right.

For the last six months, the Japanese had been fighting these same Americans and not once was there any hint the Americans had any hand grenades. When the grenades started exploding, this really shook up the enemy. They were not prepared, nor were they expecting this kind of an attack. And then above the din of battle, Gunny shouted out; *"Let's get 'em, boys!"*

Immediately, the Americans charged for the

homemade barricade, firing as they moved, heading straight for the holes created by the grenades. Then the Baker Boys ran out of ammo. The Americans were expecting a hail of gunfire from the Japanese, but nothing happened. They were about ten-feet from the barricade when Gunny saw the Japanese.

"Hey, Roger, there they are! Looks like they're coming out of hiding. Where's the bug spray when you need it."

After hearing Gunny's shout to attack, the three men in the center stood up tall, and with their Bayonets and Ka-Bars in hand, they charged at the oncoming Japanese while the scouts charged at their enemy from the right. Sergeant Stamper was shouting back to Gunny as he closed with the Japanese.

"The bug spray is at the bottom of the Zdp;pmon Sea, Al. Do you want me to announce it to the world?"

Before the sun could settle below the horizon, the battle was over. The Japanese ran out of ammo, so they did what they had been doing since Guadalcanal...they chose to die fighting rather than surrender. It took the Americans a few minutes to realize the battle was over, but once they did, the Baker Boys ripped the Japanese position apart looking, for PFC Fox, but the squad didn't find him. The chief was gone. Now Gunny was really worried.

An hour after the battle ended, Gunny was squirting sweat by the bucket-load, scared to death that something terrible had happened to Fox. When they searched the position for the second time, the Marines counted twenty dead Japanese soldiers, two of which were shot in the back of the head at close range. The two men shot in the head were Lieutenant Watanabe and Sergeant Takagi. Lieutenant Watanabe received what he wished for. Neither man knew what hit them.

After another thorough search of the area, the squad discovered they were one Japanese captain short, and one

Marine Corp PFC was missing. Now they were forced to wait for daylight to find anything else out, and everyone was feeling down. Nobody was talking. All the Baker Boys were doing was picking at the vines, kicking at the ground, and shaking their heads. "Daylight is a long ways away, Gunny."

~ ~ ~

Gunny had been following Jackson around with his eyes for about ten-minutes. The kid never seemed to stop. At the moment, he had a somewhat neutral expression on his face while he wondered around the interior of the position. His eyes never stopped looking ... and then he hesitated, and his eyes narrowed in thought. He was looking down at the base of the ridge.

The leaves of the vines where Fox was held were torn up as though a struggle took place there. After studying the scuffed-up area for a couple of minutes, Jackson looked towards the front of the position and stopped. He stared at the front of the position for a couple of seconds and then his eyes searched the trodden path all the way back to the base of the ridge, and stopped where the crushed leaves from the vines lay on the ground.

He noticed there was very little foot traffic from the ridge to the fighting positions, and there was no sign of any kind of struggle between the fighting positions and the ridge. Slowly, his head started moving left to right, up the ridge and down, his eyes motionless ... searching. His expression was no longer neutral, it was dead serious ... and then he smiled deeply.

Gunny was still watching Corporal Jackson, but his thoughts were elsewhere. It wasn't until he saw Jackson smile that he realized the kid might have found something. He was still watching Jackson when the kid suddenly put his hands together like he was about to pray, and then he pushed them through the vines, growing on the face of the ridge. And then he disappeared behind the dangling vines.

341

Gunny's mouth immediately dropped open and all he could do was stand in place, astounded. "How do they find these things?" Within seconds, Corporal Jackson reappeared from behind the vines, his pearly-whites shining brightly in the pale moonlight. For the first time in over a week, the moon was showing its face.

"They went this way, Sarge!"

PFC Bonito cringed. *Oh crap! Oh boy. Here it comes.* He was ready to cover his head and duck because Corporal Jackson just called Gunny ... *Sarge*! But nothing happened. Even Sergeant Stamper was surprised at Gunny's silence. Then the gunny spoke. His expression was about as stone-faced as anyone he knew, had ever seen. It was dead blank. Sergeant Stamper never saw it coming.

"Roger, you keep these four with you and don't get lost. I'll take Geronimo and Wounded Bird with me, and go after the chief. If you keep this ridge on your right, you'll run right into the beach. Head for the rendezvous and don't stop for anything. We don't have any money so I can't pay the Navy to wait. We'll signal when we get the chief back."

For the count of ten, the men of Baker squad were absentmindedly looking around the area for the wounded bird Gunny was talking about, until Jackson asked who Gunny was calling a wounded bird. Then the Baker Boys all caught on and fell to the ground laughing. Everyone but Jackson. He was just standing around looking dumb, wondering why everyone was laughing because of a wounded bird. Then bam. His face immediately turned red when he realized what Gunny was talking about. *I'm Wounded Bird!*

~ ~ ~

When PFC Fox started shouting at Jackson over by the kunai grass, he was knocked unconscious by a well-placed rifle butt to the forehead. So, and because of that well placed rifle butt to the forehead, PFC Fox remained unconscious throughout the entire journey to the Japanese, last stand, position. He was still unconscious when the battle started.

At first the Japanese thought Fox was faking it, so they started kicking him to, ah, wake him up, but the little scout didn't flinch or bat an eyelid. He was actually, out cold. So the Japanese grabbed him by his arms and started dragging him along until they noticed the trail his heels were leaving behind. Now they were either forced to carry him or just kill him outright and be done with it. Captain Matsui, however, wasn't ready for Fox to die yet, so they carried him.

Now he was awake and hurting. His ribs were sore to the touch, and someone was inside his head and pounding on him unmercifully, trying to get out.

The start of the battle woke him up. He sat up and went right back down. The sounds from the explosions were causing him to scream out from the pain in his head, and then he passed out. Seconds later, he was yanked to his feet and shoved face first, up against the side of the ridge. On wobbly legs, he waited for whatever was going to happen next. He felt the blindfold being tied over his eyes and a feeling of dread enveloped him. Immediately after the blindfold, his hands were tied, and he was pushed through some, *he shuddered*, crawly stuff, and for the first time since the sub sank, he felt a soft, cool, breeze that sent shiver-chills up his back.

The mouth of the cut looked exactly like the rest of the ridge face until you pushed through the vines. Once through the vines, the six-foot-long, four-foot-wide chamber narrowed down to one person only, occasionally having to scootch sideways every now and then. There were places to turn their bodies around, but Captain Matsui had no intention of putting that Yankee pig behind him, so he pushed on.

Captain Matsui couldn't see any kind of ceiling or anything low hanging, but the two men could sure feel things rub up against them. It was creepy, it was spooky, and PFC Fox had no idea where he was. The picture of where he was, didn't appear in his mind. He would have died before he entered the cut, if it wasn't for the blindfold. He hated dark cramped places, but because of the blindfold and his head injury, he hadn't put two and two together yet.

Chapter 31

Gunny was beginning to wonder if he was going to make it all the way through the cut, and if the cut actually went all the way through to the other side of the ridge. So far, he was able to skinny his way through the cut, but six months earlier he wouldn't have gone more than six-feet before he was forced to stop and head back. He was definitely sweating from the exertion. *Damn those kids. They're so skinny, they could slip between two toothpicks tied together and not touch either one.* Then, after what seemed like hours, he saw a tiny pinprick of light, and a smile spread across his face. Ten-minutes later, however, his smile disappeared.

Gunny wasn't standing at the end of the cut. He was standing in a small cavern, staring down into a dark hole, near the side of the cut. The light from the stars was coming down through a hole at the top of the ridge. Dribbling into to this dark hole was a steady stream of water. It wasn't much, but it sure came in handy at just the right time.

Looking down the hole, Gunny shuddered. *If it wasn't for the light filtering down I might have stumbled straight into that hole.* This changed his thinking about the cut. It put the fear of death in his heart. Staring back down at the hole, Gunny shook his head. "That's not how I want to go out."

The two scouts left Gunny behind shortly after they entered the cut. Gunny had only moved a couple of feet past the hole when a sudden chill hit him. *I sure hope those two spotted that hole and didn't fall in.* Then he smiled and muttered. "No. Those two didn't fall down that hole. Not those guys."

All the way through the cut, from that point on, Gunny forced himself to think back to the other missions he was on, visualizing his scouts wandering through the jungle, alive. Those visions kept him sane. The confines of the cut, almost falling down a hole, PFC Fox in the hands of an insane Jap, everything began to pull at him all at once, and he was about to explode. He was forced to move at a snail's pace and was powerless to go any faster. His patience was about gone, and he was still stuck moving through that damn crack. "Ahhh!"

Abruptly, he stopped in his tracks, stunned. He couldn't believe his eyes. Looking back, he saw the exit of the cut only six feet behind him. For the last three hours, he was so deep into his thoughts that he became oblivious to his surroundings. He had been concentrating on the visions of his scouts so hard that everything else just disappeared from his mind. Gunny was six steps past the exit before he realized he was out of the cut. Two more steps and he would have walked off the back edge of the ridge.

Looking to his left, he noticed a game trail leading into the brush, so he followed it. He couldn't go any further to his left because of the rock wall, and he wasn't about to go back through the cut. To Gunny, that will only happen once in his lifetime. Twenty-minutes passed before he found his scouts; all three of them. He almost shot one of them.

Gunny was slowly moving along the face of the ridge, following the game trail. He learned from PFC Fox that you can't go wrong following game trails. When he spotted the moving shadow, he was already too close to do anything but draw the Jap pistol and attack. So he did. All he saw was the one shadow move, nothing else. Then he hit the ground, hard. *Umph*!

"Hey Sarge, you were about to shoot PFC Bonito. I didn't think I had time to warn you before hand, so I tackled you. You're not hurt are you?"

"Get off me. *Private!*"

Gunny was deeply agitated. To Gunny, what Jackson just did was an act of *war*! You don't tackle the gunny and then walk away without a fight. To the man from Oklahoma, you only get one shot, so make it count. After that one shot, Gunny puts on the warpaint.

"We got PFC Fox back, but that Jap captain took off before we could kill him. He's a slippery cuss. I'm glad we're done with him."

Those words brought Gunny's intended attack to an abrupt halt. "You got the chief back?" Gunny's grin was huge. "Damn bugs. One just flew in my eye. Damn!"

For the first time since he joined up with Gunny, PFC Bonito saw Gunny as just a man. A man with feelings. Then he smiled and thought; *No, he's not just a man, he's a U.S. Marine Corp man ... with feelings.*

"Hey, Sarge. Are you really busting me down to private?"

Now that the focus had veered back to Jackson, Gunny turned into Gunny again. He was staring at Jackson, trying to figure out what his answer should be. *Should I bust him down to private?* Then his sourpuss expression brightened up into a smile.

"No. You can cover our rear."

Jackson's eyes widened in surprise, and then he shook his head. "You're just like Sergeant Brooks. Are you related to him?"

Corporal Jackson had a knack for pissing off his NCO's. It wasn't malicious or intentional. It just happened. He's like a little kid stuck in an adult's body. Only Sergeant Brooks figured out how to slow him down. It was an accidental discovery, like Gunny's just was, but it definitely worked ... until the next time.

Whenever Jackson pissed off Sergeant Brooks, he would just send the scout back to cover the squad's rear for a day or two, and viola, he was a whole new man when he returned to the front. He hated the rear. He would do anything to stay out front, and that includes behaving himself ... for a while. The former beanpole from Arizona spent almost as much time in the rear as he did on the scout. But when things turned deadly serious, he was always out front leading the way.

Twenty-minutes after Gunny's declared war fizzled out, the chief was on his feet again. It wasn't his wounds that had dropped him to the ground, it was complete and utter exhaustion that put him down and out. That fall-out saved his life. Captain Matsui wanted him awake and alert so he could see what was going to happen to him. The enraged captain wanted that insolent Yankee dog to see the satisfaction of revenge in his eyes, but he couldn't wake the exhausted Marine, so he let Fox lay where he had fallen. "I will see you again!"

PFC Fox was on his feet again, but he was nowhere near ready to travel yet. His body was just beginning to charge back up. It was still dark out, but on the northwest side of the ridge, the stars were softly lighting up the landscape.

The northwestern side of the ridge was nothing but rocks, scrub brush, and an occasional stunted tree. It was wide open compared to the terrain they had been traveling through. With the stars lighting up the area, it left Gunny feeling naked and exposed.

Somewhere around 0200 hours, Gunny exited the cut. Now, several hours later, and two-hundred-feet further along the ridge, the four Americans were beginning to stir after their short, hour and a half nap. PFC Fox on the other hand, had almost four and a half hours of sleep, and was showing some very serious signs of life.

He was actually feeling pretty good despite his exhausted state and his pounding head. He was ready to get off this island. He was humming right along, smiling inside. No more Japs. Now all they had left to do was meet the sub ... Immediately, his happy mood turned dark and unhappy.

"Damn, I have to get on another sub?"

Gunny and Bonito started laughing at the chief's sudden outburst. Then all his happiness was buried ten feet under when he heard even worse news. His life had been saved by another damn Apache ... "Why me?"

~ ~ ~

He was ready to go *now*! But Gunny wasn't, so Fox started fidgeting around until Gunny yanked him down to the ground ... *heel boy*! PFC Fox was like a little kid over-stuffed with energy, he couldn't stay still for very long, and it was absolutely hilarious to watch Gunny torture the chief the way he was. Fox would start to get up and Gunny would yank him back down ... *heel boy*! It was driving the little scout nuts. *"Can I at least stretch my legs?"*

"No!" Finally, at around 1000 hours, Gunny unleashed the-fox and up he sprang, headache ignored. Gunny looked at PFC Fox and shook his head ... *"kids!"*

"Wounded Bird, you take the rear. Geronimo, lead us to the promised land."

Out of nowhere, PFC Fox burst out laughing. The mention of Wounded Bird brought back the memory of Jackson's screech. The laughing, however, didn't last long, it was the pounding in his head that brought his laughing to a stop. Jackson on the other hand was red faced and shaking his head. *These guys are never gonna let me live this one down.*

As soon as Gunny was ready to move out, he told Bonito to send the signal. Two close together owl hoots told Sergeant Stamper that they made it out of the cut. The howl was to let him know that the chief was still alive and kicking.

Corporal Jackson was the only one of the four who had hung on to his rifle. He had the cuts and gouges on his face to prove it. And now, like PFC Fox, he hated small, cramped spaces … with spider webs and … ahhh! Crawly things. *Never again will I do something like that. Never again!*

Gunny started out around 1000 hours. By 1700 hours that evening, the Americans were walking on the beach along the edge of the jungle. The Baker Boys were less than a mile from where they found themselves lying after the sub sank. Comprehension was beginning to dawn on the four Americans, especially the three marines. Their stay on this rock was about over. Midnight. Seven long hours away, and this nightmare adventure would end. Twenty-minutes into their stroll, the four men rounded an outthrust of jungle and froze. *"Crap on the ground!"*

Everybody heard the whispered words, and everybody looked down for the crap on the ground. Then PFC Bonito started laughing and said; "Not the ground, you idiots, look, over there. Come on Gunny, the Japs left us some supplies."

The four men were looking at what was left of the supplies Lieutenant Watanabe had off loaded when this whole chase started. The boat driver must have gotten tired of waiting for his friends, and headed back to base. The landing craft was nowhere to be seen. Now, it was beginning to sink in, really deep. *We **are** leaving this island! In just a few hours, we will forever be leaving this piece of rock behind.* But, two things were holding them back. Sergeant Stamper hadn't arrived yet, and midnight was still several hours away.

Sergeant Stamper and the rest of the guys finally made their appearance around 2230 hours. PFC Fox couldn't keep still for some reason. He was constantly looking into the jungle, fidgeting around. Something was bothering him and he wasn't telling anyone about it. The closer it got to departure time, the more he was fidgeting around. Everyone who knew him figured something was up by the way he was constantly scouring the area with his eyes, so the squad kept their eyes on him.

The chief was like a worrisome watchdog, an old, *young* lobo, always sniffing the air for signs of danger. Even Jackson was showing signs of nervousness. By the time two hours had passed, all three scouts were now pacing about. Gunny thought it comical. *Are all of the scouts afraid of getting on another sub?* Sergeant Stamper interrupted his thoughts by tapping him on the shoulder. "Someone's coming, Gunny."

In a flash, everyone was in the jungle shadows, waiting, hoping it was their ride home. Then Gunny heard a whispered call.

"*Night Hawk!*"

Gunny didn't know what to say, so he turned to Sergeant Daniels. "What's the call-back?"

Sergeant Daniels smiled and pointed to Jackson. "He knows it, have him call it back."

Gunny looked at Sergeant Daniels for a second, and then they heard the call again.

"Night Hawk!"

Gunny continued to stare at Sergeant Daniels, and then he whispered for Jackson to answer the call. Jackson's face went pale and he dropped his shoulders letting out a sigh. "Do you really want me to do this?" Gunny just stared at Jackson until the scout weakly answered the caller. "Wounded bird."

"What?" Gunny stood straight up. "The call back is wounded bird?"

Everybody stood up and began laughing at Jackson's embarrassment. The, "Someone's coming," turned out to be extra paddlers and two Navy corpsmen in case the wounded birds needed medical attention right away. The only one needing medical attention was Corporal Jackson. He needed anti-embarrassment tabs in order to survive the ribbing he was sure to get. Then everyone's heart froze.

Without warning. Out of the jungle ran this enraged Japanese captain, brandishing his sword. He was screaming at the top of his lungs as he ran with his sword raised high, heading straight for PFC Fox. Only Jackson still had his rifle, but it was empty. Before anyone could think of what to do, PFC Fox suddenly let out what sounded like a growl, and then he took off running straight at Captain Matsui. The enemy captain was wearing the scout's knife, and the chief wanted it back.

The time was 0030 hours, but with the moon out, everyone was visible. Fox took off running and didn't slow down. He gave it everything he had, so the twenty-yard distance closed rather quickly. All of a sudden, Captain Matsui struck downward, hoping to slice Fox down the center, but he missed. If Captain Matsui had used a golf swing, he might have done what he set out to do. But instead, his downward swing allowed Fox the space to dive forward into a forward summersault, just slipping under the downward slice, the result of which, bowled Captain Matsui off his feet.

PFC Fox was up and on his enemy before the Japanese captain could regain possession of his sword again, but the chief didn't stay there long. He had his knife back, so he just stood up and backed off a couple of yards to allow Captain Matsui to regain his feet. Quick as a cat, Captain Matsui was back on his feet, with his sword in his hand. And there stood PFC Fox, staring deeply into Captain Matsui's eyes ... smiling.

As the two men circled each other, Fox said a few words to Corporal Kirby.

"Tell him to say hello to his ancestors on his way to hell."

But Corporal Kirby was a little slow on the uptake. Without warning, Gunny took action. The island. The Japs. The death of Sergeant Thomas. Everything. All of it, suddenly hit Gunny full in the face and he immediately declared war on the Japanese captain. Gunny screamed at Captain Matsui; *"You son of a bitch!"* Then he pulled out the 8mm Jap pistol he had shoved behind his belt and began firing. Captain Matsui's head snapped back from the impact of the bullet. Gunny's first shot hit the captain in the forehead, right between the L and the F, PFC Fox had carved on his forehead, the night he scalped the captain. Gunny's last two shots were to make sure Captain Matsui stayed dead. Just like an angry father shooting a perpetrator.

Cautiously, Gunny walked over to Captain Matsui's body and stood looking down at it for a long few seconds. He just stood there, staring down at the lifeless body for a few seconds, and then he cocked his head a little to the right, smiled the smile of the victor, and tossed the 8mm pistol onto the lifeless chest of Captain Matsui ... "Here's your gun back. It shoots good!"

Nobody moved when Fox took off running, including the two corpsmen. They were witnesses from start to finish. When it was over, Jackson and the rest of the men started heading for the rafts. Jackson was still shaking his head over what just happened, and then he muttered his favorite words. *"Crap on the ground!"*

Seconds later, the two corpsmen were looking for the crap on the ground. Then Gunny and his boys started laughing at the corpsmen, looking for the crap on the ground.

Thank you for reading.

Please review this book. Reviews help others find Absolutely Amazing eBooks and inspire us to keep providing these marvelous tales.

If you would like to be put on our email list to receive updates on new releases, contests, and promotions, please go to AbsolutelyAmazingEbooks.com and sign up.

Acknowledgements

Technical Advisors:
First Lieutenant Thomas Edward Clary, U.S. Army Corps of
Engineers; Viet Nam War.
First Lieutenant Raymond D. Clary, U.S. Army Air Force;
World War II.

About the Author

J. Allen Clary is currently writing books and enjoying life. He has created 21 stories in just a little over five years, with 10 of them finished. A motorcyclist until death parks his bike, he currently and forever resides at home with his wife of 36 years, along with four cats and two dogs. His oldest son works in theater, building stages. His youngest son is a U.S. Navy veteran.

ABSOLUTELY AMAZING eBOOKS

AbsolutelyAmazingeBooks.com
or AA-eBooks.com

www.ingramcontent.com/pod-product-compliance
Lightning Source LLC
Chambersburg PA
CBHW060932030726
47503CB00003B/568